# THE
# SECOND A

## By

## George Donald

## PROLOGUE

Monday mornings were always a drag, but at least she had no classes till just before lunchtime. Now sat at her dining table, she again went over the plan.

She had deliberated and undertook her study of the company for some time before deciding that the second stage of her campaign would continue at the supermarket located in Lionel Street in Birmingham; the store she had learned that was affectionately known within the company as the 'Founding Store.'

Her research indicated that the store was opened in the summer of 1951 and in tribute to its primacy, the interior of the store retained the original décor and its staff were outfitted in the first issued Chrystons uniforms. Located near to the A38 the store was directly across the road from the company's head office that occupied six storeys of the modern glass and steel building, constructed in the late nineteen sixties. Within the building over three hundred management and staff administered the one hundred and twenty-seven supermarkets and eleven thousand full and part time employees that comprised the personnel of Chrystons Supermarket (PLC) chain of food and clothing stores.

The laptop was a really useful tool for she used the AA route planner to plan her journey and decided to depart early and drive down on Wednesday morning.

Upon completion of her task she would travel home, but that time on the road would be unreasonable without stopping somewhere for a comfort break. At the break she would also have some lunch that she would prepare and take with her for unlikely as it was, she did not wish to risk being recognised in a service station food court.

She calculated the round trip, traffic problems aside, would last at most eleven hours.

She had used her computer to work out her route and traffic conditions notwithstanding, calculated she would arrive in the city centre about midday.

She had laboriously researched her destination on Google Earth, using her laptop to check out the roads and streets she would travel in the city centre and even the entrance to the head office.

Her plan was to park in the large public car park at the Museum and Art Gallery, make her way on foot via Edmund Street to Newhall Street and if all went well, anticipated arriving five minutes later in Lionel Street.

Of course she intended to take precautions and would dress down. Her visit the previous week to the charity shop in Byres Road had cost just a few pounds investing in the cheap wig, headscarf and the lengthy, outdated overcoat. She was confident that wearing such clothing and carrying a Chryston's plastic carrier bag was unlikely to attract attention for the staff would only see a woman whose purpose in the supermarket was to simply purchase shopping; milk, bread or suchlike.

She planned that after visiting the Chrystons shop she would cross the road to post the letter through the large brass letterbox in the green coloured front door of the head office, though was uncertain whether her letter would be read that day or the following day. She had no worries about posting the letter for though she assumed that like most high street stores Chrystons would have installed CCTV cameras in their supermarkets, whether or not Chrystons head office front door had such protection mattered little, for she would be in disguise.

However, before any of this could occur she had first to again visit the Chrystons food outlet located on Glasgow's Woodlands Road where she would place the first jar.

She had not randomly chosen the Woodlands Road for she had already visited the store where she purchased both jars; she smiled recalling how nervous she had been for it had also been the first test of her disguise.

No, she chose the store for on her initial visit she knew that at lunchtime it would be extremely busy with students from Glasgow University as well as the pupils from the nearby secondary school, all massing together at the fast food counter. She gambled that there would be little time for the harassed staff to pay much attention to a shabbily dressed woman with a plastic carrier bag.

Yes, she smiled to herself; lunchtime tomorrow would be the ideal time for her campaign to commence.

## CHAPTER ONE

That Thursday morning, the young clerk responsible for collecting and distributing the head office mail had been with the company for less than a month and was still finding his feet. In the claustrophobic cubbyhole he yawned as he listened to the radio playing quietly on the shelf and emptied the hessian sack onto the wide bench set against the wall that barely left his room to manoeuvre his arms. Humming tunelessly to the radio, he lazily began to distribute the dozens of pieces of correspondence to their various piles before binding them with rubber bands and throwing them into the low, four wheeled trolley he used to make his deliveries to the departments located throughout the six floor building.

By now, the procedure had become boring and his mind was on the previous evenings date with Lucy who like him had left Ark Boulton Academy in Sparkhill the previous month, but unlike him, had still to find a job.

It's not as if this is place is bloody paradise, he thought as irritably he tossed a package onto the growing pile of correspondence destined for the manager of the South East Division food packaging department.

He lifted the plain white business envelope and stared curiously at it. The typed address merely indicated it was for the 'Chief Executive Officer, Chrystons Supermarkets (PLC)'. He guessed the absence of a stamp suggested the envelope had been hand delivered and holding it in his hand he hesitated, uncertain to which department he would deliver the envelope. With a shrug, he threw it onto the pile destined for the Retail Customer Services office. "Let them sort it out," he mumbled to himself.

It was roughly an hour later that a bored Retail secretary began to shuffle through the morning mail. She stared curiously at the white envelope addressed to the 'Chief Executive Officer, Chrystons Supermarkets (PLC)' and using her slim metal letter opener, tore open the envelope at one side and tipped out the two A4 sheets of paper it contained. She glanced at the first closely typed sheet of and puzzled, read it a second time, but on this occasion her hand unconsciously reached towards her mouth.

Hastily, she pushed back her chair and made her way to the office supervisor where she placed the letter down in front of the older woman and flattened it out with her hand.

Twenty minutes later, the letter had passed through two further supervisors, three managers and the Deputy Departmental Head before it was hurriedly brought to the attention of James Hardie, the company Director of Operations and the most senior member of the Board in the building at that time.

Sat at his desk, Hardie, now approaching his forty-fourth year, had slipped off his tailor made suit jacket that hung on the chair behind him, his concentration taken by the report that he held in one hand while the other hand smoothed back his dark, thinning hair, cut short and brushed back to create a widow's peak.

The loud and unexpected knock on his door startled him and annoyed at being disturbed, Hardie beckoned his Deputy into his palatial office and snapped, "What!"

"I really think you should read this, Mister Hardie."

"What is it," he replied as he reached for the single sheet of A4 paper, then quickly scanning the typed letter, frowned and asked, "Is this some sort of a joke?"

"Ah, we're not at all certain, sir."

Hardie sighed and said, "Look, Gregory, before we give this letter credibility, did it occur to anyone to phone the Glasgow store or nip across the road to our supermarket and check the shelf there?"

"Ah, again I'm not certain sir. Shall I…"

"Yes, please and quick as you like!" Hardie snapped back as he handed the letter to his Deputy, who turning headed quickly for the door. "And let me know what you find out," he called after the retreating figure.

"Ellen," called the voice loudly from the storeroom, "Wilma says to tell you there's a phone call for you from head office. The guy says it's urgent."

Casting her eyes to heaven and exhaling deeply, Ellen Toner quickly made her way to the office located at the rear of the store and nodding at her secretary Wilma, hurried around to her office to grab at the phone lying on the desk.

"Hello, Ellen Toner here."

"Miss Toner, it's Gregory Packer, Deputy Director of Operations at head office. Sorry to call you away from the floor, but we have a question for you. It's regarding a rather bizarre letter that arrived here at head office this morning. Can you check your shelves, particularly the babyfoods for a jar of lamb and rice, aged six to twelve months. Oh and can you do this yourself without alerting any other member of staff, please."

"I'm sorry," she shook her head, "you want me to check babyfoods? Whatever for?"

"The letter we received, Miss Toner. It alleges that someone has contaminated a jar of babyfood and the contaminated jar is marked with a black cross. We believe the letter to be a hoax for we receive a few of these from time to time, but obviously…"

"Yes, I understand," she interrupted, "but is it just my store that's to be checked? I mean, is this a general threat or…"

"Another store has also been…dare I use the word, threatened. In fact, Miss Toner, the other store is the 'Founding Store' directly facing head office here and as we speak that is also being checked. Oh, and one further thing," he added, "can this be done as discreetly as possible without alerting your staff, please."

"Okay," she unconsciously nodded as she sighed, "I'll do it myself right now and get back to you, Mister Packer," then noting his extension number in Birmingham, returned the phone to its cradle and quietly muttered, "It's not as if I've not got a million other bloody things to do today."

"Is there a problem, Ellen?" Wilma's head popped in the door.

"Just a wee job for head office, Wilma," she shook her head, conscious of Packers warning and then added, "Give me a minute; I'm going to check something."

She stepped out of her office and made her way through the store towards the aisle where the baby foods were located, nodding to some of the regular shoppers she recognised who presumably lived nearby.

She had not reached the aisle when she saw Alice Greene, arms folded and standing idly between the cereal and bakery aisles as she leaned with her back against a display unit and chatted to the back store man, Eddie Redmond. Angrily she shook her head. In the six weeks since Ellen had been appointed as manager at the food outlet, if she'd told that lazy cow once, she'd told her a dozen times about standing about when she should be working, whether stacking shelves or attending to customers. As she approached them, Redmond saw her coming and the grin faded from his face as he sharply turned away to head back to the storeroom. Greene's head snapped round and seeing Ellen, her face fell. "I was just…"

Ellen held up her hand to cut off her excuse. "I don't want to hear it, Alice. This isn't the first time I've had to warn you about standing about when you should be doing your job." She indicated an almost empty shelf behind the younger woman and angrily added, "Even I can see that there's something you could be doing here. I'll see you in my office after the midday rush, Alice," she told the pale faced younger woman and without pausing, marched past her towards the aisle where the baby foods were located.

The aisle was empty as lifting her skirt slightly she went down onto one knee at the lower shelf where the jars of the popular brand of Snuckles baby foods were stacked. Peering into the shelf, she searched for the jars of lamb and rice and began pulling them towards her. Lifting each jar, her eyes narrowed as she checked the labels and to her dismay, saw that one jar near the rear of the shelf had been marked with a small black cross on the bottom of the label. Examining the lid, she pressed her thumb firmly down onto it and heard the faintest of pops as the lid depressed into the jar. She knew immediately the lid had been unscrewed from the glass jar. Had the jar been still secure she would not have been able to depress the lid with her thumb.

"Bugger," she muttered and staring at the jar suddenly wondered if she had inadvertently destroyed any fingerprints that might have been upon it.

Hurriedly, she made her way back to her office, causing her secretary Wilma to glance curiously at her as she closed the door. She placed the jar on the desk before her and now sitting in her chair, dialled the number for head office.

On his second visit that morning, Gregory Packer didn't wait to be invited into James Hardie's office, but knocked and immediately pushed open the door. Hardie glanced up from his desk to see the pale faced younger man and was about to chastise him for his impudence, but hesitated and instead said, "It's true then? They've found some contaminated jars?"

Packer nodded and replied, "In both stores mentioned in the letter, in the baby foods aisles. Both the marked jars are Snuckles brand lamb and rice, but I don't know if the contents are contaminated, Mister Hardie. My information is that both jars have certainly been opened. I've instructed the jar from our store across the road is to be brought here to my office and the manager of the Glasgow store will keep the jar there until we can make an arrangement for it to be brought here for examination by our chemists. I've also requested the MD for Snuckles call me at his convenience."

"Good, well done, Gregory," he absentmindedly replied, but his thoughts were elsewhere. The Board would need to be informed and a meeting immediately convened. He glanced down to again stare at the letter on his desk.

"Shall I inform the police about the letter, Mister Hardie?"

His head snapped up as he stared thoughtfully at Packer then sighing, slowly shook his head. "No, let's leave the West Midlands Police out of this meantime, Gregory. If word gets out about our foodstuffs being contaminated by these people..." He could only imagine the panic and ensuing problems if the public got wind of this, not to mention the nutters who would come out of the woodwork demanding exorbitant compensation payments. He drummed the fingers of his right hand on the desktop and taking a deep breath, asked, "How many people know about the letter?"

"Ah, I'm not certain who has read it, Mister Hardie. Let me see," he raised a hand and screwing his eyes tight, began to count off on his fingers, "there is undoubtedly some of the admin staff in Customers Retail Services and then there is..."

"Gregory," Hardie impatiently snapped. "Just find out who read the damned letter and bring them all here to my office. Quick as you like, if you please."

"Oh, yes, sir. Of course," he gulped quickly then quickly left Hardie's office.

He watched Packer close the door and softly exhaling, wondered as he reached for his phone who was responsible for hiring the bloody idiot.

Martin Turner hated his job. He was capable of much more than this, he thought as sitting at his desk he morosely stared at the tousled heads in the room, bent over and silently pretending they were interested in the textbooks that lay on the desks before them.

He hated the moron who was his boss, he hated having to teach the teenage illiterates of the fourth year class and considered them to be little more than unruly thugs from the surrounding council estates who he was certain would never amount to anything, anyway. They had no interest in learning and later in the year when most of them turned sixteen and entered the world without a qualification to their name, they would breed among themselves and produce more of their moronic type.

He took a deep breath and his glance took in the blonde head of Colleen Younger, seated in the front row. The pupils' desks had no vanity board and he could clearly see that slumped in her seat, her legs were astride and she had pulled her already short skirt up to rumple at the top of her slim legs. Her white coloured stockings stopped just above her knees and exposed the pale flesh at the top of her thighs and the navy coloured panties she wore. Gaping at her he felt himself become aroused and then realised she in turn was staring at him, a soft smile playing about her mouth. Slowly, as he watched she raised her arm and in a falsetto voice, said, "Please, Mister Turner, can I leave the room, sir? I need to tinkle."

Her fellow pupils burst out laughing and some of the boys called out, "Colleen needs to piss," or "Go on, sir. Col needs to take a leak."

He felt his face turn red with rage and now on his feet, screamed that they be quiet and then shouted, "Shut up! All of you!" The class ignored his cries and wagging a finger at her, he called out, "Miss Younger, leave the room! Go on, get out!"

She continued to stare at him and smiled as she took her time sliding her legs out from under the desk. Standing, she casually used her hands to smooth the front of her skirt down before saucily sauntering across the front of his desk and moving to the door.

The class erupted, jeering and catcalling and no matter what that he shouted and banged a fist down onto his desk, they ignored him.

As the young girl was reaching for the handle, the door burst open to admit his Departmental Head, Charlie McFadyen.

"Mister Turner, what's going on here?" thundered the bald and heavyset McFadyen.

McFadyen's presence was enough to subdue the uproar that faded to a whisper before dying as the pupils resumed their seats. Turner cast his eyes to the floor, angry and embarrassed even look to at McFadyen.

"Miss Younger," McFadyen turned on her, "why are you out of your seat?"

Wide-eyed, she stared at him and deliberately fluttering here eyelashes at him, innocently replied, "Mister Turner said I could go to the loo, sir."

"Then go," McFadyen stood to one side to permit her to pass and with a final and meaningful glance at Martin, he closed the door as he followed her into the corridor.

Martin resisted the urge to scream that he wanted no more of this shit, that he was finished, that the humiliation of his job was more than he could bear.

Instead, he returned to his desk and pointedly ignored the whispered sniggers.

"Please return to studying your text," he forced himself to loudly call out.

His loathing for his job and for McFadyen in particular knew no bounds.


Once more she run the Hoover over the living room carpet and rolling the cable up, cast her eyes about the room to ensure that everything was in place. It would not do for him to come home and find that the house wasn't as tidy as he liked it to be. No, she unconsciously bit at her lower lip, it wouldn't do at all.

The phone on the hallway stand rung and startled her.

"Hello?"

"Annemarie, it's me," said her younger sister, Joyce. "Thought I'd give you a wee call on my break to find out how you're doing, hen."

"Oh, fine," she forced herself to sound cheery. "Just getting the house tidied up. You know what it's like with two kids."

"Well, actually, I don't, not having any of my own."

"Sorry, I didn't mean…"

"No, you're all right. It's fine. Besides, your house *is* immaculate. God, there's never *anything* out of place and those lassies of yours are the tidiest I've ever met. I mean, I could eat my dinner off your kitchen floor," she gave a soft laugh. "I was wondering if you….listen, the real reason I'm phoning is that I've got a couple of tickets, freebies actually, for the Kings Theatre next week and I'm due a half day off. It's the matinee, a musical and maybe we could get a bite to eat after it if…"

"Oh, thanks, but I don't think so, Joyce. You know what Martin's like. He likes me to be at home when he gets in. Spend some time with me."

"Ah, okay then. Thought I'd ask," replied Joyce, but she could hear the disappointment in her sister's voice and quickly added, "Perhaps another time?"

"Yeah, fine. Right, that's me, I'll need to go, hen. Speak soon. Love you."

She was still holding the phone even though the line was dead. Slowly, she placed the phone down and leaning with her back against the wall, sighed. Joyce knew what kind of life she had with him and was always trying to get her out of the house. The thought of spending a carefree afternoon at the theatre and maybe a meal later was tempting, but the aftermath of coming home to one of his moods just wasn't worth it.

Even for Joyce.

Her glance took in the carpet stair and her eyes narrowed. She had missed some fluff on the second step and with soft exhale of breath, moving forward to pick it up she softly groaned, for her ribs still ached.


He lifted the phone and dialled an internal number that connected him with his deputy, Gregory Packer.

Without preamble, he instructed that the fourth floor boardroom be prepared, that seven of the nine Directors including himself would be convening at two that afternoon to discuss the threatening letter.

"In the meantime, Gregory, I want the contents of the Snuckles jar from the 'Founding Store' sent to our laboratory and the examination of the contents treated as urgent. If there *is* a contaminant in the product, I want to be able to inform the Board."

"What about the jar found in the Glasgow store, sir?"

He took a deep breath and replied, "Glasgow is over three hundred miles away, Gregory. How do you propose to get the jar down in time for it to be examined?"

"I was thinking that Ellen Toner, the manager of the Glasgow store could perhaps have it examined locally, sir, and the result phoned or e-mailed."

"No, Gregory. I don't think you understand. This issue *must* be kept as tight as possible. We cannot afford to have too many people know of this threat. Like I told those members of staff who read the letter; can you imagine what it would do to our customer base if it is publicly disclosed that we are selling *any* produce that might be contaminated with God knows what?"

"Yes sir, I understand, sir," Packer weakly replied.

"Now, have you heard from the MD at Snuckles?"

"Ah, yes sir," he sighed. "I'm assured that all their products are contamination free, that they leave their warehouse packaged in sealed cardboard boxes. I took the liberty of taking her into my confidence and to be frank, she informed me that if the threat is aimed at Chrystons and the products were marked while upon our shelves then really, it's our problem."

"Oh, she did, did she? Well, we'll remember that little bit of advice the next time the Snuckles contract with us is due for renewal, shall we?" he bitterly replied.

"Get the boardroom set up like I said and copies of the letter to be available for perusal by the Board," he abruptly instructed before hanging up.

Joyce shook her head and arching her back, resisted the temptation to smash her mobile phone against the wall. She drew her head back to stare at the blue sky, her eyes dismissing the grey walls of the tenement buildings around her in North Hanover Street.

No matter how hard she tried, Annemarie just could not break free from the claustrophobic clutches of that bastard husband of hers. Could not, she thought or maybe the true reason was she would not. Likely it was fear that kept her under his freakish control.

She had seen the bruises and the panic in her sister's eyes, had repeatedly tried in vain to get Annemarie to open up to her, to admit that Martin was abusing her. God, she inwardly snarled, how she hated that bastard.

To the world he seemed to be a loving and caring husband and father.

To Joyce he was no more than a manipulative and cunning abuser.

A year previously her contact with Annemarie had been curtailed to virtually phone calls only after Martin had learned that Joyce was quizzing her nieces, Paula then aged nine and seven-year-old Carol. The children were too afraid of their father to speak to her even though she suspected they had to be aware of what he was doing to their mother.

Her thoughts were disturbed by a young teenage girl who approached and hesitantly smiling, asked, "Miss McKinnon, I've just come from the office that deals with the Faculty for Leisure & Lifestyle and I was told you are the lecturer in charge of the HND course that deals with Food Science. I understand that course applications have to be submitted by the end of this week?"

She nodded and forced a polite smile. "Yes, of course."

Glancing at her wristwatch, she continued, "Look, I'm on my way back to my office. Give me twenty minutes and then come to my office. We can discuss the curriculum and if you wish, we can deal with your application then, okay?"

The girl eagerly agreed and walked with Joyce back towards the main doors of the City College.

He sighed with relief when the bell sounded and listened as the scum raced through the corridors, their howls mixed with the shouts of the teaching staff screaming that they do not run.

Do they listen, he thought? Do they fuck!

He waited for almost ten minutes to allow the unwashed masses to depart the school before wearily shoving that evenings papers to be marked into his battered brown leather briefcase. Rising from his desk, he slipped on his jacket then made his way to the door. He glanced up and down the corridor, but by then it had emptied of both pupils and teaching staff and already the cleaners were pushing their noisy metal wheeled buckets and mops along the passageways. Two of them, women wearing brightly coloured headscarves smiled cheerily and courteously bobbed their ebony faces towards him, but Martin had no time for those type of people and had little doubt all the cleaners were either asylum seekers or illegal bloody immigrants. After all, he reasoned, Barmulloch was full of the bastards, wasn't it?

He pushed open the main doors and saw that the uneven and broken concreted ground that formed the entrance to the school and led into the nearby Ryehill Road was almost clear of pupils other than a few malingerers walking towards the main gates.

Glancing at the sky he took a deep breath and again wondered for the thousandth time why he would even consider returning tomorrow to this shithole.

Well, he sullenly thought, at least I'm free for tonight and began to walk towards the staff car park.

It was when he turned the corner of the building that he saw her leaning back against his BMW, her arms folded and her school blazer lying on top of her satchel by her feet. She had loosened the ribbon on her blonde hair that now almost touched her shoulders.

"Hello, Mister Turner," she smiled at him.

He stopped and glanced about him, but there was nobody near; at least nobody he could see. He was about to speak, but then she cocked her head at the BMW and said, "Nice car, Mister Turner. I wouldn't mind a wee shot in a car like this."

He stared warily at her and then asked, "What can I do for you, Miss Younger?"

She shrugged and replied, "I was wondering what I could do for *you*, Mister Turner," then unfolding her arms, she let them dangle by her side and he saw that she had taken off her school tie and the top three buttons of her white blouse were undone and revealed her adolescent cleavage. He watched her run her tongue across the top of her upper lip and then staring at him, she added, "I know you like me. I saw you watching me in class."

He felt his throat tighten and his voice almost croaked when he replied, "I don't know what you mean. You shouldn't be here," he glanced about him again at the empty car park and in an attempt to regain some authority, added, "This is very inappropriate, Miss Younger," but his nerves were now on edge and his voice quivered.

"If that means you don't like me, Mister Turner," she pretended a petted lip, "then you won't want to come and meet with me tonight."

"What do you mean?"

"Well," she drawled, "most nights I like to go for a walk alone in the dark up in the golf course behind the Stobhill Hospital. You must know where that is, *Mister* Turner," she drawled. "The golf course…"

"I know where it is," he snapped, knowing that he should just get in his car and drive away, but something kept him there; kept him talking with her.

"There's a large gap in the fence at the hospital car park, Mister Turner. The gap in the fence leads into the golf course. It's dead quiet up there at night. I'm usually hanging about there about seven o'clock, Mister Turner."

She took a half step from the car and bent over from the waist to lift her blazer and satchel from the ground, fully aware she deliberately exposed her bra and the swell of her breasts as she did so.

He took a deep breath and forced himself to look at her face as she stood.

Swinging the satchel onto her shoulder and carrying the blazer over her left arm, she swept her free hand through her hair as she brushed past him and almost in a whisper, said, "Just in case you should be passing at that time, Mister Turner."

He turned to watch her slowly saunter off and then unlocked the door to his car. When he was seated inside the vehicle he took a deep breath and slowly exhaled. Inserting the key into the ignition, was surprised to discover his hand was shaking.

## CHAPTER TWO

Sat with her elbows on the desk and her chin resting on her clasped hands, Ellen Toner stared at the jar, now encased in a plastic food bag that lay in front of her. Gregory Packer had been quite clear that under no circumstances was she to discuss the issue with any other member of staff. Nor was she to open the jar, but to secure the jar in the store safe and he would make arrangements for its uplift, though had not provided her with any details of when or how that was to occur.

Wilma her secretary knocked on the door and said, "That's the midday rush over, Ellen," and glanced curiously at the jar in the clear plastic bag. "What's that all about?"

"Oh, eh, it's head office. They asked that I remove a sample jar of Snuckles baby food from the shelf. Apparently there's this new initiative where they want to quality test a different food sample every month," she lied with a broad smile, wondering where the hell *that* thought had come from.

"Oh aye," Wilma narrowed her eyes, recognising the lie for what it was worth, but realising that to pursue the issue would likely get her nowhere.

"Right, anything else?" Ellen cheerfully asked.

"No," Wilma shook her head and returned to her own desk.

Ellen didn't like lying to the older woman, but since being promoted just a month and a half previously from her previous post as a departmental manager at the Argyle Street superstore to the post of manager at the food outlet, she was still finding her feet here at Woodlands Road. She was aware that Wilma had been with the company for almost twenty years, having worked her way from floor assistant to the position of manager's secretary. She was now, quite literally, the second senior figure in the Woodlands Road store. However, Ellen, who had joined the company five years previously as a university graduate, was also acutely aware that Wilma was an outrageous gossip.

The desk phone rang and answering it, was relieved to hear Gregory Packers voice.

"Just to keep you apprised, Miss Toner. We have discovered another jar in the 'Founding Store' that is being examined by our chemists as I speak."

She was about to reply when the door knocked and she saw the shop assistant Alice Green nervously stood there. Raising a finger to indicate Green should wait, she said to Packer, "I have someone at my door just now, something I have to deal with, Mister Packer. Can I call you back in say, ten minutes," and accepting his agreement, returned the phone to its cradle. Waving the younger woman into her office, she bid her sit in the seat on the other side of the desk and curtly said, "Clearly, previous verbal warnings about your conduct on the shop floor have been ignored, Alice. Tell me this, is this job important to you?"

"Yes, Miss Toner, it is," replied the crimson faced younger woman. Ellen stared at her, hating herself for what she had to do. However, she knew from bitter experience that if she did not crack down on staff idleness it would spread like a virus and soon she would lose control of all her staff.

She recalled the briefing by her then store manager at Argyle Street that prior to Ellen's appointment to Woodlands Road, Alice's laziness had been tolerated by Ellen's predecessor, a young man whose main interest in the pretty shop assistant had been predatory and if the rumour was correct, he was now unemployed and involved in a divorce action with his pregnant wife. Ellen chose not to believe the risqué stories that had been bandied about regarding the Alice and the former manager.

"Alice," she slowly said. "There's an old adage..." and saw the girls face crease and her brow furrow. "An old saying," she corrected herself, "that a new broom sweeps clean. Well, I'm the new broom. In the recent past, this store has not been doing very well and I intend that situation will improve. That means that we will *all* work that little bit harder to realise that improvement, do you understand?"

"Yes, Miss Toner."

Ellen made a pretence of shuffling some papers on her desk as she continued. "You accept that I have already given you a number of verbal warnings, yes?"

Alice nodded.

"Well, as I saw this morning, these verbal warnings seemingly failed to motivate you so I will now cause you to be given a written warning regarding your behaviour on the shop floor. I must remind you, Alice that there will be no further verbal warnings and that a further written warning will result in your dismissal without reference. Do you understand?"

"Yes, Miss Toner," the girl replied in a hushed voice, her eyes filling as she fought the tears.

"Thank you, Alice, that will be all," she abruptly dismissed her.

Alice had been gone just a few moments when Wilma poked her head back into Ellen's office and said, "Do you want a cup of tea, hen?"

"I'd rather have a brandy," she sat back in her chair and sighed, but had hardly spoke when her phone rang. "Yes," she snapped, but almost immediately regretted her brusqueness and recognising the caller's voice, placed one hand over the phone speaker and turning towards Wilma, smiled at the older woman and said, "Sorry, it's a personal call if you don't mind."

When the door had closed behind the secretary, Ellen returned the phone to her ear and said, "Right then, Mister Packer. So, what are the arrangements for getting this jar down to you?"

Glancing at the kitchen clock she guessed Martin would not be home for at least twenty minutes; twenty minutes of tensely waiting.

She heard the front door open and her stomach lurched, but sighed with relief when she heard it was her daughters Paula and Carol returning from school. It wasn't often that she permitted them to return home alone, but the mother of a school pal who lived just one street away had agreed the girls could accompany her son home. Still, Annemarie was relived that they were now home safe.

"Hi, Mum," they cried in unison as they raced along the hallway towards her, their anoraks and schoolbags untidily abandoned at the door.

Her first reaction was one of horror when she realised they were still wearing their shoes and had left scuff marks on the recently hoovered carpet, but forcing a smile she enveloped them in her arms and kissed them in turn.

"Now both of you," she pretended a rebuke, "grab those jackets and bags and get yourselves upstairs to begin your homework. You know your father doesn't like a mess when he gets in."

Their faces displayed their dismay and her heart fell as they turned slowly to do as she said.

Carol turned back and said, "Can I get a drink of milk, please Mum?"

"Of course, sweetheart, I'll bring you one up," she promised and playfully slapped at their backsides, but thought only after I've hoovered this bloody carpet again.

She watched as they lifted their anoraks and schoolbags and heard them trudge upstairs.

It killed her to think of them being unhappy but, she sighed; what else am I to do?


Martin McCormick pressed the intercom button to speak with his receptionist, Martha and requested she contact Tom McEwan, one of his law firms two investigators and instructed that Tom phone him urgently.

Less than five minutes later, his desk phone rang.

"Hello, Boss, what's up," Tom cheerfully greeted him.

"Where are you right now?"

"Ah, following up that insurance claim against the bus company. Just obtaining some witness statements and a couple of photographs. Why, something up?"

"How far are you from the office?"

"Let me think, afternoon traffic," Tom paused, then said, "I can be with you in say, fifteen, twenty minutes' tops."

"Good, can you do that, but don't kill yourself on the way," McCormick dryly joked.

True to his word, Tom arrived sixteen minutes later and knocking first, pushed open the door to McCormick's office then slumped his lanky frame down into a chair opposite the lawyer and rubbed at his short fair hair.

"Right," McCormick briskly began, "let me get right to it, but first; have you anything on tonight?"

"Nothing," Tom shook his head. "Lisa was going out to dinner with her new fiancé Aiden and I was supposed to have the twins for a sleepover, but that's fell through so it's a quiet night in." He narrowed his eyes as he started at McCormick, "But you have something for me to do, don't you," he smiled at McCormick.

"I didn't know your ex had got herself engaged," McCormick was surprised. "Is it an issue with you?"

"No, not at all," Tom shook his head. "After that carry-on when Alice Foley's husband tried to frame me for the murders, you'll recall Lisa and me kind of got together again for a wee while; nothing serious, more for the twins' sake if I'm being honest about it. As you know, it didn't work out, but since the divorce we've stayed relatively friendly. No, more than that," he smiled. "I think we've become good pals. As for her becoming engaged, I've met him a few times now and Aiden seems to be a nice bloke and the twins like him and he's good to them so no, it's not an issue," he shrugged.

"I'm pleased to hear that," McCormick smiled. "Right, down to business." He leaned forward with his forearms on his desk.

"Briefly, we as a firm are associated with a prestigious law firm who are based in Birmingham. In short, while they practise law on their side of the border, we attend to any issues that their client might encounter here in Scotland. To be honest, Tom, in the three years since our retainer was agreed, this is the first time they have actually come to us for assistance. Today, I received a phone call from them outlining a problem that one of their more important clients is having."

"Who's the client?"

"Chrystons. You know, the large supermarket chain of stores. They're UK wide and traditionally sell everything from furniture to clothing to garden equipment, but about ten or fifteen years ago they branched out into food outlets as well."

"Yeah, I know they've a big store down in Argyle Street and there's that place up near Charing Cross too. I think that's food only, though."

"Yes, you're correct. On Woodlands Road. Anyway, it seems that some time today in two of their stores, one in Birmingham and the Woodlands Road store here in Glasgow, jars of contaminated baby food were discovered. The baby food is supplied to Chrystons by a subsidiary company, Snuckles Baby Foods. Staff in the Birmingham and Glasgow stores were directed to the jars by a letter that was received at the company's head office in Birmingham. I have no knowledge how the letter was worded, but my information, scant though it is, is that the letter is a threat against the company."

"Do you know who is making the threat?"

"No," McCormick shook his head and admitted, "what I'm telling you is all that I *do* know."

"So, how are we to be involved?"

"My contact with the company is a man called James Hardie who I believe is a Director. I spoke briefly with him and to be frank, he sounds a bit of a blowhard; sod spoke to me like I was some kind of lackey," McCormick scowled, clearly annoyed with this man Hardie. "Anyway, he quite specifically made it clear that there is to be no police involvement, that this issue is to be handled as discreetly as possible."

"Worried about the publicity, I suppose," Tom suggested.

"Exactly that," McCormick smiled at Tom's shrewd guess. "If word gets out that Chrystons food products might be contaminated, the financial loss would be incalculable."

"Don't Chrystons have their own security?"

"That I don't know," replied McCormick.

"So again, what's our involvement?"

"Sorry, yes," McCormick nodded. "Hardie wants the inquiry to be conducted by private investigators, both here in Glasgow and in

Birmingham. There is nothing to suggest the person or persons responsible for the threat might be from here, but he's requested that we provide a representative to sit in on their Board meeting that is to be convened tomorrow in Birmingham. And that," he grinned at Tom, "is where you come in."

"Oh. So have I time to throw a couple of things into an overnight bag?"

McCormick glanced at the wall clock and replied, "Hardie's people have arranged a seat for you on the six o'clock British Midlands flight from Glasgow. Martha has secured accommodation for you at a Premier Inn which Martha tells me," he frowned and called out loudly, "Martha! How far is the Premier Inn from the Chrystons head office again?"

The door opened to admit the large and cheery Jamaican woman who dressed in a colourfully patterned floral dress, stood with her hands on her wide hips and shaking her head, replied, "Don't you ever listen to me, Boss man? I already tell you once, didn't I? Twenty-five minutes in a taxi and," she scowled at Tom as she wagged a stubby forefinger at him, "don't you forget to bring me receipts back, you pasty faced white boy or you and me will fall out."

Tom grinned and blew her a kiss in return, earning himself another scowl as she closed the door with a bang.

"No wonder you never have any rude or cheeky clients, Martin," he turned with a grin towards McCormick.

"And she's one very capable and organised secretary too, but God help me if she ever makes a pass at me. I think I'd just surrender and let her do what she wants," McCormick returned his grin. "Right, you'd better be off…" but stopped when his desk phone rang.

Tom arose and with a wave turned to leave, but stopped when McCormick raised his hand.

"Yes, I understand," Tom heard him say, then McCormick asked the caller, "How do you spell that?"

Tom watched as he scribbled with a pencil on his desk pad and bidding the caller goodbye, glanced at Tom.

"That was one of Hardie's people, a guy called Gregory Packer. It seems that Chrystons head office has a pharmaceutical laboratory in the building where they routinely conduct tests on their food products and those of the suppliers they use. Anyway, they have tested the contents of the jar that was discovered in the Birmingham store and confirmed the contents are indeed contaminated."

"What about the jar from the Glasgow store? Any word if that too is contaminated?"

"It's still to be tested. Packer didn't say, but I'm surmising that Chrystons must be making some sort of arrangement to get it either tested here or taken down to Birmingham for testing by their own chemists."

"I suppose I could have taken it down," mused Tom, but McCormick shook his head and with a wave of his hand, said, "No, we'll let them organise that. No need for us to interfere with their own arrangements."

"What's that you were writing?" Tom pointed to McCormick's desk pad.

"Oh, it's the name of the stuff their chemists discovered in the jar. The contaminate. Something called…I'm not sure if I'm pronouncing it properly…something called Lutein," he slowly read from the desk pad.

"Lutein," exclaimed Tom. "What the heck is that, then?"

"Well," McCormick slowly drawled and brow furrowed, he stared at Tom, "according to Packer it's a food colouring, something that they obtain from plants. It's not dangerous and commonly used in food products. Curious," he shook his head.

The men stared uneasily at each other before Tom said, "Right then, I'm off. I'll phone you tomorrow with an update."


Martin Turner arrived home to the semi-detached former local authority house in Glenhead Street and reversed the BMW into the narrow driveway. Getting out of the car, he glanced along the street and shook his head at his misfortune as he wondered once more how he had come to live in such a *bloody* rundown area.

Never in his life did he imagine that he would wind up living in this shithole.

Believing himself worthy of a far better life, he could not see the homes that the locals had worked so very hard to attain as their own, the neat and tidy gardens that blossomed and thrived due to the owners' labour nor did he see the modern and polished cars that were parked outside the houses and represented the pride his neighbours had in those homes and the area in which they lived.

Martin, a snob of the worst kind slammed the door of the ten-year-old BMW and immediately regretted his action.

Even within the house she heard the car door slam and caught her breath.

He was home.

Turning back towards the car he muttered an apology and run his palm across the highly polished surface as though soothing a child. The dark blue coloured twenty-year-old, four door M3 with its Black Nappa Leather sports seats was his pride and joy and he spent more of his time with the car than he did his daughters. Not that he would permit the girls to even sit in the car. No, that's why he had bought Annemarie the old and rusting Ford Escort that now sat forlornly on two flat tyres in the roadway outside the house. The Escort was not used simply because Martin refused his wife money for its upkeep and the vehicle had not turned a wheel for over two years, was no longer taxed nor insured nor and was without a current MoT certificate.

In the kitchen Annemarie quickly tore off the apron and threw it into the cupboard before making her way toward the front door, patting her hair into shape and arriving just as he was closing it behind him. "Hi, darling," she forced a smile as she greeted him and held out her hands to take his jacket and briefcase from him.

He grunted in response then stopped, his eyes focusing on the white painted sill of the small window by the front door. A chill run through her as she watched him slowly lean forward towards the sill. She shivered as he run his forefinger along the edge.

"Did you dust this today?" he asked as he stared at the sill. His voice was barely a whisper yet still she sensed the malice behind the question.

Her heart skipped a beat as nervously she replied, "Yes, Martin, of course I did." She tried to humour him and smiling brightly added, "but you know what it's like round here."

"You're lying," he hissed and suddenly turning, took a menacing step towards her, forcing her to back against the stair banister, his hands balling into fists.

Annemarie instinctively turned her head away expecting to be struck and raised both hands to ward him off. She could feel her face turn red as she thought, how could she have been so stupid as to forget to dust the window sill?

Brutally taking her chin in his hand, he forcibly turned her face back towards him, their noses almost touching. His eyes malevolently bored into hers, terrorising her into submission.

"Daddy?" called the voice from above.

He glanced up to see Paula standing at the top of the stairs, her face pale as she stared down at him and clutched the hand of her younger sister.

He smiled and releasing Annemarie, called up to his daughter, "It's all right, darling. Mummy and Daddy are only playing a game. Come down and see me and give me a big hug."

He stepped to one side and opened his arms to the girls who hesitantly descended the stairs, both glancing nervously at their mother who quietly gasped for breath.

"Come on, down to Daddy," he commanded and ignoring his wife, enveloped them both in his arms and smothered the fearful little girls with kisses.

Annemarie turned away and stumbled along the hallway to the kitchen, the tears threatening to spill from her.


Ellen Toner turned her Hyundai hatchback from Maryhill Road into the cul-de-sac in Seamore Street and parked in a bay outside her house. Switching the engine off, she briefly stared with pride at the mid-terraced home. Almost three months had quickly passed since she moved in and yes, the mortgage was crippling her, but though it required some décor and modernisation the house had been a bargain. She glanced at her wristwatch and realised she would need to rush if she was to make the plane on time and locking the car, fumbled in her handbag of the front door keys. That's when she saw the safe keys and groaned. She'd need to stop at the store on her way to the airport and give the keys to Wilma who was acting as manager for the short time Ellen was gone. Pushing the door open, she lifted the junk mail from behind the door and dumped it onto the small hall table. Another glance at her watch told her she'd better get a move on.


Seated at his desk, his tie undone and jacket flung on a chair by the side of the room, James Hardie stared morosely at the chemists' report.

What the fuck is Lutein he wondered, but as he read on his face fell. The author of the report, aware that the analysis finding would be discussed by the Board at the next days meeting had sensibly broken the description down into layman terms, but all that Hardie and the Board required to know was Lutein was found in egg yolks and animal fats, was obtained by animals directly or indirectly from plant life and employed by animals as an antioxidant. It was used to colour chicken skin yellow and used in the chickens feed for this purpose.

In short read the report, Lutein was not in itself poisonous. However, thought Hardie, that did not detract from the threat.

His brow furrowed and he chewed at his lower lip. It seemed obvious to him the Lutein was merely a distraction, a non-lethal addition to the baby food that would easily be identified by the company chemists as a contaminant; the Lutein was a warning that if the threat was not taken seriously, the next contaminant would be more deadly.

He glanced down to the report and read that according to the author, the minute amount discovered in the Snuckles jar of lamb and rice was certainly not harmful to a child and would at the very worst, simply cause a mild gastric disorder.

It did not matter he fumed, that the Lutein was not in itself harmful. It was the threat that worried him and decided this had all the makings of a disaster.

The shareholders Annual Report was currently being prepared and while there was no likelihood of Chrystons going under, their profit margin was certainly suffering due to the growth of cheaper high street stores, much of whose products were sourced from not only the Far East, but more recently from the emerging markets of Eastern Europe.

He sat back and rubbed with both hands at his face.

Today's emergency Board meeting that included besides himself six other Directors, had insufficient cause to issue any statement or make a decision as to how the company would handle this threat. However, the two remaining Directors, one of whom was the CEO Jackson Peters were returning tonight to the UK from America and the full Board would meet tomorrow afternoon by which time the jar discovered in the Glasgow store would also have been examined.

Today's meeting had been unusually rowdy with two of the Board insisting that the police be informed of the letter and the contamination of the product, but persuasively led by Hardie the remaining Directors overruled this suggestion.

His proposal that a representative from their Birmingham based law firm and someone from their legal associates in Glasgow be present was accepted with some reluctance and ill-grace by the two challenging Directors until he explained his reasons.

"After all, gentlemen," he had said, "while I agree we must be seen to do something about this threat to our company, think about the consequences if we do go public." He had stared at the remaining six Directors in turn. "You are all aware that the shareholders Annual Report is being prepared and it does *not* make good reading. I do not believe that currently we as a company are so financially secure that we can cope with a large influx of lawsuits that will undoubtedly follow every time a child consumes a product purchased from one of our stores and then burps. Can we afford to check every single food items that we sell? I mean, who is to say that this individual or individuals do not intend further contamination of our bread, our fruit or whatever."

He had startled them by banging a fist down onto the mahogany table and forcefully stated, "I strongly recommend we *must* handle this in-house and have this individual or individuals caught and yes, if it does land us with a large bill, consider what it would cost us if we *did* go public!"

When the meeting broke up it was a disconsolate group who met in the adjoining lounge to share a glass of whatever took their pleasure, though Hardie was heartened with the backslapping support he received for his initial handling of the situation.

He sat back in his chair and reflected on the meeting.

He thought of the individual Directors who had been present and briefly considered those who had voiced their support for his actions. The tacit rumour was that the CEO Jackson Peters, who had recently turned sixty-two years of age, was due to stand down within the next year and often joked that he was ready to retire to his Spanish villa with his much younger and nubile wife. Though self admittedly one of the company's more recently appointed Directors, Hardie believed he had acquitted himself well at the meeting and wondered; would that support continue if he were to stand for the position of CEO.

His door knocked and was pushed open by his Deputy Gregory Packer, who hesitated as though bearing bad news.

"Yes, Gregory."

"Just to confirm with you, sir, that the rep from the law firm in Glasgow will be arriving in the city this evening and will attend tomorrow's meeting. Also, the manager of the Glasgow store, a Miss Ellen Toner will also be arriving later this evening with the jar of baby food. I will personally meet her at the airport and collect the jar from her to bring for examination here at the laboratory."

He stared at the young man and thought a conciliatory gesture was in order, so smiled and said, "Thank you, Gregory, and well done."

The younger man flushed with pleasure as he closed the door.

His thoughts returned to the meeting and recalled with satisfaction the Directors congratulations on his handling of the situation so far. Clasping his hands behind his head, he smiled for the thought occurred that the author of the letter might have unwittingly presented him with a unique opportunity to progress his ambition to the position of CEO.

Sitting in the front passenger seat of Martha's old and rusting Mazda, Tom McEwan flinched as she raced westwards on the M8 towards Glasgow airport. Weaving from the outside lane around a large HGV to the inside lane, she sang loudly and off-key accompanying Bob Marley who belted out his classic, 'No Woman No Cry' on the cars outdated cassette tape deck.

Bloody hell, he thought, I'm like Billy Elliot here tapping my toes looking for the brakes!

"What you worried about, pasty white boy," she turned to grin at him and displayed probably the most perfect set of white teeth he had ever seen. "You afraid ole Martha not get you to your flight on time?"

"Not get me there on time," he almost wailed. "Martha, I'm afraid you'll get me to Birmingham *without* needing the bloody flight! Can you not slow down to eighty or something?"

Martha laughed uproariously and continued to weave in and out of the traffic, ignoring the startled faces or angry horns that blasted at her.

Tom had spent several years as a police surveillance officer and was used to high speed pursuits, but this, he inwardly thought, is terrifying the fucking life out of me!

At last, Martha cut from the middle lane and narrowly missing a white coloured airport taxi, drove at speed down the off ramp that led to the airport.

He hadn't realised how anxious he was at her driving till he saw that his knuckles holding onto the handle above his door were bleach white.

Martha raced the car through the roundabout and with a screech, stopped it in the offloading bay near to the main concourse.

"There we go, my little pasty man. You get in there now and don't you forget, Tom McEwan," she wagged her finger at him. "You remember and get me all the receipts, everything. You understand?"

"Yeah," he nervously grinned, relieved to be out of the death trap that was her car and with a wave turned, but stopped and leaned back before closing the passenger door.

"Tell me this, Martha. Where did you learn to drive?"

"In Jamaica, the island of sun, laughter and good music," she grinned proudly at him.

"But you do have a British driving licence, don't you?"

She continued to grin at him and with crunch, shoved the gear stick into first and as he closed the door, called out loudly, "I get round to it one of these days!"

He watched her speed away with a screech of tyres and shaking his head, accidentally bumped into a young woman wearing a skirted business suit and knocked the overnight case from her hand she pulled behind her.

"Sorry," he began and crouched down for the handle, but the woman beat him to it and scowling continued towards the front doors.

"Aye, you're welcome," he sighed and shook his head, but stood for a few seconds to admire redheaded woman's slender figure as she strode away.

It had gone five o'clock when Tom entered the concourse that was busy with business travellers arriving at or departing from Glasgow. Martha had told him that he would collect his ticket from the British Midlands desk and with the strap of his old brown leather valise slung on one shoulder, made his way there and joined the queue of a dozen or so fellow travellers. His eyes narrowed when he saw the redheaded woman he had collided with standing halfway down the queue.

Idly, he cast a glance about the concourse and shuffled forward as the passengers were dealt with. The redhead reached the desk and was being dealt with and even above the noise from the concourse, Tom clearly heard the woman tell the ground stewardess that a ticket awaited her under the company name Chrystons Supermarkets (PLC).

As he watched, the woman collected her ticket and pulling her case behind her, headed for the domestic departure lounge.

A few minutes later, Tom collected his own ticket and smiling at the stewardess, said, "I was expecting a colleague to be travelling with me. Like mine her ticket was to be collected here at the booking desk and arranged by Chrystons. Can you tell me if she has arrived yet?"

The young woman glanced at Tom and slightly harassed at the number of passengers stood behind him, checked her clipboard and replied, "Ah, yes sir. Miss Ellen Toner. She was here a few minutes ago and collected her ticket. Now, sir, if you don't mind…"

"Of course," he offered her another smile and walking towards the departure lounge, idly wondered if the redheaded Miss Toner was carrying a jar of contaminated Snuckles baby food in her case.

## CHAPTER THREE

He glanced up at the arrivals board and saw that her flight was not due to land for another twenty minutes. Time enough for a coffee, he decided as he lazily scanned the travellers who passed him by.

A few minutes earlier than the information board indicated, he saw that the BM Airbus had landed and expected that Miss Toner would be carrying just a shoulder bag and likely to disembark quickly and be out the arrivals door within a few minutes. He felt a little foolish holding the piece of cardboard upon which he had scrawled 'CHRYSTONS', but had never met the Glasgow food outlet manager and forgotten to obtain her description. As the passengers began to stream through the arrivals door, he was approached by a very attractive and smiling redhead who stood an inch taller than his five feet seven with her hair tied back into a French plait and wearing a bottle green coloured business suit. Packer frowned a little when he saw she pulled an overnight case behind her.

"Mister Packer," she extended her hand, "I'm Ellen Toner."

He shook her hand and now a little embarrassed, said, "Miss Toner, I think there has been some sort of mistake. I thought this was to be a straightforward handover," and nodding towards her case, added, "I didn't expect that you were to be here overnight."

Her face turned pale when she frostily replied, "The ticket I was issued at the departure desk is a return ticket dated for tomorrow, Mister Packer."

"Oh, a return ticket," he repeated, now confused and shrugged with embarrassment. "I'm sorry, there must have been a mix-up at the admin office."

"Are you telling me that there is no accommodation arranged and that I'm supposed to try and find a bed for the night?"

"You can come with me and we'll see if the Premier Inn can accommodate you, if you like," said the voice behind her.

Turning, she saw a tall, slim and casually dressed man with short fair hair wearing a light blue coloured open neck shirt, chinos and a brown leather jacket who carried a bag slung over one shoulder and who was vaguely familiar. Bewildered, she stared at him and said, "Pardon?"

The man pointed towards the card that Packer still held and extended a hand towards him. Packer, equally surprised, reacted instinctively by offering his own hand and said, "I'm sorry, you are?"

"Tom McEwan from McCormick and Co (Solicitors). I'm the investigator sent down here to attend your Board meeting tomorrow morning regarding an issue you have in one of your Glasgow stores."

"I believe I know you," stuttered Ellen, "but I can't quite…"

"I bumped into you outside Glasgow airport. You dropped your case."

"No," she narrowed her eyes in recognition, "you knocked it from my hand."

"Yeah, well, regardless of that," he smiled easily at her, "I'm guessing that you have a food jar to give to this gentleman that requires to be tested, Miss Toner, and then you and I can share a taxi and we'll see about getting you a room for the night."

Her brow furrowed as she asked him, "How do you know my name?"

"I'm an investigator, remember?"

Packer was now thoroughly confused and turning to Ellen said, "Perhaps if you will give me the…" he glanced uneasily at Tom and added, "the jar, Miss Toner, and again I apologise for the inconvenience. I assure you that I will be speaking sharply to someone in the admin about this…this little hiccup."

"Well, Mister Packer," she frowned at him, "this little hiccup as you call it might just have left me stranded here overnight…"

"Don't worry about that, Miss Toner," Tom reached down and took the handle of her case from her, "if the worst comes to the very worst, you can have my room," he said, but his eyes betrayed his thoughts that he would prefer to share it.

"Wait," she told him and bending down to unzip the case, fumbled inside to retrieve the sealed plastic bag that contained the jar and handed it to Packer.

"And you're certain no other member of staff within your store is aware of this issue, Miss Toner."

"I'm certain. I dealt with it myself," she replied.

"Look," Tom interjected, "maybe it's fortuitous that we have met, Miss Toner, because you will be able to provide me with information that could help my investigation."

He saw her glance uncertainly at Packer who nodded and told her, "Mister...McEwan did you say?"

Tom nodded.

"Mister McEwan will be acting in Glasgow on behalf of the company in this issue, Miss Toner, so I see no reason why you don't comply with any questions he might have."

"Very well, Mister Packer, but this meeting tomorrow morning. If you didn't expect me to be here overnight, then I must assume that I am *not* invited?"

Packer was flustered for not only was he literally stranding this attractive woman in Birmingham overnight, he had no information if indeed she was to participate in the meeting.

"Perhaps if I might have your mobile phone number and I'll get back to you, Miss Toner."

Ellen gave him the number and holding the bag containing the jar against his chest as though it were a precious gift, Packer took his leave of them.

Tom smiled at Ellen and tongue in cheek, said, "Right then, Miss Toner we'll grab a taxi to the Premier Inn and on the way, you can tell me *all* about yourself."

He couldn't explain why he showered. It's not as if he was going on a date, not with someone Colleen Younger's age, he told himself. Yet the memory of the shapely teenager lying back against his car with her blouse open…he felt himself become aroused and slowly exhaled.

There were a thousand reasons why he shouldn't drive up to the hospital car park. A thousand reasons that screamed at him that he was being stupid, that he was risking not just his career, but his livelihood. Dressing himself in a clean shirt and denim trousers, he glanced in the mirror and thought, what the *fuck* am I doing? I'm a forty-year-old man, a teacher for God's sake, going to meet a sixteen-year-old pupil.

Yet again, the thought of Colleen and her veiled invitation overcome the rational reservations that he had.

Grabbing his jacket from the bedroom cupboard he made his way downstairs, listening as he heard Annemarie in the front room helping the girls with their homework.

"I'm going out, I've a meeting at the school," he called and lifting his keys from the small hallway table, opened the front door.

He had no need to explain further. As far as he was concerned, Annemarie did not merit any explanations from him. She was a dead loss as a wife and as far as he was concerned regretted the day that he met her. She was the stone around his neck, a slovenly cow who consistently needed to be reminded who was the boss in the house. A woman who couldn't even produce him a son.

Not that it mattered anymore, for any relationship they now had was confined to her attending his needs; his food, his washing, taking care of her daughters and trying to keep the house clean and tidy. Christ, was *that* too much to ask, he opened the car door.

Her daughters.

Yes, he had sired the girls, but really had nothing in common with them. They were their mother's daughters and always would be and the sooner they were of age and gone from the house, the better. Once that responsibility was off his hands, Annemarie would be next to go.

He was still young enough to have a life and unconsciously grinning, thought maybe that life would begin tonight.

The journey took a little over ten minutes and as he slowly drove into the darkened car park, was dismayed to see how busy it was with evening visitors, though most of the parked cars were in the bays near the entrance to the hospital doors.

Throughout the journey he had tried to persuade himself this was a really bad idea and if he were stopped or ever questioned had considered a dozen scenarios to explain why he, a forty-year-old married teacher was meeting with a sixteen-year-old pupil. In the end he had settled for the excuse that he was worried about her safety, that after school that day she had confided to him her intention to run off from home. After all as a responsible adult who cared for his pupils, all he was doing was meeting with her to try and dissuade her from running away.

If he *were* questioned, he mused, it would be the word of a slutty wee teenage girl against the word of an experienced and credible member of the teaching profession.

He dimmed his headlights as he approached the area of the car park she had described and now almost at a crawl speed drove parallel with the adjacent golf course. He narrowed his eyes searching for a hole in the wire perimeter fence.

Then in the faint beam of the cars sidelights he saw her.

Standing alone and dressed in a short black coat and knee high black leather boots, her blonde hair lying loosely on her shoulders, she was leaning against one of the fence supports and excitedly waved when she recognised the BMW.

His throat was dry and for one heart stopping moment he considered ignoring her and driving off, but as he watched Colleen walk towards the car, the coat flapped open and he saw she was wearing a short white strapless dress that barely covered her thighs.

That decided him and he pulled sharply into an empty bay and switched off the engine. Almost immediately she was at the passenger side and pulling open the door, activated the courtesy light that provided him with a better look at her.

Sliding into the seat, she pulled the door closed and said, "Didn't think you were coming, Mister Turner. Thought *maybe* you had changed your mind."

He saw that she was wearing makeup that made her look older than her years and surprised, guessed she could almost pass for eighteen or nineteen years of age. He watched as she tugged at the top of her tight dress that threatened to slip down and expose her breasts.

"So," she grinned at him as she buckled the seat belt, "where are you taking me then…Martin?"

He was about to scold her for the use of his Christian name but stopped, realising that dressed as she was and sat in his car he was hardly in a position to remind her he was her teacher.

"Where do you suggest?" he replied with a nervous glance about the darkened car park.

"We could go into town. I drink in there a lot," she bragged.

"What, you get away with it even thought you're only sixteen?"

"I look older when I'm all done up," she boasted, "and besides, it's my birthday in a couple of months and then I'll be seventeen and then I can leave that dump," she pouted. "When I leave school I'm going to get a job as a nail technician. Either that or modelling. All my pals say I've got the face and the figure for it."

Martin was confused. What the *hell* was a nail technician and wondering what kind of job that was for a girl asked, "You mean, like nails for hammering into wood?"

She laughed, a mocking laugh that set his teeth on edge and she replied, "No, silly, these kind," and holding her hand out with her fingers extended in front of him, he could see the faint light shining on her fingernails. He thought they looked like sharpened spikes.

"Anyway," she continued, "I'll probably just be a nail technician for a year or two until I'm discovered as a model, then I'll get myself a job in London, a flat and a car and probably go to America after that."

He tightly smiled. Colleen Younger was a pretty and clearly naive teenager, but with a body that belied her mental age. Already he could see she was destined to go the way of her unmarried mother and the rest of her family who were well known to the local police in the council estate where they lived. The teenagers of the Younger family were the bane of the locals lives and more than once had made the local news.

He startled when she slid her hand across to place it on his thigh and said, "If you don't want to go for a drink, Martin, maybe you'd rather go somewhere nice and quiet, just me and you."

He gulped and stared though the front windscreen, aware of his arousal at her touch and hoarsely replied, "Yes, why not, Colleen. Somewhere nice and quiet. Just me and you."

Dressed in her bath robe, Joyce stood with a glass of chardonnay in her hand staring down from the bay window of her third floor flat in Peel Street at the dark and empty West of Scotland cricket ground. Emboldened by the half bottle she had consumed, she decided to phone Annemarie, but then hesitated. Would it not be better to jump into the car and just turn up at the door? The problem was, she sighed as though already defeated, if it was Martin who answered the door there was no way he would admit her and after slamming the door in her face likely take his anger out on her sister.
She slowly exhaled and sipped at the wine.
It wouldn't be so hard if Annemarie was willing to help herself, but through the years of marriage to Martin and suffering the constant belittling and abuse that in turn Joyce was sure led to his violence, Annemarie's spirit had been broken, These days her sister was a mere shadow of the laughing girl who had loved life, the attractive girl who had worked on the perfume counter of the prestigious Buchanan Street store, who dreamed of being whisked away by a handsome man, of a happy marriage and raising a brood of kids.
She threw back the last of the wine and wiping her lips with her sleeve, turned from the window to sit heavily on the armchair.
Glancing about the large room, she smiled at the framed photograph on the side table of her two nieces, Paula and Carol.
Her smile turned to a frown and it was the photograph that decided her.
If not for Annemarie's sake, then she would do it for the girls.
Her previous fears and doubts as well as her indecision vanished; her mind now made up, she rose and went to the kitchen to refill her glass.

Tom McEwan had little chance to speak with the frosty Miss Toner during the taxi ride from the airport to the hotel simply because she chose the front seat of the Skoda Octavia while he was obliged to sit in the rear.
When the taxi stopped outside the entrance of the New Street Premier Inn, Tom insisted on paying the genial turbaned driver, but

was thwarted when Ellen pushed the fare into the driver's hand. Getting out of the car into the sudden fall of rain, he courteously tried to take her case, but hauling it from the boot she turned and quickly made her way through the doors into the reception area. He followed her and watched as she marched towards the smiling young man manning the desk then heard her ask if there were any rooms available.

The young man, Derek according to his name badge, grimaced and replied, "Let me check, Miss, but I'm almost certain that due to the pharmaceutical conference taking place tomorrow at the International Convention Centre…" and tailed off as he biting at his lower lip, his eyes scanned the monitor at the desk. Shaking his head, he took a deep breath and said, "Sorry, no. Nothing showing on my screen."

"Is there *anywhere* available in the city that you know off," Ellen asked.

Stood behind her, Tom thought there was a slight sound of desperation in her voice.

"According to the local news reports, the conference at the ICC has apparently attracted worldwide interest, Miss," Derek shook his head, "and I think it's *extremely* unlikely you will find anything available at such short notice."

"Maybe I can help," Tom slid past Ellen and giving his name to Derek, asked, "Is my room a single or double?"

Derek glanced from one to the other then typing in Tom's details, replied, "It's booked as a single, but with twin beds, Mister McEwan. Why," the younger man stifled a grin, "what do you have in mind, sir?"

Tom turned to Ellen and said, "If you're willing to pay the upgrade to double, you can share with me," then raising his hands added, "purely platonic, of course."

Aghast, she stared at him before replying, "I don't even know you!"

"You know that we're here in Birmingham on the same business, Miss Toner. There is an en suite in the room, so no problems about dressing or undressing and after all it *is* only for one night."

"What happened to Sir Galahad, the man I met at the airport who was willing to give up his room to me," she curtly reminded Tom and arms huffily folded, scowled at him.

"Ah," he nodded towards the front doors where they could see the rain now coming down in sheets. "Turns out if Sir Galahad gives up his room to the fair maiden, there's every likelihood his armour might rust out in that weather."

She turned to glance at the noisy downpour and taking a deep breath she slowly exhaled, irritably shook her head and snapped, "Fine! I'll pay the bloody extra, but please be assured Mister McEwan that this arrangement is under duress."

The upgrade made and paid for, they accepted their keys cards from the stony-faced Derek and made their way in silence to the room on the third floor.

Opening the door to the twin room, Tom stood back to permit Ellen to enter and following her into the room, said, "Look, Miss Toner, why don't we call a truce. My first name's Tom. What do I call you?"

"Miss Toner," she tersely replied.

He choked back a laugh and said, "Fine then, Miss Toner. I saw that the hotel has a restaurant and bar downstairs just off the reception area and the weather's too rotten to go looking for somewhere to eat. So as we are now officially on speaking terms and more to the point, as I am on expenses, please permit me to invite you to have dinner with me." Before she could respond he held up his hands in surrender and added, "You are not under any *duress*, as you put it earlier. It's a social offer, nothing more."

She stared at him and her shoulders drooped. Slowly shaking her head, she sat heavily down onto the bed, her knees primly together with her hands clasped on her lap and said, "I'm being horrible, aren't I? You've been nothing but kind, Mister McEwan and I've acted like a complete cow."

"Tom," he smiled at her, sensing a little light in the dark shield that surrounded Ellen Toner. He dumped his bag from his shoulder onto the floor by the nearest bed and said, "Look, why don't I head downstairs and order us a table. You take some time to freshen up and I'll see you in the restaurant when you're ready, okay?"

She nodded and smiling, simply replied, "Thanks...and my name's Ellen."

He thought her smile opened up a completely different woman and a little taken aback, returned her smile and left the room.

He had been sitting at the table in the near empty restaurant for a little over fifteen minutes when he saw her exit the lift at the reception. She had changed from her blouse and business suit into a loose fitting crimson coloured GAP sweatshirt and denim jeans and wore trainers on her feet.

Approaching the table, Ellen was oddly pleased to see Tom rise from his seat and stood back while he courteously pulled out her chair to permit her to sit.

"I've taken the liberty of ordering a bottle of white," he said, pointing to the glass in front of her.

"Thanks, that'll be fine," she tightly smiled.

He saw she had washed her face that was now free of makeup and her skin was as clear as a child's.

"I have to be honest," she leaned slightly towards him as though fearing being overheard, "I'm still a little uncomfortable about sharing the room with a complete stranger, Mister...eh, Tom."

"I understand you must have reservations, Ellen," he shrugged, "but we're both adults and for what it's worth, you have my word I will be a complete gentleman. If you like, you can even tie my hands to the bed and..." then stopped and wide-eyed, stared at her. "I'm sorry, that didn't come out the way I meant," he hastily added.

Open-mouthed, she stared at him then burst out laughing, causing Tom to join in.

They were still laughing when the young waitress arrived at the table and staring from one to the other, hid her grin as she asked for their food order.

Tom's gaffe cleared the air more than he thought for almost immediately Ellen seemed to relax and they exchanged details about each other's jobs; she telling him of her recent appointment as manager of the food outlet in Woodlands Road, of finding her feet in a store that prior to her appointment was doing so badly the company had considered shutting it down.

He explained his job as an investigator for the firm McCormick and Co. and with a sigh added it wasn't as exciting as perhaps she thought it might be.

He told her that before leaving his office in Glasgow, he had learned the jar discovered in the Birmingham store had been contaminated with a food dye called Lutein.

She knew about Lutein and was taken aback and puzzled that Chrystons would take so seriously a threat against the company when the threat was merely two jars, one of which had been contaminated with an everyday and commonly used food dye.

"It's not the food dye that's the threat," he solemnly told her. "It's the fact that someone has made the company aware that an individual or individuals have the means and the determination to contaminate any foodstuffs that are on Chrystons shelves. If the company do *not* take the threat seriously, the next contaminate might be rat poison or weed killer; in fact anything that could seriously harm or even kill a customer. Can you imagine the backlash if that happened and the company, having being aware of the threat, did nothing?"

She frowned as she nodded and he thought her frown made her appear to be even younger than he first thought her.

They skipped details of their personal lives though Tom did notice the absence of a wedding or engagement ring on her third finger. Ellen was curious about his involvement with Chrystons. Finishing her starter and pushing the dish to one side, she leaned with both forearms on the table and said, "So, an investigator. What *exactly* do you investigate, Tom?"

He laid down his spoon and replied, "In the main, there's a lot of domestic work and no matter how the television dresses it up it can be quite boring. Divorce, allegations of infidelity, whether a parent is capable of caring for a child who is at the centre of a tug of war, that sort of thing. Much of it involves attending civil court to give evidence. However, the firm also deals with business fraud or allegations of internal theft or mismanagement. My boss, Martin McCormick is a sharp guy and is acquiring a reputation in the West of Scotland not only as a prominent solicitor, but a man who is fair and can be trusted. I think that is confirmed by the fact that your company's main legal representatives here in Birmingham have associated themselves with Martin's firm and trust him as their agent to oversee their legal issues in Scotland. Martin has come a long way in the recent past. His practise started out a few years ago as a one man show, but since then he's taken on a number of associates who specialise in different aspects of the law, including criminal defence work which is another aspect of my job; interviewing witnesses and that sort of thing. There is another investigator, a man called John

Logan who like me also works for the firm. Occasionally we work together when it's a big case or for some reason the inquiry needs twenty-four-hour coverage."

"You mean like surveillance?"

"Yeah," he grinned, "like surveillance."

She pursed her lips and nodding, asked, "How did you fall into this line of work?"

"Falling in is exactly what happened," he smiled, then his face grew more serious. "I used to be a detective with Strathclyde Police, the largest of the forces that pre-dated Police Scotland. I resigned after an operation I was involved in went tits up, if you pardon the expression, and resulted in the death of a colleague. Unfortunately, though there were no charges laid against me and cutting a long story short, I was blamed for her death and really had no option but to quit. However," he sighed, but the memory still bitterly obvious, "I'm pleased to say that some years later the situation was resolved and I was cleared of all wrongdoing. It was after I was cleared that Martin offered me the job and so," he extended his hands and with a smile added, "here I am."

He frowned as he stared at her and asked, "One thing puzzles me, Ellen. Chrystons is a huge company, yet there has been no mention…well, certainly to me, of a security department; somebody that I could liaise with now that I've been tasked to assist with this threat. Why is that?"

"Well," she slowly drawled, "there is no security department *per se*. You see, a number of years ago when Chrystons weren't doing so well in the retail market and profits were falling…this was before the current CEO Jackson Peters took charge and turned things around," she explained then continued, "there was an initiative instigated by the company to bring it closer to the local consumer market. In short, the Board agreed that economically it could no longer sustain a large security department covering all the UK stores to deal with shoplifting, internal fraud or theft, that sort of thing. What the Board decided was to make Chrystons," she wagged her fingers in the air, "more approachable to the local communities throughout the UK and one of the proposals that was set in place was to empower the store managers to hire local, police vetted security companies to patrol their store. In short, it was a cost cutting exercise that made the managers responsible for their own store security."

"Is that what you do, hire local guys?"

"No," she smiled, "my store is too small to sustain a permanent security officer. If the need arises, I have an arrangement whereby I borrow a security officer from the Argyle Street store."

"And does this method work?"

"I believe so, though I have no direct knowledge of how effective this system is. The advantage of this scheme or so I'm told," she shrugged, "is that albeit Chrystons as a company contract the security firms, the cost is not as great had they maintained their own internal department. Another advantage is that the Chrystons contract is very lucrative for some of the smaller security companies so it ensures they do a good job plus if any of the security companies mess up, for example their officers make a hash of detaining anyone they suspect for shoplifting, Chrystons can legitimately wash their hands of any allegation or subsequent lawsuit and blame the security company."

"But surely there must be someone in the company responsible for contracting the security companies; somebody who collates the data for assessing the loss of profit by theft or fraud?"

"Yes, there is; that will be the responsibility of the Director of Operations, James Hardie."

Tom's brow furrowed, recalling McCormick mentioning the name and intimated, "Hardie is the guy that contacted my boss, Martin McCormick. Have you met him?"

"No," she shook her head. "Mister Hardie is a paygrade well above my own."

"Well, likely I will be meeting him," he smiled. "Now," he continued, "tell me about the jar that you discovered in your store?"

She told him to drop her a street away from the ground floor flat in Cockmuir Street where she lived with her family. He knew that a number of his pupils lived in the same area and he was keen to get away from her before anyway saw him or recognised his car, but she insisted on kissing him goodnight and shoving her hand down between his legs, asked, "When are we going to meet again, darling? Tomorrow night?"

"I'll think about it," he replied, shifting uncomfortably at her touch, his eyes darting back and forth as he scanned the street for signs of life. She stiffened and withdrew her hand and he knew he had made a mistake, that she thought he was fobbing her off. "Look," he smiled humourlessly at her, "why don't we talk about this later, eh?" "Where, at school?" she sat back in her seat and stared at him. "Don't be so fucking stupid, Martin. What if somebody saw us or found out about us?"

If nothing else, he was pleased that apparently she too didn't want anyone discovering their secret.

Her expression immediately changed. She stared suspiciously at him then continued, "You *do* want to see me again, don't you?"

"Of *course* I do," he tried to sound reassuring and added, "Let me think about when because it might depend on whether or not I can get away. From the house," he added as though inferring it might be difficult.

"Just don't take too long to think about it," she frowned at him and turning pushed open the door, activating the overhead courtesy light and brightly illuminating them both. Damn, he thought, I'll need to remember to take the bulb out of that bloody thing.

She pulled the door closed again then turning, reached for his hand and pulling him towards her, slid his hand between her bare legs and trapping it there, coyly asked, "Did you like it tonight, Martin, what we did I mean? What I did for you?"

"Yes, I did," he forced a smile, unwilling to hang about the darkened street but certain if she guessed he wanted her gone from the car she would go ballistic.

"Good," she grinned at him and released his hand, "then I promise you it will be better tomorrow night, if you can get out of the house to come and meet me."

Despite himself, he became aroused and dry mouthed watched as she again opened the door and sliding out of the car, he frowned as she noisily closing the door behind her.

He drove home a little faster than he intended, but with one eye on the rear-view mirror watching for that telltale blue light. Parking the car in the driveway he opened the door and when the interior light came on, glanced backwards towards the rear leather seat.

He must remember to give it a clean tomorrow he thought, just in case they had left any stains. The same thought brought home the reality that he had sex with a sixteen-year-old girl in the back of his car; a girl who was his pupil and a sudden dread swept through him. What if she tells someone, he thought?

What if she boasts to her pals that she shagged her teacher?

He was in no doubt he had not been Colleen's first sexual encounter and been surprised at her willingness and candour in the back seat. God, the things she had said and done; she had almost exhausted him. He allowed himself a brief smile, but the cold chill struck again when he thought of the consequences if she opened her mouth.

Yet, he thought, her comment when he dropped her off, that she didn't want anyone to find out implied that she too needed their liaison to be kept secret and further convinced him she would keep her trap shut.

Yes, he unconsciously nodded, she would keep her mouth closed, of that he was sure.

There was no other option; she had to keep silent.

Getting out of the car he locked it and went into the house. He could hear the television switched on in the front room and opening the door saw Annemarie jump to her feet.

"Martin, I'm sorry, I must have dozed off. I didn't hear you come in. Do you want some tea or something? How did the meeting at the school go?" she asked, her whining voice already grating on his nerves.

"I'm going to bed," he abruptly told her. "I've had a hard day, so it might be better if you used the spare room again."

"Yes, Martin," she meekly agreed, but her nose twitched for though he was unaware, Annemarie could smell a scent from him that she did not recognise as one of his expensive aftershaves.

He closed the door and standing completely still she listened intently, hearing him tramping upstairs and then close the bedroom door. Quickly she moved to where he had stood in the doorway and took a deep sniff. Yes, she was correct. She could smell the faintest odour of a cheap cologne.

She backed off from the odour and returned to the front room, unsteady on her feet her legs collided with the back of the couch and reached behind to steady herself.

Her brow furrowed as she wondered, what did this mean?

She had long suspected that since Martin no longer had any interest in her he was out womanising and had become used to the idea of him seeing other women. Nowadays, his only sexual demand of her was when he had been drinking or after he had watched some pornographic show on the television and wanted her to…even standing alone in the room, she blushed at what Martin made her do for him.

Her thoughts turned to the odour of the cheap perfume. It wasn't one she recognised and she sighed. It had been some time since she had the opportunity to smell any kind of scent.

She shook her head, no longer in any doubt.

He *was* seeing someone else, but that posed the question for Annemarie and for her daughters; was this a good thing or a bad thing?

## CHAPTER FOUR

Tom McEwan opened his eyes and for that brief few seconds of wakening in the semi-light of the room was disorientated, wondering where the heck he was?

Turning, he glanced at the figure in the adjoining bed and smiled. The red hair spread on the pillow reminded him of a pleasant evening that concluded with Ellen requesting he give her twenty minutes to get into bed and bidding him goodnight in the restaurant. When he had arrived in the room he thought she was probably lying awake, but did not wish to disturb her by speaking and was grateful she had left the bathroom light on to permit him to change into his nightclothes of tee shirt and shorts.

He glanced at his wristwatch and saw it was just after seven-thirty. As quietly as he could, he slipped from the bed and grabbing his bag sneaked into the bathroom. Now shaved, showered and changed into a clean clothes, he left the bathroom and with his shoes in one hand and his bag in the other was about to sneak from the dimly lit room when she called out, "Good morning, Tom."

"Ah, sorry. Did I disturb you?"

"No, you didn't. That noisy bloody fan when you were showering woke me," she grumbled.

"You're not a morning person then," he teased as he dropped the shoes and bag onto the floor and reached to switch on the kettle. She sat up in bed with her back against the headboard, her long hair tousled and falling about her shoulders and saw she was wearing a brightly coloured rugby top. Rubbing at her eyes, she said, "You wouldn't be making me a coffee by any chance?"

Tom grinned as he nodded. "Same as the restaurant? White with one sugar?"

"You remembered," she smiled with pleasure and his heart skipped a beat at her loveliness.

It was when he was handing the coffee to her that his mobile phone activated.

Glancing at the screen he saw the caller was his daughter Sophie and answered, "Hi, darling? How are you this morning?"

Because his back was to Ellen he did not see the flash of disappointment that crossed her face.

Listening as she sipped at the coffee, Ellen heard him say, "Yes, that's right, I'm down in Birmingham, but I'm looking forward to seeing you tonight and maybe you'd like to stay over? Good, then that's a date," he smiled at the phone as he ended the call.

Turning towards Ellen, he said, "Right then, I'll grab my bag and let you get up and dressed, Ellen. I'll meet you down in the restaurant for breakfast in say, half an hour. I've got an idea that you might be interested in."

She stared curiously at him as he left the room and drawing her knees up to rest her chin on them thought, just my luck; all the good ones are taken.

The buzz was rife at Chrystons head office about the extraordinary Directors meeting due to be held at eleven o'clock that morning. Reports were already circulating about the poor performance of the company during the preceding year and fuelled rumours that abound by the dozen regarding the agenda to be discussed at the meeting. These rumours included a takeover by a rival company that would inevitably lead to the sacking of hundreds of staff, the closure of many of the Chrystons stores and the most prevalent rumour of all, the disbanding of the company.

Despite all the negative rumours, none came close to the real reason for the meeting; the threat that an individual or individuals were contaminating Chrystons foodstuffs. A threat so serious that it could lead not just to financial ruin for the company, but result in someone's death.

In the absence of the CEO, James Hardie made use of the company limousine and had the chauffeur drop him at the front door of the head office. Politely greeting the elderly uniformed doorman, he accepted the courteous salute with a tight smile.

The two matronly women manning the reception desk smiled and said in unison, "Good morning, Mister Hardie."

"Ladies," he automatically smiled back, but his mind was on other matters.

The lift that conveyed him to his fifth floor office softly played the tune 'Greensleeves' and though Hardie had never previously paid attention to the tune, for some curious reason this morning it annoyed him, causing him when he arrived at his office to tell his secretary to get the bloody thing changed to something more upbeat. It was when he noticed the surprised look on the woman's face that he realised how uptight he was and guessed that the morning Board meeting was troubling him more than he thought.

Striding into his office, the tune Greensleeves kept turning over and over in his head and slumping down into his chair, he frowned.

With a flash of inspiration, he knew what the problem was.

Like the bloody tune in the lift, the company was becoming stale, outdated, old fashioned; call it what you might, but Chrystons badly needed revamped.

That was the problem, he realised; that's why so many of the cheaper, high street chain stores were hammering them at the tills. He reached for a pen and notepad while a number of ideas raced through his head and with growing excitement began to make notes.

Parking her car in a bay in the staff car park, Joyce McKinnon switched off the engine and reached for her handbag on the rear floor of the Fiesta. Scrambling in the bag, she sighed with relief when her fingers grabbed the packet of Paracetamol and the half full plastic bottle of water. Popping two tablets from the blister pack she took a quick glance around her to ensure she wasn't seen and gulped the tablets down with a swig of water. She had known it was a mistake finishing the bottle of wine before bed, but hoped her headache would be eased by the Paracetamol.

Slipping on a pair of sunglasses with lenses so dark they were almost black, she took a deep breath, got out of the car and began to make her way towards the main entrance of the college.

"Morning, Joyce," a cheery male voice said from behind.

Turning she saw it was Sandy Munro, the Departmental Head of the Faculty of Nautical Studies.

She forced a grin and thought of all days to be cornered by the handsome Sandy, it had to be the day she sported a massive hangover.

"Good morning, Sandy," she stopped and returning his greeting, waited to permit Sandy to catch up with her.

Walking together among the morning throng of students towards the main doors, Sandy quietly asked, "Well, have you given my proposal any thought?"

Joyce turned her head to stare curiously at him, then remembered. "Oh, about dinner you mean?"

"Yes," he half laughed as he pulled open the door for her, "about dinner."

She shrugged and almost apologetically replied, "Okay, why not."

Sandy stared curiously at her and almost with disappointment, said, "You'd forgotten. I mean, you'd forgotten that I asked you to have dinner with me, didn't you?"

She grimaced in agreement and shaking his head, he said, "Well, at least now I've a definite answer."

She tightly smiled and as she headed towards her department he called after her, "I'll call you about the arrangements."

"Fine," she flipped a backhand at him and strode under the overhead sign that declared she was now entering the Faculty for Leisure & Lifestyle Department.

She liked Sandy and yes, he was a handsome and charming guy, but didn't think that she was ready for a relationship so soon after…she shook her head as though to clear it, determined that today she would *not* be weepy.

It was when she reached the safety of her office with the door shut tightly behind her that she relaxed and with a groan sunk into her desk chair. She should have been sensible and called in sick, but that wasn't her style; not when she had just been in the post for a little over two months.

Besides, she had more going on than the morning lecture she was due to deliver or fencing with Sandy Munro's dinner invitation.

The wall clock indicated it was almost ten minutes to nine so she knew that Martin would have gone and reaching for the desk phone, dialled her sisters home number.

As the phone rung, she decided that she would insist that Annemarie meet with her.

What Joyce had to discuss with her was far too important to propose on the phone; far too important to be rejected with a full explanation.

He had driven to the school with his nerves on edge, compounded by the fact he had not slept a wink all night, worrying himself sick that Colleen would tell someone, one of her slutty school pals perhaps. Stopped at the red traffic light, he hammered at the steering wheel with the heels of his hands and shaking his head, gasped out loud, "God! Why was I so fucking *stupid*!"

Turning his head he saw the youthful driver of the white transit van in the adjacent lane was staring at him and while the driver could not know why Martin as upset, was grinning at his discomfort. Martin gave the driver the finger, but instantly regretted it for the drivers face almost immediately changed and enraged, Martin saw him reach for his door handle.

Just as the van driver was climbing out of his cab, the lights changed to green and Martin raced through the junction. In his rear-view mirror, he saw the driver hastily returning to the cab and heard the distant sound of horns as the vehicles behind urged the van driver to get a move on. Fortunately for Martin, the van was in a dedicated lane and obliged to turn left. He sighed with relief, pleased at having given the bastard the finger and got away with it.

"Just as well, I might have had to batter him," he muttered to himself, a little braver now that the likelihood of a confrontation with the van driver was almost half a mile behind him.

The nearer he got to the school the more care he had to take because of the couldn't care less attitude of the pupils who to the angry frustration of passing drivers indifferently wandered across the road, most with mobile phones stick to their ears.

Turning in through the gate that led to the staff car park, he acknowledged the waves of some of the arriving staff with a nod, ignoring others who he believed were simply wankers. It didn't escape his notice that his Departmental Head, Charlie McFadyen who he believed was the biggest wanker of them all, turned away to avoid eye contact with Martin.

His extreme dislike that bordered on actual hatred for McFadyen stemmed from the Departmental Head's recent annual staff appraisal of Martin that was so negative it resulted in Martin being brought before the Head Teacher and counselled about his future not only in the school, but with the council's education department.

And all because those little shits just don't listen and have no interest in what I'm teaching them, he inwardly snarled.

He forced himself to be calm and getting out of the car, was about to lock it when he glanced towards the metal fencing that separated the car park from the senior pupils' entrance gates.

That's when he saw Colleen and two of her pals, their heads together and giggling as they watched him. He inwardly sneered. Three teenage tarts with the same dyed blonde hair, the same white blouses a deliberate size too small to show off their pubescent tits, the same short skirt and white socks to just above the knees.

Christ, they're trying so hard to be individual and yet their make-up was so thick it looks like they used a plasterer's trowel to apply it.

He almost sniggered out loud as he thought the girls looked like they've come off the same Barbie production line. Don't they have fucking mirrors in their homes, he wondered?

But then as he watched, his stomach lurched and his imagination run wild. Was the stupid wee slut telling them about him? Was she disclosing what they had did in the back of his car.

His throat felt tight and locking the car, he turned to walk towards the main entrance, avoiding glancing at them but aware that on the other side of the fence the three girls were keeping pace and would arrive at the doors at the same time.

He considered bending down and pretending to tie his shoelaces, but they would probably wait for him so decided to brazen it out.

Mounting the four steps towards the wooden doors, he pulled one open and tightly smiling, held it open to permit Colleen and her two friends to pass by.

Colleen gave him a knowing smirk while the other two girls, deep in whispered conversation, ignored him.

He exhaled slowly and continued to hold the door for two staff members, nodding at their thanks and giving him the opportunity to watch the short-skirted Colleen head off along the wide corridor towards her classroom.

Gritting his teeth, he realised that somehow today he would need to corner Colleen and find out exactly what she was telling her pals.

He glanced up from the breakfast table to see that once more Ellen Toner was dressed in her bottle green coloured business suit, but with a fresh blouse and her hair loosely hung about her shoulders. He stood to draw out her chair, but she waved him back to his seat and sat down.

"I haven't ordered for you…" he began, but had hardly spoken when the waitress appeared and noted Ellen's order of plain omelette and coffee.

"So," she leaned forward with her elbows on the table and her clasped hands supporting her chin, "what's this idea you have?"

"Well," he drawled, "I'm invited to your company's Board meeting as the representative of my firm, but I believe that as the store manager where one of the two contaminated jars was discovered, you should also be present."

"And your reasoning behind this idea that I gatecrash the meeting?"

"I haven't yet had the opportunity to visit your store nor have I had sufficient information to make any assessment as to why your store might have been chosen by the culprit or culprits. I'm of the opinion that the Board meeting might have some questions for me that currently I am unable to answer, so I would like *you* to be present to permit me to interrogate you when these questions are thrown at me. Besides," he shrugged, "there's no reason I can think of why you shouldn't be in attendance at the meeting."

"Interrogate me? That sounds a bit chilling," she smiled then jokingly asked, "Am I a suspect, Mister McEwan?"

"Everyone's a suspect, Miss Toner," he stone facedly replied, "until such times that they are eliminated from my inquiry."

She softly smiled and nodding, "Yes, Tom, I understand why you might think it would be a good idea for me to attend, but don't you think you will be going against the Board's wishes about me being there?"

"I don't work for Chrystons, Ellen. If your company want me to deliver a full and professional service, they will have to abide my wishes too."

"Okay, I'll come with you, but don't be surprised if I'm asked to sit in the waiting room outside the meeting. If I've learned one think about working for Chrystons it's that there's a pecking order and managers of minor food outlets like me *do not* usually sit down at the table with the hierarchy."

"Okay, I get that, but you will be there at *my* invitation and I'm the guy that they will be asking to identify or catch the bugger who's threatening them."

The waitress laid Ellen's food order down before her and thanking the young woman, she turned towards Tom. Cocking her head to one side as she squinted at him, she said, "You don't seem like a man who is comfortable toeing the line, Tom McEwan."

He shrugged and replied, "I've lived most of my adult life living within the boundaries; within the rules and regulations I mean, but sometimes it's more practical to do what's right rather than what's accepted. Does that make sense?"

"Oh, I know *exactly* what you mean," she sighed, her head unconsciously lowering a fraction as she stared down at her latte and idly stirred with her fork at the omelette.

He didn't want to press her and suspected that her response had nothing to do with whether or not she was invited to the Board meeting, but that something more personal was on her mind.

"Penny for them," he said at last.

"What? Oh, yes, sorry," she blushed and smiling at him, took a deep breath. "I was miles away."

"So, you agree that you *will* come with me this morning?"

"Yes, at your insistence, I agree," she nodded.

"Good, that's settled then," he grinned at her and called the waitress over for the bill.


Annemarie returned the phone to the cradle. It was with some reservation that she agreed to meet with Joyce in the city centre for lunch, but insisted that they finish for two o'clock. What she didn't tell her sister was she had to be home in plenty of time to check the house over before Martin returned home, that she dreaded that he might once more accuse her of being slovenly, that if he believed the house looked untidy it would result in another slapped face and verbal abuse.

Now on her knees and running the damp, yellow duster round the skirting boards, she considered telling Joyce of her suspicions, that Martin was having yet another affair, but knew what Joyce's predictable reaction would be.

If she had told Annemarie once, she had told her a thousand times; leave him, bring the girls with you, come and live with me till you find your own place.

She sat on the floor, leaning her back against the wall and bit at her lower lip.

It was easy for Joyce to say, to advise her big sister to leave her husband when *she* didn't have the same commitments, but almost immediately regretted her unkind thought.

Joyce had also been through her own awfulness, she sighed, remembering the wreck that had been her sister just two years previously when Kieran had been killed. The elderly man driving the car on Byres Road was as much a victim as was the keen cyclist Kieran and did not survive the heart attack that caused him to collide with Joyce's fiancé.

She had tried to help or as much as Martin would permit her, conscious that with both their parents deceased she was Joyce's only living relative, but had not been as much a source of comfort as she would have wished. Annemarie still harboured a sense of shame that Martin refused to attend the funeral, boasting he neither liked nor had any time for Kieran. The truth however was that Kieran had been a wonderful partner to Joyce and wasn't afraid to openly confront Martin and tell him just what kind of bullying bastard he was.

The last time the sisters had met some was some weeks previously when without Martin's knowledge, Joyce had called unexpectedly at the house. Panicking that Martin might suddenly return home, Annemarie flushed with embarrassment, remembering that she had said some unkind things and her sister had left, both hurt and angry. She had cried with frustration because she knew in her heart that Joyce worried about her and the girls and only wanted to help, but realistically, how could she?

Martin held all the cards. It was *his* house, *his* income for he refused to permit her to work and as he constantly reminded her, *his* daughters for whom he would fight tooth and nail in court if she ever considered leaving him.

Her eyes narrowed. If he was that interested in keeping Paula and Carol, why then did he never spend time with them and persistently refer to them as Annemarie's daughters?

But she knew what the answer to that was; the girls were merely bargaining chips; something he would hold over her if she did ever dare leave him.

James Hardie went over the notes he had made for that day's Board meeting and briefly considered that if it went as well as he expected and on the basis of yesterday's plaudits from his fellow Directors, he might just find himself being seriously considered as the next CEO. He had one last thing he had to do and called his Deputy, Gregory Packer's number to confirm that the briefing notes had been typed up and a copy available for each of the board members and invited guests.

He glanced at the clock. Another hour before the Directors were to assemble in the boardroom. Time enough for him to make some phone calls to his fellow Directors and remind them of their tentative promises to support him when the CEO position did become available.

He glanced again at the wall clock and with soft smile considered that perhaps there might even be time to phone Lesley to remind her that he had missed her when she had been away.

## CHAPTER FIVE

The taxi dropped Tom and Ellen at the front door of Chrystons where after identifying himself, Tom was handed a visitors' badge. The receptionist however was confused when Ellen also provided her name as well as her company ID card.

"I'm sorry, Miss Toner, but I don't see your name on my list," she stared at her computer screen and slowly shook her head.

"Miss Toner is with me and might I add that your Mister Packer will verify her presence, if you care to phone him," Tom smiled in the certain knowledge the young woman would not wish to disturb Gregory Packer in what Tom inferred was obviously a clerical mix-up.

"Of course," the receptionist nervously smiled and after agreeing to care for their luggage, handed Ellen a visitors' badge and instructed them how to make their way to the boardroom on the fourth floor.

Once safely travelling upwards in the lift, Ellen smiled and said, "You were chancing your arm there, Tom McEwan. What if she *had* phoned Gregory Packer?"

"Then I would just have to had persuade him you are vital to my inquiries, Miss Toner," he returned her smile with a grin.

The lift stopped and the doors opened onto an expensively furnished corridor with art deco furniture and fittings.

"Ah, glad you could make it," Gregory Packer stepped forward to meet them, his hand outstretched as he stared uncertainly at Ellen Toner.

Before he could ask, Tom said, "I invited Miss Toner to the meeting, Mister Packer. I believe her knowledge of the Woodlands Road store and its patrons might be of use to my inquiries in Glasgow.

"Indeed," Packer nodded, but Ellen suspected he wasn't convinced as he led them along the corridor towards the boardroom.

Pushing open one of the two large oak doors Tom and Ellen followed Packer into a bright and airy room where it seemed that no expense had been spared. The table that dominated the centre of the room could easily accommodate thirty people rather than the nine Directors that comprised of the Board of Chrystons Supermarkets (PLC).

Eight men who to Tom all seemed to be in their late fifties onwards were seated around the table quietly speaking among themselves. A young woman wearing the uniform of the company's 'Founding Store' stood deferentially beside a table on which rested bone china crockery, flasks of coffee and tea and bottled water.

"Can I get you anything," Packer indicated towards the young woman.

"Coffee, please," smiled Tom.

"Nothing for me," replied Ellen.

Packer indicated two seats together at the table and beckoned the young woman forward, ordering coffee for Tom.

"We should be commencing anytime," he courteously smiled at them. "We are awaiting the arrival of Mister Peters, the CEO and Mister Hardie, the Operations Director."

One of the seated men, tall and whippet thin with grey hair and a dark, neatly trimmed moustache, wearing a dark suit arose and approached Tom with his hand outstretched.

"I heard the accent," he grinned. "You must be Tom McEwan. I'm Gavin Blakestock, Chief Investigator for Blakestock Inquiry Agency. I'm retained by the law firm representing Chrystons. How do you do?" he introduced himself in a thick, Brummie accent

Tom rose to shake Blakestock's hand and introducing Ellen, learned that Blakestock was to make local inquiry regarding the threatening letter and the contaminated jar discovered in the 'Founding Store."

"Sadly, no leads meantime," Blakestock sighed, running a hand through his thick hair. "I went over the CCTV footage, but of course without even a rough time or date there is nothing to suggest when the jar was tampered with."

"Did the jar belong to the batch that was on the shelf?" asked Tom. Blakestock smiled and stared keenly at the younger man.

"Good question, Tom. You're the first to bring that up and no, the jar didn't belong to the batch on the shelf. In fact, my inquiry so far has discovered the jar's Codex Alimentarius...." he stopped and smiled light-heartedly at Tom's bemused expression.

"What Mister Blakestock means, Tom," interrupted Ellen, "is that all foodstuffs have an internationally recognised standard, a code of practise if you will that relates to all food, their production and food safety. In layman terms it's to do with the traceability of food, its packaging, handling, all sorts of issues regarding the movement of food and includes identifying when there is a suggestion that foodstuffs have been tampered with. For example, jars that pop will suggest the lid has already been removed and the contents are no longer airtight sealed."

"We could go on at length with an explanation that took me over an hour to read last night," it was Blakestock's turn to interrupt, "but Miss Toner seems to have summarised it nicely. Anyway, what I'm trying to say is that the unique packaging code imprinted by the manufacture on the lid of jar discovered in the 'Founding Store' here in Birmingham came from a batch that had been delivered to your store eighteen days ago, Miss Toner," he turned towards her. "I can also tell you that the jar you brought down yesterday is from the batch that was delivered to your store."

Tom took a deep breath. "So in short, both adulterated jars were probably purchased or stolen from the Woodlands Road store in Glasgow and it seems likely the jar discovered in Glasgow was either bought in the store, contaminated then returned to the store or else contaminated *in* the store."

"Correct, Tom," beamed Blakestock.

The door opened to admit two men, one of whom immediately made his way to the chair at the top of the table while the other man sat in a chair opposite Tom and Ellen. At a nod from Gregory Packer, the young uniformed woman stood by the refreshments quickly left the room as Packer closed the door behind her before taking a seat at the table.

The silver haired and tanned man sat down, his hands clasped together on top of the shiny surface of the oak table and waving his fellow Directors to their seats, said in an authoritative voice, "Thank you all for coming at such short notice. Now," he glanced curiously at Tom and Ellen, "I have previously met Mister Blakestock and it's nice to see you again," he nodded to Blakestock with a smile, then added, "but might I ask who you are please?"

Gregory Packer stood and nervously said, "Mister Peters, might I introduce Mister Tom McEwan who is retained by the Scottish law firm and will represent our interest in this matter in the Glasgow area and Miss Ellen Toner, the manager of the Woodlands Road store where one of the contaminated jars was discovered."

Peters stared at Tom and Ellen in turn, then nodding a greeting to them both, addressed the assembled group.

"We find ourselves with a dilemma. The receipt of this threatening letter and subsequent discovery of the two contaminated jars of Snuckles baby food is not in itself a major concern; however, the content of the letter…" he gestured towards James Hardie who had accompanied him into the boardroom. Hardie in turn nodded to Gregory Packer and they all watched Packer literally jump from his seat and stride towards a computer laptop that sat upon a table by the door. Packer's fingers danced across the laptop keyboard causing a large white screen to slowly descend from a hidden recess in the ceiling and which took up most of the wall at the far end of the table. Pressing a button on the wall, the curtains on the panoramic windows slid closed plunging the room into twilight.

James Hardie rose to his feet and moving along the table towards the screen, began, "Gentleman," he paused and then correcting himself, added, "I do beg your pardon, Miss Toner. A copy of the letter is enclosed in the briefing pack that lies before you. However, Gregory will now display the letter that started this nonsense," and nodded to Packer who pressed a button on the keyboard. The screen lit up and displayed the one-page letter that was now large enough to be easily read by those who remained seated.

Tom's eyes narrowed as he read the letter typed in italics:

*To Jackson Peters,*
*The Chief Executive Officer of Chryston's.*
*Two jars of Snuckles baby foods have been adulterated and placed in the stores located at the 'Founding Store' in Birmingham and in the Woodlands Road store, Glasgow.*
*For identification, both jars have been marked with a black cross on the label.*
*We suggest you retrieve these jars without delay.*
*We represent those women Chrystons has wronged.*
*We represent those women that your corrupt company has used and exploited throughout the years.*
*We will have our revenge and this revenge will be monetary.*
*We accept that you will be unable to identify all the women Chrystons has cheated and ill-treated.*
*We accept that the recompense Chrystons will pay will not fully make up for the hurt Chrystons has caused.*
*However, this recompense will be paid to the list of twenty women's charities that are attached.*
*To each of these charities Chrystons will 'gift' fifty-thousand pounds.*
*We instruct Chrystons inform the media and publicise these 'gifts' to inform us of your cooperation with our demands.*
*Failure to act in accordance with our demand will result in further food products being adulterated and distributed by our members throughout your UK stores.*
*Failure to act in accordance with our demand will ultimately result in the death of a Chrystons customer(s).*
*Failure to act in accordance with our demand will result in copies of this letter being forwarded post mortem of your customer(s) to the media.*
*Should you decide to inform the police of this letter, we will know.*
*You have seventy-two hours from receipt of this letter to act in accordance with our instructions.*

*We are Penthesilea.*

Still stood beside the screen, Hardie turned to the those assembled and assuming that all had read the letter, said, "A separate sheet was attached that listed the twenty charities, a cop of which you will also find within your briefing pack."

Chairing the meeting, it was Peters privilege to ask the first questions and turning towards Blakestock, said, "So, Gavin, who or what exactly is Penthesilea?"

Blakestock opened his hands and replied, "As far as my limited inquiry has established with my former colleagues in the West Midlands Anti-Terrorist…"

"Wait a minute!" Hardie almost shot out of his chair. "Are you telling the Board that despite my…I mean, despite *our* insistence of no police involvement at this time, you contacted and informed your former colleagues of this…this…"

"Calm yourself, Mister Hardie," Blakestock raised a hand and smoothly replied, "I merely spoke with a few trusted people in the intelligence community who have no idea why I wanted the information. Suffice to say I inquired about the name, if it represented any individual or group. Let me assure the Board, at no time did I mention Chrystons."

"And what answer did you receive?" intervened Peters who to Tom seemed curiously calm and unflustered by the potential threat facing his company.

"According to my source, all databases were checked and it seems that nobody has the slightest inkling who might be using this name that quite obviously is a pseudonym."

"What about the name itself?" Hardie butted in.

"Well, as likely you might have already discovered yourself, a tentative check on the Internet provided me with the information that apparently the name Penthesilea refers to an Amazonian Queen, noted for her participation in the Trojan Wars. By all accounts a brave and heroic figure in Greek legend and mythology. There is of course a lot more information, but nothing that identifies the author or authors of this letter. The name of course suggests the *gender* of the author that may or may not be true."

The man seated next to Ellen raised his hand and asked, "The continuing reference in the letter to these unknown women that alleges our company has wronged. Is there a likelihood that this person or persons are or has been employed by the company?" Peters turned and stared pointedly for a response from a portly man sitting to his left who blustered, "That's just not possible to determine. I mean, we employ thousands of women in all sort of situations within the company, from sales assistants to…to…" he turned and with a raised hand indicated towards Ellen, "…to store managers."

But none as Directors, she inwardly thought.

"As for doing these women wrong, without any knowledge of what the alleged grievance is, how are we to know what these supposed wrongs are?"

"There *is* the question of the salaries," a Director seated opposite Tom quietly commented.

Beside him, Tom could almost feel Ellen bristle.

"That was resolved last year, Frank," Peters smiled at the Director, Frank Kennedy.

"Yes, but don't forget the problems we had with the union when they demanded we compensate the women for the years that we underpaid…"

"Frank," Peters snapped a little too sharply as he smiled humourlessly, then paused and drew breath before continuing. "We are well aware of what the union demanded of us, but consider this. Had the company paid out that ridiculous figure that the union believed was owed to our female employees, we would not have survived and our competitors would surely have overtaken us. Not only would the company gone under, but in consequence the female employees the union believed they were helping would have become unemployed."

"As the union continue the claim and threaten to do today," murmured Hardie in a low voice, but not so low that it wasn't heard by everyone in the room.

"Exactly," Peters forcefully seized upon the comment. "Now, I'm not so interested in what we *should* have done all those years ago, but what we intend doing today to stop these people." He took a deep breath as he paused and addressing everyone in the room, continued. "In my absence, the Board had decided to accept Mister Hardie's decision that we do not involve the police either here in Birmingham or in Scotland." His eyes narrowed. "Whether that proves to be a wise decision or not, remains to be seen. However, Mister Hardie is quite adamant that in the meantime we employ our own investigators to bring a resolution to this issue. Mister Blakestock," he turned towards the older investigator. "How exactly do you intend resolving this issue?"

Blakestock took a deep breath and shaking his head replied, "It seems to me Mister Peters you have two options. The first option is to pay the one million pounds…"

"Not an option!" Hardie startled them all by slamming his hand down onto the table.

"Please, James," Peters smiled tolerantly at the younger man, "control yourself."

"Well then," Blakestock continued, "the second option is to give me and my Scottish colleague Mister McEwan the two days we have before the deadline to make our inquiries; before another food product is contaminated and if the persons or persons responsible for this threat are to be believed, contaminated by something far deadlier than food dye."

"How will you go about your inquiry?" asked Hardie.

Blakestock turned towards Tom and smiled mischievously.

"Mister McEwan?"

"Well," Tom flushed, taken aback at being drawn into the discussion and slowly drawled, "my first step will be to return to Glasgow where with the help of Miss Toner, your Woodlands Road store manager, I will interview the staff and try to determine if any of them have knowledge of the contaminated jar being planted in the store and of course, check whatever CCTV might be available. Mister Blakestock informs me that both jars were from a batch delivered to the Glasgow store. It's time consuming, but," he half turned towards Ellen and eyebrows narrowing, asked, "between the date of delivery of the batch to the store and the time the jar was discovered, I assume you retain till receipts that will indicate when that particular type of foodstuff passed through your cash machines?"

"Yes," she nodded, "but bear in mind there is the possibility the jars were shoplifted."

"Agreed," Tom nodded, "but I need to start somewhere."

"When you interview the staff, Mister McEwan," interrupted Hardie who leaned across the table, "you will of course maintain some illusion that will not infer the threat to the company?"

"Of course, sir. I'll think of something," he smiled.

"And what do you propose to be doing here in Birmingham, Mister Blakestock?" Hardie turned towards him.

"I seem to have drawn the short straw, Mister Hardie, for I'll be sitting at a desk here in your company personnel office going through all your files to try and find a disgruntled employee or former employee who just might be the author of your letter, though my instinct tells me that Mister McEwan will be the busier of the two of us. However, with his cooperation," he nodded to Tom, "we will do our level best to try and to solve this issue as quickly as possible though…"

"Though?" Peters peered at him.

Blakestock sighed and continued, "My instinct is to involve the police, certainly the Anti-Terrorist unit here in Birmingham and their colleagues in Scotland. The resources they have available…"

"Again that is not an option, Mister Blakestock," Hardie firmly raised his hand.

Peters stared at his Director of Operations and slowly nodding, said, "Mister Hardie seems to be quite firm on this issue, Mister Blakestock. With you and Mister McEwan acting for the company, I sincerely hope we can keep this matter in house. I assume if we were to involve the police there is a strong possibility the media would learn of our problem and then God help us; every Tom, Dick and Harry would believe we are a target for extortion, not to mention our competitors who would likely take full advantage of the issue. So, on this issue I bow to Mister Hardie's initial decision, Mister Blakestock. No police."

"It begs the question, Mister Peters," Tom raised his hand. "If Mister Blakestock and I are unsuccessful in locating the person or persons responsible within the time left to us, how will you deal with the problem then?"

Peters frowned and abruptly replied, "That young man will be decided at the next meeting. According to the letter we have seventy-two hours from its receipt so allowing for the time that has passed, I assess that the deadline is set for ten in the morning, this forthcoming Saturday. Therefore, I am scheduling our next meeting for that time, two days hence."

Standing, he nodded politely to Ellen and said, "Miss Toner, gentlemen, this meeting is concluded. Thank you for your attendance and your tolerance."

Peters turned towards Hardie and said, "James, a word in private, if you please." However, Hardie raised a finger requesting Peters permit him a moment or two and beckoning Gregory Packer over, spoke briefly and quietly with him.

It was as Tom, Ellen and Blakestock were about to leave the boardroom that Packer approached and invited them to his office on the third floor.

Packer escorted them not to the lift, but to stairs that were set behind a fire door and led them down to a corridor that was in contrast to the opulence of the fourth floor.

"This is where the real work gets done," he joked as he pushed open a door and nodding to his secretary, pushed open a second door into his office.

The room was larger than Tom expected and while Packer fetched two extra chairs from the outer office, Tom saw a photograph on the desk of a smiling and relaxed Packer with a young, pregnant woman who held a child in her arms.

Now comfortably seated, Packer sat behind his desk and addressing Gavin Blakestock, said, "Mister Hardie believes that it might be in the company interest Mister Blakestock if you were thought to be conducting some sort of audit when you are working within the personnel department rather than have the staff become suspicious."

"Not a problem," agreed Blakestock.

"Mister McEwan," smiled Packer. "Mister Hardie wishes you to inform him nightly of any progress you might make. I can provide you with…"

Tom held a hand up to stop him and said, "I understand that you as a company are anxious for an update. That's perfectly natural and reasonable; however, if I'm to devote my full time to this inquiry and remember we only have two days at the most, then I might not have time to be running about giving updates, Mister Packer. That said though, if I discover anything that is of immediate interest, I will inform my boss Martin McCormick, who in turn will contact Mister Hardie. Is that okay with you?"

Ellen saw Packer swallow with difficulty and suppressed a smile, guessing that the nervous man would not look forward to relating Tom's refusal of Hardie's instruction.

As though recalling something, Tom then said, "Mister Packer. I don't pretend to be an expert on protocol when it comes to Board meetings, but isn't it rather unusual not to have the minutes of the meeting noted?"

"That was a decision taken by Mister Hardie," Packer slowly replied.

"Right then," Tom didn't question the response, but wondered exactly why Hardie did not wish the meetings decisions recorded. Quickly he got to his feet and extending his hand towards Packer, said, "All it remains is for us to say goodbye and we'll head for the airport and catch our return flight." He turned to Blakestock, who taken by surprise, was rising to his feet and said, "I'll phone you, Gavin, and we can exchange information."

"Better still," Blakestock replied as they left Packer's office, "I'll run you to the airport and we can talk on the way."

Stepping down from the bus in George Square, Annemarie Turner quickly made her way across Queen Street towards the Counting House pub restaurant located on the corner of Queen Street. She had never been inside the former flagship of the Bank of Scotland and entering through the main door in St Vincent Place, was immediately impressed by the internal size of the ornate and vaulted building. Feeling a little overwhelmed as she glanced around the busy lunchtime crowd, she saw her sister Joyce waving from a nearby table and in her hurry to greet her, almost knocked over a waiter carrying a heavy tray of food.

"No problem," the young man grinned at her and deftly landed the tray on a table full of men wearing business suits.

"Joyce," she hugged her sister to her and with a relieved sigh, sat down on the vacant seat. "Sorry, I'm a wee bit late, the bus...."

"Never mind, you're here now," interrupted Joyce. "Now, I'm on the bell so what are you having," she asked, handing Annemarie a large and comprehensive menu.

Annemarie slipped out of her jacket and hung it on the back of the seat.

"Can I have..."

Joyce reached across and placed her hand on her sisters and softly said, "You can have what you want, but first," she reached for the bottle of wine in the silver bucket and pouring the wine into a glass, continued, "let's have a wee toast. To you Annemarie, for *finally* coming into the city and meeting me." She stared solemnly at her sister and added, "I do miss you, you know. We really need to do this more often."

Annemarie took a deep breath and replied, "I know. It's just that…well, you know what he's like, Joyce. I don't always get the opportunity. Martin likes me to be there when he gets home."

"Like a bloody slave," her sister vehemently spat out.

"No, you don't understand…"

"Look," Joyce got to her feet, her hands flat against the table surface as she stared down at her sister, "today is supposed to be about us enjoying lunch, Annemarie. I don't want it to turn out to be another argument about your relationship with Martin. I'll order the food. Table forty-one. Right, baked potato with tuna and side salad okay with you?" she added, but didn't wait for a response and hurried away from the table as Annemarie stared after her. At the bar, ordering the food from a helpful young waitress she mentally cursed herself for even mentioning the bastard. In the years of their marriage, Joyce had never known her sister to be anything but servile with Martin Turner, yet still it infuriated that he had such a hold over Annemarie.

If only she still had Kieran…

She slowly exhaled and paying for the meal, forced herself to remain calm. Turning, she adopted a cheery smile and made her way back to the table.

Annemarie had hardly touched her wine.

"I've paid for the bottle," Joyce jokingly grinned. "Let's do it in and maybe get another. I've taken the afternoon off and left my car at the staff car park, so why don't we get pissed," she teased as she sipped at her wine.

Annemarie stared sadly at her, resigned to the fact that no matter how hard Joyce tried, she could not enter into the same spirit as her younger assertive sister.

"I think he's having another affair," she quietly admitted.

Joyce hesitated, the glass hallway to her lips. Slowly she lowered it to the table and deeply inhaled. "How do you know?"

Annemarie lowered her eyes to stare at the table, the shame of her admission weighing heavily upon her shoulders.

"Little things that I've come to recognise, but mainly when he come home last night he was smelling of her scent; some cheap stuff," she suddenly grunted.

Joyce glanced about her, but the nearby diners were more interested in their own conversations that listening to Annemarie's quiet voice. "Do you know who she is? Someone at the school, maybe?"

"I've no idea and does this sound odd," she stared peculiarly at Joyce, "I don't really care."

Wordlessly, Joyce reached across the table to take Annemarie's hand in hers.

"Do the girls know any of this?"

Annemarie's head jerked up and her eyes burned fiercely. "No, of course not," she snapped, "and nor will they. My God, as if they haven't..."

"As if they haven't enough to worry them, living with their father? Is that what you were going to say, Annemarie?"

She didn't respond, but bit at her lower lip, suppressing the tears that threatened her.

Joyce was dismayed. This wasn't going well, not at all as she had planned.

She stared at her sister and was about to tell her, but startled when the young man hovered beside her, the tray with their food order in his hands. Laying the plates before them and with a cheery smile that they enjoy their meal, he moved away.

Joyce had lost her appetite and glancing at her sister, saw that apparently so also had Annemarie.

They sat in an uncomfortable silence, each picking at their food until Annemarie said, "I can't leave him. I mean, where would I go," then raising her hand, added, "and don't say we'd move in with you. Your flats lovely, but it's not large enough for the four of us. Besides," her voice dropped almost to a whisper "Martin told me that even if I left, he would never let the girls go with me."

"He's bluffing," she snorted. "Don't kid yourself, Joyce. You run after him hand and foot. You cook and clean and he doesn't do a bloody thing in that house. Can you really see him holding down a full time job while running a home? Doing the washing, the cooking, getting the girls to school and picking them up? Unless he's changed since that last time you told me, he can't even iron a bloody shirt, let alone anything else!" she bristled.

"No, Annemarie; he's treated you like a skivvy for all the years of your marriage, so if you leave Martin he would be bloody lost, I tell you!"

"But what if he tried to keep the girls…"

"How long would he last, looking after two wee lassies?" Joyce was almost leaning across the top of the table now, hissing her encouragement to Annemarie. "You get yourself out of there and get your life back!"

She slowly sat back in her seat and stared into her sister's eyes.

"He's still slapping you around, isn't he?"

"It's…" Annemarie took a deep breath. "it's only when I'm not doing the cleaning properly or maybe if his meal…"

"And that justifies it, does it?" Joyce snapped back at her.

A sudden burst of uproarious laughter from an adjoining table startled Annemarie who turned her head away, too embarrassed to admit that Joyce was correct, that there was no justification for the way Martin treated her. Why, she wondered, have I put up with this for so long? Why have I allowed myself to become like this, jumping every time he speaks to me, worrying myself sick in case he finds something that displeases him? For the girls, I tell myself, but that's not the real reason. It's because I'm too afraid to leave.

"I wish I was more like you," she tried to smile at Joyce, but her voice broke and the tears had begun to slowly trickle down her cheeks.

"Is everything all right?" said the voice.

Joyce turned to see a waitress holding a tray of drinks and staring uncertainly down at Annemarie.

"We've just had some sad news," she replied and tapped at her mobile phone lying on the table, the lie easily tripping from her lips.

"Oh," the waitress turned and nodded towards the door in the far wall. "The ladies are down the stairs through that door if you want to use it," she softly said and with a sympathetic smile, moved away.

Annemarie dabbed at her eyes with a handkerchief. "Sorry," she took a deep breath. "I'm a mess, aren't I?"

"No, big sis, you're a woman who made a bad marriage and coming to terms with the fact that you just *might* have a way out," Joyce softly replied and then tapping her fingernails nervously on the table, added in a low voice, "and that's the real reason that I wanted to meet with you today."

The subject of their conversation was seated in a comfortable armchair in the staff lounge at the school, having cried off dining room duty and idly listened to two male colleagues of the English Department discussing a pupil.

To Martin Turner's surprise, he overheard the teachers mention Colleen Younger's name. His interest peaked when he heard one of the teachers relate, "Tried it on last week with me, the wee tart. Sat in the front row during my class and when I glanced over at her she deliberately lifted her skirt up with one hand and started rubbing the top of her knickers. Knew exactly what she was doing too. Fairly took me by surprise, I can tell you. She's a right dangerous wee shite, that one."

"Aye," agreed his colleague. "I remember when her three older brothers were attending here. Nothing but trouble, the lot of them. I heard that one of the brothers, Sean I think it was, did time for assault and I know the polis were in here a few times about their behaviour in the school. Did you mention it to the Deputy Head, what she was doing I mean?"

Martin's stomach lurched and he held his breath, endeavouring to catch the response.

"Oh aye, I thought I'd better say something. You know what some of these young lassies are like. Look at them the wrong way and they're alleging all sorts of impropriety. They let their imaginations run wild and before you know it, they're giggling with their pals and suddenly you are the focus of their adolescent hormonal attention. Get you hung, so they would; dangerous wee bitches."

"What did the Deputy say when you told her?"

"What do you think she said? The fucking usual, that I was to just ignore it," and they both laughed, but without humour.

Martin lost interest when the teachers conversation turned to football, but his heart was racing and his mind was in a panicked state as again he remembered what he and Colleen Younger had done. A rivulet of sweat began to trace its way down his spine and he almost jumped from the chair when a female teacher said, "Finished with that newspaper, Mister Turner?"

He stared wild-eyed at the young woman who returned his stare, her eyes betraying her curiosity at his reaction.

"Oh, yes, of course," he handed her the paper that now lay unattended upon his lap.

With a smile, she took the newspaper and returned to her seat.

His face flushed, he turned away embarrassed and rising from the armchair, made his way out of the room and headed towards the main doors and some fresh air.

His wristwatch told him he had fifteen minutes left before the afternoon classes and pushing open the doors, stepped outside.

Standing there, breathing deeply, he thought again of seeing Colleen that morning with her two friends.

What was it the English teacher had said? Giggling with their pals? His brow furrowed and he worried about what she might have said, what she might have told them.

Jesus Christ!

His throat felt tight and not for the first time he realised what kind of situation he had got himself into.

Sex with a teenage pupil.

It wasn't just a firing offence; it could even lead to prison!

His chest hurt and his hands began to tremble and to stop them shaking, forced them into his jacket pocket.

The door behind him swung open and to his surprise it was his Departmental Head, Charlie McFadyen.

Forcing a smile, he turned and said, "How are you, Charlie."

"Fine, Martin, just fine." McFadyen stared curiously at him. "You however look like you've just seen a ghost. You feeling okay?"

"Ah, just a touch of a cold coming on," he lied. "Eh, right, better get back in. I've forth year for the first period and you know what those toe rags can be like," he attempted a heart grin, but stopped when McFadyen said, "A word, please Martin."

"Yes?"

"It has come to my attention that you might be feeling a little uncomfortable dealing with some of the fourth and fifth year pupils. I've had some…well, to be honest, some concerns that when you are dealing with the classes, they can be a bit rowdy. Is there anything wrong, anyway I can be of assistance, Martin?"

"Who exactly has raised these concerns?" he asked and coldly stared at McFadyen.

Not a man easily intimidated, McFadyen replied, "There's no beating about the bush, Martin, but some of your colleagues have complained that the noise coming from your classroom can be a little distracting. In short, I will be grateful if you exercise a little more restraint and…" he took a deep breath, "if you are unable to control those buggers, then I will have little option but to refer the matter to the Deputy Head."

"Fine, do what you must," Martin snapped at him and turned away, his head reeling, tears of rage biting at his eyes and his fists clenching.

Returning to his classroom, he seethed that they were all out to get him.

They knew that he was better than them, that he was wasting his talent at this shitty dump. The bastards!

By his own admission, Martin believed himself to be the best teacher in the school, far too good to be working in a dump like this among these cretins and by cretins he didn't just mean the pupils!

McFadyen was picking on him because the Departmental Head knew that Martin was superior to him simply because McFadyen was the most useless bastard of them all!

Had he no idea what it was like trying to teach these ignorant shits! These council illiterates who had no ambition, no interest in learning and no future!

He was much too qualified for this place, far too educated!

Pulling open the classroom door, he slammed it behind him and making his way to his desk, that's when he saw the note sticking out from under the lid.

He snatched at it and unfolding it, chilled to the bone when he read:

*Martin, meet me tonite at the same time, same place. Dont forget what we did. Luv and kisses. Cxxx*

His hands clenched and crumpling the letter, tore it into little pieces and dropped it into the waste basket. Staring down, he thought that it was odd, his briefcase lying beside the waste bin was unlocked. He reached down and lifting it onto his desktop, searched through it to see if anything had been removed, but his small pay as you go mobile phone, his pen, work notebook and paperwork all seemed to be there.

Slumping down into his seat, his eyes narrowed as he considered Colleen's invitation. He wouldn't go to meet her. He would ignore the letter and just not meet with her.

There was nothing she could do, he reasoned. It was her word against his that anything happened.

He thought back to the conversation he had overheard in the staff room.

If anyone asked, he would laugh and say that he was simply the focus of a deluded teenager's obsession.

Yes, that's what he would do and smiled with relief as though a great weight had fallen from his shoulders.

The bell rung for the start of that afternoon's classes.

He shook hands with Gavin Blakestock and both agreed to keep each other apprised of any developments.

"And it was very nice meeting with you, Miss Toner," Blakestock smiled at Ellen.

"Likewise," she coyly replied and waved with Tom as the tall man headed back to his car.

Pushing their way through the doors that led to the concourse, Tom said, "Wait here with the bags and I'll book us in," returning a few minutes later to inform her with a smile, "I managed to sweet-talk the lassie into giving us adjoining seats.

"I don't know if I'm happy about that," she pretended to be annoyed.

"What, the adjoining seats or sweet-talking another woman," he grinned at her.

As he turned away she caught her breath. Following him towards the security gate, Ellen promised herself that if he continued with his flirtations she would soon put a stop to it. Tom was certainly an attractive man, but there was no way she would again involve herself with a man who was already in a relationship; not after the last fiasco.

Once through the airport security, they headed towards the departure gate and shortly after that were seated upon the plane.

Tom turned towards her and said, "Now that we have some time together, can you give me a bit of background on your company? I mean, I was a bit taken aback when there was mention at the meeting about some sort of union involvement regarding back pay for your female employees. Needless to say, it could be very relevant if the letter should be authentic, that this person or group calling itself Penthesilea is indeed acting on behalf of the women."

She stared in surprise at him. "What, you mean that you think there is a likelihood the threat might not be genuine, that this could all be some sort of a hoax?"

Tom shrugged, his brow furrowing and fingers clasped as he replied, "Obviously I can't with any certainty say one way or the other, but before you give me a background of your company, let me tell you about *my* experience of extortion. A few years ago while I was still a serving officer, my surveillance unit dealt with a similar threat to a large UK food company. On that occasion the threatening letter was delivered to their head office that was located in London. That company very wisely chose to immediately involve the Metropolitan Police in London who in turn contacted Strathclyde Police in Glasgow and also the West Midlands Police in Coventry; the three cities where some contaminated sandwiches were subsequently discovered. In his letter, the extortionist pretended to be a political organisation opposed to and railing against capitalism, but the truth was he was simply trying to induce the company to pay him a small fortune, about half a million pounds if memory serves correctly." He paused and rubbing at his forehead, continued. "Anyway, the point of the story is that most extortionists work alone and in reality, have little chance of getting away with the money simply because money creates a paper trail that is usually easy to follow. Of course there is also the difficulty of the extortionist successfully collecting his ill-gotten goods. Handovers of sums of cash are easy to monitor by surveillance units. If the money is instead transferred to an account operated by the extortionist, it's even easier to follow the transaction through the banking system."

"But you're forgetting," said Ellen, "this threat demands the money be given to women's charities so the extortionist is not personally gaining from the deed."

"That's the most curious thing," his brow wrinkled. "All this trouble to screw your company for a million pounds, but no profit for the extortionist? I'm sorry," he shook his head and pursing his lips, added, "but it doesn't make sense and just doesn't ring true to me. No, I think that's really, really odd."

The plane began to taxi to the runaway and their conversation was interrupted by the cabin crew going through the emergency procedures.

"So, tell me about your company and the union problem."

"Well, Chrystons have been operating since the two Chryston brothers Abel and Jonas started the company in 1906," and smiling at him, added, "Part of the management graduate trainee programme is knowing your company history. Anyway, like most retail organisations, the work force is mainly comprised of females. I think at the minute women make up about two thirds of Chrystons work force, but up until a couple of decades ago the work force was *predominantly* female who served under male supervisors and managers. It is only in the last two decades that women have been appointed to the positions of supervisor and latterly," she smiled, "store managers and area managers."

"But not as Directors," he rightly guessed.

"That will come in time, I'm sure. About ten years ago and before I joined the company," she continued, "because of the outrageous disparity in salaries, the union forced the issue of equal pay for women employed by Chrystons. Up to that time Chrystons had sweetened the women's salaries with a company card that entitled them to discounted clothing and food which worked out to be a lot cheaper for the company than paying them the wages of their male colleagues. There was also a non-contributory pension scheme for the women that settled a small pension upon them if they worked for thirty years or more with the company, thereby ensuring company loyalty."

"So what you're telling me is that rather than pay equal salaries, the company profited by rotating the staff's wages thus ensuring the staff remained as customers as well as employees?"

"Exactly," she smiled. "The money the company saved on keeping the women's salaries low far exceeded that small loss of providing the women with discounted goods and a small pension. But then things changed. The younger generation fought for equal rights and the union became involved and forced Chryston to pay the same salary that they were paying the men."

Tom saw her eyes narrow and said, "But?"

"Equal salary meant an end to the company card and also an end to the non-contributory pension fund."

"So, they got you women in the end then?" he joked.

"Sadly, yes which is why I am of the opinion that the author of that letter just might be a Chryston employee or a former employee, Tom."

The plane engines reached a crescendo and he saw her face pale. Reaching down, he tried to take a reassuring hold of her hand, but was a little surprised that she pulled her hand away and curtly told him, "Thank you, but I'll be fine."

A few moments later they were airborne and Ellen relaxed.

However, Tom had the distinct feeling that any camaraderie they might have experienced in the preceding hours was now gone.

## CHAPTER SIX

On the bus home Annemarie Turner worried herself almost sick. She still couldn't believe what Joyce had proposed. The enormity of it scared the daylights out of her and yet Joyce had seemed so persuasive and so confident that it would work.

The few miles to her bus stop passed without her seeing a single one, so wrapped up in her thoughts was she.

"The girls," Joyce had continually urged her, "think about the girls, Annemarie. Do you want them growing up in a house where the norm is for their father to verbally and physically abuse their mother? Is that what you want? And think about this. When will he start his abuse with the girls? At what age will Martin decide the girls can be beaten too?"

She wasn't stupid and realised her sister was blackmailing her; using her children as leverage to urge her to leave Martin, just as he was using them for her to stay.

Dear God, she thought; what am I to do?

There was nobody she could ask, no one to turn to for advice.

The horrible thought that also passed through her head was that no matter what decision she made, the die had been cast; Joyce had already commenced her plan.

With a start she realised she was approaching her bus stop and hurriedly made her way to the door, holding onto the steel bar and oblivious to the admiring glance from the driver for it had been a long time since Annemarie had noticed anyone admire her.

Stepping down from the bus, she quickly made her way to Glenhead Street, her hands shaking as she searched her handbag for her keys. Opening the door she checked her wristwatch and saw that she had just time to vigorously brush her teeth to erase any trace of the half glass of wine she had drunk before she headed off to collect the girls from their school.

With a last glance at the hallway and mentally crossing her fingers she had not missed anything, she locked the front door and hurried off.

Arriving home to his Dennistoun flat, Tom paid the taxi off, but not forgetting to ask for his receipt. Turning towards the close he inwardly grinned. It wouldn't do to get on the wrong side of Martin McCormick's secretary, Martha.

He thought back to saying cheerio to Ellen Toner at the airport just after he had arranged to call the following morning at her store. It puzzled him that she had reverted to the cool and politely distant Miss Toner before walking off to collect her car and even though he had mentioned he lived in the city had not suggested offering him a lift, but instead to his surprise told him to have a pleasant evening. Women, he shook his head as he inserted his key into the front door; he would never understand them.

Dropping his overnight bag in the bedroom, Tom's first action after switching on the electric kettle was to call Martin McCormick and standing with his back to the worktop, said, "Hi Martha, it's Tom McEwan. Can you put me through to Martin, please?"

He smiled and reassured her, "Yes, I've got all the receipts and that includes the bar bill for fifty quid."

He grinned at her loud and outraged response before she paused, realising that he was joking. Calm now and warning him not to tease her again, she put him through to McCormick.

"Tom, I assume that's you returned from the Brum?"

"Yeah, landed forty minutes ago and came straight home," he replied with the phone tucked under his chin while he spooned coffee into a mug. "There's not much I can do today so I'll get a fresh start tomorrow. I've the girls staying with me overnight."

"Give them a hug from their uncle Martin," replied McCormick. "Now, anything new to report?"

"Nothing, Martin, other than the fact that I'm not too happy that this is a genuine threat to Chrystons."

"Why, what's troubling you?"

He didn't immediately respond, wondering how he would explain a gut feeling, then said, "Like I told you when I left the meeting this morning, the letter demands a million quid to be distributed to women's charities, but nothing for the supposed extortionist. That is definitely weird. I mean, I know that nowadays you deal mainly with civil law, but you *have* dealt with criminal law too. So tell me this, have you *ever* in your career heard of a situation where the bad guy sets out to get nothing from the crime?" He didn't wait for a response, but added, "No, I think there's something else going on here."

"You could be wrong. It could be some crackpot that believes they are doing this for the greater good and genuinely believes in their cause; making Chrystons suffer for the alleged harm they did to their female employees."

"What, like a criminal philanthropist?" Tom smiled, then added, "Maybe and that's why we have no other option than to run with the threat as it stands. However, before I commit myself, you're my boss and before I do anything else I want to run something by you."

"And that is?"

"The Board of Chrystons are adamant there should be no police involvement and I do understand their reasoning. If it became public knowledge their foodstuffs were being poisoned, they could lose untold revenue as well as their customers' trust. In fact, when their local investigator, a man called Gavin Blakestock informed their Board he had made some discreet inquiry with former colleagues in the West Midlands, one of their Directors, James Hardie, the guy you spoke with on the phone, went off his nut."

"So, what is it you're suggesting, Tom?"

"I think that to protect ourselves and the firm, Martin, we should have our own discreet contact with the local cops because if indeed this *is* a genuine threat and Chrystons refuse to pay the demand and lose a customer to a poisoned food product, we as a firm might be in deep shit if it comes out that we had prior knowledge of the threat. If nothing else, it wouldn't do our credibility as a firm any good."

McCormick deliberated for a few seconds then unconsciously nodding to his phone replied, "You think we should have a quiet word with my cousin, Lynn Massey?"

Tom knew Massey, a Detective Chief Inspector with Police Scotland CID and one of the smartest officers he had ever come across. However, he replied, "No, not Lynn. If we brought her into this and it *did* go belly-up, it could land her in serious bother with her bosses. I was thinking more of having a quiet and *very* unofficial word with Danny McBride."

"Your pal in the Criminal Intelligence Unit?"

"That's him. Danny could be useful and knows when to keep his mouth shut. If I ask him nicely he could also make a check for us regarding any disgruntled employees that my inquiry might throw up when I visit the Woodlands Road store tomorrow."

"I take it that you will have *carte blanche* when you visit the store?"

"Yes. According to the Board the local investigator Gavin Blakestock and I will have the full cooperation of those Chrystons staff who are in the loop. As well as that, I travelled down with the Woodlands Road store manager, Ellen Toner and ah…well," he grinned, "we kind of had to spend the night together."

There was a definite pause before McCormick replied, "I expect you'll explain that one when you come to the office. Right then, I'll leave you to get on and needless to say, keep me apprised of any development."

"Right, Martin, cheers," Tom signed off.

Idly stirring his coffee, he thought again of Ellen Toner and was wondering what he might have said or done to offend her when the front door of the flat was knocked.

To his delight, it was Tom's two daughters carrying their overnight cases and with his ex-wife Lisa stood behind them.

"I won't come in, Tom, I'm meeting Aiden for dinner; the cancelled dinner from last night," she smiled then added as she wagged a warning finger at him, "Remember, Dad. Any nonsense from these two taking advantage of you and I'll deal with them tomorrow."

He grinned in response, pleased that he and Lisa were comfortable in their new found relationship and told her, "I've a job on early tomorrow, but I'll have them dropped off in plenty of time at the school before I go. Have a nice night and tell Aiden I said hello."

"I will, thanks," she smiled and giving the girls a goodbye hug, turned and went down the stairs.

Closing the door, he took a deep breath and rubbing his hands together, said, "Right, who's for takeaway pizza and for the tenth time, wants to watch 'Frozen'?"

Reversing her car into an empty bay, Ellen Toner sighed with pleasure at being home. It did occur to her that she might pop by the store and check that everything was running smoothly, but decided instead to phone Wilma Clark, confident if there were any issues she would have contacted Ellen. Busybody or not, Wilma was a competent woman and if rumours were true about Ellen's predecessor, it wasn't the first time she had been left to manage the store.

No, decision made she got out of the car; tomorrow would be fine to start back.

She walked the few yards to the front door and arching her back, looked forward to a nice steamy bath. The Premier Inn hotel room shower was excellent, but there was nothing like relaxing in one's own bath and thoughtfully smiled; preferably with a glass of Pinot Blanc close at hand.

Within fifteen minutes, the mail opened, overnight bag put away, the courtesy phone call to Wilma dealt with, travel clothes in the wash basket and now wearing just a dressing robe, Ellen was leaning over the bath in the steam filled room placing a cautious hand under the hot tap.

Turning off the tap she stepped gingerly into the bubble filled scented bath, but first ensured the glass of wine was reachable.

With a pleased sigh she sank into the deep waters and closed her eyes.

Her thoughts turned to Tom McEwan, but he was obviously with someone and for that reason she determined she would never consider him in a romantic sense.

A very nice man she decided, but then again, Paul Williams had been a very nice man too.

Yes, she sighed at the memory, Paul *had* been a nice man right up till the time she discovered that the west end flat where they regularly met and that he pretended he rented was in fact owned by his friend; that he *actually* lived with his artist wife and son in their neat little semi-detached house in East Kilbride.

Bastard!

She flushed with embarrassment, annoyed with herself that even after almost a year she was still so very, very angry that she had been so deceived.

For three months he had lied to her.

Three months!

How could she have been so naive?

She unconsciously shook her head and sighed.

She hadn't been naive, she had been trusting and in love.

Well, her brow furrowed, that wouldn't happen again and certainly not with a man who is involved with another woman, regardless of how attractive and appealing he is. For that reason, Mister McEwan would *not* figure in her thoughts.

Not at all.

She sipped at her wine, but try as she might Tom McEwan still beset her thoughts and angrily she shook her head as though to clear it.

Damn him.

The heat of the bath, the journey and the glass of wine began to take its toll and her eyes drooped.

Oh, oh, better get myself out of here before I drown, she smiled and stood to dry herself off.

But still, tomorrow's meeting at the store with Tom occupied her thoughts.

Ellen Toner, she inwardly chastised herself.

What *is* it with you and men?


She caught a taxi back to her flat and throughout the journey worried herself almost sick that she might have placed too much stress on Annemarie, that by divulging her plan her sister would give in to the pressure and inform Martin of Joyce's intentions.

No, she tried to convince herself. If Annemarie did not wish to go through with the plan she would simply ignore everything that Joyce had told her; not inform Martin, simply because to him knowledge was power and it would give him more cause to apply his strangling hold over Annemarie.

Not the first time she wondered how her sister had managed to land herself such a nasty piece of work like Martin Turner when she had so many suitable men knocking on their parent's door to ask her out. Joyce was aware that she was herself a good looking woman, but had always accepted being in Annemarie's shadow though never had she been jealous. Quite the contrary for she was immensely proud that Annemarie, the less academically qualified of them both, landed herself a job working in the beauty department of the prestigious Frasers store in Glasgow's Buchanan Street. She smiled when she recalled that even among the lovely women who worked there, the attractive and cheery Annemarie had stood out and was popular among her colleagues.

Why then, Joyce shook here head, did she accept Martin's proposal of marriage when she could have done so much better for herself. The civil wedding had been a complete disaster, with Martin insisting that their father pay for it, but that all the arrangements would be made by the penny-pinching Martin. It transpired the only invited guests were Annemarie and Joyce's parents, a couple of aunts and an uncle and their spouses, but no one from Martin's family who he later described as just a bunch of freeloaders. Even his so-called best man made an excuse and hurried off after the meal. Much later Annemarie confided to her sister that Martin did not associate with his family for he believed that he had, as he said, outgrown them.

The so-called reception was held in a restaurant where the staff simply shoved a number of tables together at the rear of the small room they shared with other diners. She recalled that dressed in her finery, her mothers face burned with shame at the cold faces of her two sisters and her brother.

Paying off the cabbie, she wearily climbed the stairs to her third floor flat and aside from the half glass Annemarie drunk, regretted finishing the full bottle of wine.

The phone in the hallway was ringing when she opened the front door and at a rush, grabbed the handset and gasped, "Annemarie?"

"Eh, no," said the voice, "it's me, Joyce. Sandy Munro. Were you expecting another call? Do you want me to call back later?"

"No, Sandy, you're fine," she replied, slumping down onto the small seat at the telephone table.

"I'm calling about dinner. The arrangements, I mean. I was wondering if you might be available this Saturday evening?"

"Saturday? Yes, I think so," she replied.

"Great then. Say, seven-thirty?"

"Yes that will be fine, Sandy."

"Right, see you then."

"Oh, Sandy," she quickly said and could not but smile.

"Yes?"

"Where?"

"Where what? Oh, sorry; yes, of course," she heard him laugh. "I've booked a table at the Ingram Wynd in Ingram Street, if that's okay. I was thinking that if I'm to take the lecturer in Food Science to dinner it had better be somewhere that serves good food."

"Ingram Wynd sounds perfect," she replied and agreeing to meet him there, ended the call.

He would never know, but if nothing else meeting Sandy for dinner would likely give her the opportunity to relax for she had planned that Saturday was to be a very busy day.

Still seated at the telephone table, she thought about Sandy. She had heard colleagues describe Sandy as such a lovely man and with bright academic future ahead of him. Joyce was acutely aware that he was so different from Kieran, both in looks and temperament. Since losing Kieran in the accident Joyce had virtually ceased all her social activity and though had received more than a few dinner invitations from men, Sandy was the first invitation she had accepted. Why she did accept on this occasion, she couldn't exactly say, but she did like Sandy and knew that he would not pressure her. He just wasn't that kind of man.

She sighed and hoped that he wouldn't be too disappointed for right now romance was the last thing on her mind.

The Head for the Maths Department Charlie McFadyen was a worried man.

Word had reached his ears that one of his female students was bragging about having had a sexual liaison with a male teacher.

Of course rumours abounded and flourished in such tight a knit community and some of these young girls, the way they flaunted themselves in front of the male students let alone the male staff; he unhappily shook his head at the thought.

McFadyen, who was known throughout the school for his principled Catholic beliefs, inwardly admitted though wrong it might be, it was not unheard of to overhear some of the younger and less experienced male staff discuss the physical attributes of their teenage female students; comments he would quickly and very harshly crack down on.

Now seated at his desk in the empty classroom with his elbows on the desktop and his chin resting on his folded hands, McFadyen considered the informant, a sixth year Prefect and exemplary student whose ambition was to achieve all her Higher Grades and apply for teaching college. A bright and unassuming individual, he knew the girl was not known to carry tales, but on this occasion she believed what she had overheard in the first floor female toilets was worthy of reporting. The Prefect had her own concerns for being uncertain who the male teacher might be, she brought the information to her female form teacher's attention.

No, she had apparently told Miss Carson, she neither knew nor recognised the voice of the bragging girl and no names had been mentioned.

Inexperienced in such issues, Miss Carson decided she had no recourse other than to inform her Departmental Head and thus McFadyen was brought into the circle. According to Julia Carson, the Prefect had been initially reluctant to admit she had been in a toilet cubicle smoking when she heard the girl whisper to what sounded like two of the girls' friends and even that had been when the three girls were leaving the toilets.

"And what exactly did she hear," McFadyen had asked Miss Carson, pretending interest, but already half convinced himself it was just another attempt by a female student to impress her pals.

However, when the blushing Miss Carson related the Prefect's tale of the unknown girl meeting the teacher the previous evening and screwing him in the back of his fancy car, as Carson described it, a sense of apprehension overtook McFadyen.

What concerned him was that it seemed the Prefect believed the story to be true and knowing what a smart girl the Prefect was, despite her smoking issue, McFadyen believed *her*.

Instructing Miss Carson to inform the Prefect that for now she was to keep this information to herself, McFadyen's problem was that having been informed of the allegation, how he would go about making the inquiry to identify the female student. If indeed he were to find this student and deal with her, he would then have little option but to confront the male member of staff and thereafter set the ball rolling to involve not just the Education Department, but the police.

"That's the phone for you, Danny," the civilian analyst called out across the room.

"Right, thanks," Detective Inspector Danny McBride replied and leaving his desk at the top of the room, made his way to the analyst's desk beside the large computer server.

"DI McBride here."

"Danny, it's Tom McEwan. Can you talk?"

In Tom's background he could hear the sound of children loudly singing 'Let it Go' off-key and replied, "You sound like you have the twins overnight and let me guess; it's takeaway pizza and the film 'Frozen'."

"That's why you're a detective," laughed Tom. "Aye, Lisa dropped them off earlier and while they're happily stuffing their faces I thought I'd catch you at the office."

McBride grinned and responded, "I'm not really *that* smart, Tom, it's just that you're so bloody predictable. Can you not take they twins out to a McDonalds now and then? Isn't that what divorced Dad's do? So, what is it you want?"

"What, I can't call my pal to see how he's doing?"

"I told you, McEwan, you're too bloody predictable. I know you're not inviting me out for a pint tonight because you're childminding your weans and…"

"No, you're right about that," interrupted Tom. "I'd need to give you a weeks notice so you could submit a written request to Brenda for enough cash to buy a round."

"I'll tell her you said that," McBride tried to sound annoyed, but failed and asked, "Now, what can I do for you?"

"It's work related. I need to meet with you and discuss something. My problem is I'm working on a time limit and I could use your advice…maybe your help as well."

McBride glance at his wristwatch and grimacing, said, "I'm finishing here at Gartcosh in about half an hour. I usually catch the train to Queen Street," but then stared at a detective whose head was bowed over his desk. "Tell you what, one of my guys here lives in the east end of Glasgow. I'll get him to drop me on Alexandria Parade and I'll grab a chip supper and come up to your flat."

"What about Brenda, won't she be expecting you for your dinner?"

"I'll give her a call and she can pick me up later before she puts the wean down for the night. Do you want me to bring a couple of cans of lager in?"

"Maybe for yourself," Tom replied, "but not for me, not when I've the girls overnight. You *can* bring me in a fish supper though."

"I knew there would be a catch somewhere," sighed McBride, who added, "I'll get them a bag of chips between them. Is it okay to bring them a bar of chocolate as well?"

"If you want to remain their adopted uncle, I wouldn't risk *not* bringing them chocolate."

"Right then, I'll see you in about an hour and a bit."


In fact, it was almost and hour and a half before Danny McBride arrived at Tom's flat in Craigpark Drive.

"Traffic," he explained as he handed over the aromatic bag of fish suppers and chips and with a wide smile, greeted Sophie and Sara and to the glee of the girls, as if by magic produced two bars of Cadburys chocolate from his coat pocket.

Squealing with delight they run back into the lounge to continue watching the cartoons while McBride hung up his coat then followed Tom through to the kitchen.

"Tea with these or did you bring in lager?" Tom asked as he tipped the suppers onto two plates.

"No, I hate drinking alone so tea will be fine," replied McBride, settling himself into one of the two chairs at the small kitchen table.

Tom placed the plate down in front of McBride and sat opposite.

Though the two men had been friends for just a couple of years, they had bonded and developed a trusting relationship that encompassed both their friendship and working lives.

"So, what's up?" asked McBride.

During the following ten minutes, Tom outlined the inquiry that currently involved him and stressed that while he was happy to relate the circumstances to McBride, he did not wish to officially involve his friend.

"In short, I'm seeking your advice on how I should handle this. That and I would be extremely grateful if you were in a position to assist me off the record as it were, with any information that might identify this individual or group calling themselves Penthesilea."

"It doesn't ring any immediate bells, Tom, but remember; I'm involved in the acquisition, collation and distribution of *criminal* intelligence. Yes," he slowly nodded, "sometimes my work spills over into the intelligence held by the Counter Terrorist Intelligence Unit but to be frank, it's often a one-way street. My mob might feed them Intel that assists them, but they don't always return the favour." He grinned and added, "It's what you might call a bone of contention between us, particularly if they have Intel I could use but don't share because they don't fully trust my people."

Tom returned the grin and replied, "So, things haven't changed that much. It's still a case of my ball and you're not playing?"

"Something like that," McBride nodded in agreement then his expression changed as he asked, "You're meeting the manager tomorrow at her store in Woodlands Road?"

"Ellen Toner, yes."

"Is she a suspect?"

Tom's brow furrowed. "They're all suspects until I decide otherwise, but my gut feeling is no, she's simply an employee caught up in the issue. I thought that while we were in Birmingham we had built up some kind of rapport, but when we arrived back in Glasgow, she reverted to being the cool, icy woman I first met." He shook his head and narrowing his eyes, added, "I don't know what, but I think I annoyed or said something to upset her."

"Good looking?" smiled McBride.

"Very, but a bit out of my league I think."

"So, what's your plan for tomorrow morning?

"I was thinking I would check the CCTV first then if that produces nothing speak with the staff who are on duty and at worst, obtain a list of names. Any chance you might run them through your system?"

"You *do* know that because of the Data Protection Act, every time an operator signs on to our system to do a background check, it's logged and there has to be a reason for the check?"

"I thought that your department was outside the legislation?"

"No," McBride shook his head. "That only applies to the CTU people. But," he sighed and placed his cutlery down onto the empty plate, "if you are willing to provide me with the go-ahead, I can create a report that will give an explanation for my assisting you." He paused and contemplated for a few seconds before adding, "Something along the lines of information received regarding a potential threat to Chrystons."

Tom was about to argue that Chrystons had insisted there was to be no official police action, but McBride held a hand up and continued. "The report would for the meantime be for my eyes only and list you as my confidential informant. I would then be able to justify having one of my trusted people carry out the checks and the report would remain allocated to me alone. That way if anything broke and as you fear someone *was* poisoned or harmed in the future, you can honestly say that the police were informed, but at the time there was insufficient information or justification to carry out a full inquiry. If the threat dies and goes away, there's no harm done and the report gets shredded. How does that sound?"

Tom smiled and toasting McBride with his mug of tea, said, "As always Danny, your advice is invaluable."

The bell rung to signal the end of that day and thankful that his last period had been free to catch up with submitted homework, Martin Turner sighed with relief.

Another day finished in this place, he idly glanced about the empty classroom.

Stuffing his lunch container into his briefcase, he grabbed his jacket from the back of his chair and opening the door, joined the swarm of pupils noisily making their way through the corridors towards the exit doors.

Pushing and shoving at each other in their excitement to get out of the school the pupils in general ignored the frustrated shouts of the teaching staff.

It was when he arrived outside the main doors that Martin saw Colleen Younger standing alone, her head bobbing back and forth as she searched the throng of pupils and staff exiting the door.

Seeing Martin she smiled and her hand started to rise as though to wave, but turning away and ignoring her, he quickly made his way across the yard to the staff car park entrance.

Fifteen minutes later Martin Turner arrived home, still a worried man that he might have incurred the wrath of Colleen Younger by ignoring her.

Who knew what went through a teenage girl's head, he thought as he locked the car and strode to the front door.

"I'm home," he sharply called out and hanging up his coat on the hooks by the door, saw Annemarie nervously step out from the kitchen to greet him.

"Martin," she forced herself to brightly smile, "how was your day, dear?"

"The same as every other bloody day," he snapped at her and added, "fetch me a cup of tea through to the lounge. I'm sitting down to read my newspaper."

"Yes, dear, right away..." but she got no further for he slammed the lounge door behind him.

Turning back into the kitchen, she slowly exhaled and reached to switch on the kettle.

In the lounge he slumped into the armchair, the newspaper resting ignored and folded on his lap. His eyes narrowed as he wondered what Colleen would do when he failed to turn up tonight.

He thought again of his explanation if their encounter should ever become known. He had decided that no matter what she said, he would completely refute her story and was confident that he would be seen as the more credible individual for after all, who was Colleen Younger but a sixteen-year-old tart from a well-known scum family.

Yes, he settled more comfortably in his armchair; that little chapter was over and grinned at the memory of her squirming under him on the backseat of his car.

It was later that afternoon when Charlie McFadyen had just arrived home that he thought about it. Like he said afterwards, it wasn't a serious thought, nothing to keep him awake that night, just one of those peculiar things that sticks in the mind.

When the bell rung to conclude that days schooling, he had been standing on the steps by the main door supervising the departure of the pupils and nodding to the staff who were leaving through the main entrance to the school. Maybe it was nothing or maybe it was that his suspicions had been aroused by his earlier conversation with Miss Carson.

Whatever it was, it caused him to recall seeing the fourth year girl Colleen Younger standing alone near the large wrought iron gates that led out into Ryehill Road and being puzzled at the girl's furious expression, while idly wondering to whom her displeasure was directed.

## CHAPTER SEVEN

After dropping his twin daughters at their school, Tom McEwan made his way through the city traffic to the Chrystons store in Woodlands Road.

Parking his Toyota Yaris in the nearby Ashley Street, he walked round to the store entrance and was directed by a young male shop assistant to Ellen Toner, who was in the warehouse at the rear supervising a food delivery.

"Morning, Miss Toner," he smiled at her, watching as she held a clipboard in one hand and a pen in the other.

"Mister McEwan," she formally greeted him, but without returning his smile. "Perhaps you could wait in my office. I'll be with you in a few minutes," and turned away to continue checking off the pallets as they were offloaded by the driver and the warehouseman.

He sensed he was being dismissed and returned through the warehouse to the shop floor where the same assistant directed him to the office.

Seated at her desk, Ellen's secretary Wilma Clark raised her head to stare imperiously at the interruption. "Can I help you?"

"Hi, I'm Tom McEwan. Miss Toner asked that I wait in her office."

"Why?"

"I'm from head office. I'm conducting an unofficial staff audit," he smiled at her.

"What? I wasn't told anything about this," she began to bluster, but stopped when the door was pushed open by Ellen who said, "Wilma, I'll be in conference with Mister McEwan here for about ten minutes. Could you rustle up a coffee for us, please?"

Wilma's cheeks turned red and with ill-grace, nodded as Ellen led Tom into her office.

"Is that the first line of defence," he quipped as he closed the door behind him.

"Wilma is very good at her job and quite rightly, wondered who you might be wandering about the office area," she tightly replied as she moved behind her desk to sit down. He recognised the rebuke, but made no comment as he drew out a chair to sit opposite her.

"So, how do you want to begin?" she asked.

"I saw that you have CCTV cameras covering the front door and in the store. Do they happen to cover the area where the jars were taken from and for what period of time do you keep the discs?"

Her brow knitted and she shook her head. "I have eight cameras covering different aisles that operate on a roving time delay; by that I mean there is one disc that records each camera on a fifteen second snapshot of what the camera is pointing at, but regretfully none at that section. To comply with Data Protection, the discs for the cameras are stored here in Wilma's office, however," she stared at him and continued. "I *thought* you might wish to know what recordings we have so when I arrived this morning, I checked and discovered the cartons containing the jars were delivered here within the last three weeks." Opening a top drawer in her desk, she brought out a plastic wallet of DVD discs and handing it across the desk to him, said, "I collected the discs that cover the period from the delivery to the time the jars were discovered. I'm sorry to tell you it's eighteen discs." She pointed to a small TV and player in the corner and added, "You can use that, if you have to. To comply with Data Protection, all the cameras are focused on Chrystons property. Now, as for where the cameras are located, they are primarily situated to cover the front door, staff entrance at the rear of the building, three in the warehouse and docking area for the delivery of goods that again is located at the rear of the building and the remaining two to protect the vulnerable products such as alcohol and high-priced meats. The alcohol and high-priced meats are our most prized products for the shoplifters," she added by way of explanation.

"That's seven," he replied.

"Camera number eight is located above the three tills. Unfortunately, like most large retailers, Chrystons attribute a high percentage of loss is either by staff theft or passing items through at a lower price or not passing them at all through the till."

"Isn't the bar code meant to deal with that? I mean, doesn't the till recognise the price when the product is passed through the machine?"

"Ideally, yes," she sighed, "but like I said, that's if the operator *does* pass the product through. One of the common scams by staff is that the product is simply slipped from the basket straight into the customer's bag without going through the bar code machine, hence the camera above the tills."

"So, there is three options. First option is if whoever bought the jars then paid for them, there will be a record in the till receipt The second option is if they were stolen then no receipt. The last option is a member of staff is involved and passed the jars across the till, hence the sale would not be recorded."

"That about sums it up, yes. What's your thoughts on the matter," she asked?

Tom shrugged and replied, "I don't believe the jars were stolen. If the culprit were caught shoplifting the jars, then that would completely foul up their plan from the outset. I think it's unlikely a member of staff would take the risk when the jars could so easily and legitimately be purchased. So, that leaves the first option. All it remains for me is to find out when the jars might have been purchased and try to match the time and date with the recordings you have of customers entering or departing through the front door."

She half smiled and said, "I assume you don't relish the idea of wading through hundreds of till receipts?"

"Not particularly," he agreed.

"Well, the good news is that these days we're computerised. All the tills are linked to my desktop here," she patted the top of her computer.

"What does that mean?"

"Well, as the store manager I have to know what products are selling well and what products are *not* selling so well and that permits me to arrange my food product orders as I require, so when an item is legitimately sold here in the store, the bar code is recorded in a data programme. Therefore, if as you suspect the items were purchased, I should be able to research the programme and discover when and how many jars of Snuckles baby food were sold within the eighteen days I spoke of."

"Well," Tom grinned, "that *would* make my job a lot easier."

"What about the staff, will there be any requirement for you to speak with them?"

"I shouldn't think so at this time simply because I don't have the right questions to ask them. I mean, asking them if they recall somebody buying or stealing two jars of baby food really won't get me very far," he shrugged.

"Right," Ellen turned to her desktop computer and signing onto the company network, said, "if you give me five minutes I'll get on with downloading the information you need."

Just then the door was knocked and opened almost immediately by Wilma who scowling, wordlessly handed in a small tray upon which lay two mugs of coffee, a sugar bowl and jug of milk. Turning she closed the door loudly behind her.

"I've always had a way with women," grinned Tom, however, the joke fell flat when it was ignored by Ellen who thought that the charming Tom McEwan would *not* charm her.

Still puzzled at her cool attitude towards him, he turned his head to stare idly at the Chrystons annual planner chart that was pinned up and covered most of one wall in the small office.

She couldn't but help herself and almost acerbically, asked, "Did you have a nice evening?"

"Yeah," he absent-mindedly answered. "Takeaway pizza and another session of the film 'Frozen.' I'm beginning to think I know the plot backwards and as for that *bloody* song," he grimly smiled as he shook his head.

Ellen stopped typing and stared at him. What the hell was he talking about, she wondered, then carefully said, "I'm sorry; you watched a children's movie last night?"

"That's what you do with children, Miss Toner," he returned her stare, in turn wondering what the heck *she* was thinking.

"Oh, I thought…" she began, but stopped and resumed typing.

"You thought what?" he pressed her.

"Sorry, nothing," she shook her head, a little confused now and stared at the monitor, unwilling to meet his eye. But then inwardly taking a deep breath, asked, "I thought you were having a night at home with your girlfriend or partner," her voice slowly tailed off.

He paused before answering, wondering why Ellen Toner thought him to have a girlfriend or partner.

"No, my night was with two little women. Twins in fact. Sophie and Sarah. My eight-year-old daughters. Their mother dropped them off for a night with their Dad, hence the pizza and 'Frozen' film...*and* that bloody song."

He almost startled as a notion crossed his mind. Where did she get the idea he might be seeing a woman? Could it be that the cool Miss Toner might be interested in him after all, but thinking him involved with someone else wasn't prepared to be anything but officious with him?

"No, I've no girlfriend or partner," he continued with a soft grin. "Divorced yes and pleased to say it's as amicable as a divorce can be which is fortunate because it means I get to see my daughters without any fuss and no need for a court to decide when and where."

"Oh," she simply replied and continued to stare at the monitor, but try as she might could not prevent the flush that crossed her face or the funny sensation in her tummy.

"That's my personal life exposed now, Miss Toner. Tell me about you now. Hubby or boyfriend lurking in your background?"

"No," she quickly responded, but almost immediately regretting that she replied too quickly before adding, "There was someone a while back, but that fell through. Right, here's the information I'm looking for. I'll print it off and you can have a working copy," she hurriedly told him and pressed the print button.

"How many jars are we talking about?"

"During the parameters I have set the store sold one hundred and forty-seven jars of Snuckles baby food."

"Are you able to discern how many jars were lamb and rice?"

"Unfortunately, all the jars are bar coded at the same price, but give me a minute and I'll try to work out..."

Almost in frustration, she admitted defeat and shaking her head, told him, "Look, Wilma's far better than me at working the IT side. Are you happy to have her conduct the search? She might be able to give you a more accurate number."

Tom agreed and calling the dour Wilma into her office, Ellen explained what was required of her.

"Is this about the jars that were tampered with?" she asked.

Tom and Ellen stared at her as Wilma suddenly smiled and said, "I've been with Chrystons a lot of years now and I've got pals in the head office. One of them gave me a call on the QT to tell me about the threat. It's not *that* big a secret, you know."

"Evidently not," agreed Ellen and sighing, explained what was needed and asked Wilma to conduct the search.

The older woman took no more than a couple of minutes.

"Well," Wilma's eyes narrowed as she stared from the monitor to Tom and then back at the monitor, "according to the unique bar code on the jars, between the time and dates set by Ellen I can tell you that twenty-six jars of Snuckles lamb and rice were sold and of these sales," she leaned forward to peer closely at the screen, "as far as I can see only four sales were of two or more jars together. Do you want me to print out the time and dates of the sales?"

"Please," Tom delivered her a grateful smile and to his surprise, was rewarded by a return smile. "There you go," she said as she printed out the sheet she raised her hands palms outward and added, "Now Ellen, before you ask, as far as I'm aware nobody else in the store knows about the threat to the company and as far as my pal in the head office tells me, there's a few people whispering about it, but nobody has all the details."

"Wilma," Tom continued to smile at her, "you have no idea how much time and effort you have saved me. Thank you, I'm very grateful."

Her grin almost dazzled him and arising from Ellen's chair, returned to her own office.

"Right, with this printout from Wilma and these DVD discs," he moved his chair towards the TV and DVD player in the corner and added, "I'll get started."

Gavin Blakestock was getting nowhere. Wearily he rubbed at his face and realised that his task was simply hopeless. No matter how many employee records he had so far waded through he knew it was unlikely he would identify any culprit from the scant information the files contained.

He glanced about him at the cupboard like room he had been allocated and decided that enough was enough. His best option was to visit the 'Founding Store' across the road and speak with the staff in the vain hope that perhaps one might have seen something suspicious in the last couple of weeks.

He wondered how Tom McEwan was getting on and though not someone who was usually quick to judge, had already decided he liked the younger man. He glanced at his wristwatch and decided he would phone Tom later and exchange any update they might have. With the knowledge that the contaminated jar must have been placed in the 'Founding Store' within the last eighteen days and though it narrowed the time frame down a little, he realised it was still a considerable length of time for a staff member to recall one customer between those dates. It can't do any harm to at least try, he thought. Straightening his tie and grabbing his overcoat from the desk by the window, he slipped it over his arm and headed out from the room.

Sitting at his desk Martin Turner was grateful that the first period that morning was free and permitted him to catch up on the third year homework.

Flipping through the pupils' jotters, he savagely stroked his red pen through page after page of detailed work. It neither occurred nor bothered him that his disdain for the efforts of his pupils not only disheartened them, but that his actions was in itself a form of bullying. Not one jotter escaped his red pen nor did he add any constructive criticism for what he perceived to be their failure to grasp and understand his teaching of the subject.

The door opened and turning, he was immediately apprehensive when he saw Colleen Younger quietly enter the room. Standing with her back to the closed door, she said in a low and accusing voice, "Why didn't you meet me last night? I was stood there like a fucking numpty for almost an hour!"

Fearful of a confrontation in his own classroom, Martin choked a nervous reply, "This is not the time to be talking about it, Colleen! Now get to *fuck* out of here before somebody comes in!"

"Meet me tonight," she hissed and turned to open the door, but with her hand on the handle, turned back towards Martin and added, "You'd better!"

"Wait," he called out, then eyes narrowing, said, "Who did you tell about me? About us, I mean?"

Colleen didn't immediately respond, but her lips curled into a sneer before she told him, "Come and meet me tonight, I'll tell you all about it, who I *might* have told, okay? Just don't forget. Same time and the same place."

With that she was through the door and gone.

He sat there staring after her, his eyes wide with fear. His plan and carefully thought out excuse to deny any relationship with her was forgotten in the dread of discovery. His hands were clenched into fists and his chest hurt as he tried to breathe. Slowly, he exhaled and forced his knees together to stop them shaking.

God, what a fool he had been! But then he thought about it for really, it wasn't his fault. It was her fault; yes, he decided, it was Colleen's fault. It was the way she had forced herself upon him.

What he had to do now was decide; should he meet with her or call her bluff.

Exiting a room almost twenty metres away in the long and quiet corridor, Charlie McFadyen turned to see the fourth year pupil and wondered *exactly* what Colleen Younger had been doing in Mister Turner's classroom. His brow furrowed.

Didn't Martin say he would be going to the staff room to mark some homework?

Charlie McFadyen was an outstanding teacher and very proficient at his job as the Maths Department head, however, he was not a police officer and it didn't occur to him to link what he saw and the problem that was troubling him, so shaking his head, he turned and made his way towards the Deputy Head Teacher's room to inform her of the allegation that one of the male staff was allegedly having a sexual liaison with a pupil. On his way there he sighed, already predicating her response; it's just another one of these stupid girls making up stories to get attention from her pals, she would likely tell him, and is simply a load of nonsense.

No, the Deputy Head would choose not to believe what the school Prefect had overheard for it was common knowledge that the Deputy Head did *not* like dealing with problems.

Annemarie Turner did not sleep well. Not that she ever slept well, these days; always fearful of Martin coming into the spare bedroom and finding some reason or other to disturb her, whether it be one of his unreasonable sexual demands or simply to get her out of bed to fetch him a cup of tea.

But last nights lack of sleep was not just about what Martin might want, it was about what her sister Joyce had suggested.

Annemarie had tossed and turned all night, the ramifications of the idea too awful to contemplate if it did not go as Joyce planned. Seated at the small kitchen table, the cup of coffee cooling in her hands, she gently stroked at her cheek.

She had not been quick enough that morning to butter Martin's toast. He had been overly long in the shower and she had waited nervously in the kitchen, aware that he had to depart the house by eight-thirty at the latest. Though he drove past the girls' primary school, it would not occur to him to offer them a lift, regardless of what the weather might be. No, getting the girls to school was Annemarie's job he told her and besides, he didn't want sticky fingers and their dirty shoes all over his leather seats.

When at last he came downstairs and discovered his toast was not on the plate, he slapped her. Not hard enough to cause any real damage, but hard enough to leave the imprint of his hand as a reminder that she was too slow and too slovenly for a man like him.

It was the casual indignity of the slap that decided her. What is it again that they call it, she wondered; yes, she nodded, the final straw.

Wearily she pushed herself up from the table and walking into the hallway, lifted the phone. It would be so much easier with a mobile, but as he persistently told her that was a luxury that could only be afforded for him.

Her hands trembled slightly as she dialled, but she was so nervous she had to redial the number twice. Forcing herself to concentrate, at last she dialled correctly and when the call was answered, asked to be put through to the extension number.

"Joyce," she caught her breath and her eyes widened, "it's me. Look, I'm sorry to call you at work…yes, yes," she stammered, "what you…suggested. I've not been able to think about anything else." Taking a deep breath, she choked back her hesitation and said, "Yes, let's do it."

Chrystons Director of Operations James Hardie replaced the phone into its cradle and smiled with pleasure.

The Director of Finance was on board, finally confirming his support for Hardie when at last the CEO Jackson Peters finally stepped down.

However what Hardie did *not* intimate to the Director of Finance was that he fully expected Peters to step down a lot sooner than the end of his contracted term.

Hardie had spent all the previous evening contemplating the worst case scenario.

If indeed this Penthesilea carried out the threat and a customer *did* suffer some gastric distress or even die from consuming some kind of poison that was contained within one of the company food products, it would serve not only to cause the demise of Peters career, but paradoxically help Hardie to achieve his goal as CEO. By his reckoning, Hardie believed that when the shit quite literally hit the fan and the media got a hold of the story that Chrystons knew about the threat but did not warn the public, Peters would have little option but to resign as CEO, leaving Hardie to reluctantly step into the fray and bring the company back from the brink of disaster.

Yes, he sat back in his padded leather chair and nodded. It was a win-win situation; he could either wait the few months till Peters retired or better still, wait for a few days to pass the deadline. When Chrystons failed to accede to the extortionists demands the extortionist, this Penthesilea or whoever they were, would undoubtedly carry out their threat and poison a food product. He accepted that the initial consequence for the company will at first be catastrophic and reasoned that to begin with the company would take a massive profit loss, but within a few months or a year at the latest Chryston stock would again be on the rise. If nothing else, Hardie's two decades of experience in retail had taught him the public have short memories. All it would need was a firm hand on the tiller, a captain of industry who knew what he was doing.

He smiled, for he was determined that the captain will be James Hardie.

He glanced at the clock and saw it was approaching ten o'clock. His eyes narrowed for if he recalled correctly, Lesley usually finished her daily workout at the gym about now.

A moment later he had called her number and left a message on her mobile phone. With the confidence of a self assured man, he had little doubt she would meet with him at their favourite hotel and that, he smiled, would be the best start to the day a man could get.

Pressing the button on his intercom he informed his secretary he would be attending a business meeting and return about two, that if she urgently needed him he would have his mobile with him.

With increasing excitement, Tom McEwan pressed the rewind button and watching the digits on the bottom of the television screen, stopped the recording two minutes before the time that he first saw her.

Unconsciously, he leaned forward a few inches to stare at the screen and pressed the play button, impatiently waiting for the recording to change from the display of the warehouse and staff entrance cameras to the CCTV camera that was located above the entrance to the store. Again he checked the printout in his hand and realised that the woman, for that was certainly how the figure was dressed, must have entered the store just a few moments before the purchase of the two jars. Unfortunately, the till receipt indicated the purchase had been made with cash.

Yes, he almost cried out, there she was hovering uncertainly just inside the door as though undecided whether to fully enter. He quickly pressed the pause button and the woman froze, but unfortunately the picture clarity was streaked with lines and he mentally cursed. He was no expert but didn't believe that the picture could be cleaned up to provide a better image.

However, what it did indicate was the woman in the picture whose grey coloured hair was mostly hidden beneath a dark coloured scarf, wore a dark coloured overcoat that hung almost to her shins and carried what seemed to be a Chrystons plastic carrier bag that when she walked, flapped against her leg and appeared to be empty. It was the coat that aroused his suspicion. Ellen had signed him into her account on her desktop and when Tom conducted a quick Google search had discovered that three days previously when the woman was recorded on CCTV visiting the store, the weather had been unusually warm.

At no time did the woman glance up causing Tom to suspect the woman was either avoiding the possibility of CCTV cameras or had previously visited the store and was aware of the cameras locations. His gut told him that it was her, but without any significant evidence he knew he was merely guessing. However, he also knew that if he was correct in his assumption, that the woman was wearing the coat and headscarf as a disguise, then it was likely she might be wearing the same or similar disguise when she had visited the Birmingham store.

Fetching his mobile phone from his pocket, he dialled the number for Gavin Blakestock.

"Tom, nice to hear from you. How are things?"

"Fine, Gavin, fine. Look, are you still sifting through the personnel records at the head office?"

"No," he heard Blakestock first sigh, then his voice quickened as he said, "I gave that up as a bad idea. I'm over at the 'Founding Store' across the road speaking with some staff. Why, do you have something?"

Briefly, Tom described what he had discovered in the Woodlands Road CCTV recording and matching the till receipt, believed he had a possible suspect.

"Give me a description of what she was wearing and I'll get right onto it," snapped Gavin, fetching a notebook and pencil from his inner jacket pocket.

The door opened to admit Ellen Toner who stared curiously at Tom as he issued his description to Gavin and saw him indicate she bring a chair across and sit beside him.

"Right, Gavin, if you agree I think there is every likelihood that the woman probably visited your store down there either in the twenty-four-hour period before or after visiting Woodlands Road."

Ellen saw him nodding as he finished, "I'll expect to hear from you. Bye."

Ending the call, he turned to her and smiled as he pointed to the screen where the recording was paused and showed the woman stood frozen by the front entrance to the store.

"Might be nothing, might be something, but that woman was very hesitant when she entered the store. Stood about for a good twenty seconds glancing back and forth before the camera shot changed. What might be significant is that the till receipt for the purchase of two of the jars occurred a few minutes later."

"Is she recorded leaving the store?" Ellen asked.

Tom shook his head. "I couldn't find her departing through the front door so I'm guessing by the time the camera located above the door was again recording, it missed her leaving."

"Bloody system," she quietly replied.

He turned to grin at her. "That's been my experience, unfortunately. Whether a large company like Chrystons or a corner shop, most businesses install CCTV because it cuts down their insurance premiums, but it's human nature that they usually go for the cheapest option. Incoming and outgoings I believe you guys call it."

Ellen returned his smile. "If I had my way I would revamp the whole system, but I'm at the mercy of the accountants." Her eyes narrowed as she peered at the screen. "Do you really think that's her, the person or one of the group calling themselves Penthesilea?"

"I really can't say for certain, Ellen," he shook his head, "but it's the best lead we have so far. If Gavin Blakestock can match the description to a similar woman visiting the Birmingham store, then it's a real possibility. I'll continue checking here if you don't mind me using your office, until I hear from him. Now, can I print out the photograph? Do you have that facility?"

"Wait a minute," she stood and opened a small cupboard. "I have a small, portable printer that attaches to the computer, but unfortunately because the CCTV records in black and white, that's what it will print."

"That'll be fine. I don't hold out much hope that anyone will remember the woman, but I'll print off a photo to show to your staff and also capture the image and send it to Gavin's phone too."

"Right then," she stood up from her chair and brightly said, "I'll have a sandwich and some tea sent in for your lunch."

He watched her leave the office and the thought crossed his mind that maybe the ice maiden was melting just a little.

## CHAPTER EIGHT

The pen she held limply in her hand hovered over the report, for the moment forgotten.

Joyce McKinnon's mind was in turmoil.

She almost couldn't take it in that Annemarie had agreed to the plan. The straight forward truth was that though Joyce had already set the first phase of the plan in play, she hadn't really believed that she would be carrying out the next stage and that's what worried her.

Nevertheless, it needed to be done. She couldn't back down now and leave her sister in the hands of that heartless bastard!

But it was more than just Annemarie now; it was the girls too.

Paula aged ten and Carol, just eight years old. They had the right to grow up in a home without listening to their mother being verbally abused and beaten, a right not to be constantly afraid. That Martin would use them as barter to keep Annemarie in line was not just despicable, but downright contemptible and indicated just what kind of man he really was.

Man? She inwardly scoffed, recalling the old adage that typified men like Martin as a man among children, but a child among men.

He was a bully of the worst kind.

Her desk phone rung and startled her into dropping the pen that then rolled off the desk.

Damn, she muttered and lifting the phone, said, "Miss McKinnon, how can I help you?"

"Just checking that we're still on for our dinner date on Saturday night," said the voice.

Sandy Munro heard the sharp intake of breath and with a sigh, added, "What?"

"Just kidding. I haven't forgotten," she replied, mentally crossing her fingers and her toes for of course, with everything else going on she *had* forgotten.

"Right," he slowly drawled and then to remind her, said, "Seven-thirty, tomorrow evening, Ingram Wynd. Are you sure you don't want me to pick you up?"

"No, either I'll drive or call a taxi," she answered, her eyes narrowing.

"Okay, see you there then," he replied and hung up.

She slowly replaced the phone, her mind calculating that if she left just after eight o'clock that morning and just in case there was a hiccup she would take her evening clothes with her. Besides, the trip would be much shorter this time and subject to the traffic she could easily be back in Glasgow for seven-thirty.

Ideal, she thoughtfully nodded and getting out of her chair, got down onto her knees to hunt for the dropped pen and wondered why inanimate objects *always* seem to find their bloody way to the most inaccessible places.

It was as he thought. The Deputy Head Teacher, useless cow that she is, didn't want any fuss and dismissed his information outright.

Returning to his own office, he knew that by informing the Deputy he was in the clear; the matter was now officially out of his hands, but shaking his head he also knew he wouldn't let it go. If one of his colleagues *was* taking advantage of a vulnerable teenager, then Charlie McFadyen's conscience would not permit him to let the matter rest. No, he would make his own inquiry and find out the truth and if as the Deputy opined it was a load of shite, then so be it; no harm done.

On the other hand, he pushed open his room door, if indeed there was some sort of dalliance between a teacher and a pupil, he would see that the bastard was nailed to a cross.


Ellen Toner decided that she would take her lunch with Tom and selecting two packs of sandwiches from the deli section, run them through the till. Making her way back into the outer office she glanced through her open door and saw Tom remained sitting at the television screen, leaning forward and apparently concentrating as he run DVD's though the player.

Boiling the kettle, she made three coffees and handing one to Wilma, took the other two and the sandwiches through to her own office, using her backside to close the door behind her.

"Grub up," she smiled at him.

"Ah, thank you," he replied, but his thoughts were elsewhere as he accepted a pack of sandwiches and a coffee from her.

"Any further forward?"

"No," he shook his head, tearing open the pack. "If I'm honest, I'm too caught up thinking this woman is likely our suspect," he held up a six by four inch black and white photograph, then pre-empting her next question, added, "I'm still waiting to hear from Gavin."

Almost on cue his mobile phone rang and fumbling with the sandwiches, almost dropped them as he snatched the phone from Ellen's desk.

"Gavin," he greeted Blakestock and winked at her.

"Tom, bit of good news for you. I received the photograph on my phone you sent down and thanks for that. As you suggested, I've scrolled through the CCTV recordings in the 'Founding Store', the day each side of the time you noted in the Glasgow store. Cutting a long story short, I happened upon a woman fitting the description and similar in appearance to the photograph. Yes," Tom heard him sigh, "I realise the photo isn't very clear, but I'm as satisfied as I can be Tom; it's the same woman."

Tom tried to contain his excitement and gave a thumbs up to Ellen.

"I'll e-mail you a photograph for comparison purpose and I'm pleased to say that the quality of the CCTV down here is far better than what you had to work with."

"Great, thanks, Gavin," Tom was about to end the call when Blakestock interrupted and said, "That's not all the good news Tom. I've kept the best bit to last."

"And that is?"

"Well, sometimes as you probably know, we get lucky. I spoke with several staff members down here and after your information I was in the fortunate position of having the photograph to show them. Anyway, one young shop assistant, a college student working part-time, recognised the woman from the photograph and told me she had thought the woman was quite nervous and offered to assist her only to be told that no, the woman was fine."

Tom could feel his excitement rise and asked, "What else did the assistant have to tell you, Gavin?"

"Turns out the assistant is in her second year of a City and Guilds beauty therapy course and apart from remarking the woman had a Scottish accent, is almost certain she was far younger than the grey wig and dark glasses she wore. In fact, the assistant is positive the woman had deliberately dressed down and tells me the woman's skin was far younger than the clothes she was wearing. Must be a female thing," Blakestock drily added.

Tom decided not to pass *that* comment to Ellen.

"So, if indeed this mystery woman is our suspect, she has a Scottish accent and was probably wearing a disguise to hide her true age, hair colour and the dark glasses presumably to hide her features."

"That's what I'm thinking, mate."

"What's your gut feeling about all of this, Gavin?"

There was an anxious pause and for a second, Tom had thought the call had disconnected before Gavin replied, "Are you alone?"

"Yes, well, no. What I mean is, Ellen Toner is sitting with me," he turned to glance at her. "I'm in her office."

"She's a manager employed by Chrystons, Tom. Do you think she can be trusted?"

Tom smiled at Ellen and replied, "Yes Gavin, I believe she can be trusted."

"In that case then, put me on speaker," requested Blakestock.

"Right Gavin, you're on."

"Okay, well, you're asking about what I really feel about this threat. If I'm honest and Miss Toner, I'm trusting you will be discreet about any comments I make."

She leaned forward to reply into the mobile held by Tom, "You have my word, Mister Blakestock."

"First of all, I consider Chrystons are making a huge mistake not bringing the two constabularies into this. I believe that the signatory of the threatening letter, this Penthesilea, is *probably* just one individual. What I do *not* believe is that this individual is so big-hearted to make the threat on behalf of women employed by Chrystons. As far as the information about Chrystons female employees being exploited; well, no great secret there. It is common knowledge that Chrystons had its difficulties with the union and it was extensively reported in the media over the years so can easily be researched on the Internet. No, I'm of the opinion that there is some underlying reason for the threat, but frankly I have no idea nor can I guess what that underlying threat is. What I *do* think is that by not involving the police, if this individual carries out the poisoning of a food product there is every likelihood that when the media learn of the Boards decision not to alert both the police and the general public as I am certain they undoubtedly will, the ensuing outcry will utterly destroy Chrystons as a company. So, far from representing the women of Chrystons as this individual claims, when your company collapses, Miss Toner, they will in fact be responsible for perhaps several thousand employees losing their livelihood."

A couple of seconds elapsed before Tom replied, "Not to steal your thunder, Gavin, but I was thinking something along the same lines. About some kind of second agenda, I mean. However, you've taken it a bit further. I hadn't considered that the people employed by Chrystons would suffer as you suggest." His brow knitted as he added, "Your hypothesis is that the underlying reason might be an attempt to bring down Chrystons? Is it possible that a rival company might be responsible for the threat?"

"Who knows, Tom, but I seriously doubt that any legitimate company would resort to such a criminal act simply in the name of business. What I am confident about is when we *do* trace this woman, we can ask her, eh?"

Both Tom and Ellen smiled at Blakestock's optimism.

"What's your next move, Tom?"

"Well, on the back of your discovery, I'll quit wading through the DVD's here and when I print out your copy of the woman's photograph, I'll show it to the staff in the store here; maybe jog a memory. How about you?"

"If indeed this woman *is* Scottish and given that the jars were purchased up there, I did consider travelling to Glasgow to help you make some local inquiry. However, if the letter is to be believed the deadline set by Penthesilea expires tomorrow and if you are happy for me to represent both you and I, then I will remain here and attend the Directors Board meeting and at least we now have something to report. Whether the Board decide tomorrow to accede to the demand or not is something that is out of our hands."

"Yes, of course I'm happy for you to represent us both," replied Tom then decided that a little honesty wouldn't go amiss. Conscious of Ellen's presence and her position as a Chrystons store manager, he took a deep breath and informed Blakestock, "Last night I spoke with a mate of mine, a Detective Inspector who is a trusted friend. Quite unofficially of course. Danny is the head of a criminal intelligence unit that operates out of the Scottish Crime Campus at Gartcosh. I requested that he assist me locally by checking out the name Penthesilea and also agreed to run any checks on any suspects that we come across."

There was a pause before Blakestock replied, "I think we should keep that little piece of information to ourselves. However, I do agree with you, Tom, for after all the police have access to all sorts of intelligence that might assist us. Yes, a wise decision, my friend."

Tom turned to Ellen who was frowning, but behind the frown he detected the hint of a smile.

Agreeing to keep each other updated should anything else turn up, Tom and Blakestock ended the call.

Turning to Ellen, Tom said with a sigh, "I really believe the police should be involved. Knowing what I did and you being employed by Chrystons, does that put you in some sort of compromised position?"

Ellen slowly shook her head. "Only you and Mister Blakestock know what you did and I won't be telling anyone, so no. As long as we keep the information to ourselves it won't compromise me at all."

"Good," he suddenly smiled at her and said, "I'll print that photo out now and we'll show it to your staff."

Seated at his desk in the intelligence suite, Danny McBride had checked all the criminal databases for any reference to Penthesilea and come up blank.

Lifting the phone he dialled an internal number and spoke with his contact in the Counter Terrorist Intelligence Unit suite, calling in an overdue favour.

Five minutes later the return call disclosed that no, the CTIU had no knowledge of any person or group calling themselves Penthesilea.

"Why the inquiry, Danny?"

"Just a confidential tip from a friend."

"Anything that might concern my mob?"

"If it does, you're my first phone call," he assured his contact and ended the call.

Sitting back in his chair, his hands clasped behind his head, he was irritated that he had nothing to report to Tom.

The ball was in Tom's court and he would just need to wait for anything else that his friend might turn up.

Thankful that his remaining periods that Friday did not include Colleen Younger's fourth year class, Martin Turner was distracted and irritated that the teenager's veiled threat he meets with her than night could worry him so.

He was convinced in his mind that she had told one or more of her friends about him and whether walking through the school corridors or seated here at his desk, was conscious of every pair of eyes.

Yet though he deeply regretted the madness that overtook him that night in the back of his car, he remembered Colleen and her naked body and becoming uncomfortably aroused, shifted in his chair to ease himself.

He quickly glanced at the bowed heads of the third year class, relieved that none seemed to have noticed his discomfort.

He slowly exhaled and decided that he would meet with her to tell her that it was over, their brief encounter was simply that.

He would tell her that if indeed she had told her friends and continued to tell tales about him he would ensure the police were informed that she was spreading malicious gossip. For after all, he again told himself, who in their right mind would take the word of a young tart like her against that of a highly respected teacher.

Besides, after he had thoroughly cleaned the back seat of the car there was no evidence, nothing that could possibly connect him to her.

Yes, his confidence grew. That's what he would do.

Meet her tonight and end it before it really got started.

Getting off the bus in West George Street, Annemarie decided that strict budget or not, she was having a coffee to calm her nerves and made her way to a nearby café.

Seated at a table in the busy café, Annemarie glanced at her wristwatch, a gift from her now deceased parents when as a teenager she achieved her dream of working in Frasers.

Sipping at the coffee, she saw she had almost an hour before meeting Joyce to collect the package and for the first time in such a long while felt curiously upbeat and decided she had time to do a little window shopping.

Joyce McKinnon took advantage of the midmorning break to visit the large storeroom in the rear of the building where the products used in the Food Science lectures and projects were stored. As the senior lecturer in the subject she had her own passkey and aware that while security cameras were located throughout the campus, none covered the entrance at the storeroom and there was no requirement to log any visit to the large room.

Assuring herself that there were no students lurking about illicitly smoking or secretly courting in the corridors leading to the storeroom, she let herself in the main door and quickly made her way to the last aisle where ignoring the warning signs, she lifted a large, plastic box. From the box she withdrew a small polythene bag and placed it into the handbag she carried over her shoulder.

That done, she returned to the main door and was locking it when she glanced at her wristwatch. Good, she thought. Fifteen minutes before she was due to meet with Annemarie and hand it over. Time enough to permit her to walk down to George Square and…

"Joyce. Sorry," Sandy Munro raised a hand, his briefcase held in his other hand. "I didn't mean to startle you."

"Sandy," she forced a smile.

"Time for a cuppa?" he asked.

"No, sorry. I'm meeting someone," then seeing the curiosity in his face, explained, "My sister, Annemarie."

"Ah, right. Okay then," he slowly passed her by, his face expressing his relief that apparently he was not in competition for her favours. "Still on for tomorrow, though?"

"Absolutely," she grinned and thought, I'm gushing like a schoolgirl, before waving cheerio and turning away.

Taking a deep breath, she quickened her step and continued making her way along the corridor while thinking, of all the *bloody* people to meet when I'm leaving the storeroom!

It continued to prey on his conscience and he though he had uttered a silent prayer and even considered consulting his parish priest about the issue Charlie McFadyen knew that to involve an outsider, even his priest, would be wrong.

No, he had decided that he would deal with the problem.

Tom McEwan wasn't too disappointed that none of the Woodlands Road store staff recognised the woman in the photograph.

"According to the rota there are members of staff who were on duty that day, but off today," Ellen tried to be helpful.

"I'll leave a copy of the photo with you. You can show them the photo when they resume, but I'm not holding out any great hope. I'm sure you'll think of something to tell them about why you're showing them the photo. Right then," he lifted his jacket from the back of the chair, "I'm heading back down to my office in Pollokshields. I'll leave you my card that has the office number and my mobile number on it. If for any reason you need to contact me," he stared at her, his words hanging between them like an invitation. Later, when she thought about it, she could not believe that she had been so forward when she replied, "Oh, but I owe you dinner."

He grinned and nodding to the empty sandwich packet in the waste bin, replied, "I thought you bought the lunch?"

"Yes, well, a pack of sandwiches and a cup of coffee hardly costs what you must have paid for dinner," she gruffly replied, embarrassed and regretting that she had raised the matter.

"Miss Toner," he smiled tolerantly at her. "If you are asking me to dinner, then yes, I accept and would certainly enjoy having a meal with you. However, my only stipulation is that you permit me to foot the bill. Our last meal was paid for by my employer as a business expense, so I would *not* like to deceive you."

"I always pay my way and for your information, I'm not a woman that's easily deceived, Mister McEwan," her eyes twinkled as she thought, not again anyway.

"So," he pointed to his business card she held in her hand. "Perhaps when you get a minute sometime later today, you might consider giving me a call and I'll book somewhere."

"Perhaps," she pouted and closed the door behind him.

## CHAPTER NINE

It was beginning to haunt him for try as he might, Charlie McFadyen could not get it out of his head that one of his male colleagues had been or was having an inappropriate relationship with a student. Sitting at his desk with a list of the teaching staff in front of him, his forefinger danced down the list of twenty-four male names and smiled when his finger passed by his own name.

At each name, he considered the possibility the teacher was *the one* and either marked a cross against a possible suspect or dismissed the name for a variety of reasons; too old or too this or too that. Sighing, he rubbed at his forehead when he reached the bottom of the list and counted off six names with crosses beside them.

Staring at one name in particular, he circled the name and his eyes narrowed. He had never liked the man and thought him to be an overbearing fool; the sort of pompous individual who gave teaching a bad name.

Idly tapping his forefinger against the mans name, he knew that if he were to approach and confront the teacher, quite literally McFadyen's arse would be out of the window. All it would take would be a complaint of false accusation by the teacher and not only would the Deputy Head be on McFadyen's case for not obeying her instruction to drop the issue, but likely the teaching union would also get involved.

He arched his back to relieve the ache and bit at his lower lip as he wondered; how the hell was he going to broach the allegation with him?

Annemarie passed the small bag from one hand to another before deciding to hide it in the bottom drawer in her room, confident that Martin wouldn't discover it there.

Quickly she raced round the house, checking that everything was in its rightful place. Pulling on her coat, she prepared to leave the house to collect the girls from school.

Martin Turner watched the first year class quietly leave his classroom, daring them to even smile. He preferred working with the first years; they were so very easy to intimidate.

Stuffing some papers that he needed to mark at home into his briefcase, he stood and shrugged into his jacket and loosened his tie. He decided he would wait that extra five minutes before leaving the classroom to permit all the pupils to be clear of the yard. There was no sense in risking another embarrassing encounter with Colleen.

The door opened and he turned, surprised to see Charlie McFadyen stood there.

"Mister McFadyen," he began, his brow creasing with worry and his mouth suddenly dry.

"Martin, I wonder if I might have a quiet word," said McFadyen, closing the door and indicating he return to his seat.

"Of course," he replied, his voice wavering as his throat tightened and he fought to breathe. Reaching behind him, he nervously slumped back down into his chair.

Stood with his hands clasped in front of him, McFadyen stared at him as though uncertain how to begin, then quietly said, "Some information has come to my attention. Something that has caused me some concern."

"How…how can I help?" he swallowed with difficulty, his throat barren.

McFadyen continued to stare uneasily at him.

"There has been an allegation that a member of the teaching staff of this school has or is currently engaging in sexual activity with a student. As you are one of the longest serving teachers in this establishment, I thought I would speak directly to you. Now Martin…"

He thought he was about to pass out, but then McFadyen slowly continued, "…just how well do you know young Brian Polson, the trainee teacher who recently joined the English Department?"

Tom McEwan handed Martha the receipts that he had collected from his Birmingham trip. Peering closely at them, she waved one and eyes narrowing, said, "What is this one, you bad boy. Two meals? You trying to be Martha's *big* boy?"

He grinned at her and replied, "Business expense cultivating a member of Chrystons staff, Martha."

She waved another receipt at him and trying with some difficulty to suppress a grin, asked, "And this one. Breakfast for two. Just how much cultivating did you do, you *very* bad boy?"

"Not what you think, you *bad* minded lady. Miss Toner and I had to share a room…" and held up his hands as he added, "purely platonic, I assure you."

The door to Martin McCormick's office opened and he came out, shaking the hand of a middle-aged woman.

Tom watched the woman walk past toward the front door then turning saw the lawyer beckon him into the office.

Closing the door behind him, McCormick returned to his seat behind the desk and waved Tom to the chair opposite.

"Right, what's the update?"

Passing a copy of the photograph of the woman across to him, Tom said, "This is a possible suspect for Chrystons threatening letter; in fact, she's the only real lead we have so far. I'm liaising with a local investigator who like me is a former cop called Gavin Blakestock," and proceeded to brief McCormick on the inquiry so far.

"This Board meeting tomorrow. You're not attending?"

"No," Tom shook his head, "there's really no need. Blakestock can handle that and report the Board's decision at the deadline. Besides, it would be an unnecessary expense and frankly I don't think I would gain anything from attending except a belt round the ear from Martha."

McCormick grinned and then tilting his chair to one side, clasped his hands behind his head and staring keenly at Tom, said, "So, tell me about you having to share a room at the hotel with this woman Ellen Toner."

Descending the stairs of the small but discreet hotel, James Hardie reached into an inner pocket of his jacket and retrieving his wallet, withdrew three fifty pounds notes.

While paying for the three-hour rental of the room, a tall and willowy woman wearing a tight fitting yellow coloured dress and carrying a matching short jacket and handbag over one arm, large sunglasses that hid most of her face and a silk scarf tied about her short auburn hair, descended the stairs and without acknowledging either Hardie or the manager, strode out through the front doors.

The manager cast a brief, admiring glance at the departing woman and in a low voice, told Hardie, "Sir, on your previous visit your, ah…" he hesitated before continuing, "your *fiancée* misplaced an earring." Reaching beneath the desk, he fetched a small white envelope and handing it to Hardie, earned himself an extra twenty-pound note.

Placing the envelope in his pocket, Hardie nodded his thanks to the manager and walking through the front door, breathed deeply.

Caught up in the pleasurable memory of his sexual encounter with the athletic Lesley, Hardie was too preoccupied to notice the man in the fawn coloured raincoat and tweed cap standing in the bus shelter across the busy road who busily photographed him.

Driving home, Martin Turner was in a rare good mood and almost joyfully beat his hand against the leather cover of the steering wheel in time to the music for the radio.

He could not believe his luck. That fool McFadyen, taking him into his confidence had unwittingly presented Martin with a real opportunity to deny any rumour or accusation by Colleen of their affair.

Affair?

He almost laughed out loud. One shag in the back of his car could hardly be described as an affair; more of an extra-curriculum lesson in carnal activity, he giggled at his own humour.

If he was ever challenged about him and Colleen, he would simply respond that he had heard rumours about young Brian Polson, the perfect patsy. He shook his head.

Who would have thought McFadyen would suspect that wimpy, four-eyed bugger?

He took a deep breath of satisfaction and thinking of Colleen lying in the back seat, was again aroused.

His mobile phone, tucked into an inner pocket in his briefcase chirruped twice to inform him he had received a text. Strange he thought, but almost immediately dismissed it. He didn't permit Annemarie to have a phone and the only texts he usually received were from the service provider offering deals or points or other such crap. Still, his curiosity got the better of him and reaching across to the passenger seat, scrambled with his fingers and drew the briefcase towards him. He was reaching into the inner pocket of the briefcase for the phone and momentarily took his eyes off the road. Just as his fingers closed over the phone to lift it out of the pocket, he inadvertently swerved across the centre line and incurred the wrath of an oncoming car that sounded its horn. Alerted to the danger Martin briefly panicked and in his haste to return his vehicle to his own lane, dropped the phone that skidded across the seat and dropped down between the front passenger seat and the door, wedging itself in the seats mechanism.

Bugger it, he thought and angrily dismissed the text message that almost got him killed.

His thoughts turned again to Colleen. Yes, he would meet with her tonight; maybe even after he shagged her he would infer that *Mister* Polson had been asking about her and hint that the young English teacher probably fancied her. He smiled. Yes, being the wee tart she is, that would interest her and it wouldn't be difficult to steer her towards Polson. Then if she ever opened her mouth about her and Mister Turner, it would be the simplest thing to deny her accusation as the fantasy of an adolescent female Walter Mitty. After all, he was a trusted and respected member of the teaching staff for hadn't his own Departmental Head confidentially discussed such an issue with him, a pupil who was pursuing a teacher?

Yes, it had all worked out nicely.

One last meeting with Colleen and all his concerns were over.


Ellen Toner turned and twisted the business card she held in her hand. It didn't seem right that *she* was to phone Tom. Wasn't the man supposed to contact the woman and ask *her* to dinner?

Well, she thought, I suppose in a *way* he did ask me to dinner.
Or did he, she mused.
Oh, bugger it she decided and reached for her mobile phone.


The man in the fawn coloured raincoat and tweed cap arrived in
Wellington Road in the Edgbaston area of Birmingham and getting
out of his car, whistled at the sight of the impressive mansion located
behind the wrought iron gates. Pushing the bell attached to the
speaker on the wall at the gate, he gave his name and informed the
housekeeper he was there to meet with Mister Peters.
A few moments later, the gates gave an audible click as they were
unlocked and striding through, the man quickly made his way up the
gravelled path towards the double oak doors.
It wasn't the housekeeper, but Peters himself who met with the man
at the door.
He was not invited into the luxurious residence, but wordlessly was
handed a buff coloured envelope and in exchange handed Peters a
small digital camera card.
It was, it seemed to the man as he turned away, as though the very
act of meeting with him repelled Peters.
No matter, he grinned as he made his way back through the gates;
the thousand quid was worth the snooty bastard's scorn.
Politely declining his elderly housekeepers offer of a cup of tea,
Peters made his way upstairs to his expansive study located in the
room that was directly above the front entrance to the house.
Settling himself into the desk chair that faced the panoramic window
overlooking the driveway, he switched on the laptop and when it was
booted up, inserted the digital camera card into the side slot.
Taking a deep breath, he opened the card and discovered the man
had taken over one hundred photographs in three distinct groups that
appeared as three files on the screen.
Peters drew back his head, his back suddenly aching and almost with
reluctance, double-clicked on the first file of photographs.
As he moved through the photos in the first file and then opened the
second file, Peters marvelled at the sharp quality and wondered how
the hell the man had managed to obtain such clear shots through the
hotel window, presuming he must have obtained a vantage point in a
building opposite the room.

Though it displeased him, he could not but admire the supple dexterity of the naked woman as she cavorted on the bed with a grinning James Hardie.

It pained him that after his suspicions were aroused he had caused James to be followed and such photographs obtained. It was particularly upsetting, for it had been Peters who introduced James to the company and nurtured him throughout his almost meteoric rise to the position he now held. However, he sighed unhappily, this was business and he would not permit anyone, James or otherwise, to usurp him as CEO before he was prepared to stand down.

He was gazing at the last group of photographs when he heard the crunching of tyres on the gravelled driveway and then the slamming of a car door.

Quickly he removed the digital card and placed it into his trouser pocket before closing down the laptop.

The door to his study opened and his wife strode in and with a smile, clasped her arms around his neck before kissing him on the crown of his head.

"Darling," she gushed, "how has your day been?"

"My day?" he smiled and gazed up at her, resplendent in her bright yellow coloured dress. "My day has been very interesting. Very interesting indeed, Lesley."


Tom McEwan decided there was little point in conducting any further inquiry for that day and instead settled himself into the little used office used by him and the firms' other investigator, John Logan. Besides, he argued, there was paperwork from other cases that he had to catch up with.

It was while he prepared the witness statements for an ongoing internal fraud inquiry at a Glasgow city centre precinct, his mobile phone rang.

He smiled when he saw Ellen Toner's number on the screen.

"Thought you had maybe changed your mind," he greeted her.

"I nearly did, but a debt is a debt."

"I told you, you owe me nothing but if you insist, then forget paying for a meal. A couple of hours of your company will suffice," he replied.

"You simply ooze charm, don't you?" she teased him, then added, "Right, if you're not otherwise engaged why don't you book somewhere for this evening and I'll meet you there. You can text me the time and venue."

"Seems like a plan," he smiled at the phone and ended the call.

The statements for the time being forgotten, he wondered at the sudden change in Ellen Toner's attitude towards him and decided that certainly for this evening, he would walk on eggshells.

He had just finished the call with Ellen when his phone again rang and the screen showed the caller to be Danny McBride.

"Sorry, Tom," his friend began, "absolutely nothing on the criminal databases and according to my CTIU contact, nothing on their databases either."

"Well, at least you tried and I'm grateful for that."

"Well," McBride drawled, "that's not to say that this individual or group Penthesilea doesn't exist. Remember, Tom, you told me that the letter insisted no police involvement. It *is* possible that this Penthesilea might previously have raised their head above the parapet and targeted another company or companies, but the threat was not reported to the police; perhaps because either they were paid off or simply ignored."

"It's a possibility, Danny, but how I would go about checking that I'm not certain. However, while you are on I've obtained a photograph of a possible suspect," and recounted both his and Gavin Blakestock's success in obtaining the vague description and the photograph.

"So your suspect has what sounds like a Scottish accent?"

"That's what Blakestock learned, yes."

"And of course the two jars were purchased in the Woodlands Road store. Well, maybe two and two make five, but that sounds pretty damn convincing that you have a local connection, Tom."

"That's what I'm thinking. The woman in the photo isn't identifiable from the picture, but again Blakestock's chat with the shop assistant down in Birmingham suggests the woman was wearing a disguise anyway. What I'll do is forward Blakestock's e-mail to you and you can have a look for yourself. In the meantime," he smiled, "I've a date tonight."

"Are you going to burst and give me a name or should I guess?"

"I'd rather wait and see how tonight goes before I start bragging," Tom replied.

"Well, no matter. Good for you, Tom. It's about time you got yourself back into the world. Let me know how it goes," McBride said and ended the call.

Annemarie ushered the girls' upstairs to get on with their homework and for the tenth time, checked the stew she had prepared.
Stirring the pot, she shook her head at her own cowardice. It was the same routine every evening. She dreaded Martin coming home, wondering what kind of mood he would be in and invariably suffered either a snide comment or on occasion a slap or kick to her backside because of some mistake she had made with the housework, the food or any menial thing that he judged to be untidy. She couldn't take any more, she told herself; Joyce was absolutely right. If she didn't do something she would end up either hospitalised with a mental illness or worse.
She didn't realise she was crying till she saw a tear fall with a small splash into the stew. Wiping her eyes and her nose with her sleeve, she hurried to a mirror.
Martin didn't like her looking anything but happy when he come through the door and pinching her cheeks, forced a grin.
God help me, she silently pleaded to her reflection.
What have I become?

Sitting at her dining table with her laptop opened before her, Joyce McKinnon planned Saturday mornings journey to Manchester. Using the AA routemaster, she read that the trip was three and a half hours, but decided to add an extra hour each way to compensate for traffic problems and any hiccup she might encounter when delivering the second letter and the pie. Leaving her house at eight o'clock and with a journey of nine hours at the very most would return her to Glasgow in plenty of time for that evenings date with Sandy Munro. Tracing her finger across the screen that displayed a map of Manchester city centre, Joyce saw that the large Chrystons store was located in Quay Street. Just as she had done in Birmingham, she planned to park her car in a public place, deciding on the Museum of Science and Industry in Liverpool Road that was served by an NCP car park. After donning her disguise in the museums toilet, she would walk the short distance to the store.
Everything she needed was ready.

The individual chicken pie she had purchased that afternoon in the Argyle Street store was in her fridge and not yet marked with an X or adulterated with the poison. That could wait till she was in the toilet in the museum and slipping into her disguise. The less time the poisoned pie was available for purchase, the better.

She considered several options for the recipient of the second typed letter and trawling through the Internet, decided to deliver it to the BBC Radio station in Oxford Road that she discovered was a little under ten minutes driving time from the museum car park. She reasoned that not only would it be quickly passed to the police who presumably would contact Chrystons immediately, but it would also alert the media to her threat.

She shivered nervously for it was her greatest fear; never did she intend that any innocent member of the public be harmed.

Once again she read through the letter that warned of the poisoned pies in the Manchester's Quay Street and Glasgow Argyle Street stores, though of course when they searched the Argyle Street store they would find nothing.

Almost as an afterthought, she opened up several UK news websites and as she fully expected, there was no mention that Chrystons had acceded to the demands of the letter she had posted to the head office. It pleased her that this was just as she had foreseen; Chrystons did not intend surrendering to the threat.

Still, she thought, the deadline she had set did not expire until Saturday; time enough for the Board of Chrystons to pay one million pounds to the women's charities, but not in keeping with her plan, she frowned.

Fear settled upon her at the thought, her worst nightmare, that Chrystons capitulated and paid the money.

It was not about money nor was it about Chrystons.

At the outset, it had simply been a daydream; a desire to remove Martin Turner from the life of Annemarie and her nieces.

She snarled, for the very thought of the bastard made her grind her teeth in revulsion.

A more spiteful man she had yet to meet; a bully of the worst kind who believed himself to be superior not only to women, but to anyone who crossed his path.

A man who barely scraped through his teaching exams and who would never amount to much in life, but who was happy to sneer at and belittle anyone else's success.

Martin, who thought himself to be God's gift to women and who on one occasion had even tried to sexually assault Joyce when his wife was pregnant with their first daughter.

She remembered the occasion as though it were yesterday.

Annemarie had been confined to the maternity ward in the city's Victoria Hospital with a bleed.

Joyce, carrying a newly purchased buggy and struggling up the flight of stairs to the one-bedroom flat in the Gorbals, found him half drunk then panicked when he locked the door behind her and slobbering all over her, grabbed at her breasts.

She recalled the satisfaction of kneeing him squarely in the balls and then seeing him doubled up in pain, whimpering and pleading not to tell her sister.

Joyce was disgusted and did not tell Annemarie for the simple reason her sister had enough to endure, living with Martin.

It wasn't long after the birth of Paula that she began to see the bruising on Annemarie's wrists, the marks on her neck and though she denied anything untoward had occurred, it was evident to Joyce that her husband was hitting her.

Annemarie begged her not to challenge him, that anything Joyce said to Martin would simply be the worse for her sister.

It was a long time coming, but the daydream if she could call it that neared its end. Her plan to free her sister from the clutches of that sadistic bastard was almost over.

Reality for Martin Turner was about to set in.

All it needed was for Chrystons to refuse to pay the money and for Annemarie to sustain the courage to follow her part of Joyce's plan.

Standing in Sauchiehall Street outside the small Italian restaurant to the west of Charing Cross, Tom McEwan again glanced at his watch. A Hyundai hatchback pulled slowly past him and parking in a nearby bay, he watched as Ellen Toner exited the driver's door. Dressed in a knee length lemon coloured dress with her collar length red hair pinned back and carrying a dark coloured shawl and handbag over one arm, he couldn't explain why but thought tonight he was the luckiest guy alive. It had been a long time since he had been on a date and was uncertain how to greet her; however, Ellen took the initiative and smiling, reached forward and kissed him on the cheek.

"You look…" he took a deep breath and exhaling, returned her smile and almost lost for words, said, "…just wow!"

"I aim to please," she grinned and nodded as he courteously held open the door to permit her to enter the restaurant.

The booked table was set to the rear of the dimly lit restaurant and afforded them some privacy.

She couldn't explain why but was comfortable being with him and through the meal, though at first hesitant, grew more confident and began to disclose chapters of her life. To her own surprise, she even admitted the hurt and anger of her failed relationship with Paul. Sheepishly she added that having overheard Tom's phone call that morning in the hotel room, she had thought him to be involved in a relationship.

He smiled and understood then why he had thought her to be cool towards him.

In turn, he explained his divorce that had resulted because he had believed himself to be in love with a fellow cop, shocking Ellen when he disclosed the woman had been later killed by her murderous husband. The murder had in turn led to his resignation from the police and almost destroyed his life. "And so," he smiled humourlessly at her, "I now find myself employed as a private investigator currently trying to identify an extortionist."

"Let's not talk business," she shook her head and staring at him, added, "I'd prefer to hear more about you. Tell me about your daughters."

She could not have chosen a more accepted subject and he made her laugh when he described his twins and their antics.

"Their mother is a lovely woman," he sighed, "and a fabulous mother."

Ellen had a short, tingling feeling of jealousy about his ex-wife until he added, "But she's marrying a man who I have met and he's a really nice guy. He's good to the girls, too. I'm happy for them both."

He idly stirred at his coffee and then asked, "Nobody special in your life just now?"

"Nobody special…right now," she smiled at him and teased, "Why? Are you applying for the job?"

"Well," he drawled, a little taken aback by her forwardness, "I'm a bit busy at the minute, but I could probably fit you in *somewhere*. Maybe, I dunno, twice a month?"

"You are *so* generous, Mister McEwan."

A comfortable silence fell between them, broken when Tom said, "I've enjoyed tonight. Being here with you, I mean. I'd like to do it again sometime."

"I'd like that to," she softly replied and holding her breath, reached across the table and taking a hold of his fingers, entwined them with her own. She was relieved that he in turn squeezed her fingers too.

"It's maybe a bit too soon to invite you back to my flat for a coffee," he smiled at her.

"Yes, maybe just a bit," she agreed with her own smile.

Annemarie was surprised at Martin's demeanour when he arrived him. He sounded, she hesitated to use the word, almost cheerful.

As usual he took his meal on a tray in the lounge watching the evening news programme and curiously, did not utter one complaint. She wasn't fooled though. Something was going on though of course she daren't ask and he would never divulge.

When she collected his tray he told her he was going out; a school issue he said, but she knew otherwise.

To meet his latest floozy, she guessed and likely that was why he was so cheery.

She wasn't upset, not even remotely. A night without her dour husband ordering her around like a servant, forced to remain in her small room or with the girls in their bedroom while he sat watching the television; no, she would not miss him when he was gone.

Now she could hear him upstairs showering.

She made a decision. She would await his return home and just as she had done the other night, try to detect the smell of that cheap scent from him.

In the bedroom she shared with mother, showered and wearing just a bath towel about her, Colleen Younger laid out the short, black leather skirt she had bought at the Barra's market on top of the twin bed alongside a low cut white blouse with pop buttons that could easily be undone. With a satisfied smile she knew that if she also wore her leather boots Martin would not be able to resist her.

From one of the two drawers used by her in the gaudily painted chest of drawers, she fetched out a thong and without undoing the towel, awkwardly slipped it on. From the same drawer she lifted a black coloured plunge bra she had borrowed from her mother's drawer and dropping the towel to the floor, slid her arms through the straps.

She had both hands behind her to fasten the bra when she heard the creak and turning, saw her brother Sean standing in the doorway, leering at her.

"What the fuck…get out!" she screamed at him.

Sean didn't move, but continued to run his eyes up and down her body.

"Nice tits, wee sister," he grinned then added, "Who's getting a feel of them tonight?"

She bent to lift the towel and covering herself, hissed, "I'll tell Ma what you're up to, you fucking pervert; so fuck off!"

"Give me a wee feel at your tits and *then* I'll fuck off," he casually replied.

Striding quickly towards him, she grabbed the edge of the door and slammed it closed, then heard him laughing uproariously as he went through to the front room.

She was shivering but with rage, not from the cold. It wasn't the first time the bastard had sneaked a look at her when she was undressed and no matter how many times she complained, all her mother would reply was that it wasn't Sean's fault. All those years he had been in the jail had changed him, that he didn't mean any real harm.

Complaining to her mother was a waste of time anyway. If she wasn't pissed she was out of her head on coke or away staying the night with her latest boyfriend. Everybody on the council estate knew that Patsy Younger was anybody's shag for two cans of Carlsberg Special or a gram of coke.

She knew there was no use asking her other brother for help. William was as twisted as Sean and when puberty had crooked its finger, Colleen had quickly learned to avoid being alone with any of them when they had been drinking. The only one who ever listened was Chic, but he was doing time for drugs.

Slipping the blouse on, she vowed that tomorrow she would get the money from her Ma and buy a lock for the bloody door.

Pulling on the tight skirt, it got her thinking. It occurred to her that teachers were well paid and if things went well tonight with Martin maybe she could talk him into getting a flat for her. Her eyes narrowed as the daydream took over. Maybe even leave his wife and live with her. After all, in a couple of months she would be seventeen and leaving school; then she would get herself a job and earn her own money.

She breathed in and zipped the skirt closed and then patting at her tummy as she inspected her reflection in the wardrobe mirror, another idea crossed her mind. She stared down at her stomach and grinned at the thought; pure wicked it was.

She slyly smiled for her new idea might be one that Martin could not possibly ignore.

The subject of Colleen Younger's new fantasy was now dressed in a casual shirt, chinos and carrying a light fawn coloured jacket. He closed the front door without bothering with a farewell to his wife or children.

Martin Turner had the plan laid out in his head. He would meet Colleen as arranged and drive her to the same isolated road beside the Cawder Woods north of Bishobriggs. On the way there he would turn the conversation round to her friends and ask her if she had told anyone about them, what they had done. When they got to the woods he would park the car, manoeuvre her into the rear seat, shag her one last time then tell her of the interest in her by one of the teaching staff, Brian Polson. She was so gullible and desperate for affection that he didn't believe he would have any problem persuading her to switch her attention to the dim witted, trainee English teacher.

He would also dissuade her from telling Polson of her relationship with Martin, that it might put him off Colleen and he was certain she would not want that.

Yes, he started the car engine.

Convinced of his own superior intellect and that he had planned it perfectly, he made his way to the rendeavous with his sixteen-year-old pupil.

In the privacy of his study and though it pained him to do so, Jackson Peters scrolled through the photographs again.

His intention had been to stop James Hardie from usurping his position as CEO, but staring at the naked form of his wife with Hardie between her long legs, he coldly changed his mind.

Now he would utterly destroy the bastard.


It took Martin a little over fifteen minutes to reach the location and in the dimmed headlights he saw Colleen, again wearing the long coat but on this occasion buttoned tightly against the chilly wind and the slight fall of rain.

Getting into the passenger seat, she leaned across to kiss him on the cheek.

In a short time, he had driven to the narrow, unregistered road that run beside the Cawder Woods and parked the car in complete darkness.

"Why don't we get out and get into the back seat," he smoothly suggested.

"Okay," she nodded and exiting the passenger door, slipped off her coat and leaving it folded on the front seat, shivered in the cold before climbing into the rear of the car.

Fumbling and pawing at her Martin soon had her blouse undone and groping at her naked breasts with one hand, with the other hand was pushing her back down onto the seat when she placed her hand on his chest and said, "Stop the now, Martin. I want to talk to you."

"We can talk while we're doing it," he replied, his voice shaking with lust.

"No!" she forcibly replied and snatching at both his wrists, wriggled and sat up with her back to the door.

"Okay," he sighed and pushing himself from her into a sitting position, asked, "What is it?"

"Do you like me?"

"Course I do," he nodded in the darkness, impatient to have her naked before him.

"No, I mean *really* like me?"

By the faint moonlight that shone through the window he could see the top of her exposed breasts and reaching forward, began to stroke them. "Yes, Colleen, I *really* like you. Why?"

"I was thinking," she slowly replied as taking his hand, she guided it to between her open legs, "we could do every night if you thought about us getting a flat."

"A flat?" he was bemused and grinned at her naivety. "What do you mean by us, Colleen? I'm married and besides, you're still a schoolgirl."

"I'll soon be seventeen and when the term finishes, I'll be leaving that dump," she huffily replied and sitting back against the door, closed her legs, trapping his hand.

He pulled his hand away from her and stared in confusion. Did this wee tart think that he was serious about her? For fuck's sake, was she out of her mind?

Despite her youth, Colleen was no fool and intuitively sensed his rejection.

"And there's another thing," she angrily began to pop the buttons closed on her blouse, now playing her trump card. "The other night when you fucked me you didn't use any protection, did you Martin? I'm not on the pill. What if I'm pregnant? Have you thought about that!"

Being the conceited and arrogant man that he was, Martin Turner was not used to being spoken to like this by anyone and certainly *not* a sixteen-year-old tart! He stared at her, a cold fury creeping over him. Who the *hell* did she think she was!

Almost instinctively and without thinking, he slapped her across the face.

It wasn't a hard slap simply because the confines of the car prevented him from drawing his hand back too far; however, what it did was release an animalistic fury in the teenager. Stunned by both his reaction and the slap, Colleen was for a second speechless, but she was a Younger and brought up in a family where domestic and casual violence was a part of everyday life. With a shrill scream, she attacked him. Clawing at his face with her long, false nails, her face a mask of virulent hate, all the misery of her youthful years went into that assault and spitting out her vehement and cursed opinion of Martin, she was on top of him within a second.

In self defence and completely taken aback by her assault, Martin was fortunate that when he fell back against the door on his side of the car, he managed to seize Colleen's wrists, but not before she had raked his left cheek with her nails causing a slight and superficial wound.

Screaming at him, her saliva striking his face, Martin wrestled with her on the bench seat of the car, his legs kicking up to the roof. In her effort to butt Martin to the face, Colleen miscalculated and by sheer bad luck, found herself twisted onto her back on the seat under the heavier Martin, her head jammed in the corner. Still holding her wrists, Martin had by now lost all control of his actions and releasing one hand, grabbed Colleen by the hair. Twisting his fingers into her hair he began to rhythmically bang it hard against the unyielding solid plastic side of the car. Stunned and bleeding from a head wound, Colleen's resistance slackened, but there was no let up from the enraged Martin.

Now on top and astride the dazed girl, he released his grip on her other wrist and placed both hands about her throat and began to squeeze.

Still snarling, Colleen reached both hands for his face then her eyes widened and realising she was choking tried to prise his hands from her neck, but there was no stopping Martin who teeth now gritted, continued to squeeze the life from her.

All the perceived wrongs he had suffered, the failings of his life; all the hate for everyone who didn't agree with him, who didn't see him for the man he really was, were in that grip.

Though she could not know what was happening, the small blood vessels in Colleens eyes began to pop as the pressure being applied prevented oxygen from reaching her brain. White spittle dribbled from her mouth as her futile effort to stop him lessened and slowly, staring at him, she succumbed to his throttling of her.

Martin was still squeezing at her throat when he realised she had gone limp and with horror, breathlessly removed his hands from her throat.

Still astride her, he was puzzled why his trousers felt damp and sniffed curiously at the pungent smell of urine. Lifting one leg he realised that in death, Colleen's bladder had emptied and soaked both them and the seat and the carpet of his beloved car.

"Dirty fucking *bitch*!" he screamed and began to pummel her face with his fists, causing the dead girls nose to burst and spray him and Colleen's face with blood.

He sat back on the other side of the seat as Colleen, no longer pinned to the seat by the weight of Martin, slowly slipped down to lie gracelessly on the floor between the front and rear seats.

The moment of madness now passed, he stared in almost incomprehensible shock at her lifeless body and screamed, an unbridled screech of frustration and terror.

She can't be dead, he thought, his mind racing with the enormity of what he had done.

"It wasn't me," he began to sob. "It was her fault. She made me," his voice whined as his nose began to run, the tears almost blinding him. Opening the door, he tried to step out backwards from the car but instead stumbled and twisting around as he fell, his hands and knees took the full force of his fall. His chest heaved and his stomach rebelled as a wave of nausea swept over him and he heaved his stomachs contents onto the ground. His body shook as the adrenalin kicked in and forcing himself to stop breathing he listened for any sound, but other than traffic travelling on the road some distance away, he heard nothing. Wide-eyed he stared about him, but the darkness enveloped him and the car like a cloak. Sitting there beside a puddle of vomit, his first thought was he had to get Colleen out of the car; he had to save himself.

He had to get rid of her body.

When Ellen offered to pay for the meal Tom would have none of it and calling for the bill, settled payment and then escorted her to her car.

"You'll be at the store tomorrow morning?"

"Yes, Saturdays can be busy," she unlocked the door and pulling it open, turned to face him. "Why, do you intend visiting the store?"

"I'll get by there at some point. If nothing else, then to let you know what Gavin tells me has occurred at the Board meeting."

"Good, I'll see you then," she stared at him then having dreaded the awkward moment, reached forward and kissed him on the cheek.

"Is that all I get?" he grinned at her.

"For now," she coyly replied.

Parting, she swallowed hard and slipped into the driver's seat as he closed the door.

Driving off, she glanced in the rear-view mirror to see Tom waving. Watching the departing car with a smile, he walked on Sauchiehall Street to the taxi rank near to the casino. As he made his way there he reflected on how the evening had gone. He liked Ellen and was comfortable with her, smiling as he unconsciously touched his cheek where she had kissed him goodnight.

Of course, she was right; it was early days and he was curiously pleased she had declined his invitation to have coffee back at his place.

Definitely a woman with principles, he smiled.

Climbing into the rear of the hackney cab, he sat back and after providing the driver with his address, he closed his eyes and wondered what tomorrow might bring.


Seated at his desk in the study of his luxury city centre apartment, James Hardie nursed the brandy glass and thought again of his bright future.

Tomorrow morning's Board meeting was to be the most important of Hardie's relatively short, but extremely successful career. Himself and Jackson Peters aside, he now had the tacit support of five of the remaining seven Directors. When this threat went public as he knew it surely would, the company would undoubtedly falter for several months or even perhaps as much as a year, during which time a disgraced Peters would have no option but to resign.

He smiled in anticipation of the pleas from his fellow Directors that he assumes the role of CEO, that he saves the company and in doing so, save them.

With false modesty at their belief in him, he would accept their nomination.

Sipping at the brandy, he glanced at the wall clock and his gaze slowly fell to the desktop photograph of his wife and two daughters.

Margo had been a rare beauty, but in recent months had let herself go, he shook his head and thought if she ever got round to tidying herself up again, maybe she could find someone else.

He wouldn't be mean and would initially settle a monthly sum on the dull bitch and his daughters; perhaps find them a house somewhere and in due course, agree Margo file for a divorce that he would not contest.

A bit of inventive accounting would hide his true income, though for the sake of their daughters he would be magnanimous and not leave his wife struggling; at least, not until such time she found herself a job.

He smiled at the thought of once again being free to pursue women without the constraint of marriage.

Such thoughts turned to Lesley Peters.

Of course once he had ruined her husband, Lesley would have no further use for Jackson and likely being the woman she was, turn her attention to where the power and the money was; power and the income that as the CEO would then be his.

Yes, he reached for the bottle of brandy, tomorrow's Board meeting would be very interesting indeed.

He drove like a man possessed, unaware how fortunate he was that no patrolling police car saw him speed through the city towards Glenhead Street; the one aim in his mind to get home.

He screeched to a halt in the driveway and sat there, the engine still racing, his hands tightly gripping the steering wheel.

Had a doctor examined Martin Turner at that moment he would likely have been diagnosed as a man who had suffered some profound shock.

Slowly, his heart still beating wildly in his chest, he relaxed but unaware that his speedy arrival had attracted the attention of his wife who nervously peeked from behind a hallway curtain and who wondered why he continued to sit in the car with the engine running.

He switched on the interior light and glanced at himself in the rear-view mirror then with shaking hands gently touched the scratch on his left cheek. He tentatively rubbed with his fingers at a spot of congealed blood, relieved that the slight wound had stopped bleeding.

Though he had used Colleen's coat to soak up what he could of her urine, he grimaced for the car still smelled and the memory of wiping dry the seat and carpet almost made him gag.

He would have to get up early tomorrow morning, he realised and give the interior of the car a deep clean; remove any trace of her.

He closed his eyes and shivered, again seeing himself dragging her limp body from the car and stumbling as he pulled her along, dumping it several yards into the wood.

In his haste he hadn't even covered her over, fool that he was!

His brow creased and his fists clenched.

Fuck! He had forgotten to ask her who she had told of their relationship.

Calmer now, his fear and worry now turned to anger. Anger that the little cow had trapped him into a relationship.

It was all her fault, he seethed. He wouldn't be in this position if she hadn't seduced him. That was it!

She had seduced him, flashing her knickers and her tits at him!

It was all her fucking fault and she got what she deserved!

He glanced at the house, seeing the front room light was still on.

He turned on the cars interior light and fetching a handkerchief from his pocket, spit onto it and dabbed at the mark on his cheek, but only succeeded in making it more visible.

Taking a deep breath, he got out of the car and locking it, went into the house.

Annemarie stood in the hallway by the kitchen door and he saw her expression change from a frozen smile to a curious glance at his cheek.

"What!" he snapped at her and daring her to question the scratch stopped at the bottom of the stairs, his hands bunching into fists as he glared at her.

"Eh, nothing, Martin. Do you want anything, tea or…"?

"Nothing," he sharply interrupted her and making his way upstairs, added, "I'm going to bed so keep the bloody noise down."

"Yes, Martin," she meekly replied.

She waited a full fifteen minutes, standing almost motionless in the kitchen as she listened intently to him first use the bathroom, then make his way into the bedroom.

She wondered at the scent from him, unable to place the strange smell. It was almost like…but no, she decided. It couldn't be that.

Her curiosity had been aroused by the scratch on his cheek. Had his latest floozy done that? And was that some kind of dark staining on his jacket, his blood perhaps?

Biting at her lower lip she made her decision. Tiptoeing to the front door, she lifted his car key from the sill of the window at the bottom of the stairs and quietly unlocking the front door, her eyes narrowed in curiosity. "Not like him," she quietly muttered as she sneaked out to the car, surprised to see the interior light remained on.

Her heart beating wildly in her chest, she unlocked the car and almost immediately, stepped back at the pungent smell of pee that escaped the interior of the car.

As quietly as she dare, she closed and locked the door, her mind a confusion of thoughts.

Returning to the house, she felt curiously pleased that seeing the scratch on Martin's face and the smell from his car seemed to confirm to what she intended for Martin the following day.

She had just closed and locked the front door and turning was unprepared for the fist that struck her, causing her to scream and fly backwards, cracking her head off the closed door. She instinctively knew that her eye was badly hurt and as she slid wordlessly down to the floor, Martin grabbed her by her cardigan and pulled her forward onto her knees.

"What the *fuck* were you doing in my car!" he hissed at her and slapped her hard across the face.

Though only a few seconds had passed since she was struck, already she could feel her eye swelling and staring in terror at him, sobbed.

"The light. You left the wee inside light on in your car."

He stared at her with maddened, suspicious eyes but then remembered; he had switched on the interior light when he dabbed at his cheek, but under no circumstances would he admit his mistake to Annemarie.

"In future, you nosey, prying *bitch*, come and tell me! Stay out of my car!" and threw her to the floor before turning to stomp noisily up the stairs.

On the top landing, awoken by her scream, her daughters stood in their nightdresses and clutched at each other as they stared down at their mother who now lay sobbing on the floor, standing to one side when their father without acknowledging them brushed past them to return to his room where eyes narrowed, he grinned.

By good fortune, it had worked out nicely; the girls will have heard the argument and saw the fight and if they're asked, they will say their Daddy fought with their Mummy and he can claim that's how he came by his scratched cheek.

**CHAPTER TEN**

Saturday morning broke in Glasgow sunny and bright, however, a squall of rain greeted the early morning travellers in Birmingham. Getting ready to attend the meeting, Gavin Blakestock showered and dressed and as he did most mornings in the privacy of their bedroom, bent over to lightly brush away the strands of hair covering his sleeping wife's cheek and gently kissed her good morning. Her eyes opened and turning her head, she smiled and told him to take care. Making his way downstairs, he checked his mobile phone for messages, but found none. Heading into the kitchen to prepare a light breakfast he wondered if he should phone young Tom McEwan, but decided against it, preferring to wait till after the meeting when hopefully he would have something to discuss.

In her Peel Street flat, Joyce McKinnon hurriedly dressed and listened to the radio weather forecast while she finished her cereal. Boiling the kettle, she prepared a flask of coffee and added this to the bag that contained her prepared sandwiches and the chicken pie. Patting at her pocket she ensured she had the black marker pen similar to the one she had given to Annemarie.
With a final glance around the kitchen, she took a deep breath and left the flat to travel to Manchester.

The girls had slept huddled with their mother in the narrow bed in the spare room while their father occupied the double bed in the larger room.
The older girl Paula had said little but her sister Carol, unable to understand why Annemarie's face was all swollen and red and why her Daddy had hit her Mummy had sobbed and wept through the first hour. At last, she fell into a fitful sleep hushed and wrapped in her mothers arms while Paula, crushed against the wall in the narrow bed, had stayed awake a little longer, fixedly staring at her mother till finally in the early hours, sleep took her too.
Morning dawned bright through the flimsy curtain and still wearing her clothes from the day before, Annemarie awoke in the cramped bed from her troubled sleep and saw that Paula was also awake.
"I want us to go away," she softly whispered to her Mum. "I don't like it when he hits you all the time."
Annemarie's lips trembling and at first too emotional to reply, simply nodded and finally said, "Don't worry, darling. Daddy doesn't really mean it. He's just a wee bit upset."
The door suddenly opened and Martin, dressed in an old shirt and denim trousers, gruffly said, "Are you going to lie in all day? I need my breakfast."

He didn't wait for a reply, but turned away leaving the door ajar. Without disturbing the sleeping Carol, Annemarie wearily arose from the bed and forcing a smile, told Paula, "Stay where you are for now, darling. When Carol wakes up, both of you come downstairs for your breakfast. I've an idea," she brightly said, "we'll all go into the city centre today for a wee bit of shopping."

"I don't want to go if he comes too," her daughter's eyes widened with fear and her head lifted from the pillow as she stared at her mother.

"No, I mean just you, Carol and me," she reassured the little girl. Paula slowly nodded and lay her head back down, but all the while staring wide-eyed at her mother.

Before going downstairs, Annemarie slipped into the bathroom and after peeing, studied her face in the mirror. Her reflection showed a tousle haired woman whose left eye was badly swollen, her eyes bloodshot and who looked exactly what she was; a beaten and abused victim of domestic violence.

With a sob, her hands grasping the enamel washbowl, she fought the tears and sniffing, carefully washed her hands and face.

Preparing herself she made her way downstairs where the front door lay open. Peeking out, she saw Martin with the rear doors of the car open. A basin of soapy water lay on the ground and Martin appeared to be inside the car, cleaning the upholstery.

She didn't call out, but he turned and seeing her, climbed out of the rear seat and followed her into the kitchen.

"What happened to your eye; did you fall against something?" he said, staring pointedly at her and then reached forward to tightly take her chin in his hand as he peered at the bruising.

Unconsciously she started to raise a hand to her eye but stopped, playing the game she had so often played before.

"Yes, Martin, I fell against something."

"You need to be more careful in future," he warned her and roughly shook her chin before adding, "I'll be in within a couple of minutes. Have my breakfast ready," and left her alone to return to cleaning the car.

She breathed slowly, the tension ebbing from her and again wondered; how had he come by that scratch and why was he concentrating on cleaning just the back seats of the car. Her nose wrinkled at the memory and she thought, why did his car reek of…she almost laughed, for she had thought it smelled of piss. Her mind was a confusion of thought and with his breakfast cooking in the electric frying pan, decided she had time to put a wash on. Walking into the hallway, she opened the door to the tight cupboard under the stairs where she kept the wash basket. To her surprise, Martin's light coloured bomber jacket and chino trousers lay crumpled on top of the pile of clothes, Carrying the basket through to the washing machine, she bent down on to her knees to sort out a load. It was then she noticed the dark, almost copper staining on the front of the jacket and some spots on the front of the chinos; not a lot, but, she wondered, was it small spots of dried blood? She remembered his cut cheek and was about to shove the jacket and chinos into the machine, but some instinct stopped her. She was unable to explain why, but decided that she would keep the jacket and chinos back and with a fearful glance towards the front door, shoved them both deeply into the bottom of the plastic basket.

Since early that morning, James Hardie's deputy Gregory Packer stood patiently at the entrance foyer of Chrystons head office, waiting to greet the Directors and provide them with a copy of the briefing report prepared by the two investigators.
Glancing at his watch, he saw it was now nine-forty and almost on cue, James Hardie walked through the doors.
"All here are they Gregory?" he snapped at the younger man, accepting the briefing report as he walked swiftly towards the elevator and obliging Packer to hurry after him.
"All except Mister Peters, sir. The investigator, Mister Blakestock is here too. I've arranged for…"
But Hardie was already in the elevator and the doors slid shut, cutting off Packer's statement.
Packer took a deep breath and silently wondered how much more he could take of his boss's indifferent arrogance.
Turning, he almost collided with Jackson Peters and was about to apologise when Peters said, "Good morning, Mister Packer. Ah, the latest development, I assume and might I ask, how are you today?" he smiled as Packer handed him his copy of the briefing report.
Striding with Peters towards the elevator, Packer replied he was fine and wished that Hardie was blessed with the same manners and

courtesy as was Peters. He pressed the button to take them to the fourth floor.

As the elevator silently glided upwards, Peters turned towards him and asked, "How long have you been with the company now, Mister Packer?"

"Just over eleven years, sir. I commenced my career as an office junior and," he smiled, "here I am today."

"And let's hope you have *much* more to achieve," Peters stared at him as he returned his smile and then to Packer's astonishment, pressed the hold button that brought the lift gliding to a smooth halt between floors.

Turning to Packer, Peters stared at him with keen eyes and said, "Before we continue, Gregory, I wonder if you and I might have a *private* word?"

A little under five minutes later the doors slid open on the fourth floor.

Packer politely stood back to permit the CEO to exit the elevator, but his mind was in a whirl. What was that chat about and why did the CEO wish to discuss Mister Hardie's accounts and banking details? Wasn't that information already available to the CEO? And, he caught his breath; was that a veiled suggestion from Peters that he might be destined for further promotion?

A little confused by what had just transpired, he followed Peters to the Board Room but stopped outside the door when Peters turned and quietly said, "I've enjoyed our little chat, Mister Packer, but I do hope that I might rely upon your discretion; that you keep what we discussed between us," he stared meaningfully at the younger man, then added, "Perhaps some time later today you might call upon me at my office with the information that I need?"

"Yes, sir, of course sir," Packer replied and then followed him into the boardroom.

The Directors were all gathered around a small side table that held coffee pots and crockery. It didn't escape Peters notice that most, but not all, were laughing at something Hardie had obviously said.

"Good morning, gentlemen," the CEO loudly called out and making his way towards his chair at the top of the table, invited the rest to join him.

Carrying their coffees, they took their seats with Gavin Blakestock joining them and seated at the end of the table.

"This further extraordinary meeting is called to order to discuss the threat against the company," Peters formally opened the meeting and added, "I assume by now you will all have had the opportunity to peruse the information that was discovered by Mister Blakestock and his associate." Turning to Hardie, he stared at him and said, "James. Your decision not to involve the police. Does that still stand?"

Hardie was taken aback by the question, but having taken a stance, nodded and replied, "It certainly does, Jackson. I believe that to involve the police would not only be a great mistake, but foolhardy. While we on the Board can trust that there will be no leak to the media from any of the Directors, we cannot trust our staff and certainly not the police. My God, if previous media reporting is anything to go by," he cast a jovial glance around the table and then pointing to the Director seated opposite, added, "the bloody police leak worse than that old motorboat Frank has docked in Bristol Harbour!"

The loud laughter than erupted at the expense of the red-faced Director, Frank Kennedy, charged with Media and Public Relations, echoed about the room.

Peters smiled tolerantly at the joke, however, his discreet though brief conversation with Gregory Packer had suggested to Peters that the Director was not liked by Hardie and formed the opinion that Kennedy was likely being singled out for jest by Hardie because Kennedy was not a supporter in Hardie's campaign to usurp Peters as CEO.

Calling the Board to order, Peters glanced at the ornate wall clock and said, "The time has just gone ten o'clock, gentlemen. We have passed the deadline that we believe was set by our mystery extortionist. If as James has correctly assessed," he inclined his head towards Hardie, "we have just called Penthesilea's bluff. Are you all in favour of continuing with the decision made by our esteemed Director of Operations?"

Gavin Blakestock cast an eye about the table and it seemed to him that while five of the Directors almost immediately raised their hands, the remaining two that included Frank Kennedy, first glanced at Peters before slowly raising their hands.

As CEO, Peters declined to vote but smiling, said, "Thank you gentlemen. We will follow the course of action instigated by Mister

Hardie. Mister Blakestock," he called down the table, "It is my desire that should either you or your colleague, ah, Mister…"

"Tom McEwan, sir."

"Indeed, Mister McEwan. Should there be any further developments regarding the full identity of the woman whose photograph you have obtained, I wish to be immediately informed. I will ensure you are provided with a direct contact number."

"Of course, Mister Peters."

"I suggest that in the meantime to use the adage, the ball now lies *firmly* in the court of that female individual or the group calling themselves Penthesilea. We will await any development and regardless of what next occurs, we will re-convene here at ten am on Monday. Are there any questions? No? Then gentlemen, again, thank you for your attendance and enjoy the remainder of your weekend."

Standing, Peters beckoned towards Blakestock and above the noisily shuffling of chairs, called out, "Before you depart, can I have a word, Mister Blakestock?"

He followed the CEO to the corridor and then to Peters private office. Indicating that he sit, Peters opened a drinks cabinet and fetching out a decanter of whisky and two glasses, inclined his head in offer towards Blakestock who raised a hand to decline. Pouring two fingers into a chunky crystal cut glass, Peters sat opposite Blakestock and asked, "Tell me, Mister Blakestock, in your considered opinion what will be this Penthesilea's next move?"

"Frankly sir, I have no idea. However, I maintain it is a mistake not to involve the police."

"Quite so, but *that* was a decision taken by James Hardie prior to my return to the UK and one the Board seem determined to abide by. Now about the threat and the next move; if you *were* pressed to offer an opinion, truthfully, what would that opinion be?"

Blakestock took a deep breath and replied, "As you are aware from the briefing report, Tom McEwan and I have discovered that the suspect is possibly a Scot and in all probability is female, though that can't be ascertained because the suspect wore a disguise. You ask for my considered opinion, Mister Peters?" He leaned forward and stared at the CEO. "The length that the suspect has gone to, purchasing the jars and depositing them in the stores in Glasgow and Birmingham, delivering the letter to you head office here all seems to me to be a determined effort to extort the money from your company. Your company's failure to pay the one million pounds will likely be accepted as a challenge and I believe that the suspect, who both Tom McEwan and I believe to be working alone, will continue the campaign against you but with greater intensity."

"A rather chilling opinion, Mister Blakestock," sighed Peters.

"You asked for the truth, sir."

"Yes, I did, didn't I?"

However, Peters had been involved in business all his life and his intuition told him that Blakestock was holding something back. Staring keenly at him, he asked, "Is there something that perhaps you *might* have overlooked, Mister Blakestock? Something you are *not* disclosing?"

Blakestock smiled and slowly shook his head for he had the distinct feeling that Peters was a more astute fellow that he had given him credit for.

"You have to understand sir, it's nothing definite, nothing that either Tom or I can put our finger on. However, we are both of the opinion that there is some sort of second agenda with our suspect. Neither of us believe that the suspect," he paused and continued, "this Penthesilea is so altruistic that they are waging this threat for the benefit of the women employed by Chrystons."

"And this agenda might be?"

"Absolutely no idea, Mister Peters," he shook his head, "but given a little more time, Tom and I might find out."

"Unfortunately, time is a commodity we do not have so let us hope that Mister Hardie was correct in his opinion that we do not bring the police into this," Peters frowned, then asked, "Tell me this, did Mister Hardie at any time privately seek your opinion? What I mean is, did he take any account of both you and Mister McEwan's previous knowledge in police responses to this sort of situation?"

Blakestock drew a deep breath and before replying, considered what he was being asked. "Mister Hardie seems committed to his course of action, Mister Peters," he diplomatically replied.

"Indeed he is, he most certainly is," muttered Peters and thoughtfully sipped at his whisky.

Tom McEwan pushed open the door to Chrystons Woodlands Road store, surprised to discover that though it was just after ten in the morning the place was already crowded with shoppers.

Staff hurried back and forth and he decided that Ellen would be too busy for coffee and was about to leave when he heard his name called.

Ellen, wearing a black business skirted suit with her Chrystons name tag on the left breast and her red hair tied back into a ponytail, waved at him from an aisle, but before she could greet him, was stopped by a customer.

Tom waited patiently for a few minutes till Ellen had dealt with the shopper and then smiled when almost breathlessly, she said, "Thank you for last night, I had a lovely time."

"Me too. I hope we can do it again, soon."

She stared curiously at him and then said, "How do you feel about a home cooked meal, say tonight at my place?" then quickly raising her hands, added with a pretend frown, "but just the meal, nothing else."

He grinned and nodding, was about to reply, when another customer holding a can, hesitantly sought Ellen's advice.

Turning to the front door, he called out, "I'll come back later when you're not so busy."

Distracted, Ellen waved, but he was already gone.

Annemarie and the girls got off the bus in West George Street. She had used what little makeup she had to tone down the bruising, but was conscious of the sympathetic stares she was getting from not just the driver, but the passengers too.

Taking their hands, she fought the panic that threatened to overtake her and tried to make light of their walk, persuading her daughters not to step on the lines in the pavement. Distracted from their mother's apprehension, the girls got into the spirit of the improvised game and before long were giggling and hopping from paving stone to paving stone.

Approaching the busy pedestrian precinct in Argyle Street, Annemarie felt her stomach tensing and unable to stop shaking, decided that she had better walk off her nerves before entering the store.

Her sister's instructions had been quite specific, insisting that Annemarie would shop in the Chrystons store and purchase what she needed there.

It wasn't where Annemarie would normally shop for delicious though they might be, the tight budget permitted by Martin didn't stretch to the pricey foods that Chrystons offered.

It took her a full twenty minutes before she calmed down and only then because she realised the girls were becoming bored as they walked the city centre streets. Taking a deep breath, she pushed open the front door of Chrystons and collected a plastic shopping basket from the foyer area, handing it to Paula who insisted she carry it.

The fine hairs on the back of Annemarie's neck were bristling for she was aware that she was passing under the CCTV camera at the door. Following Joyce's instruction, she stopped within a few feet of the door and fumbling with her handbag, as though by accident dropped it to the floor. Before she could bend down, a middle-aged, uniformed store security officer hurried forward from a small desk and with a smile, stooped with the girls to retrieve the handbag and its spilled contents.

"There you are, Madam," smiled the security officer, taking pains to avoid staring at her bruised and discoloured eye.

"Thank you," Annemarie shook her head as though at her foolishness and as she had practised, added, "the more hurry, the less speed."

With the girls holding hands as they trailed a few feet behind, she walked forward into the store, surprised that her voice had not faltered as she feared and slowly exhaled with relief.

The store was crowded and now ushering the girls in front of her, she made her way towards the food department, recalling Joyce's instruction that she should speak with at least one more member of staff. It is important, Joyce had told her, that you are seen and remembered shopping in the store.

Annemarie stopped when she saw the teenage female shop assistant in an aisle with a price labelling gun. The girl was using the gun to attach the small stickers on to cans that she then stacked onto a shelf. Annemarie swallowed hard and forcing a smile, said, "Excuse me, can you direct me to where I can purchase a pie?"

"Meat pie or a fruit pie, Madam?" the young girl turned and was about to brightly ask, but like the security officer, tried in vain to ignore the pleasant looking woman's bruised eye.

"Oh, chicken pie, please."

"In the freezer section, second aisle on your left. Shall I show you, Madam?"

"No, if you just point me in the direction," she smiled.

The girl directed her and turned to continue labelling the cans, but not before returning Carol's shy wave.

Annemarie thanked her and made her way to the refrigerated aisle where with a deep breath, she fetched an individual chicken pie from the chest freezer.

It occurred to her then that Joyce was correct about the two members of staff, though couldn't have known it wouldn't be difficult for the security officer and the young assistant to recall the woman with the black eye.

She spent another ten minutes in the store purchasing a few other items and a packet of cheap sweets for the girls before making her way with them to the till.

Standing in the queue, she was again conscious of the small orb that contained the CCTV camera located in the ceiling above the tills and though it unnerved her, deliberately stared up as though glancing about her.

She paid cash for her purchases and mindful of Joyce's firm instruction carefully folded the receipt into her purse.


Arriving in Manchester city centre, Joyce followed the SatNav's directions and arrived at the NCP car park earlier than she anticipated.

Parking the car, she fetched the plastic bag containing her disguise and the chicken pie from the car boot and entered the museum at the Energy Hall before heading directly towards the toilets, located beside the Energy Café.

She heaved a sigh of relief when she found the ladies' toilets to be empty and entering a cubicle, nervously peed before donning her disguise. For a heart stopping second, she thought she had forgotten to bring the black marker pen but there it was, caught in a fold at the bottom of the plastic bag. Marking the chicken pie with an X she stuffed her driving jacket into the bag with the pie and carefully listened, but nobody had entered the toilets. Taking a deep breath, she left the cubicle and retraced her steps to exit the museum.

It took just a few minutes to walk to the Chrystons store on Quay Street.

She did not hesitate at the entrance but forcing herself to be strong, pushed open the main door and ignoring the bored security officer who sat at the small desk reading a newspaper, lifted a plastic basket from the pile beside the door.

Conscious of the overhead CCTV cameras, she kept her head down and made her way to the Food Court where she quickly found the freezer section.

Now was the most dangerous part of her plan.

She had already practised her manoeuvre and moving along the fridges experienced a slight panic, for she was unable to find any individual chicken pies of the type she had purchased in Glasgow. Then with a sigh of relief, saw several dozen stacked neatly in a glass windowed fridge beside boxes of quiche. She fought the temptation to glance around for members of staff who might be watching her. Reaching into her bag just as she had practised in the flat, she deftly removed the marked pie and placed it at the back of the pile while lifting one from the front that she placed in her basket. Quickly standing upright, she made her way to the tills where with head down and trembling hands, she waited in the queue to be served.

It was fortunate that the woman at her till was engaged gossiping with her colleague and took no apparent notice when Joyce placed the pie onto the conveyor belt, but then the woman startled and peered at the note Joyce handed her.

"Oh, that's a Scottish fiver, isn't it love," she frowned then turning, loudly called out to a supervisor, "Can we accept Scottish notes, Beryl?"

Shocked, Joyce almost fainted and thought her legs were about to buckle beneath her, but was relieved when the supervisor called back with a laugh, "Yeah, no problems, pet, as long as it's not a forgery."

"Sorry about that, my dear," the cashier apologised with a fixed smile and handed Joyce her change.

Her throat too dry to respond, Joyce forced a weak grin and almost grabbing at the pie, hurried from the store.

Shit! she thought.

It never occurred to her that a Scottish note might attract attention. Shit! Shit! Shit!

In the fresh air, she took a moment to steady herself and then speedily made her way back to the NCP car park.

She could not change out of the disguise yet for she still had the letter to deliver and again with the use of the SatNav drove to the BBC premises located in Oxford Road. Though the drive was supposed to take just under five minutes, the Saturday traffic added precious time to the journey and almost fifteen minutes passed before an increasingly nervous Joyce arrived in Oxford Road. The road itself was busy and she spent another five minutes finding a parking bay and that almost a full two minutes walk from the premises.

At last she arrived at the location, but to her horror discovered the building had been demolished and the site was just a wasteland of debris. She glanced about her as panic overtook her; yes, this *was* the correct address.

"No, no," she softly muttered as disbelievingly, she shook her head. All her carefully laid plans, her research on the Internet. It was about to all fail because of this!

Confused, she stared down at the sealed envelope she held in her gloved hand and dread set in.

What the hell was she going to do now?

He decided to drive himself to meet with her and taking her advice, parked the car in the public car park that served the Museums and Art Gallery before walking the short distance to Colmore Street. It had been his idea to meet where there was little likelihood of anyone they knew seeing them together. Arriving at the Starbucks, he could see through the window that the place was half full and pushing open the door, selected a table near to the back of the coffee shop. He took off his Burberry coat and smiling at the young assistant, ordered coffee for two and placed the bulky brown envelope on the seat beside his. With a fleeting look about him, he was pleased that nobody took any particular notice of him and glancing at his wristwatch, realised he was a little early for their meeting, but smiled when he saw the dark haired Margo push open the door. He stood to greet her and saw the indecision, or perhaps it was curiosity, register on her face.

Making her way to the table, he continued to smile, but saw that since they had last met some months previously she seemed to have lost weight and thought there was a lacklustre appearance in her mode of dress. Yet, he mused, there was no doubt Margo was still a very attractive lady, even if she seemed to be a little jaded.

He placed both hands lightly upon her arms and leaned forward to kiss her cheek, his eyes narrowing at the faint but discernible smell of body odour that emanated from her and thought perhaps she had hurried to meet with him. He guessed that her marital problems with James were affecting her far worse than he feared.

"Jackson, how are you?" she wheezed as she sat heavily down on the chair.

"I am very well, thank you my dear. But you Margo. How are you? And the girls, how are they?"

He watched as her throat tightened and she forced a smile, her jaw clamped tight and guessed she was close to tears. Taking a shallow breath, she replied, "Under the circumstances, I am as well as can be expected, I suppose and as for the girls; you could say confused is how I would describe them."

"You know then," he asked, but not unkindly.

She nodded, not trusting herself to speak and at last muttered, "I *know* there is someone, but not who."

"Has he said anything, given you any idea of…"

"Said anything," she snapped back, then almost immediately, contritely added, "I'm sorry, Jackson. It's just that…well, I've been a bit stressed recently."

She shook her head and in a low voice, said, "He hasn't said anything. I just know. It's the little thing; the scent on his shirts, the unexplained absences. His attitude towards the girls and me. He's not just indifferent to us, he's…well, I suppose the word is dismissive. He just doesn't care anymore. Not about the girls and me, anyway."

She sat rigidly in her seat as her eyes narrowed and peering accusingly at him, almost with anger, said, "Why did you ask to meet me, Jackson, and why here? Has he told you anything? You know, don't you? Does he intend…"

He raised his hand to quiet her and paused, allowing her time to compose herself. When he thought her sufficiently calmed, he replied, "I suspected for some time, Margo, that James was having an affair. I also suspect…no, I firmly believe that James intends leaving you and your daughters." He decided if he were to persuade her to agree to his plan he must be blunt and added, "He intends divorcing you, Margo."

He took a deep breath and continued, "I have reliable information that James is conniving to leave you with the minimum settlement that the divorce court will permit." He did not disclose that his information came unwittingly from James's own Deputy, Gregory Packer. "How he intends presenting his case to the divorce court, I have no idea; however, what I do know is that you might be able to…how shall I put this? Circumvent his intentions."

It seemed to him that by confirming her worst fears, she visibly sunk even lower into the seat and with defeat in her eyes, simply asked, "How would I do that, Jackson? James is so much smarter than I am."

He smiled softly and replied, "James *might* be smarter than you, Margo, if you believe that, but is he as smart as a good divorce lawyer?"

He lifted the sealed envelope from the empty seat next to him and passed it across the table to her, but kept a firm hand upon it as she stared curiously at it.

Margo, her eyes now filled with unshed tears, tried to speak but words failed her.

"I have one request of you should you choose to accept my help," he spoke softly, but clearly.

She did not understand why Jackson Peters, the man she believed to be James close friend, would choose to help her, but her eyes widened with sudden interest and taking a deep breath, she replied, "What request?"

He thought he detected a faint stirring of hope in her response and said, "This envelope contains all you need to beat James in any court, no matter what kind of case he brings against you, but I will request of you that you take no action in the meantime. Let me be quite clear, Margo," he shook his head, "no action whatsoever. I have my own agenda to attend to first and if you should go from here to challenge James with the contents of this envelope, it will undoubtedly interfere and ruin all that I intend."

He paused and softly smiling, continued. "I realise, Margo, that the next few days will be overwhelming for you. You have much to consider and frankly, I don't believe you will logically think your options through. I am of the opinion that if you immediately challenge James about what you learn today he might try to persuade or even coerce you into making decisions that in the long term, you *will* regret. Yes, you are correct to have believed me to be James's friend, but for the next day or so I ask you to trust me."

She shook her head, fighting the tears and said, "I'm no match for him, Jackson. You know me; you know that I could never stand up to him."

"Yes, my dear, but what you have to realise is that you are not alone."

It was time now to disclose to her the terrible truth.

"The other woman, Margo. You never suspected who it is?"

"No," she fervently shook her head, "never."

"Then it is my painful duty to inform you that James is currently and has for several months having an affair with my own wife, Lesley."

She stared at him, aghast; the realisation suddenly clear why Jackson Peters was so eager to help her.

"I've known for some time," he continued, "but it did not suit my plans to confront either Lesley or James; at least," he smiled, "not till I set in motion certain details."

"What details, Jackson?"

"In the envelope," he nodded to it, "you will find a legal document that can be served on James."

He saw her eyes narrow with curiosity and added, "You must understand, Margo, I have been planning this for some time now and I have taken the liberty of making certain arrangements for both you and your daughters as well as my own behalf. I assure you, my dear, that such arrangements will prove to be to your satisfaction."

He could see that she remained worried and continued, "Perhaps you will be relieved to know through the chambers of your new divorce solicitor, whose details I have included in the prepared synopsis in the envelope you have there, I have contracted a company to ensure that you and your daughters will not be harassed by James. Again, the details are in the envelope. You will also find a small cardboard wallet that contains copies of photographs. I regret that you might find these photographs…" he carefully considered the correct word and with some hesitation, added, "explicit. I regret you might find yourself terribly upset when you view them. Once the shock of seeing the photographs has passed, Margo, consider them to be the main ammunition in your pending lawsuit. I have included copies of these photographs and if you should decide to…how can I put it, present them to James, that will be your decision."

He sipped at his coffee and then said, "Everything I have planned, all that I told have you, Margo; it all depends on both of us acting in concert and so I must ask you for now, hurt and betrayed though you undoubtedly must be, to bide your time. I ask you that for the next few days, to trust me."

She didn't immediately respond, but composed now, asked, "How long do you wish me to wait?"

"Till I phone you and as I said, I suspect that will be some time within the next few days, possibly even Monday."

"I can wait that long," her lips trembled slightly as she vainly attempted to smile.

"Good. Now, my dear," he leaned forward and patted gently at her hand, heartened by her new found vigour, "if I might be so bold, may I offer you some advice about how James should be confronted with your new information?"

Martin Turner stared hard into the rear of the car. It was as clean as he could possibly get it. Every little piece of leather seat, every fibre of the carpet, scrubbed and dampened in a heavily diluted bleach soak.

As satisfied as he could be there was no longer any trace of Colleen Younger in his car, he threw down the cloth into the basin and closed both rear doors.

He was still angry that the dirty wee bitch had peed on his seats and carpet and involuntarily shivered in disgust. For that alone she deserved to die.

Leaning back against the handrail of the two steps that led up into the front door, he took a deep breath and moving towards the rear door, opened it and took a deep sniff. Good, it no longer smelled of her. He'd stop at a garage and get one of those lemon scented things that hung from the mirror; that should mask any lingering odour.

Idly he wondered how long it would be before anyone stumbled upon her body. He had half considered going back and making a better job of covering her up; maybe even burying her, but decided against it. It was far too risky. It only needed somebody else up there nosing about and he couldn't risk being seen.

He glanced at his wristwatch and wondered where Annemarie and the girls had got to. Not that he was too bothered. If she took them with her it left him free to do his own thing. He spent enough time with bloody kids when he was working to be around them on his days off.

Confident that now she was dead there was nothing to connect him to Colleen, he decided he would have a shower. Even the thought she might have told her pals of her relationship with a teacher or even named Martin no longer worried him. If he was challenged about it he would strongly deny such an accusation and simply laugh it off as her fantasy.

Yeah, he smiled. Maybe he'd go out into town tonight for a beer. He smiled, perhaps pull a bird.

Ensuring the car was locked, he turned and went indoors.


The sixteen pensioner members of the Balornock Old Farts Walking Club chatted, laughed and giggled among themselves as they made their way through the nature trail in the Cawder Woods. Dressed in their multi-coloured anoraks, bobble hats and each member wearing stout walking shoes or boots and carrying a small back pack, they ambled along at a sedate pace enjoying the serenity and peace away from the bustling inner city life.

One of their members, Tommy, wisecracked he was away into the woods for a pee and laughingly called out to ask if any of the seven female members among the group would like to come and hold it for him?

The good-natured derision and jeers that followed him into the bushes caused him to snigger and taking a deep breath, he unzipped his cargo trousers. Fishing about in his underpants for his willie he stopped and eyes narrowing in the dim light caused by the overhanging trees, peered at what looked like an overcoat lying on the ground.

With a start, he jerked back and as he later stated to the officers who attended his frantic phone call, "When I saw the lassies feet sticking out from under that coat, I was that shocked I peed down the inside leg of my trousers."

# CHAPTER ELEVEN

The call received by the police and in turn forwarded to the local divisional CID was responded to by a Detective Sergeant and Detective Constable who were informed a body had been discovered by walkers in Cawder Woods. Unfortunately, the location of the walkers and the body had no reference point and hopelessly lost, it was a full twenty minutes of driving along dirt tracks before they encountered an elderly lady. Breathlessly, the excited woman told the officers her group had wisely split into smaller parties and extended in a large circle from the body to widen the point of contact and to bring the officers to the location of their discovery.

Within an hour, the area was sealed off by Police Scotland and a full Scene of Crime and Forensic examination was underway.

During that time, Detective Inspector Murray Fitzpatrick of the Kirkintilloch CID arrived and stood by the blue and white tape that denoted the SOC search area. Assuming charge of the inquiry, he was updated by DS Anne Leitch, a diminutive woman with collar length dark hair who dressed in an encompassing white Forensic suit, was referring to her notebook when she told him, "Young lassie, sir, maybe in her teens, discovered by they walkers," she stopped and pointed to a group of pensioners who stood or sat near a police van, drinking from flasks. "Sherlock...I mean, Doctor Watson is up there the now, but first indication is that victim was strangled and dumped there."

"What do you mean, strangled and dumped there? Strangled yes, I understand that; but are you telling me she was strangled here and left where she lies or strangled elsewhere and dumped here?"

Leitch gritted her teeth and refusing to rise to the bait, took a deep breath. The DI was a stickler for protocol and lived in a world governed by rules, regulations, procedure and formality. Worst of all, Fitzpatrick was a spiteful man and not slow in picking on some poor unfortunate subordinate who he believed crossed him. Due to retire anytime soon, as far as Leitch was concerned the sod could go yesterday.

"Sorry, sir," she carefully replied. "According to the doctor, the victim was strangled, yes. She was *discovered* here, but it has *not* been determined if she was murdered here or murdered elsewhere and then dumped here."

"That's better, Sergeant; lets get it right first time, eh?" Fitzpatrick coldly rebuked her.

It briefly occurred to Leitch it might be worth her career to break the bastards nose, but she kept her cool and politely asked, "What's your orders then, sir?"

"My orders, Sergeant?" he glanced about him at the hive of activity and said, "I'm sure you have enough experience to be getting on with what you are doing, so continue with the search and fetch me a suit. I'll want to see the body when Doctor Watson has completed her examination." He turned and nodded towards the pensioners. "Ensure that those peoples details are correctly noted and they are to be informed to make themselves available to provide statements."

"Already done, sir," she replied.

"So, you *do* have some idea how to conduct an inquiry, Sergeant." Leitch was seconds away from telling Fitzpatrick exactly what she was thinking when she saw the SOC supervisor beckoning towards her.

"Excuse me, sir, I'm wanted," she snarled and left him to fetch his own Forensic suit.

Leitch walked towards the edge of the sterile search area where the supervisor was bent down examining the ground.

"I'm not certain, Anne, and it might depend on how long Sherlock believes the body has been lying there, but if you recall there was a wee bit of heavy rain last night. If I'm right, these are fresh tyre tracks and it looks to me like the vehicle that made the tracks has stopped, reversed here and drove back that way," she pointed down the track. "Course, could be nothing; after all, this *is* the Cawder Woods."

She saw the confusion in Leitch's face and explained. "There's a lot of shagging goes on here at night time," the woman grinned and turning, stared at Leitch as she added, "unless it's changed any since *I* was a teenager. Aye, I've had a few delightful evenings in the back seats of motors up here," she continued to grin at Leitch.

Leitch decided not to question how delightful those evenings were, but instead asked, "What do you propose? Photographing the tracks?"

"That and I'll take a plaster cast and yes," she narrowed her eyes at Leitch, "we still do that these days."

"Anything else of note?"

"Well," the SOC officer hesitated, "there is what seems to be the remains of somebody's puke, but because of the rain the fluid has…diluted I suppose is the best way to describe it, then drained into the ground."

"Is it possible to obtain DNA from what remains of the vomit?"

"Well," the SOCO hesitated, "all glands are made up of epithelial cells. These are the cells that line your mouth and the oesophagus; you know, your food pipe or gullet to give it its common name. As for obtaining DNA from what's left," she shrugged, "it will depend how much damage is done by the acid and enzymes in the stomach to the DNA and I suspect it's unlikely we'll get anything from the vomit, but don't you worry," she grinned, "I've the very man for the job."

Leitch watched with a quiet smile as the SOCO called over a junior colleague and instructed him to collect some vomit for testing.

It seemed obvious to Leitch the man thought the job distasteful and muttering under his breath, walked off to collect a sample.

"Sergeant Leitch! With me, now!" Fitzpatrick, now dressed in a white Forensic suit, loudly shouted.

"There's your lord and master calling," teased the SOC officer.

"Aye, right," Leitch shook her head and turned away to join Fitzpatrick as he lifted the tape and strode to where the dead girl lay.

Doctor Elizabeth Watson, affectionately known as Sherlock by the CID officers she assisted, was similarly attired in a Forensic suit and down on both knees, her hooded head bowed as she examined the victim.

"Good morning, Doctor," Fitzpatrick greeted her as he stood a few metres back from her. Over Watson's shoulder, he saw the body of a young blonde haired woman lying on her back, wearing a white blouse that had opened to her navel, a short black leather skirt and black leather boots. Leitch noticed the stud buttons of the blouse were irregularly closed as if buttoned in haste. To one side of the body lay a lengthy, black coat that appeared to be mud stained.

Watson turned her head and almost groaned when she saw him stood there and politely, but formally replied, "Morning, Mister Fitzpatrick," then seeing Leitch, smiled and with warmth added, "Good morning, Anne."

"Sherlock," Leitch acknowledged her with a grin, aware that the use of Watson's nickname would rile the DI.

"I understand you have a preliminary cause of death, Doctor," said Fitzpatrick,

"From the marks on this girl's neck and the popped blood vessels in her eyes, it seems to me she has been strangled and if I'm not mistaken, by the use of hands for there appears to be finger marks on her skin. If as I suspect bare hands have been used there is a possibility that the Scene of Crime people who swabbed her neck might have lifted ectodermal tissue and therefore the likelihood of obtaining her killers DNA. As well as the abrasions, there is the very slight marks where her assailant's fingernails have broken the skin. My tentative examination suggests the Hyoid bone is broken and would be characteristic of her being throttled. She also has a slight head wound," Watson pointed with a forefinger, "that had bled, but I'm of the opinion it's superficial and not the cause of death; perhaps enough to stun her, but no, it doesn't seem bad enough to have caused death," Watson shook her head. "She's still wearing her underwear, if you can call a thong underwear," she sighed, "but I'm reluctant to remove the underwear at this time, so I am uncertain if there was any sexual activity prior to her death. That will be determined at the post mortem examination and in light of these facts and obviously subject to a more detailed PM examination. However, you will undoubtedly noticed that her blouse seems to have been undone then buttoned again, but the studs are not buttoned in the proper order," she glanced at the detectives, hiding a grin when she saw Leitch nod, but from Fitzpatrick's face it was apparent he had not noticed it. Watson continued, "For your purpose, Mister Fitzpatrick, I can officially pronounce life extinct and as a preliminary cause of death I conclude this young woman was murdered by strangulation."

She turned and nodded to the tape that led through the woods to the track a mere ten metres away. "It seems to me from the drag marks that I saw approaching the body and the fact the heels of her boots are clogged with mud that she was dragged from the track and dumped here."

"I believe regarding the drag marks we should permit the Scene of Crime officers to come to that conclusion, eh Doctor?"

Watson bridled at the censure, but held her tongue and tightly smiled. Like Leitch, she was well aware of Fitzpatrick's cold insolence and besides, though she hated to admit it, he was correct. It was not her job to determine such facts, but believed no other CID officer she worked with would make such a rude comment.

Still, it that didn't stop him being an obnoxious bastard.

Rising to her feet, she said, "Well, Mister Fitzpatrick, there isn't much more I can do here under these conditions other than to confirm the death and for the time being, though the post mortem examination will of course be more accurate, I can tentatively put the time of death between late evening yesterday and the early hours of this morning. That timing is calculated by her body temperature and the fact her coat that covered her is wet, probably by the heavy rainfall while her inner clothing is dry."

"Does she have any identification upon her body?" he asked.

"Mister Fitzpatrick," she closed her medical bag and coolly replied, "I wouldn't dream of searching this young woman for such information. Isn't that the job of the Scene of Crime personnel?" Nodding her farewell to Leitch, she turned and walked off, but mentally scoring a point.

Leitch fought to stop from laughing as the red faced Fitzpatrick turned and angrily snapped, "Get me the SOCO supervisor here. Now!"


Seated at his desk in Martin McCormick's law offices, Tom McEwan was frustrated that there was little he could do other than await the phone call from Gavin Blakestock to report the outcome of the Board meeting.

With an old transistor on a shelf softly playing in the background, the midday news bulletin had just begun when Tom's mobile phone rang. The screen indicated it was Blakestock and pressing the green button, he greeted him.

"Gavin, pleased you called. How did the meeting go?"

"As you might have guessed, the Board rejected any consideration the police be involved so as it stands, we're at a stalemate until such times either nothing happens or there is another letter or report of a contaminated food. In short," he sighed, "nothing to report."

Tom couldn't explain where the notion came from, but he thoughtfully asked, "Was that guy Hardie still bulldozing his way through the meeting? It seemed to me," he explained, "that though Jackson Peters is the CEO it's Hardie that determines how this threat will be dealt with."

"Curious you should ask that," Blakestock replied. "When the meeting concluded and I should tell you that there will be a further Board meeting on Monday that I believe we both should attend; anyway, after this morning's meeting, Peters took me to his office where we had a rather strange conversation." He paused and Tom guessed Blakestock was considering his response before he continued, "From what he said and what he *didn't* say, it seemed to me that Peters is a lot shrewder than I first imagined, though why wouldn't he be? I mean, after all the guy's the CEO of a major UK retail company."

"So, Gavin, what was it that Peters said?"

"Well, quite naturally he asked my opinion about the threat and I related our thought that perhaps there might be some sort of second agenda by the extortionist, though of course I was unable to tell him any more. But, Tom, it was the *way* he spoke about James Hardie that made me feel…I can't really explain. It was as if he hopes that this

Penthesilea succeeds, almost as if the threat succeeds it will bring Hardie down, regardless of how it affects the company."

Tom was puzzled. "Surely though, Gavin, if the threat succeeds it will be Peters head on the chopping block. He will be the first casualty."

"And conversely perhaps *that's* what Hardie is hoping for," Blakestock quietly replied.

The call concluded with both agreeing that as Gavin was the first point of contact with Chrystons if anything untoward should occur, he would in turn contact Tom; otherwise, they would meet on Sunday night at the Premier Inn in Birmingham prior to Monday's Board meeting.

Switching off his mobile Tom smiled for he had been half expecting Gavin to make some comment about Ellen Toner and that might have been awkward.

In her desperation, Joyce had come to a decision. Risky though it was she could not risk the possibility that a member of the public might purchase the poisoned chicken pie and she needed it found straight away; she needed it taken off the shelf.

Fetching the black marker pen from her coat pocket, she wrote upon the sealed envelope in upper case letters.

Taking a deep breath she watched the elderly Indian shopkeeper through the newsagents' front window as he served the woman and handing her the change, waved goodbye and with a smile watched her leave the shop.

Joyce turned away with her head down when the woman passed her by. Taking a deep breath she pushed open the door of the shop and approaching the counter, she kept her head down but heard the man say, "Hello, can I help you?"

She didn't reply, but still keeping her head as low as possible placed the envelope upon the counter and turning, quickly left the shop. The man was puzzled and shaking his head at the woman's strange behaviour lifted the sealed envelope.

Turning it over he read the message, '*DELIVER TO THE POLICE IMMEDIATELY!*' and his blood chilled. In his time the elderly shopkeeper had faced threats from violent drunks, teenage thieves, racists and the occasional irate customer, but for some odd reason the letter he held worried him greatly. Hands shaking and knowing that at his age he could not possibly catch up with the woman, he decided his best course of action was to phone the police…and some instinct told him, quickly.

Hurrying, but careful not to attract unwarranted attention and now almost a hundred metres from the shop, Joyce breathed again and crossing the road, continued to quickly make her way towards her car.

In the kitchen brewing himself coffee, Martin Turner froze at the midday radio news bulletin announcing the discovery of a woman's body in woods outside Kirkintilloch. Suddenly dry mouthed, he listened to the commentator reporting a large police presence in the area that was now cordoned off, adding that no further details were available. He slowly glanced down at his hands, surprised to see them shaking and reaching behind him for a kitchen chair lowered himself slowly down into it.

They found her, he thought. It had to be her.

They can't know it's me; there's no evidence, he tried to convince himself, but doubt and paranoia were knocking at his conscience and his legs began to unaccountably shake.

All his prepared excuses, his denials, his reasoning; now that she had been found they all seemed so hollow, so unbelievable.

In the empty house his lips began to tremble and fear set in as the tears of self-pity began to roll down his cheeks as he worried about his future.

Like a well oiled machine, the Police Scotland response to the discovery of a murder victim commenced with the setting up of an incident room in the Kirkintilloch police office located in Southbank Drive in the town. The modern, square built building that is part of the East Dumbarton area of responsibility included a CID unit commanded by Detective Inspector Murray Fitzpatrick who oversaw his officers with a ruthless efficiency; so much so that Fitzpatrick's boss, Detective Chief Inspector Lynn Massey, who worked out of the divisional headquarters at Baird Street in Glasgow, frequently dealt with transfer requests from his staff.

In a little over two hours following the discovery of the body, the incident room was set up and included a full HOLMES (Home Office Large Major Enquiry System) that would be overseen by the Fitzpatrick's senior Detective Sergeant, Anne Leitch, who would fulfil the dual role of office manager and supervisor of the small staff comprising both police and civilian HOLMES operators and analysts.

Importantly, upon a table set up in a corner of the room, the tea and coffee fund was also in place.

In his office in the CID suite, DI Fitzpatrick sank into his chair. He did not invite DS Anne Leitch to sit, but as a junior officer kept her standing in front of his desk as he folded his hands onto his narrow chest.

"Right then, Sergeant, what do we know so far and please be concise."

Fighting the urge to snap back at him, Leitch reported that a bus ticket dated the previous evening was discovered in the victim's coat pocket and had been given out as an Action to be investigated regarding the route and time it was issued. However, there was no other identifying items or marks upon the body and a search of the area failed to locate any handbag. "No visible tattoos, sir, but of course a fuller examination will be conducted at the PM. I have agreed with Doctor Watson that the PM has been set for four pm, this afternoon."

"You have arranged for the body to be removed to the mortuary at the Queen Elizabeth University Hospital I assume."

"Yes sir, of course."

"Just checking, Sergeant, just checking," he smiled humourlessly at her pale face.

Leitch continued, "I have one of the HOLMES team currently researching the missing persons file for anyone fitting the victim's description, but so far no hits. At the minute, the team are assembling and await your briefing, sir."

"Good, I will be with them shortly."

"Sir," she turned to go, but opening the door stood back to admit Detective Chief Inspector Massey who smiled and said, "Hello, Anne. Nice to see you again. How is the family?"

"They're all fine thanks, Ma'am. My oldest girl starts secondary school in a few weeks and her wee sister is now primary three."

"My, God, they grow up so quickly, don't they," Massey returned Leitch's smile and companionably added, "They're not babies for long, are they?"

Fitzpatrick got to his feet, silently bristling that the DCI was gossiping with a subordinate when there was a murder to solve.

"Can I get you a coffee, Ma'am?"

"I'd love one, please Anne. Milk only."

Nodding, Leitch turned away and closed the door as Massey greeted the DI with, "Good Morning, Mister Fitzpatrick. I was passing so thought I'd drop by and find out about your murder. May I?" she pointed to a chair.

"Yes, Ma'am, of course," he sullenly replied and when she was seated, sat back down in his own chair.

He didn't like Massey and was aware the feeling was mutual, but she had never given him any opportunity to complain about her attitude towards him. At least, not yet.

Over the next five minutes he recounted the known facts about the discovery of the body in Cawder Woods.

"So, no identification as yet?"

"No Ma'am, not yet. If the woman or rather the girl, for she seems to be no older than a teenager, is not identified by tomorrow morning I will, with your permission of course, consider a public appeal."

"Yes, I agree. That seems to be the best course of action. Now, about resources. How can I help?"

Annemarie and her two daughters got off the bus and holding her girl's hands, they slowly began to walk the few hundred metres towards their home; the building where they lived, she corrected herself, not their home, for a home is where my girls and I are supposed to feel safe and protected.

While Carol skipped along beside her, she realised her oldest daughter Paula was dragging her feet so turning towards her, smiled, "When we get home, why don't you get one of your games out and the three of us will sit down and have a nice time together."

Paula turned and stared up at her mother. "Will *he* be there?"

"Who, Daddy? Yes, of course he will, but you know he's not fond of board games so…"

Paula stopped and lips trembling, snapped back, "I don't want to go home. I don't want him to hurt you again!"

Carol stared curiously from her sister to her mother, sensing that something was wrong.

An older woman, a neighbour she thought, was passing but grimaced when she saw Annemarie's bruised face and wordlessly continued walking.

"It was just a little argument," she smiled at Paula, her mouth dry. "Daddy didn't mean to…"

"He did, he's always hitting you!" The little girl began to wail, setting off her sister who also began to cry.

Annemarie laid the shopping bag onto the ground and bending down onto one knee, embraced both the girls who wrapping their small arms about her shoulders, hugged her, their tears falling onto her bare neck.

Her eyes fell to the shopping bag and it was then she determined that if there had previously been any doubt in her mind about what she had to do, no matter what happened to her, she resolved she would not risk her daughters' happiness or their wellbeing.

Safely returned to her car, Joyce McKinnon tore off her wig and wriggling out of the old coat, sobbed with frustration. Her carefully prepared plan to deliver the letter to the Manchester BBC radio station had fallen through and now it all depended upon an elderly Indian man calling the police.

No matter what happened next she was helpless to influence the outcome for now, the die was cast.

The beat constable acknowledged the call and being only a few hundred metres from the newsagents, ambled along to collect a letter. He glanced at his wristwatch. He was due to take his break soon and if this was a bloody hoax, he wearily shook his head.
A few minutes later he took the letter from the equally puzzled shopkeeper and eyes narrowing at the message on the outside, tore the envelope open. Retrieving the single A4 sheet of paper he began to read the typed letter and his mouth fell open.
"Jesus!" he mumbled and snatching at the radio clipped to his stab proof vest, called his control room.

In response to the constable's frantic radio message, the duty officer at Greater Manchester Police (GMP) control room reacted swiftly and caused a patrol car to be speedily dispatched to the Chrystons store located on Quay Street.
Arriving within minutes, the two patrol officers secured the assistance of staff and were quickly led to the frozen food aisle where they poked among the chicken pies. Uncertain *exactly* why they were checking chicken pies for one with a mark on its labelling, nevertheless to their surprise discovered one at the rear of the pile that was easily identifiable by the large black cross written on the packaging.
Sensibly, the male officer instructed his female partner to attend at the CCTV room where she seized all the DVD discs that recorded the main doors and frozen food aisles for the preceding week. Reporting the discovery of the marked chicken pie, the male constable was instructed to preserve the location and informed that the CID were now en route.

**CHAPTER TWELVE**

Tom McEwan hated having nothing to do and it made him feel impotent; nothing to do he sighed and plenty of time to do nothing. There was no sense in phoning Gavin Blakestock for like Tom, he too was playing the waiting game.

Getting into his car he drove towards Charing Cross and then to Woodlands Road where by chance he found an empty parking bay near to the Chrystons store.

The rush of Saturday morning customers had dwindled and a staff member escorted him to Ellen's office.

To Tom's delight, Ellen seemed genuinely pleased to see him and switched on the kettle. "Wilma's off today," she explained, "so I'm it, as it were."

A few minutes later, seated together in her office, he related Gavin Blakestock's phone call.

"So to summarise, it's just a waiting game?" she nodded.

"That's it in a nutshell," he sighed and then smiled. "I really enjoyed last night *and* I'm looking forward to tonight."

"Yes," she stared meaningfully at him, "but remember what I said, Tom. Dinner only."

He raised both hands in the surrender position and smiled. "Got that. I'll bring wine, so all I need now is your address."

He could not know then her invitation to dinner was a huge leap for Ellen. Family aside, she had not yet invited anyone to her home and particularly not a man. Her disastrous relationship with Paul had been conducted at her old rented flat or the flat she believed was occupied by him.

Staring at Tom, she smiled. If she got this wrong, she inwardly thought, then I'm giving up on men for good and scribbled her address on a sheet of paper.


Now returned home to his large, detached house in the fashionable Westfield Road area of Birmingham, James Hardie reflected on that mornings Board meeting. He was more than pleased the meeting had gone well, so well in fact that Jackson Peters himself had acquiesced to James's original decision not to involve the police. Yes, he smirked, old Jackson had even agreed they continue with the decision he had made. The old sod couldn't know he was playing right into James's hands. He now had five of the seven Directors onside who were prepared to support him if it came to a boardroom fight. As for they other two wimps, he smiled as he recalled embarrassing Frank Kennedy and that tub he called a boat, they would not stand against him in the face of such overwhelming odds;

not if they wished to remain as Directors and with the commensurate salary it provided.

He could hear his wife and daughters in the lounge; oh for peace, perfect peace, he sighed and then wondered what Lesley was up to. Jackson had gone home, of that he was certain and he guessed that Lesley was not a woman to spend her Saturdays sitting at home with her aging husband.

Reaching for his mobile phone, he smiled.

The GMP CID officers who had attended the call to Chrystons store in Quay Street had the suspect chicken pie conveyed to their headquarters and being Saturday and with no staff in the laboratory, the duty Forensic scientist was called out.

Grumbling that he had just three holes left in his match, the scientist had little option but to travel to the Headquarters at Central Park, on Northampton Road where still grumbling, he snapped on plastic gloves and stared curiously at the pie that now lay on a metal examination tray on his workbench.

"What exactly am I looking for here?" he asked the stony-faced detective.

"Fuck knows, Jim, but here's a copy of the letter that started the whole bloody thing."

Jim took the sheet of paper in his gloved hand and reading it, turned to the detective and said, "This is a joke, right? Some kind of hoax?"

The detective stared keenly at him and said, "That's why you're paid the big bucks, Jim. Have a bite of that pie there and if you fall down dead, we'll know it's a genuine threat."

"Yeah, very funny," he sighed and added, "Right, give me an hour and I'll have something for you."

"An hour? Will it take that long?"

Jim snorted and replied, "If I'm here less than an hour, my call-out rate drops so yes, it *will* take an hour."

He heard the door open and his wife and daughters quietly come in. Sitting in the lounge watching the horse racing, three empty cans and two full cans of lager on the floor and another almost full that was held in his hand, Martin Turner had never been interested in gambling, but nevertheless liked watching the racing.

"Annemarie!" he loudly barked.

She hadn't time to even take off her coat and sighing, forced a smile as she pushed open the lounge door.

"Martin?" she brightly replied.

"Where did you go you with the kids," he asked, his attention taken by the final

furlong on the television.

"In town, shopping for your dinner."

"What are you making me?"

"Chicken pie. The kind you like; a nice one I got you from Chrystons."

"Chrystons? What the hell are you spending money in there for? What else did you buy there?" he turned angrily towards her. "Have you any idea what shopping costs these days?"

Like you do, she thought, but instead replied, "I only bought your dinner and a sweet for the girls," she mumbled, anxious lest he would demand a look at the receipt.

"Yeah, well, I was thinking of having a curry before I went out tonight."

She was about to protest, but thought better of it. It didn't do to argue with Martin when he had been drinking...or at any time, she gently massaged her eye.

She felt deflated and was about to close the door when he called out, "Okay, I'll have the chicken pie. Make it now because I need to get myself ready if I'm going out," then added, "and keep those bloody kids quiet! I'm trying to watch the TV here!"

In the hallway, her daughters stared fearfully at her, but she smiled and told them to go upstairs and play their games and she would be up soon.

Then with a relieved smile playing upon her lips, she hurried into the kitchen to warm up the oven.


By late afternoon, the police were no further forward in identifying the young woman found murdered in Cawder Woods.

Murdered, for the post mortem examination carried out by Doctor Watson had definitely concluded the victim was strangled. The head wound observed by Watson at the locus was, as she correctly surmised, superficial and did not contribute to the victim's death. Watson was also able to inform the attending Senior Investigating Officer, DI Murray Fitzpatrick that the victim was not a virgin, though there was no indication she had been sexually active immediately prior to her death.

The only positive outcome of the PM, as far as Fitzpatrick was concerned, was a sample of what appeared to be a minute scraping of dried blood removed from under the victim's fingernail on her right hand. That and a phone call he received at the mortuary from the Forensic department confirming that the swab taken by the SOC at the locus was indeed skin cells that were removed from the victim's neck where she had been throttled; skin cells as Doctor Watson rightly concluded, that were undoubtedly from the hands that strangled her.

The fingernail sample, along with the victims clothing and other samples removed from the body, were in due course sent for examination to the Forensic Laboratory located at the Scottish Crime Campus in Gartcosh.

There being little else that the inquiry team could accomplish that evening, they were stood down for the night.

Citing a problem at work, Chrystons CEO Jackson Peters graciously declined an offer for he and his wife to attend dinner that evening at a close friend's house. Seated in the lounge in his favourite armchair, he told her of his decision.

"But darling," pouted Lesley, "staying at home on a Saturday night is so *boring*." Throwing her arms about his neck, she stared keenly at him and said, "Would you mind terribly if I went out? Perhaps to visit Jackie, maybe have a girls' night in? You know how down she's been since that bastard walked out on her."

"Of course not, my dear," he smiled at her. "You run along and have a nice time. Please give Jackie my regards."

Kissing him on the top of his head, Lesley made her way upstairs and in the privacy of her bedroom, sat at her dressing table while she scrolled down the directory of her mobile phone till she arrived at the number she sought.

"Jackie darling, it's me" she smiled at her reflection, delicately tapping a finger at her lips. "I need a *teeny* little favour; just in case later this evening you should receive a phone call from Jackson."

The GMP detective who conveyed the suspect chicken pie to the Forensic scientist interrupted his evening meal of meat sandwiches and returned to the laboratory in response to Jim's phone call. The scientist, wearing a white lab coat, gloves and seated on a high stool, pointed to the pie that now lay dissected before him on his workbench.

"I thought you said you'd be just an hour?" the detective asked.

"That's what I thought too, mate," replied Jim, chewing at his lower lip, "but to be honest, I half expected this to be a bloody hoax. Well," he sighed and held up a glass phial, "it most definitely isn't a hoax. This pie *is* contaminated and while I'm not one hundred percent certain exactly what the contaminate is, what I can tell you if my examination is correct is that it *is* bloody poisonous!"

"You're kidding," replied the startled detective.

"No, I'm not," he anxiously shook his head. "But let me also add that the toxicity of whatever this stuff is, according to the charts I have and the tests I completed, seem to indicate it is some sort of mineral based poison and I stress I'm guessing here, but possibly one of the toadstool fungus."

"Toadstool?"

"Yeah, toadstool as in mushroom. What I suggest is that if you can get it authorised I will have this specimen sent over to the Toxicology Department at the Royal Infirmary, but being Saturday they'll need to call someone out too."

"I'll have to see what the boss says about that," replied the detective and then added, "Doesn't the ingredients of the pie include mushroom?"

"Not according to the label," replied Jim with a shake of his head.

"Well, could it be a manufacturing fault? An ingredient mistakenly added at the factory or wherever these things are made?"

Jim pointed to the copy letter and added, "Let's not forget that, too."

"Yeah, of course, you're right. Okay, I'll get onto my boss and let him know. I'm guessing he'll want to inform Chrystons and the guys up in Glasgow about the threat," sighed the detective.

"One thing before you go," said Jim, handing the detective a sheet of paper. "Can you sign my work chit to confirm the hours I've been here?"

He liked to eat his dinner in front of the television and had kept a can of lager aside to have with his meal.

The door opened and Annemarie carefully carried in the tray, the aromatic smell of the chicken pie wafting through the door.

Setting the tray down onto his lap, unusually he muttered, "Thanks," but was distracted by the evening news reporting the discovery of a woman's body in the Cawder Woods in the north side of the city. The newscaster then passed the item to the female reporter on the scene who dressed in a warm anorak and wellington boots, continued the report. In the reporter's background, Martin could see the police blue and white tape that hung between the trees and a uniformed constable standing guard who deliberately ignored the TV cameras.

Backing off to the door, Annemarie held her breath till her chest hurt, wondering why the news item was so interesting for curiously, Martin normally attacked his food like a five-year-old. Yet still he intensely watched the news bulletin and it was only when the news item changed she saw him lift his cutlery.

Closing the door behind her, she began to nervously shiver.

Annemarie's sister, Joyce McKinnon, worried all the way home and by the time she was on the M74 on the final approach to Glasgow city boundary, she was no less worried.

What if the shopkeeper had ignored the letter and tossed it in the bin?

Jesus! How could I have been so stupid, she began to beat at the steering wheel with her hand as the salty tears flowed freely from her.

The dashboard clock told her she still had a couple of hours before she was due to meet with Sandy Munro, but how could she possibly go out to dinner feeling as she did?

She took a deep breath. Like it or not, she had to continue the ruse, to pray that the shopkeeper had contacted the police.

Dear God, just this once, let things work out in our favour; let Annemarie and girls have a chance at a normal life.

Please God, she silently prayed to a deity she had long forgotten, just this once!

The manager of the Chrystons store in Quay Street, Manchester was interviewed by a senior police detective from GMP who showed him a copy of the letter handed to a local shopkeeper. No, the manager assured the detective, he had no previous knowledge of any threat to his company.

While this was happening two detectives from Police Scotland were similarly interviewing the bewildered manager of the Argyle Street store in Glasgow, but again he had no knowledge of any threat. Though the e-mailed copy of the letter the detectives handed the manager stated that a second contaminated chicken pie was to be found in his store, a thorough check of the stock on sale or in the fridges in the storeroom failed to find any such chicken pie marked with an X.

At closing time, Ellen Turner left the securing of the store to the warehouseman and carried her bag of groceries to her car.

She decided to keep the meal plain and simple; a good old fashioned meal that she couldn't mess up and still found it bizarre that though she had known Tom but a few days, she was so keen to impress him. Gunning the engine, she pulled out into the traffic and began to make her way home.

Seated at the small table in the kitchen, Annemarie smiled humourlessly as her daughters wolfed down their fish fingers and chips, but she herself had no appetite and was satisfied with a cup of tea. Joyce had warned her that Martin would not immediately feel the effect of what she had given him, but it was likely that later in the evening and certainly within the next twenty-four house he would experience diarrhoea, nausea and perhaps even vomiting.

She was nervously tapping her fingers on the tabletop, but startled when he loudly called out, "Annemarie." Jumping up from her seat she saw the look of panic on Paula's face and shook her head. "It's nothing, love," she assured the wee girl and hurried through to the lounge.

"Here, take this, I'm finished," Martin told her and handed her the tray.

The plate was empty. He had eaten the full meal.

Turning towards the door she almost sighed with relief. It no longer mattered now what she felt for him she thought, for she had committed the capital crime.

She had murdered her husband.

# CHAPTER THIRTEEN

Within a few minutes of the agreed time, Tom McEwan arrived by taxi at Ellen's townhouse and paying off the driver, fetched the flowers and bottle of wine from the rear seat.

She answered the door dressed in a long flowery dress, her hair again pinned back and with a light cardigan over her shoulders. "Even after nearly three months, I'm still trying to come to terms with the central heating," she joked.

Accepting the flowers with a big smile, she invited Tom up the short flight of stairs to the lounge that was located on the first floor with windows overlooking the parking bays at the front of the house. In one corner of the room a small extending table was set for dinner.

"Kitchen and a bedroom on the ground floor, lounge, bedroom and bathroom here on the middle floor and two small rooms and a toilet and shower on the top floor," she explained and smiling at the enthusiasm in her voice, Tom realised how proud she was of her home.

"Lot of house for one person," he grinned.

"Well, yes, maybe; but it's also an investment for my future," she replied and left him to pour the wine while she tended to the meal.

"Can I help at all?" he called down the stairs.

"No, I figured you'd be on time so it's all ready," she called back and a minute later, appeared in the lounge with a tray. "Here we go," she laid a plate down in front of him. "I thought chicken pie, potatoes and veg would be okay with you?"

"Love chicken pie," he grinned at her and as they toasted each other across the table, his mobile phone rang.

He glanced at the screen and said, "I better take this, it's Gavin Blakestock."

"Gavin," he said, "I'll put you on speaker. I'm with Ellen," he bit at his lower lip trying not to laugh at her expression.

There was the slightest of pauses before Blakestock replied, "Ellen. How are you, my dear?"

"Fine, Gavin; thank you," she replied, narrowing her eyes and pretending annoyance at Tom.

"Tom? Sorry to interrupt whatever you and Ellen might be up to, chum," he said with a hint of amusement in his voice, "but I thought

I should call you. I have an extraordinarily important update I must share with you; with you both."

Martin Turner, showered and dressed, decided that after having drunk a few cans it just wasn't worth the risk taking the car into the town centre. Instead he instructed that Annemarie order him a taxi and getting into the minicab told the driver to take him to the Merchant City.

During the short trip he checked his wallet to ensure he had plenty of cash. The advantage of dealing with his income meant that he knew exactly what money he had to socialise at weekends. What he gave Annemarie to get by was, as far as he was concerned a necessity and after the household bills were settled, what remained was his for after all, wasn't he the one out grafting for it five days a week?

The minicab dropped him in Albion Street and licking his lips, he made his way to the Irish themed pub on the corner at Bell Street. Pushing open the door into the throng of patrons, he made his way to the bar and ordered his first drink. With a pint in his hand, he cast his eye about at the women, oblivious to the fact that the half dozen cans he had consumed in the house were taking their toll and he was already more than a little tipsy. Abruptly and quite unexpectedly, he loudly burped and giggled at his own surprise. An attractive woman in her late thirties stepped up to the bar beside him, her nose wrinkling at the noxious smell he had just breathed out. Turning towards her, Martin slurred, "Hi there, doll. Can I get you a drink?"

The woman peered at him and with disgust, shook her head and replied, "No thanks, pal. I'm with somebody," then beckoning over a barmaid, proceeded to give her drinks order to the young woman. Martin shrugged and turning away, stage whispered to a man standing nearby, "Must be a fucking lesbian," and grinned at his own humour.

The woman overheard the comment and pulling him around by the shoulder, demanded, "What did you just call me?"

"Never said a word, hen," he slurred again.

From out of the crowd, a heavy set, shaven headed man, his attention attracted by the woman grabbing at Martin, appeared swiftly beside them. Taller than Martin by a good six inches, the man grabbed him by the jacket lapel and bending down to be almost nose to nose with him, growled, "That's my missus. What did you say to her?"

"Called me a lesbian," sniffed the outraged woman.

The man turned to the woman and replied, "Did he?" and drew back a fist to punch the now terrified Martin, but fortunately it was just then that two stewards had seen the pending trouble and grabbing the burly man hustled him away while a third steward grabbed at Martin and said, "You've had enough, pal. You're out of here."

Leading the unresisting Martin by the arm, the steward half pulled him away from the bar through the amused crowd towards the door while the woman loudly called out, "You'd better not be out there, pal, when they let my man go!"

Tipsy or not, the frightened Martin took off as fast as his legs would carry him and stumbling along Bell Street into Candleriggs, experienced a sharp pain in his abdomen. Now bent over, grasping at the wall for support, a sudden wave of nausea hit him. Clutching at the pain in his guts and believing that the beer he consumed was taking its toll, he inadvertently careered solidly into a lamppost, bursting his nose that sprayed blood over his shirt and almost knocking himself silly. A group of young men walking past began to laugh and jeer at the drunken Martin as without warning, he violently vomited onto the street.

He thought he was choking to death and reached up for help, but the men stepped round both him and the puddle of vomit and ignoring him, continued on their way.

Two couples passing by hesitated at the sight of the bloodied drunk and as one of the women went forward to bend towards the stricken Martin, her partner pulled her by the arm and said, "If he's stupid enough to get into that state, hen, he deserves to look like a right idiot. Come away, let's go."

It was at that point Martin's body shuddered and he passed out.


The meal was temporarily forgotten as Gavin Blakestock recounted the latest information, telling Tom and Ellen that the managers of the Chrystons stores in both Birmingham and Glasgow, as well as the police from those cities, had contacted the duty commissionaire at Chrystons head office.

Blakestock related that complying with a previous instruction the commissionaire in turn relayed these calls through to the CEO Jackson Peters who had contacted Blakestock and requested he visit Peters at his home. Blakestock continued, "It seems that another letter was discovered by the Greater Manchester Police though I'm not yet certain yet how they came by the letter, but a copy was e-mailed by the GMP to Mister Peters, who requested I attend here and meet with him at his home. Reading it, I can tell you the letter refers to a contaminated chicken pie that thankfully was intercepted in a Chrystons store in Manchester city centre. The letter also indicated a second contaminated pie was placed in a city centre store in Glasgow, but the Glasgow police have intimated that after a search of the store, nothing was found. Of course it *might* be a diversion, some kind of cruel hoax regarding the Glasgow store, but the worst case scenario is that the pie has already been purchased by a customer."

"The pie that was recovered; is there any indication on this occasion what the contaminate is?" Tom asked.

"The contaminate is yet to be fully identified," Blakestock slowly replied, "but first indications from the GMP is that the contaminate *is* extremely toxic."

"Good God!" exclaimed Ellen. "Then that means…"

"Yes, my dear," Blakestock interrupted. "It means that *if* there was a pie in the Glasgow store then some poor bugger up in your area quite possibly has or is about to ingest a toxic substance contained in the pie."

"What is Peters saying to all this?" Tom asked.

"*Mister* Peters, who is through in the next room," Blakestock quietly warned, "is currently on the phone with a Mister Kennedy who I understand is his public relations Director authorising an immediate notification to the media to warn the public of the threat. Frankly, I'm pleased that without recourse to his Board he has taken the threat so seriously and actually told me that no matter what damage is done to the reputation of Chrystons, he will not have someone's death on his conscience." Blakestock allowed this comment to sink in and then added, "What he has requested of you, Tom, is that you liaise with the Police Scotland and with his authority identify yourself as the representative of Chrystons. You are to provide them with any relevant information that you might have and you are to fully cooperate with them. In essence, be totally transparent regarding the threat." Blakestock paused and then added, "Needless to say I suspect you might find them to be a little acerbic as they have not previously been informed of the threat, but I am sure you will be able to deal with that, young Tom. Might I also suggest you contact your source in the police intelligence community and bring him up to speed, if simply to warn him of the latest development."

Tom glanced at Ellen and eyes narrowed, asked, "Have you a printer here in the house?"

"Yes, in the room upstairs I use as a study," she nodded.

"Gavin," Tom said, "you have a copy of the second letter. Can you forward it to me too? It means I will have something I can bring with me and refer to when I speak with the local CID."

"Yes of course. As I told you Mister Peters was forwarded his copy by the GMP, so I'll forward it to your e-mail address, Tom."

"Thank you. You said the contaminate has not been identified yet. Is that ongoing?"

"Well, you'll appreciate we are getting the information third hand, but I understand the GMP Forensic people have concluded the contaminate is mushroom based and as we speak, the GMP are having a sample analysed at the Toxicology Department at one of their local hospitals. Mister Peters was promised a copy of the result as soon as the GMP have it. Again, when I receive a copy I'll e-mail it to you."

"So once more, Gavin, it's a waiting game," Tom bitterly complained. "We sit about waiting on some poor soul being admitted to hospital or worse from the effect of eating a contaminated chicken pie when this could have so easily been avoided if Chrystons…" he paused, "No, not Chrystons; that mouthy bugger James Hardie had immediately chose to alert the public to the threat."

"I understand your frustration, Tom," Blakestock replied, "but it's not quite as simple as that. We both know what the outcome would have been for the company and besides, it might simply have driven this Penthesilea underground to strike another time, perhaps at a different retailer or company. Remember our discussion," he added. "We both suspect that extorting Chrystons is merely the means for Penthesilea's second agenda, whatever that might be."

"You're right, of course," Tom sighed, "it's just that I feel so…so bloody helpless!"

"Well, perhaps at the moment," the older man commented, "but we are slowly building up a picture of this individual and with the police services now aware of the inquiry, we now have considerably more resources at our disposal. Anyway, there's not much more we can do at this time of the evening, Tom, so I suggest that unless anything else develops tonight, you and the lovely young Ellen enjoy the remainder of your evening. I'll get that e-mail sent right away but for now, goodnight to you both," he ended the call.

Tom slowly exhaled and almost as one, both he and Ellen lowered their glance at the cooled food and grimly smiling, she said,

"Perhaps I should phone for a takeaway, Tom. I'm no longer in the mood for chicken pie."

With Martin out of the house, Annemarie had access to the television and DVD player and cuddled together on the couch, watched one of the girls' favourite films. However, while the girls laughed and sang along to the film, Annemarie's thoughts were elsewhere. According to Joyce, Martin should feel no effect from the pie for anything between a few hours and twenty-four hours, but savagely thought it was far too long. She hoped he was already feeling the ache in his stomach and fervently hoped the bastard was suffering.

Glancing at the time on the wall clock, she guessed by now he would be well and truly pissed, perhaps even meeting with his latest girlfriend.

Not that she particularly minded Martin having a girlfriend. The more the mystery woman occupied him, the less Annemarie had to worry about when he got home.

She almost shuddered in disgust. His perversions were getting worse…and painful too.

"Are you okay, Mummy?" a worried looking Paula broke into her thoughts.

Gently stroking her daughter's hair, she smiled and replied, "I'm fine, darling. Honestly. And feeling better every minute that passes."

The senior of the two late shift detectives on duty at Stewart Street CID suite in Glasgow city centre phoned Mickey Farrell, the duty Detective Inspector, at home to inform him of the circumstances of the call they had received from the Greater Manchester Police.

"We attended at Chrystons down in Argyle Street, boss, and spoke with the manager there. He didn't have a clue about any threat, but I've been back onto the polis at Manchester, their Central Park office in the city centre. They told me they had got hold of a threatening letter that said there was a poisoned chicken pie in a store down there and one up here in the Argyle Street store. Anyway, cutting a long story short, we turned over the Argyle Street store, but there was nothing there. However, the GMP have got a poisoned pie and are taking the threat seriously and sent their sample of the pie to the…wait till I read this; oh, yeah, the Toxicology Department at one of their local hospitals. I also phoned Chrystons head office down in Birmingham and spoke with their duty commissionaire. I told him about our negative search then he gave me a phone number for one of their bosses, some guy called Peters and I phoned and had a word with him too. That's it, so far. How do you want us to proceed?"

"Do we have a copy of the letter?"

"Aye, I requested that the GMP send a copy up and it's in my e-mail file. I've read it through. It's typed and signed by some mob called Pent…Peth…Penti…Jimmy," he loudly called out, "how the *fuck* do you pronounce that name again?"

The detective called Jimmy grinned and taking the phone from his neighbour's hand, said, "Hi, boss, Jimmy here. It's pronounced Penthesilea. I looked it up in the Wikipedia and it's something to do with the Amazons."

"What, the company?"

"No," Jimmy grinned, "the women that used to fight with the ancient Greeks. The ones that supposedly cut off one of their tits to use their bow better, you know?"

"No, not really," replied the puzzled Farrell who wondered why this was relevant. "But first things first. Is there anything more we can do tonight?"

"No," Jimmy shook his head. "If there was a poisoned pie in the Argyle Street store, it's been sold, so we just need to wait till somebody arrives at a hospital throwing their guts up or complaining they've been poisoned."

"Right then, if there's nothing more we can do tonight, there's no sense in me leaving this curry I'm sitting in front of," sighed Farrell, "so unless something else occurs tell your neighbour to print off a copy of the threatening letter. When that's done leave a full explanatory note with the copy for the dayshift tomorrow and call me if anything else crops up."

Willie the detective might have been more than a little surprised if he had known at the time of his call to the Detective Inspector, two of his uniformed colleagues, patrolling on foot in the Candleriggs area of the Merchant City had happened upon the prone and unconscious Martin Turner.

Constable Victoria Fallon, Vicky to her family, friends and colleagues, puckered up her face as she approached the comatose Martin. "My God, he's in some state."

Her neighbour, Constable George Shaw waved a hand in front of his face and replied, "If we call the van to take this bugger back to Stewart Street, the Inspector will have a fit. He's not just puked, Vicky; I think he's shit himself too."

"Aye," she knelt down beside Martin and opening her mouth to avoid breathing through her nose, took off her cap and fanned it in front of her face. "You're right," she agreed. "He's had a bowl movement and pissed himself too. Must've been a hell of a night. His nose is burst too. A fight, you think?"

That's when Shaw noticed the blood staining on the lamppost and pointing at the staining, nodded and suggested instead, "No, probably bumped into this."

A group of rowdy students passing by began to jeer, but were suddenly silent when Shaw gesticulated to the prone man and loudly called out, "Any more noise from you lot and you're getting the jail and going into the van with him! So shut it!"

"Here we go, it's Stephanie Spielberg," Fallon, angrily shook her head and stared threateningly at two middle-aged and inebriated women, one who now had her phone out and was using the camera to record the officers. Though it nauseated her being so close to Martin, she sweetly smiled at the women and said, "Ladies, could you possibly just *fuck off* before I decide to give you the jail too?"

"Bloody cheek of her, forgets it us that pays her wages," sniffed the phone camera woman, but it did the trick for both turned away and noisily grumbling, walked off.

"George, I don't think this guy's just drunk," said Fallon with one hand on Martin's forehead. Her brow furrowed and fighting the nausea from the overpowering smell, added, "My God, he's burning up. I really think we should get an ambulance."

Ellen signed Tom McEwan onto her computer then stood back while he accessed his e-mail inbox. Selecting Gavin Blakestock's new message, he opened it and printed it off. Handing the printout to Ellen, Tom read the letter on the screen.

*To Jackson Peters,*
*The Chief Executive Officer of Chryston's.*
*You have failed to accede to our demand and now your company must face the consequence for ignoring our claim.*
*Two individual chicken pies sold by your company have been adulterated with a highly dangerous toxic substance.*
*The consumption of this substance will result in death.*
*We are not without soul or conscience and give you the opportunity to prevent these deaths.*
*The adulterated pies will be distributed today by our members in the Chrystons stores located in Quay Street, Manchester and Argyle Street, Glasgow.*
*Your failure to remove these adulterated pies will result in the death of Chrystons customers and you will be held accountable for these deaths.*
*Should you decide to inform the police of this letter, we will know.*
*If you again fail to accede to our demand, we will consider contacting the media and reserve the right to do so.*
*We will contact you again in seventy-two hours with a further demand.*
*Do not fail a second time.*
*We are Penthesilea.*

"Brief and to the point," sighed Ellen.
Tom's eyes narrowed as he read the letter a second time.
Ellen stared curiously at him. "What?"
"Something's just not right about this," he shook his head.
She glanced at the printout in her hand and again at Tom and said, "It seems pretty straightforward to me."
Tom turned to stare up at her. "What was it that Gavin said about the Manchester police again? They had come into possession of the letter, something like that?"
"Yes," she agreed, "something like that."

He poked a forefinger at the screen. "This bit here where it says *'Should you decide to inform the police of this letter, we will know.'* That to me suggests they *don't* want the police involved, yeah?"

"Yes," she slowly agreed.

"So, how did the police down there get a hold of the letter?" Turning to the computer he used the search engine to obtain the phone number of the GMP headquarters in Manchester.

"Why the headquarters?" Ellen asked.

"Gavin told us that the GMP Forensics people were examining the chicken pie. I realise that I'm guessing here, but I suspect the Forensics people work out of the HQ so it's likely that's where the city centre CID work from too," he grinned at her and added, "Keep your fingers crossed."

A moment later he was being transferred through to the CID suite and explaining who he was, switched his mobile phone to speaker and asked if he could speak with the detective who had dealt with the incident at Chrystons in Quay Street.

"That would be me," said the deep voice. "How do I know that you're not the press, Mister McEwan?"

Tom thought quickly and replied, "The labelling on the pie was marked with a large black X. You spoke with the commissionaire at Chrystons in Birmingham who transferred you to Jackson Peters, the CEO. The letter was signed Penthesilea. You sent a copy…"

"That's enough, Mister McEwan," interrupted the detective. "I'm satisfied you are who you say. Now, how can I help you?"

"Gavin Blakestock, my colleague down in Birmingham was uncertain how you guys came to be in possession of the letter."

"Well curiously enough the envelope was addressed to the police and it had immediately marked on it. Hand written, I might add. It was handed into a shopkeeper on Oxford Road here in Manchester. The beat man who attended the call tore open the envelope and we've sent it to our SOCO boys to try and lift some prints, but they're not too optimistic. Apparently the old gentleman it was handed to has his prints all over it."

"Any description of who gave him the envelope?"

"No, mate. Says it was a woman in a long coat, but she was in and out of his shop in seconds. She didn't say anything, just dropped the envelope on the counter and scarpered. I know the old duffer; he's run the shop for as long as I can remember. A decent man, but long in the tooth if you know what I mean."

"Does there happen to be CCTV in the shop? I mean, is it a large store?"

"No," the detective laughed. "It's a small newsagents and I don't know if there is a CCTV camera but these days, with the amount of bother in that area there just might be," he sighed. "Look, tell you what I'll do. The shop is open tomorrow and I'm on dayshift, so I'll pop round early doors and if there is a camera I'll see if I can get a photograph for you. If I do, give me your e-mail address and I'll send it to you."

Tom related his e-mail address then further requested that the detective photocopy the pies packaging and send a copy of that too. Then he asked, "Oxford Road. Is that a main road down there in the city?"

"Well, it *is* a busy old road; an arterial road that leads into the city centre so catches a fair amount of traffic. Why do you ask?"

"It just seems odd that the letter should be handed to an elderly shopkeeper. What's on the road near to the shop that might be considered a significant building?" asked Tom, not certain himself why he asked the question.

"Significant building? Not sure what I can tell you," the detective was puzzled then continued, "Round that area there are shops with flats above them, some houses, more shops," he paused and then said, "There used to be the BBC radio building close by, but that was demolished...let me see, about three, maybe four years ago. It's a building site nowadays."

"BBC radio," Tom slowly repeated, then thanking the detective, ended the call. Turning to Ellen, he tightly smiled. "I know I'm out on a limb here, but I think that letter was intended for the BBC radio building. Remember that the first letter threatened to send the second letter to the media?"

"Yes," she slowly drawled,

"I'm of the opinion that the second letter was meant to be delivered to the BBC radio station, but whoever the courier was, this woman probably, she didn't know the building had been knocked down. That to me suggests somebody who isn't local to Manchester; maybe the Glasgow connection again."

"You think this woman travelled down to Manchester from Glasgow to deliver the letter and what, plant the chicken pie in the Manchester store? Isn't that one heck of a journey?"

"Yes, it is," he nodded and then continued, "but it also suggests to me that if I'm correct, this woman is trying to give out a sort of smokescreen that Penthesilea is a group, a network if you like, rather than an individual. If I *am* correct, it means the chicken pie was likely purchased up here too. I can't imagine the woman risking adulterating the pie in the store or purchasing it then returning to the store. No, that would be too risky for her. Now, if we have the," he turned sheepishly towards her, "what do you call it again?"

"You mean the Codex Alimentarius. Ah," she smiled knowingly, "and that's why you want a copy of the packaging?"

"Yes. If we have the…" he grinned at her, "*details* of the packaging we might be able to trace the pie to the store where it was purchased and if we can do that…"

"Maybe we can obtain some CCTV footage," she finished for him and to his surprise, bent down and kissed him.

Standing upright, she patted the top of his head and eyes shining, smiled as she said, "That's for being a clever boy. Now, food; Indian or Chinese?"


The ambulance crew that arrived at the Candleriggs to collect the unconscious Martin Turner took one look and smell of him, then decided before they lifted him into the ambulance to attire themselves in plastic aprons and face masks. Lastly they laid a large plastic sheet across the stretcher bed.

"We're going to be *really* popular with the casualty staff when we bring this guy in," grinned one of the crew to Constable's Shaw and Fallon.

Fallon lost the toss and informed her control room that she was accompanying the unconscious man to the Royal Infirmary, then borrowing a spare facemask from the crew, climbed into the rear of the ambulance.

Grinning widely, Shaw waved her goodbye and continued on his beat.


The ambulance crew wheeled Martin Turner into a cubicle just as the Casualty Ward Sister arrived and snatched back the curtain, her face like thunder.

"What the *hell* have you brought into my ward this time?" she demanded, turning her head to one side and grimacing at the strong smell.

"The polis called us to the Candleriggs, Sister," shrugged the paramedic as he held on to Martin who though still unconscious, was groaning as he turned and twisted on the stretcher bed and attempting to bring his knees up to his chest. "The guy's stinking; shit and pissed himself and he's had a right bevy as well, but in fairness the cop was correct. He's got a temperature that's way beyond normal and seems to be in severe abdominal distress. I really think he should be seen by the doctor."

"Well," unhappy though she undoubtedly was by the stench from the patient the Sister gritted her teeth and replied, "Before we do anything we had better try to get him cleaned up a bit. What's his name?" then without waiting for a reply, loudly called for a nurse.

"Something Turner, I think. The cop who called it in is at the reception," the paramedic continued. "She searched him in the back of the ambulance and she has his wallet. She's booking him in with the Dragon Lady now."

Constable Vicky Fallon was sat in the reception area with the middle-aged receptionist Constance Meikle, known unofficially throughout the Central Division as the Dragon Lady due to her strong halitosis and her preference for heavy tar cigarettes and men in uniform; the younger the better.

Fallon had Martin's wallet open on her lap and was responding to a call on her radio.

"Aye," she read from a driver's licence, "tell the Sergeant the injured party is a Martin Turner, aged forty years and I have the address as 401 Glenhead Street over in the Possilpark area, I think it is. He has been drinking, but was unconscious and there was some cause for concern regarding his health."

She didn't add that it was she who had the cause for concern and listened as the controller informed her that the local division would send a cop to inform the next of kin about Martin being conveyed to the hospital.

"Now then," the Dragon Lady peered closely at Fallon, "tell me all about that *handsome* young man you work with?"

Sat in a cubicle in the dimly lit and very busy Ingram Wynd restaurant, Sandy Munro sighed and staring at Joyce McKinnon, said, "Maybe this wasn't such a good idea after all."

She startled and said, "I'm sorry, what was that?"

He smiled softly and replied, "You seem very distracted tonight, Joyce. I said maybe this dinner *wasn't* such a good idea."

"No, it's me who should be sorry," she smiled in return. "I have a lot on my mind."

Munro took a deep breath and asked, "Anything that you might care to share? To discuss?"

She stared at his handsome, concerned face and thought; how can I tell you that I orchestrated a terror campaign against a major UK retail company? How would I explain that everything I have done was for the love of my sister and my nieces? How could you possibly understand, you kind and thoughtful man?

Instead, she slowly replied, "I've never spoken about my family. My parents are both deceased and that leaves just me and my older sister, Annemarie and two nieces, Paula and Carol," she softly smiled. "Lovely wee girls that I adore. There are a couple of aunts still alive, but we're not in touch," she sighed. Then her face darkened as she continued, "Annemarie is married to Martin. He's a maths teacher in a secondary school over in Barmulloch somewhere."

She paused, fighting the anger, her hands clenched on her lap beneath the table.

"Martin hits Annemarie," she tightly said. "Hits her and terrorises the children. Gives her the minimum of money to keep house. Won't permit her a mobile phone, doesn't allow the children to travel in his precious *bloody* car! No," she shook her head, "regardless of the weather, Annemarie has to walk or bus them everywhere. Won't even allow my sister any money for personal items, you know, feminine things. She has to scrimp and scrape for those off the meagre housekeeping he gives her. But him? Oh, nothing is too good for Martin Turner," she snapped. "*He* always has money in *his* pocket for *his* nights out, getting drunk and chasing other women!"

Munro quickly glanced at the nearby tables, seeing that Joyce's rising voice had attracted more than a few curious stares.

"I'm sorry I asked. It must be very upsetting and painful for you."

"Nowhere near as painful as it is for Annemarie," she muttered, then shook her head, suddenly feeling deflated. "No, Sandy, it's me who should be sorry. I'm ruining your night. You've arranged this lovely dinner and here I am pouring out my problems…"

"A problem shared is a problem halved," he grinned at her then more seriously, asked, "Does your sister have the opportunity to leave? Take the kids and just go?"

"You think I haven't suggested that?" she snapped at him, then tightly closed her eyes and clenched her teeth, immediately regretting her outburst. "God, Sandy, I'm so sorry. Here you are trying to be helpful and I…" her eyes brimmed with tears.

He reached into a pocket and handed her a folded handkerchief. "Look, why don't you go and freshen up and I'll settle the bill. It's a nice night out; we can take a wee walk, maybe find a quiet pub. You got a taxi here, didn't you, so no reason why you can't have a glass of wine."

Not trusting herself to reply, she forced a smile and nodded before arising from the table and making her way downstairs to the ladies.

True to his word Tom McEwan didn't press his attention upon Ellen Toner, but instead decided that the way forward was to take things slowly, for Ellen was a woman he definitely wanted to get to know a whole lot better.

Her store was closed on Sundays and much as he wished to spend time with her the following morning he begged off seeing her, explaining that with the new developments in the inquiry it was more than likely that all morning he would be involved either meeting or liaising with the police.

However, aware that he was to attend Monday mornings Board meeting at Chrystons, Ellen suggested he drive to her house in the afternoon for a late lunch, park his car there and she would then drive him to Glasgow Airport.

With a smile, he agreed.

Arriving home, he switched on his desktop computer and slowly exhaled with satisfaction. The Manchester detective was true to his word and had forwarded a Photostat copy of the chicken pies packaging. Printing off a copy for himself, Tom then forwarded the e-mail with an explanatory note to Gavin Blakestock. His copy he would give to Ellen, tomorrow and by the time he attended the

Board meeting, she would be at work and hopefully have phoned him with details of where the pie was purchased.

Pouring himself a finger of Glenfiddich, he settled into an armchair and reflected on his evening with Ellen. He sensed when he arrived she had been a little nervous, but she had quickly settled down and the night had gone well; the ruined dinner aside, he smiled.

Joyce had firmly instructed there was to be no phone calls between them; at least not for a few days, but if ever Annemarie needed to hear her sisters reassuring voice, it was now.

She startled when the doorbell rang and almost fainted with shock when she opened the door and in the light from the porch lamp, saw the stoutly built policewoman stood there.

"Missus Turner?" the middle-aged and world-weary Sergeant asked, wisps of grey hair escaping from beneath her cap, her eyes betraying her concern at Annemarie's bruised eye that was now a rainbow of vivid colour.

"Yes?"

"Does a Martin Turner reside here?"

"Yes, Martin is my husband."

"Oh, is he," the Sergeant dryly replied, then added, "We've had information, Missus Turner, that earlier this evening your husband was admitted unconscious to the Royal Infirmary. I'm sorry, but I've nothing further as to what happened to him or what his condition is, but I can give you the phone number if like," the Sergeant added, then she angrily pointed to Annemarie's face and almost with a growl, asked, "Did he do that to you, hen?"

Taken aback, Annemarie unconsciously reached up and stroking at her eye, gulped as she nodded.

Tight-lipped, the Sergeant reached into a pouch on her utility belt and handed Annemarie a business card. "That's me, Missus Turner. If you need somebody to speak with, I'm at the end of a phone and don't worry, it *will* be in total confidence."

Taking the card back from Annemarie's hand, the Sergeant lifted a pen from the pocket of her stab proof vest and wrote the hospital number on the rear of the business card before returning it to Annemarie.

"Thank you," she replied, her voice almost a whisper.

The sergeant was about to walk away, but stopped and turning back, asked, "Do you have transport to get to the hospital, hen?"

"I have two wee girls in bed sleeping, so I won't be going tonight. I'll just phone for now," and nodding to the BMW parked down the driveway, added, "and yes, I do have transport, thank you."

The Sergeant nodded and made her way down the path as Annemarie closed then locked the door.

Her stomach was churning and her legs shook so much she slowly settled down onto the second step of the stairs, her arms tightly wrapped about her.

So, he was in hospital.

It had begun.

## CHAPTER FOURTEEN

Sunday morning broke with low cloud cover over the City of Glasgow and with a fine, almost wispy drizzle falling.

Detective Sergeant Anne Leitch quietly departed the house in Neilston, leaving her husband still snoring, their youngest daughter cuddled in beside him and their oldest girl asleep in the adjoining room.

She was the first to arrive at the incident room and placed the half dozen local newspapers on a desk to be trawled through later by one of the analysts for any mention of the murder. While the kettle boiled, Leitch switched on all the HOLMES computers and listened to the tape recorder plugged into the hotline phone, but the machine counter indicated no messages. Finally, with her coffee she sat down at the office managers desk with a printout of the synopsis of incidents that had occurred in the division through the night.

There was nothing among the incidents that seemed to indicate anything remotely connected to the murder nor any reference to a report of a missing female.

The murder team staff began to arrive between eight and nine, most immediately making their way to the tea and coffee table. Punctually at nine o'clock, DI Murray Fitzpatrick arrived in the incident room. Striding through his staff without greeting anyone, he crooked a finger to beckon Leitch into his office.

Taking off his coat, he hung it on a hook before settling himself behind his desk and addressing Leitch who stood by the door, said, "Is there any news about the murder, Sergeant?"

"Good morning, sir," Leitch replied, but the courtesy was lost on Fitzpatrick as she laid the synopsis on his desk for his perusal. "No, sir, no update about the murder."

"Assemble the team. I will brief them as to their duties in ten minutes. I don't wish to be disturbed till then," he curtly dismissed her with a wave of his hand and picked up the synopsis.

"Yes, sir," she sighed and closing the door behind her, passed the word round the disgruntled detectives and civilian staff.

Leitch had barely reached her desk when the phone rang and identifying herself was surprised to find the caller was DCI Lynn Massey.

"Morning, Anne. How are you today?"

"Fine, Ma'am, thank you. How can I help?"

"What time is the DI having his briefing?"

"Just under ten minutes."

"Right," Massey slowly drawled. "No word yet as to who the dead girl is?"

"Nothing yet, but the DI was speaking about a media appeal today."

"What about the DNA that was taken from her. Nothing there?"

"There's been no response from the Lab yet, Ma'am. It might be that they're waiting to send their report of the girl's DNA together with the report about the material found under her nails and the skin cells."

"Yes, possibly," Massey paused, then continued, "Look, I tried the DI's phone, but he wasn't at his desk," said Massey.

Leitch didn't admit that likely the bastard just refused to answer the phone.

"Here's what I'd like *you* to do, Anne. It's imperative we get this girl identified so I'll phone the Lab and set a fire under their backside. We can worry about the report for the material under the girl's nail, later. In the meantime, please arrange for someone to hotfoot it out to Gartcosh right now and fetch the report about the girl's DNA. I'll ensure it's ready and waiting. Oh, and when you see Mister Fitzpatrick, you can explain I tried to contact him, but get the courier off before you do that."

"Yes, Ma'am, no problem," Leitch slowly replied, her eyes narrowing as she glanced at the closed door where Fitzpatrick most assuredly sat behind his desk.

As she returned the phone to its cradle, she wondered why Massey would entrust her with that task rather than going through the DI? And why get the courier off to Gartcosh *before* she was to inform Fitzpatrick of Massey's call?

Still puzzled, she glanced up and called a detective to her.

Wearing a dressing robe and huddled over his desktop computer, Tom McEwan's first phone call that morning was to Gavin Blakestock and together, while Tom munched on toast and sipped at his coffee, they discussed the events of the previous day.

"So, you think that the woman who handed the letter into the shop might be our suspect, Tom?"

"Every likelihood, Gavin. When the GMP detective starts duty today, he's promised he'll try and obtain a photograph, but only if the shop has a CCTV system. There's nothing in my e-mail yet, but I'll continue to monitor it."

Blakestock then confirmed receipt of the photocopy of the chicken pie packaging.

"If the Codex Alimentarius..." he stopped and remembering Tom's previous confusion, teasingly laughed as he continued. "I mean the little numbers of the packaging."

"I *know* what you mean," Tom smiled.

"Well, if as you suspect young Tom, the pie was purchased in Glasgow, that more or less confirms all our suspicions. It's a Scottish plot to undermine a successful English company!"

"Now you're just being racist," Tom laughed.

"Right, you *are* coming down for tomorrow's Board meeting?"

"Actually, I've just booked another night at the Premier Inn and a return flight. I'm departing on the late afternoon flight and should arrive in Birmingham about six-fifteen."

"I'll pick you up at the airport and we can have a chinwag on the way to your hotel," suggested Blakestock.

"That's kind of you," replied Tom.

"Yes, that and you can tell me all about your date with the charming Miss Toner."

Tom decided he liked Gavin Blakestock and thought that regardless of how the inquiry played out, he would maintain contact with the older man, both on a professional and a personal level.

His next phone call was to Danny McBride's home where the call was answered by McBride's wife, Brenda, herself a former civilian analyst for the police but now a fulltime housewife and mother to their baby son.

"Hello, Tom. Haven't seen you in a while. How are you?"

"Doing well, thanks Brenda. Is the man about?"

"He's in the shower. Shall I call him?"

"Eh, no. Would it be any problem if I was to call by and visit with him for an hour?"

"Of course not. Have you had breakfast?"

"Just toast and coffee."

"Well, every other Sunday is our fry-up day and today is it. We'll be eating in about an hour if you want to join us?"

"Yes, please," he happily grinned, but more about the expectation of one of Brenda's cooked breakfasts than meeting with her husband, "I'd like that."

Ending the call, he was about to check his e-mails one more time before heading for the shower, but stopped to turn on the radio and that's when he heard it.

The junior doctor stared down at Martin Turner and frowned. Washed clean the previous evening by two disapproving nurses and now dressed in a hospital gown, the patient had not regained consciousness but continued to moan throughout the night, continuing to expel more bodily fluids as he no longer had any control of both his bladder and his bowels. The duty consultant who initially examined Martin had been baffled and other than issuing an instruction that blood be taken for analysis, further instructed that the patient be given pain killing medication and be continually hydrated to compensate for the expulsion of his bodily fluid. Circumstances prevented the consultant from following up his diagnosis for he was then obliged to hurry off to deal with the multiple victims of a serious road accident before finishing his shift and was now off duty without again having had the opportunity to check up on Martin. Now completing his seventeenth hour on duty, the young doctor yawned and turned to the equally young nurse to tell her, "I really believe this man should be transferred to the Acute Receiving Ward. Whatever it is that's wrong with him and I confess, I don't have a bloody clue, at the rate his temperature continues to rise I expect his head to explode anytime soon."

The nurse stifled a laugh.

"Has his preliminary blood work been returned yet?" he asked her.

"Not to my knowledge, doctor. But you know what it's like. It was Saturday night so there will have been the minimum of staff on and there was a lot of patients came through the doors, particularly about the time of that big motorway traffic accident."

He nodded and yawning again, turned and walked off towards the rest room, hoping to catch forty winks and unaware that the young nurse stared adoringly after him.

"Perhaps if you concentrated more on your work, Nurse," the Sister had silently crept up on her, "we might get a little more done."

Lifting the chart from the bottom of the bed, the Sister frowned when she read the nightshift consultants decision to admit the patient for 'observation meantime'. It wasn't appendicitis, for the old scar on his abdomen indicated that had already been removed. Yet from the way the patient writhed and trembled it was most definitely something abdominal. A twisted gut, perhaps?

She raised an eyebrow. Like it or not, she was calling the dayshift consultant down and this time she needed the bloody man to make a decision. She couldn't afford to have a patient occupying a bed in casualty for too long.

"That's a woman at reception saying she's the patient's wife, Sister," said the young nurse at her elbow.

"Well," snapped the Sister, "either she is the patient's wife or she's not. What is it?"

The nurse gulped and blushing, nodded, "It is the patient's wife, Sister."

In the casualty staff rest room, the BBC (Scotland) news was about to end when the commentator repeated the bulletin that warned the public of a threat to Chrystons Supermarkets (PLC), that a chicken pie sold in the Glasgow Argyle Street store was possibly contaminated with a toxic substance and a photograph of which was displayed on the screen showing a similar chicken pie. The commentator reported that police advised any person who had purchased such a chicken pie contact them immediately, then referred to the phone number for Stewart Street office which scrolled across the bottom of the screen.

The junior doctor was suddenly fully awake and staring wide eyed at the television screen, almost jumped from the two chairs he had been sprawled across and startling two nurses, raced to the internal phone on the wall by the door.

Clutching her daughter's hands, Annemarie was stood by the reception desk when the Sister arrived.

"Missus Turner, you're the wife of Martin Turner?"

"Yes," she nervously replied, conscious that the woman was staring at her bruised eye.

The Sister forced a smile. "Perhaps you might like to come with me to the relatives' room. We can speak privately there."

In the ward, the junior doctor waited impatiently for the consultant who used to the histrionics of his junior colleagues, deliberately took his time travelling down to the casualty ward.

In the relatives' room, the world weary Sister smiled at the two small girls and instinctively thought of Annemarie as a woman who seemed cowed and downtrodden.

"Your husband was brought in yesterday evening, Missus Turner. From his notes I understand he was discovered unconscious in the Merchant City area. He has not as yet regained consciousness and to be frank, we do not know what is wrong with him. I must ask you, is there any likelihood your husband might have consumed or partaken in drugs or is he on some sort of prescribed medication?"

"No, he doesn't take any medicines and as for taking drugs…"

Annemarie hesitated for really, she had no idea what Martin got up to when he went out. Glancing down at her daughters, she took a deep breath and replied, "No, I don't know if he would take anything like that. I do know that he does drink a lot of alcohol at the weekends," and any other time he can she thought, but didn't admit to it.

"Well, if you wait here for a few minutes, Missus Turner, I'll try to contact the duty consultant and I'll find out if he is available to speak with you," the Sister got to her feet and thinking to herself, but only if the lazy, arrogant sod can get off his arse.

However, unknown to the Sister, the consultant actually had arrived at the ward and now stood with the junior doctor, listened to him recounting the news item.

"I do believe you're going off at a tangent, my dear chap. Poisoned? Have you any idea how ridiculous that sounds?"

Behind him, the Sister quietly approached.

"I mean," he continued, "how the *devil* would we go about trying to establish what he ate last night unless we ask *him*," he almost guffawed, pointing at the unconscious patient.

"Or perhaps you could just ask his wife. She's in the relatives' room," hissed the Sister.

DI Murray Fitzpatrick was about to commence his briefing for that day when Anne Leitch asked if she could have a quiet word in his office.

Clearly annoyed at the disruption to his briefing, he waved for him to follow her and turning, said, "Yes, Sergeant, what is it that's so important you believe you need to interrupt me?"

Explaining that DCI Massey had earlier tried to contact him, Leitch related the circumstances of Massey's call and ended with her telling him of sending one of the team to collect the DNA report from Gartcosh.

"And you are telling me *now* when you knew fine well I was *at* my desk?" he angrily barked at her.

"Well, you were at your desk when she phoned you…sir. And, if you remember, you instructed you did not wish to be disturbed…sir," she pointedly reminded him.

"Well, that delays the briefing for we have little option but to await the arrival of this report," he angrily hissed at her.

It was the annoyance on his face that made her realise why Massey had bypassed him.

As the SIO, Fitzpatrick should have realised that identifying the girl was of vital importance and insisted the DNA report be treated with the utmost urgency, not simply waited for both reports to be returned together.

Fighting to keep her face straight, Leitch turned and left his office. She inwardly grinned at the thought that Fitzpatrick realised as she also now did that he had *really* fucked up.

The question now was, who would he vent his anger upon?

Detective Inspector Mickey Farrell had plans for Sunday; plans that included picking up his girlfriend Diana, a police station assistant who like him was off duty that day; driving her to Callendar, parking the car, hiking up one of the hills for an hour or so to work up an appetite then returning to the village and having lunch at one of the pub restaurants on the Main Street, then back to his flat for some romance.

Well, that was the plan, but then his mobile phone rang and his heart sank.

"Boss, it's Willie McGuigan at the office. Am I disturbing you?"

"You've phoned me, Willie. Of course you're bloody disturbing me," he growled. "What's up?"

"The late shift left a note about a poisoned chicken pie and that they had phoned you, boss. So, I'm calling to update you about what's happened."

"And that is?" sighed Farrell, guessing his day out with Diana was now cancelled.

"It seems that there was a guy, eh…" McGuigan searched for the name in his notebook, "Martin Turner, aged forty, was admitted to the Royal last night. At first it was thought by the cops that found him…"

"Found him?"

"Aye, apparently young Vicky Fallon and her neighbour, eh…oh aye, George Shaw; they found him lying unconscious in his own vomit down in the Candleriggs; he had shit and pissed himself too and they thought he was just steaming drunk."

"Sounds lovely," interjected Farrell.

"Aye," McGuigan sniggered. "Anyway, when they examined him they realised he wasn't well or something and got him taken to the Royal, but the doctors didn't know at first what was wrong with him. He was detained overnight then sometime this morning though I'm not sure how they worked it out, but it seems they now know he was poisoned by the chicken pie that was sold down in Chrystons down in Argyle Street."

"How did you find this out, Willie?"

"The staff at the Royal phoned the control room. I'm here in the office dealing with the overnight crime reports, but my neighbour Kenny Ross is down at the casualty now. He phoned me."

"This guy, Turner. Is he likely to prove fatal?"

"Uncertain, Boss, though apparently he is still unconscious. I phoned the GMP dayshift in Manchester and they are still waiting on the result of what the poison is. They sent the stuff to the…"

"Yeah, I know. Some hospital down there. Jimmy told me last night."

"Aye, well the guy I spoke with in the GMP told me they don't have a result as yet what type the poison is, but the doctors down at the Royal are sending a specimen to their own Toxicology Department, so we might get a result from them. They're not certain what specific treatment to give Turner because like I said, they don't now yet what the poison is. Kenny told me all they can do meantime is hydrate him and give him painkillers."

"Turner; has he a family?"

"Kenny spoke briefly with Turner's wife at the hospital, but she had her children with her so he didn't get much from her other than to confirm that she served her man the chicken pie last night for his dinner. She's away home and accompanied by a police woman. Kenny stayed on at the Royal to get statements from the staff just in case Turner snuffs it."

"Is the wife a suspect?"

There was a definite pause before McGuigan answered and Farrell did not miss the sharp intake of breath. "Kenny doesn't *think* so, but he did say that she's sporting one hell of a sore eye. It seems her man probably used her as a punch bag. Anyway, he's told the cop that's with her to keep her eye on Missus Turner till we get there."

"Right," Farrell wheezed, "I'll get dressed and be in to the office in about twenty minutes or so. Tell Kenny to stay at the Royal and update us regarding Turner's condition. I'll pick you up and we'll visit Missus Turner."

"One thing before you go, boss. The BBC news broadcast an alert this morning and it's on the radio as well about the possibility of someone buying the chicken pie and warning the public to contact us if they bought the pie. Anyway, someone down at the Royal must have contacted the media because Kenny told me the reception has been fielding calls all morning about Martin Turner."

"Shit, exactly what we need," growled Farrell. Ending the call, he sighed and then scrolled down the directory for Diana's phone number. Maybe if he offered to take her to dinner tonight, it might lessen the disappointment; his more than hers, he sighed.

James Hardie glanced at the digital clock on the bedside table. He liked his Sunday morning long lie and wondered who the hell was disturbing him.
Reaching for the mobile phone, he could hear his wife and daughters laughing downstairs and gritting his teeth, longed for the day he could be rid of the three of them.
"Hello," he snapped at the caller.
"Good morning, James, I hope I haven't disturbed you?" Jackson Peters soothingly asked.
"Not at all, Jackson, I was just getting out of the shower," Hardie lied as he swung his legs from the bed and stood up. "What can I do for you?"
"Oh, bad news I'm afraid. I have just had a phone call from the police in Manchester. It seems they in turn were contacted by the Glasgow police, the CID, who informed them that a man has been admitted to a Glasgow hospital suffering from the effects of consuming one of our chicken pies. According to the detective I spoke with, his information was that the pie had been purchased in our Argyle Street store in the city centre of Glasgow. I believe we must assume that the pie was poisoned."
An icy chill run down Hardie's spine.
"Is the man…dead?"
"Apparently no, he isn't, but though the detective has no information as to the mans current condition, I intend contacting our Mister McEwan in Glasgow and have him make some local inquiry. I will of course keep you apprised of what I learn. Again, so sorry to have disturbed you with this awful news."
As he finished the call, Jackson Peters could not but smile at the misfortune about to descend upon the head of James Hardie.

Annemarie offered to make the young policewoman a cup of tea or coffee, but she declined.
It never occurred to Annemarie that being aware her husband had been poisoned, the police officer was simply being cautious and wary of accepting *anything* from Missus Turner.
In the kitchen, she took a deep breath and forced herself to be calm.

He had looked so vulnerable and helpless, lying unconscious in the room with tubes in his arm and an oxygen mask strapped to his face. She boiled a kettle and prepared a coffee. Joyce had said the police would want to ask her all sorts of questions and told her stick to the truth as far as she could; it would be easier to remember.

Her glance took in the pies packaging she had removed from the recycle bin that was now sealed in a clear plastic bag the cop had handed her from a pouch on her belt. "It's important you place it in the bin then be seen to remove it from the bin," Joyce had said.

Her legs began to shake and she sat down onto a kitchen chair, silently praying that she must get through this; not for her own sake, but for her daughters' sake.

The two girls sat in the lounge facing the policewoman, their eyes wide. It was Carol the youngest who shyly asked, "What's your name, please?"

The young cop smiled and said, "My name's Julie. What's yours?" Their shyness overcome, the girls vied for Julie's attention with question after question.

In the kitchen, Annemarie could hear their excited chatter and for the first time that morning, smiled.


Tom McEwan had just settled into the dining chair and waiting expectantly for Brenda's cooked breakfast, briefed her husband Danny McBride on what had occurred since the last time they spoke. "This warning that's being broadcast. Who authorised that?" asked McBride.

"My contact down south told me it was the CEO, Jackson Peters, so I can only imagine that he's had a real scare and decided to play safe and," he shook his head, "not before time."

He frowned when the mobile phone in his pocket activated and not recognising the number on the screen was surprised to hear Jackson Peters voice.

"Mister McEwan, Gavin Blakestock provided me with your number. Are you free to speak?"

"Of course, Mister Peters," he replied, and raised a 'one minute' forefinger to Danny McBride. Rising from the table, he made his way into the hallway.

In a few, short but informative sentences, Peters related his phone call from the Greater Manchester Police and the admission of a man to a Glasgow hospital who was suspected of consuming a poisoned chicken pie.

Tom informed Peters that he had heard the warning being broadcast on the local radio, but he was unaware of the victim being admitted to hospital.

"I trust therefore that you will be able to make further inquiry and update me as you believe necessary, Mister McEwan?"

"Yes, sir, of course. On this number?"

Peters confirmed his phone number and ended the call.

Tom was thoughtful and pleased that Peters, unlike his fellow Director James Hardie, was confident in Tom's ability without requesting a blow by blow update.

Returning to the McBride's dining room, he said, "Sorry about that guys. That was Jackson Peters, the CEO of Chrystons. It seems that some guy has been admitted to the Royal here in Glasgow and is suspected of eating the poisoned chicken pie.

"How dreadful," said Benda. "Will he live?"

"I don't know," he shook his head. "Mister Peters information was a bit sketchy. However, once I've eaten I'll need to head down there and try to obtain some details. It seems that I'm to be the local representative for Chrystons so likely I'll call into Stewart Street and speak with the CID too. Danny," he turned to McBride, "your previous knowledge, what I told you; I mean it won't come back and bite you in the..." he stopped, but Brenda smiled and in a voice dripping with sarcasm, finished for him. "His arse, you mean? Don't worry about that, Tom. The way he's been knocking back the fry-ups and curries these days, there's plenty of arse to go round."

"Aye, very funny," her husband scowled and jokingly added, "It's not *that* when she's buying a new dress or wanting me to take her out to dinner, I can tell you. That's when I suddenly become the perfect husband. As far as Brenda is concerned, Tom," he nodded with a sigh towards his wife, "I'm just a walking wallet."

He ducked to avoid the teacloth that flew across the table and grinning, turned back to Tom and continued. "Anyway, regarding your information, I've sort of semi legitimised my inquiries on your behalf and likely with the issue being public now, I will be able to be more open with you about anything I learn."

Tom dabbed at his mouth with his napkin and taking a last mouthful of tea, pushed back his chair and stood up. "Brenda, as always, that was delicious."

Fetching his coat off the couch, he headed for the door, but not before adding, "The next time we eat, why don't you guys organise a babysitter and we can go out in a foursome? See you," then left before the stunned Brenda could get a question in.

Hearing the front door closed, she turned to her husband and eyebrows raised, said, "A foursome? *What* haven't you told me, McBride?"

He sighed and raising his hands as though barring further questioning, quite blatantly lied, "I have no idea what he's talking about."

The inquiry team lounged about in the incident room at Kirkintilloch police office, refused permission to leave by DI Fitzpatrick who sat morosely in his office awaiting the return of the detective dispatched to Gartcosh.

At last, the door opened to admit the harassed detective who strode across the room to deliver the sealed report to DS Anne Leitch.

The DI's door was torn open and Fitzpatrick sharply called out, "That will be for me, I believe!"

Staring at the young detective as though daring her to respond, the woman caught Leitch's subtle shake of the head and without comment, handed the envelope to the DI who beckoning Leitch into his office, closed the door behind her.

Without speaking or even looking at Leitch who remained standing, he sat down behind his desk and lifting a letter opener, deliberately took his time slicing open the envelope.

Fetching out the report, he read it over and then sighing, said, "It appears that while the deceased is not known to the DNA database, there is a familial identification; a male called Sean Younger, aged twenty-three who is assessed by the Laboratory to possibly be a sibling. The parental address is Cockmuir Street. Task two of the team…" he paused and peered at Leitch. "No, on second thoughts, Sergeant. *You* take one of the team and go yourself. Establish if our victim is related to this man Younger. I trust you do know what information I will require?"

"Yes, sir," she refrained from retorting like she *really* wanted to, but instead asked, "but what about the briefing?"

"I will attend to that," then handing her the report to file, dismissed her with a wave of his hand and added, "now please, just go!"

It was only when Leitch returned to her desk and quickly read through the report that she saw the Forensics also resulted the tests on the vomit discovered at the murder scene; disappointingly, they were unable to obtain any DNA from the sample they examined.

After collecting Willie McGuigan from Stewart Street police office, DI Mickey Farrell drove them in his own car to Glenhead Street to interview Martin Turner's wife.

The policewoman Julie was known to them and requesting that she continue to entertain the children in the front room, they sat on the two kitchen chairs in the kitchen while Annemarie stood with her back to the worktop.

It was obvious to both detectives that she was nervous, but mistakenly believed that her anxiety was concern for her husbands wellbeing.

"Couldn't half murder a cup of tea," smiled Farrell in an attempt to put the edgy woman at ease. Smiling tensely, she turned to fill the kettle at the sink. Farrell caught McGuigan's attention and pointed to his own eye. Though he already knew the answer, he had to ask and said, "If you don't mind me saying, Missus Turner, that's some eye you've got on you there, hen. How did you come by that?"

Keep lies to the minimum, she remembered Joyce telling her; stick to the truth as much as possible.

Gently touching her face, she softly replied, "My husband. He punched me."

Farrell said nothing, but simply nodded. She could not know that the large, stocky built former rugby player detested men who hit women; in fact, detested bullies of all sorts. He took a deep breath and said, "I understand that you bought the chicken pie that you served your husband for his dinner last night. Is that correct?"

"Yes," she nodded, "I bought the pie and the veg in Chrystons. The potatoes came from the Coop. I served him the pie, potatoes and the veg with gravy as well. The police lady next door, she said I had to keep the wrapping from the pie," she leaned across McGuigan and lifted the bag containing the wrapper that she handed to Farrell. "This is it here. I had put it in the recycle, but…" she tailed off. Farrell glanced at the wrapper, seeing the black X marked upon it and pointing, asked, "Did you do this to the packaging, Missus Turner?"

"No, of course not," she shook her head, her throat tightening.

"Did you notice this when you bought it?"

"No, I can't say I did," she hesitantly answered and swallowed with difficulty, inwardly cursing her forgetfulness, for the black marker pen lay in the kitchen drawer not more than an arms length from the detective. Why oh why didn't I get rid of the bloody pen!

Farrell stared at the X and sighed, guessing there wouldn't be much evidence that the Forensics would be able to obtain from the wrapping. If the individual who drew the X was as clever as he believed, they would have worn gloves. The only fingerprints would likely be those of Missus Turner. Still, they would need to take hers for elimination purpose.

His eyes narrowed as he stared at the anxious woman who was carefully pouring the boiling water into the teapot. It was natural she worried about her husband though when he glanced again at her wounded face it escaped him why any woman would put up with a bastard that beat her.

McGuigan's mobile phone chirruped, disturbing Farrell's thoughts. Rising from his seat, McGuigan moved into the hallway to take the call.

"Missus Turner," Farrell smiled, "that's two pretty wee girls you have there. How old are they?"

He watched as first she seemed confused by the questions as though it might be some sort of trick, then Annemarie visibly relaxed and placing two mugs of tea onto the table, sat down in the chair vacated by McGuigan.

"Paula the oldest, she's ten and Carol's eight," she returned his smile. "Do you have children, Mister Farrell?"

"No," he shook his head. "My wife and I weren't blessed."

"Well, you don't seem that old. Maybe there's still time."

He continued to smile, not wishing to embarrass her by admitting he had been a widower for several years, albeit recently now had a new girlfriend.

The door opened and McGuigan, his eyebrows raised, simply said, "Boss."

"Excuse me," Farrell rose from the table and followed the DC into the hallway, pulling the door closed behind him.

"That was Kenny Ross on the phone. He's back at Stewart Street and has taken a phone call from the GMP in Manchester. It seems that the sample they sent to the Toxicology Department at hospital down there has been identified. He has all the details and I can't pronounce the proper name, but Kenny says it's known as Death Cap. It's a highly poisonous mushroom."

"Are the Royal Infirmary doctors aware?"

"Aye," McGuigan nodded. "Kenny phoned them before he called me. He says that Turners condition has slightly worsened and from being unconscious, the doctors have now placed him in an induced coma."

"So," Farrell thoughtfully nodded, "for the minute we're dealing with an *attempted* murder, but if Turner proves fatal…"

"It's murder," nodded McGuigan.

## CHAPTER FIFTEEN

DS Anne Leitch and her neighbour, DC Bob Stevenson, a quiet spoken and well mannered man in his late forties and known throughout the divisional CID as Jumbo because of his outstanding 'elephant' memory, arrived at the ground floor flat in Cockmuir Street. The only indication they were at the correct flat was the name scrawled in felt tip pen upon the chipped and battered door. After banging her fist against the door, Leitch nodded at the damage to the locks, a clear indication they were not the first officers to call upon the Younger family.

The door was opened by a tall, lanky youth with long greasy hair and wearing a football top that declared his loyalty to Rangers FC.

Glaring at the officers, he said, "What the fuck you lot want now?"

Leitch took a deep breath, realising almost immediately that was a mistake if the smell from inside the house was anything to go by.

"I'm looking for Mister or Missus Younger. Which one are you?"

The sarcasm was lost on the youth who shouted, "Ma, it's the polis," then closed the door.

Leitch glanced at Stevenson who grinned and shook his head.

The door was then snatched open by a second, older youth who scowling, asked, "What do you want?"

"What I want is to come in and speak to an adult," hissed Leitch and without waiting any further, pushed against the door, knocking the youth backwards.

"Here, you can't just…" was all the youth managed before Stevenson, using his body, forced the youth against the wall and staring into his eyes, said, "We're the CID, but maybe you guessed that so play nice or me and you will fall out, sonny."

The youth gulped and shouted, "Ma! Get your arse out of your bed! The polis is in the house!"

Leitch turned and stared with beady eyes along the dark and narrow hallway at the sound of a toilet flushing and guessed the first youth was disposing of some drug or other, but wisely decided that for the time being was a second issue.

A bedroom door opened and a woman, gaunt in appearance and wearing a faded and stained dressing gown, peered at her son and the two officers.

"What is it?" she slurred. "What the fuck do you want at this time of the morning?"

Leitch was tempted to tell her what time of the day it really was, but held her tongue and instead asked, "Are you Missus Younger?"

"Aye, Patsy Younger. What of it?"

"Is there somewhere we can speak privately?"

Patsy tried to focus, then shook her head as though to clear it and turning, waved a hand for Leitch and Stevenson to follow her.

"I'm coming too," snapped the youth, who added, "I'm her son, Sean."

The detectives realised that Sean was the familial match for the deceased who ironically was about to be identified because of Sean's drug and assault convictions.

With Sean Younger tripping behind them, the detectives followed Patsy into the lounge and Leitch's first thought was, how the hell can people live like this.

The cheap, flimsy curtains were still closed though the overhead light was switched on, giving the room a claustrophobic feel. The humid stench of unwashed bodies, stale alcohol, cigarette smoke and other undefined smells almost turned Leitch's stomach and not for the first time wished she had dabbed some perfumed hand cream under her nose before entering the flat.

"Sit down if you want," Patsy invited the officers as she herself slumped down onto the couch.

That's when Stevenson noticed the school photograph in the plastic frame and catching Leitch's eye, nodded towards the flimsy ledge above the two bar electric fire.

Leitch strode across the room and lifted the five by seven inch photograph that showed a young girl aged about fourteen, her blonde hair hanging unbound about her shoulders and staring with a broad smile at the camera.

"Missus Younger, who is this girl?" Leitch quietly asked.

"What the *fuck* do you want to know for," Sean demanded, his hands curling into fists.

Stevenson took a step towards him, but Leitch raised a hand and holding the photograph towards Patsy, again asked, "Missus Younger. Please. Who is this girl?"

Her hands shaking, Patsy was trying to light what remained of a crushed cigarette and peering at the photograph, almost with indifference, replied, "That's Colleen, my daughter. Why, what the fuck has she done now? Is she arrested? Is that why you're here?"

Against her better judgement, Leitch decided to risk sitting on the stained couch, immediately conscious of the body odour given off by the older woman. With a brief glance at Stevenson, she said, "Missus Younger. Patsy. I'm very sorry to have to break the news, but it's my sad duty to inform you that this girl, your daughter Colleen. She's dead. Colleen was found murdered yesterday morning."

"What the fuck...murdered? No! Who the..." snapped Sean and shaking his head, took a step towards Leitch, but was suddenly confronted by Stevenson who to his credit did not react confrontationally, but instead raised his hands disarmingly to halt the younger man.

"We're not the enemy here, son" he softly said. "We're here to break the bad news and ask for your help," while firmly staring into Sean's eyes.

Sean gulped and stepped back, nodding as he slumped into a wooden chair.

The younger youth who upon their arrival had disappeared into the toilet and who they learned was William Younger, stepped into the lounge and stared sullenly at the officers before wordlessly sinking down and curling up on an armchair.

The next few minutes were taken up by Leitch noting in her book Coleen's personal details; her date of birth, school attended, when and who last saw her.

Sean volunteered she had last been seen by him on the Friday evening and described the clothes she had been wearing. His description of Colleen's bra raised Leitch's eyebrow, but she didn't respond for that was a comment she intended keeping to herself for the time being. Better to get what she could before quizzing about how he came to know that particular piece of information.

"Sean, when she left the house was she carrying any kind of bag, a handbag, maybe?"

"No, I didn't see her leave." He shook his head. "I don't think she ever carried a handbag, not that I remember anyway."

"What about a mobile phone? I don't know any young woman these days who doesn't carry one," she softly smiled.

Sean's brow furrowed. "Aye, she did have a phone, but she never had any credit on it; she was always asking me for a bung. I think…" his brow furrowed and raising a hand, added, "Wait a minute," before disappearing through the door. He returned a moment later with a mobile phone in his hand. Leitch took it from him as Sean told her, "It's nearly dead, just one bar of power left and the screens cracked too."

"I'll take it anyway," Leitch replied and slipping it into her handbag, retrieved a brown evidence label that she had Sean sign. "Chances are that our technical guys might get something from it."

"My wee girl, my poor wee lassie," Patsy continuously mumbled, shuddering as she rocked herself back and forth on the couch before turning to Sean and telling him, "Can you fetch me a smoke, son? There's some fags on top of the cabinet in my room."

Leitch considered that Patsy's trembles and shivers were not so much the shock of the bad news, but rather the need for either an immediate alcohol or drug injection.

When Sean returned with the fags, he lit one for both his mother and himself.

"Does anyone in the house drive or have the use of a vehicle?" she asked him.

"Only if we want to go joyriding," William sneered, then giggled.

"Shut the fuck up, you!" Sean snarled at him, taking a step forward, his fist raised as though to strike his younger brother. "This is serious, you stupid twat!"

Stood to one side, Bob Stevenson decided not to intervene if Sean did indeed clout the stupid younger brother. As far as he was concerned, the younger guy deserved a smack round the head.

Suddenly cooperative, Sean turned to Leitch and shaking his head, continued, "No, Missus. Nobody here has a motor."

"Who else lives in the house, Sean?"

"Just my Ma, me, Colleen and that *fucking* idiot," he nodded towards William. "Wee Chic's the youngest brother, but he's in Polmont for getting caught with half a bar of grass. It wasn't his first conviction for the dope so he's doing a six-month stretch. Been there, what…" he turned questioningly towards his mother, "six weeks now, Ma?"

"Charles? Aye, he's been in about that time, son."

Leitch made a note in her book and turning to Patsy said, "Do you know who Colleen's friends are, Patsy?"

"No, not really," she sniffed. "She kind of kept herself to herself, if you know what I mean. You know what young lassies are like these days, hen."

Leitch took Patsy's response to mean that not only did she *not* know what was going on in her daughter's life, she probably didn't give a shit either.

She looked questioningly towards Sean, but he shrugged and head drooping, also shook his head.

Tight-lipped she made a note in her book and turning to Sean, asked him, "Did Colleen have a boyfriend? Anybody special in her life? Somebody she might have mentioned."

He stared at Leitch with narrowed eyes before replying, "Not that she mentioned, no, but on Friday night before she went out," he unaccountably blushed, "I went into her room…I mean the room she and my Ma share; I was looking for fags. She was getting dressed. That's how I knew what she was wearing. She was getting herself all dolled up and I was kidding her on; you know, teasing her, that she was going out to meet somebody and to get her hole," he stopped and stared uncertainly at Leitch before adding, "What I mean is…"

"It's okay, Sean. I know what getting her hole means."

"Anyway, she got right angry and told me to fuck off out of the room. I didn't see her after that, but when I was in here watching the television I heard the door bang and that's how I knew she was away out."

Well, thought Leitch, that explains why he was able to describe the bra, but suspected that fags weren't the real reason he went into the room. What it did though was suggest that the dead girl was sexually active, confirming Sherlock's finding at the PM.

"So," her eyes narrowed, "Colleen didn't say she was meeting anyone?"

"No, but young as she is…was, I mean, Colleen's a looker…" his brow furrowed. "I mean, she was a looker."

Maybe it was Sean's use of the past tense, Leitch wasn't certain, but Patsy began to softly weep, using the sleeve of her dressing gown to wipe at her eyes and her running nose.

Leitch arose from the couch and formally said to Sean, "Again, I'm sorry to be the bearer of such bad news, however, it also falls upon me to request that a member of the family, presumably yourself Sean and your mother if she wishes," she turned towards Patsy before continuing, "attend at the mortuary to make a formal identification of your sister. I'll make the arrangements and if you can provide me with a contact phone number, I'll be in touch."

"Aye, no bother," he quietly replied, then fetched a mobile from his tracksuit pocket and related the number to Leitch.

She was about to turn to leave the room when Patsy sniffed and bleary-eyed, thoughtfully asked, "With her getting herself murdered, does that mean I can make a claim for criminal compensation?"

Stunned, Leitch could only stare wide-eyed at Patsy for a few seconds and almost in disbelief shook her head as she left the room.


It was when they were seated in the car outside the tenement building that Bob Stevenson, shaking his head and tightly gripped the steering wheel, angrily said, "I just don't get it, Anne. How the hell can people live like that? And as for that *bloody* woman. Calls herself a mother? Criminal compensation? Trying to make some money from her daughter's murder? Nearly twenty-seven years in the polis," he slowly exhaled through pursed lips, "and I'm still shocked at some of the people I meet. Dear God, why are women like that even allowed to have weans!"

Seated in the passenger seat, Leitch decided that to respond would only infuriate him further. She knew that Stevenson was a committed family man with teenage children, a regular attender at his local Baptist church and privately thought him to be a good man. Patiently she waited till he calmed down then said, "That comment, Jumbo; I mean, the description by the brother of the victim's bra," she sighed. "I have to admit…"

"That you thought her brother was maybe interfering with the wee lassie?"

"Aye, it did cross my mind," admitted Leitch.

"We'll never know," he shook his head, "but I don't think that lassie had an easy time of it, living in that house. The brother Sean; he looks like he's been around the block a couple of times and as for that younger brother. God forgive me, but that wee shite should have been drowned at birth." He slowly then added, "I know that I'm guessing, but when you look at that motley crew, that wee lassie Colleen; she's maybe found somebody she thought she could trust. Somebody that she thought might give her the affection that she should have got from her family."

"Aye," Leitch sorrowfully replied. "Somebody she thought she could trust who killed her."


The consultant charged with the poison case glanced at the printed e-mail that had been received at the Royal Infirmary. Turning towards his registrar, he said, "I have never been involved in any case where this…this," he peered though his bifocals at the sheet of paper, "Amanita Phalloides has been ingested by a patient. You?"

"No, never," the registrar shook his head.

"Hmmm. Well, if I deduce correctly from what our colleagues in the Toxicology Department tell us, Mister Turner here," he nodded down at the unconscious patient, "is in serious danger of liver and kidney damage and *that* only if he survives. According to the journals I've researched, the symptoms are initially gastrointestinal and appear pronounced within two to three days. However, according to his wife, from the time of consumption of the poisoned pie to his collapse, it seems our Mister Turner's condition deteriorated within a relatively short period after ingestion; some hours, in fact. Curious, wouldn't you agree?"

"Perhaps his consumption of a large quantity of alcohol accelerated the rate of deterioration? I mean, is it possible that the alcohol has exacerbated the condition; flushed the poison through to the liver and the kidneys that much faster than had he *not* been drinking?"

"Possible, but to be frank," the consultant shrugged, "I know so little about the condition that I would be guessing and that is not reassuring, is it?"

"No sir, it's not," agreed the registrar. "How do you wish to proceed?"

"For now, all we can do is keep the poor chap hydrated and continue the induced coma. Based on the recommendation of our esteemed colleagues in Toxicology and if as we are informed there *is* the likelihood of damage to the liver and the kidneys, it will do no harm to have him started on a regime of Silibinin. If nothing else, it can do no further damage." Returning the clipboard to the frame on the bottom of the bed, he shook his head but before turning to walk off, added, "Keep me apprised if his condition should change; no matter where I will be."

Driving to his flat to pack his overnight bag, Tom McEwan decided to take the time to phone and update his boss, Martin McCormick. "Sorry to call you at home on a Sunday, Martin, but I believe you should know what's happening so far."

"I saw the twenty-four-hour news bulletin on the TV. I take it the man admitted to the Royal Infirmary is a victim of this group you're hunting, Tom?"

"Apparently so. I've spoken with Danny McBride and he's agreed to stay onside should any information come through his intelligence department. I've also spoken with my counterpart down south, Gavin Blakestock and I'll be seeing him this evening to share what we know prior to tomorrow mornings Board meeting."

"That should prove interesting. I wouldn't mind being a fly on the wall at that meeting," mused McCormick.

"And," Tom continued, "I had a phone call this morning from no other than Chrystons CEO, Jackson Peters. He's instructed his media people to open up to the press, so there should be plenty of stories in tomorrows papers."

"Anything else?"

"I don't see any point in going to the Royal Infirmary; for one, we both know the staff won't give out information to anyone who is not a relative. However, once I've packed a bag, I'm heading into

Stewart Street to liaise with the CID there. They're the local office for the hospital and Chrystons in Argyle Street is on their patch, so I'm certain they'll have the inquiry. I have Mister Peters authorisation to present myself as the local representative for Chrystons. I'll introduce myself and tell them what I know and hope for an exchange of information. If I'm lucky, I'll get a sympathetic hearing; if not, I'll get flung out on my arse."

"One thing occurs to me, Tom. Regardless or not whether this man in the Royal dies, it's likely that Chrystons will be facing some form of litigation and as their local legal representative, it will probably fall to me to deal with any subsequent lawsuit. If you can, try and obtain the victims next of kin details. It would help tremendously if I was able to speak with the man's next of kin at the earliest opportunity and try to defuse the situation before some ambulance chaser gets there. Right, anything else for me?"

"That's pretty much it. I used my own Visa card to book my flights and overnight accommodation and I am flying down this evening. I'm catching the last shuttle and I'm booked into the Premier Inn again. Maybe you can give Martha a heads up so I don't catch flak from her when I get back," he grinned.

"I'm not telling her that," McCormick joked. "I'll send her an e-mail instead. The sod frightens me too, you know," then added, "Before you go, Tom. You previously mentioned that there might be a second agenda to this whole issue. Do you still feel that way?"

There was a distinct pause before Tom replied, "After I speak with Gavin Blakestock, I might have a better answer for you, Martin."


Annemarie stood at the front door, watching the detectives and the policewoman return to the car parked outside. Her arms were clutched around her and she shivered, though she was not cold. She watched the detective who questioned her, the man called Farrell, get into the driver's seat. She thought about his questions. He had been straightforward and brief and nothing he said had given her any cause to think he suspected she might have told him anything but the truth. No, he had been more sympathetic than suspicious and as she closed the door, she gently touched her eye. Ironic she thought, that by punching her Martin had unintentionally caused the police to see her as a victim, not as a suspect for his murder. Murder.

That's what it was if he died and she shivered again.

Following Joyce's instructions, she decided that it was time for her to again call the hospital for an update.

She had no sooner lifted the phone when the door was knocked and she almost dropped the receiver in fright.

Paula and Carol run excitedly from the lounge shouting in unison, "It's auntie Joyce, it's auntie Joyce," and run to pull open the front door.

She stood there dressed in a lemon coloured tracksuit, her dark hair pulled fiercely back into a ponytail and a plastic carrier bag in her hand.

Hugging her nieces to her, she glanced over the heads at her sister and Annemarie saw there were tears in her eyes.

"Right," she took a deep breath and sniffed as she reached into the plastic bag. "Who's for a bar of chocolate?"

The girls eagerly grabbed their bars and were busily unwrapping them when they were ushered back into the hallway by their mother, who then guided them into the lounge, telling them, "Switch the television on if you want."

Turning, her tears began to fall as she stared at Joyce who dismayed, hesitantly raised a hand to gently stroke at Annemarie's bruised eye before also bursting into tears and enfolding Annemarie into her arms.

Together, the two sisters hugged tightly as their tears dampened each others necks.


Ellen Toner decided to have a lazy morning and was sitting on her couch in her pyjamas with a coffee watching television and considering whether to put on a colours wash when the story broke about the poison victim.

Startled, she reached for the remote and wound the news item back to again catch the beginning. Housework was forgotten as her mind raced, her thoughts turning to Tom. By now he must be aware of what had happened, of that she was certain and began to feel a little miffed he hadn't contacted her. She thought about challenging him when he arrived as arranged later that afternoon, but then contradicted herself; Tom had far more to do than phone his girlfriend. She slowly shook her head, then smiled.

His girlfriend.

That's how she now thought of herself.

Almost on cue her mobile phone rang and lifting it from the side table, to her surprise saw on the screen the caller was Tom.

"I was just thinking about you," she grinned at the phone.

"Ellen, can't stay on for long," he briskly said. "I'm just about to walk into the police office in Stewart Street in the city centre here. Listen, there's been a development…"

"I know, I saw it on the television. The man admitted to the hospital."

"Yeah, that's right. Look, I'm just pushing through the doors here, so are we still on for later this afternoon?"

"Yes, I'm looking forward to it, so I'll see you then," she unconsciously nodded at the phone.

"Right, bye and I…" he stopped, aghast at what he almost blurted out.

On her side of the call, Ellen almost stopped breathing. Oh my God; was he about to say…no, she slowly exhaled and simply replied, "Bye."

She stared at the phone in her hand, a curious feeling in her stomach.

The civilian bar officer phoned Tom's name through to the CID suite and a few minutes later, a burly detective arrived at the foyer minus his suit jacket, his shirt sleeves rolled up and tie undone.

"DC Kenny Ross," he identified himself, his eyes appraising Tom. "What can I do for you, sir?"

"Tom McEwan," he handed Ross his business card. "I work for a law firm as a private investigator, but I'm currently acting on behalf of Chrystons Supermarkets (PLC) regarding the threat against the company. I wonder if I might speak with someone who is engaged in the inquiry."

Ross held the card between his forefinger and thumb and scowled as though the very thought of dealing with a private investigator repelled him.

"What exactly is that you want to speak about, Mister McEwan?"

Tom didn't bother asking if the detective was involved in the inquiry, but guessed he was being given the onceover before being passed along the line.

"I was contacted this morning by the CEO of Chrystons and I might have some information that could be useful to your SIO. So, do I get to speak with him or not," Tom crisply replied, making Ross aware that he wasn't going to be fobbed off.

Ross didn't immediately respond, but stared keenly at Tom before replying, "Don't I know you?"

Tom inwardly clenching of his stomach. He had left the police under a cloud and though some years later he had later been totally vindicated, guessed there must be some officers who hadn't heard the news that he was innocent of everything that had been said about him.

His face deadpan, he admitted, "I was in the job a few years ago."

Ross again glanced down at the business card and to Tom's surprise, broke into a wide smile. "Tom McEwan. Yes, I remember now," he nodded. "You were involved in the inquiry when Poet Burns got murdered, right?"

"That's right," Tom nodded, pleased that the ice had been broken, but uncertain whether he wished to be reminded of that time.

"Couldn't have happened to a better bastard; Poet Burns getting his," remarked Ross who then added, "Come away through, Tom. I'll stick the kettle on while we wait. The boss is DI Mickey Farrell and he should be back here anytime and you can tell him what you have."

Arriving back at the incident room in Kirkintilloch police office and before they got out of the parked car, DS Leitch instructed Bob Stevenson to have an Action created by the HOLMES team and assigned to him. Thereafter to was to take the phone directly to the Forensic Technical Department at the Crime Campus in Gartcosh. "And Bob," she told him, "stress the urgency of this inquiry. If the dead girl used her phone at all in the recent weeks, please ensure they immediately contact the incident room here with any information they can glean from the phone and where possible, contact details for those persons she was in touch with. We're still building up a profile and even if her killer isn't one of the called numbers, we need to discover who she contacted for those individuals might have information that will lead to the killer."

She stared curiously at his soft smile and then she sighed and shook her head.

"Sorry, Bob. I'm forgetting you've been doing this longer than me and here's me trying to teach you to suck eggs. I'm an idiot and I unreservedly apologise."

"Don't worry about it, Anne," he grinned at her. "For a minute there I thought I was hearing that bumptious bugger Fitzpatrick."

"Oh my God," she was genuinely horrified. "Don't tell me I'm turning into that smug shit," she wailed.

"No, not at all," Stevenson continued to grin at her. "In fact, there's those among us who wonder how you manage to cope working for that bampot. I've seen some good bosses in my time and some bad bosses," his grin faded as he slowly shook his head, "but I have to tell you, Murray Fitzpatrick must be one of the worst I've encountered in my lengthy service. In fact," he grinned as he opened his door, "the word is that he's such a tight-arse he tucks his shirt tails into his underpants."

Leitch laughed as Stevenson added, "Right then, I'll have a pee, collect an Action like you said and them I'll be on my way."

While Bob Stevenson made his way to the Gents, Anne Leitch headed for the DI's room and getting the nod from one of the civilian analysts that he was at his desk, knocked on the door before entering.

Fitzpatrick glanced up and then without acknowledging her, lowered his head to continue reading the report in his hand.

"You have some news for me, Detective Sergeant?"

"Yes sir," she bristled, aware that she would not be invited to sit. Over the course of the next few minutes Leitch related the circumstances of her and Bob Stevenson's visit to the flat in Cockmuir Street and the success in identifying their victim.

"So, the brother is of the opinion that our victim, albeit she was a schoolgirl, was sexually active. Is that correct?"

"Yes, so he thinks, sir."

"Well, that seems to bear out Doctor Watsons finding at the post mortem and one can hardly be surprised that our victim found herself murdered if she was out late at night, how shall I put it…offering herself?"

A cold fury swept through Leitch and staring at him, her teeth gritted, all reason went flying out the window as she replied, "With respect sir, I believe that comment about the victim is totally unwarranted. You have absolutely no right whatsoever to judge that wee lassie! None of us know anything about what kind of life she lived! How dare you…"

"No, Detective Sergeant! How dare you…" he was rising angrily to his feet, but the past months of offensive comments and behaviour by Fitzpatrick now boiled over and the outraged Leitch would not be silenced.

"You sanctimonious shit!" she shouted, her hands now flat on his desk as she leaned towards him. "You opinionated, chauvinistic, ill-mannered, torn-faced…"

The door opened behind her and a woman's voice loudly cried out, "If you *please*! Both of you!"

Her body shaking, Leitch stood upright and turning, saw Detective Chief Inspector Lynn Massey stood there, her face chalk white as she stared in turn at them in turn.

Slowly, Massey closed the door and pausing, took a deep breath before quietly telling them, "The whole office out there can hear every *bloody* word! You two are supposed to be the senior officers conducting this inquiry and you seemingly cannot conduct yourselves properly. How the *hell* are the team supposed to take direction…"

"I must apologise…" Leitch began, but was stopped dead by Massey who hissed, "*I'm* speaking, Mister Fitzpatrick! Do not interrupt me!" Massey rubbed at her forehead and slowly exhaled. "I accept that officers under my command might not socialise together or even like each other, but I do expect them to be professional when they are employed working together. I also expect my officers who hold rank to be exemplary in their attitude towards those *they* command. There is a team of hard working detective and civilian personnel out there in the incident room," she forcefully pointed at the closed door, "who deserve leadership and motivation, not their bosses squabbling like fishwives!"

She paused for breath and stepping forward to stand beside the DI, again stared from one to the other before quietly adding, "Will you two be able to work together to find this girls killer or do I need to replace you both for *believe* me, DI Fitzpatrick and DS Leitch, I most certainly will *not* hesitate to do so!"

There was a pregnant pause before Fitzpatrick replied, "I am certain DS Leitch and I can continue to work together and will of course provide the team with the leadership that you desire, Ma'am."

"DS Leitch," Massey turned sharply towards her.

As they both stared at her, Leitch was about to respond that Massey could do with her as she wished for there was no way she would serve under Fitzpatrick, but to her surprise, saw the faintest and subtlest indication of Massey raising her eyebrows.

Was it some sort of warning, some hint or other? She couldn't be certain, but it was enough to decide her and nodding, she instead replied, "Of course, Ma'am. The inquiry comes first."

"Good," Massey exhaled and then with a humourless smile, added, "What occurred in here will not be discussed elsewhere. DS Leitch, would you excuse us for a moment? I need a private word with the DI."

"Of course, Ma'am," she replied and pulling open the door, closed it behind her. Stepping back into the incident room she was acutely aware that all eyes were on her as she returned to her desk.

Tensely, she forced herself to concentrate on the returned Actions that were in her wire tray, none of which progressed the inquiry and that was fortuitous, for Leitch was so blinded by rage that she was incapable of concentrating on anything other than her loathing for Fitzpatrick.

Forcing herself to calm down, she took a deep breath and glanced up as a few moments later, Massey opened the DI's door and beckoning to Leitch, began to make her way to the incident room exit.

It wasn't until both women were in the car park and standing beside Massey's car that she spoke.

"I'm disappointed, Anne," but then shrugged and added, "Disappointed, but not surprised."

"Ma'am?"

"Losing it with Mister Fitzpatrick like that; it isn't healthy for the inquiry, the team who all heard you both *or* for your career." She stared meaningfully at Leitch as she continued, "I'm well aware that you have been working, how can I put this…" her voice changed to a hiss, "under some *pressure*, but I expect my Detective Sergeant's to rise above goading and chauvinism. We as women have worked fucking hard to be treated as equals in this job, Anne and I don't want your personal gripe with your DI or any histrionics to set us back! You have to understand as a DCI that I must be seen to support my Detectives Inspectors. You are worth far more to me as a Detective Sergeant than as a uniform Sergeant, but believe me Anne, if I learn of any more differences between either of you, I will *not* hesitate to return you to uniformed duties. Now, do I make myself clear?"

She paused to let the threat sink in, then in a softer voice, continued. "That's the kicking delivered. It would serve you well to take cognisance of what I have said and in particular," she sighed and placed a hand on the younger woman's arm, "your career. I already have you marked for better things, Anne. Frankly, I do *not* wish to assume the duty of SIO in this murder inquiry so I *need* someone on this team who knows what she is doing. Can I trust that you will not let me down?"

"Ma'am," Leitch quickly nodded.

Massey turned and getting into her car, waved as she drove off. The message was clear.

The DCI did not trust Fitzpatrick to competently handle the inquiry and it was down to Leitch to keep things on track. All she now had to worry about now was when DI Fitzpatrick was around, to keep her back to the wall to avoid the knife.

## CHAPTER SIXTEEN

DI Mickey Farrell was looking forward to a coffee when he strode into the CID suites general office and glanced curiously at the fair-haired man sitting with DC Kenny Ross at one of the desks.

"Boss, this is Tom McEwan" Ross introduced him. "He's asked to speak with you regarding the poison pie issue. He's the representative of Chrystons," and handed Tom's business card to Farrell.

Eyes narrowing, Farrell recognised Tom's name and glancing at the card, also recognised the company name of Martin McCormick and Co.

"Tom McEwan," he slowly repeated than staring at him, waved the card. "You the guy that works for Martin McCormick alongside that limp legged bastard John Logan, the former cop?"

"That's right. I understand John's a friend of yours, Mister Farrell," replied Tom with a smile.

"Aye, he is," admitted Farrell with a nod, "a very good friend, though it pains me to admit it, but friendship doesn't win you any favours, Mister McEwan, nor does it entitle you to information. You *do* understand that?"

"Completely, Mister Farrell. However, I am willing to trade information…" he stopped and with a sigh, shook his head, "No, that's not correct. I'm willing to provide you with any information you need. If you decide to reciprocate by assisting me with information for my private investigation then that will be to my advantage, but it's not a swap. You're investigating a crime so you are entitled to know everything that I can tell you. I'm at your disposal."

Farrell stared at him then suddenly grinned. "That's the answer that wins you a watch, Mister McEwan…or can I call you Tom?"

"Tom's just fine," he returned Farrell's grin.

The DI turned to Ross and said, "If you can rustle up a coffee for me, Kenny, I'll be grateful and…" he raised his eyebrows at Tom, who shook his head.

"Right, we'll be in my office," and turning, led Tom through the corridors to his own room. Slipping off his coat and settling in his chair behind his desk, Farrell said, "I know something about you, Tom, from my mate John Logan. If you call me Mickey, it makes things easier. Now," he folded his fingers to make an arch in front of his nose, "what can you tell me that's going to assist me to catch the bugger who poisoned the man in the Royal Infirmary?"

Seated across from each other in the narrow kitchen while the two girls watched television in the lounge, Joyce McKinnon and her sister Annemarie Turner together decided that it would seem suspicious if Annemarie did not visit Martin in the hospital.

"After all, it's only natural you would want to know how your husband is faring," Joyce said. "Besides, I'm not going home tonight. I'll stay here with the girls while you're away to the Royal. Maybe even spend a couple of days until Martin…" she stopped and took a deep breath. She had been going to say, "…until Martin's dead," but even now after all that had happened, she still couldn't quite believe that her plan was working, that soon Annemarie and the girls would be free from the bastard!

"Staying here with you; I mean, that's also quite natural, isn't it? Your sister supporting you in your time of need. I've taken the next few days off work to support you, so nobody would find that odd, would they?"

"No, you're right of course and," she smiled, "you know how the girls have missed you."

"Yes, like I missed them…and you too, big sis," she smiled, trying so desperately not to cry again. "Right," Joyce sprung up from her chair and lifting the kettle, began to fill it from the tap as she said, "We'll have another coffee and then you can tell me again *exactly* what questions the CID asked you?"

The CEO of Chrystons, Jackson Peters had spent much of the day in front of the television twenty-four news channels during which time he also fielded calls from his fellow Directors who in turn were receiving information from the managers of those stores that were opened that Sunday.

In short, the complaints and allegations from customers were rapidly increasing; customers who believed or falsely alleged to have purchased tainted foodstuffs from Chrystons.

Of course, Peters understood that among those who genuinely complained would be the imposters whose sole aim was to screw the company out of some form of compensation, however, he already had a plan in mind for dealing with these charlatans; a plan that he would reveal at tomorrow's Board meeting.

His mobile phone that lay on the couch beside him rung and glancing at the screen, though he did not recognise the calling number, thought that given the circumstances in which he found himself today decided it might be prudent to answer the call.

"Hello?" he hesitantly asked.

"Mister Peters, it's Tom McEwan calling from Glasgow."

He could hear the sound of traffic in the younger mans background and almost with relief, replied, "Mister McEwan. Have you some news for me?"

"Nothing that yet identifies the culprit, I regret to inform you, but I have made contact with the local police here in Glasgow. I've spoken with the investigating officer, Detective Inspector Farrell and made him aware of all details regarding our female suspect and intimated my interest on behalf of your company. From Mister Farrell I've learned the name of the victim who continues to be detained at the city's Royal Infirmary; Martin Turner, a forty years old schoolteacher. Turner's married with two children. He…" the line crackled as though the signal was lost, then returned.

With his pen hovering over a notepad, Peters said, "I'm sorry, Mister McEwan, I lost you briefly. What was that about the victim?"

"Mister Turner remains in a critical condition and is in an induced coma with some concern for his life. I have the consultants name, Mister Peters, and I will bring full details for tomorrow's meeting."

"You intend coming down for the meting, then?"

"Yes, sir. I arrive tonight and will liaise with Gavin Blakestock. I regret I won't have the facility at the hotel to type out a synopsis of what I have learned, but will be able to give your Board a verbal update if that's okay with you, sir."

"That will be fine, Mister McEwan. Now, have you made contact with the victim's family?"

"No sir. My boss, Martin McCormick who is your company's legal representative here in Scotland suggested that if I obtain the next of kin's details, he would be better disposed to deal with them. However, it's likely that I will accompany him at that time, probably tomorrow afternoon when I return to Scotland after the Board meeting."

"This detective you spoke with. Has he any information as to who might be responsible, Mister McEwan?"

"Not a scooby…sorry, I mean, not a clue, sir. However, after I speak with Gavin I intend pursuing more vigorous inquiry here in Glasgow and with the assistance of the local CID hopefully obtain more information. Look, I'm sorry, Mister Peters, but I'm having some difficulty hearing you…"

"Don't worry, Mister McEwan," he interrupted. "Whatever else you have to tell me can wait till tomorrow. Thank you and goodbye."

Ending the call, he stared thoughtfully at the phone before laying it down onto the couch beside him.

The young investigator had not provided him with any further information of which he was not already aware other than the Board now had the name of the victim to discuss and how they would deal with the fall-out when the man died, as undoubtedly he must.

From his research on the Internet he had learned that Amanita Phalloides…this so called Death Cap mushroom apparently ingested by the victim caused horrendous damage to the internal organs. Detached though he was from the victim, nevertheless Peters shuddered at the horror of what the victim was enduring and felt some remorse for the poor man and in particular, for his wife and children.

He sighed and realised that though it was more than likely some Board members would object, the company must be seen to be humbled by the death and make all necessary reparation to the mans family.

On that he would insist and argue if not for compassionate reasons, then to publicly demonstrate the company's regret that it occurred with one of their products.

His thoughts turned towards his Director of Operations, James Hardie and he glanced at his watch.

Lesley had left almost an hour ago, purportedly to attend a nearby cinema.

Curious, as he smiled humourlessly, that just as Lesley was pulling out of the driveway he called James's mobile phone and it went straight to the answer service. Even more curious, he grimly smiled, that when he called James at home his wife Margo had been informed by him that her husband was attending an impromptu and urgent meeting with his CEO.


Seated at his desk, DI Murray Fitzpatrick was still bristling over the exchange of words with his Detective Sergeant. Bloody woman, he thought. Uppity beyond her service or her experience. He should have slapped her down long before now; kept her in her place. That was the problem with the modern police service; too many women in positions of authority and his thoughts turned to Lynn Massey. Another upstart who no doubt used her feminine wiles to her advantage for after all, why else would someone her age be promoted over more skilled detectives such as he.

He could feel the tension in his body and beneath the desk, his legs began to tremble.

Opening the drawer of his desk, he reached in and glancing to ensure his door was closed, fetched out a small plastic bottle of pills.

Tipping two of the little red coloured tablets into his hand, he swallowed and washed them down with a mouthful of cold tea.

Licking at his lips, he took a deep breath, almost immediately feeling a little better, but still angry.

The door knocked and he sharply called out, "Come!"

It was Leitch with a report in her hand.

"Sorry to disturb you, sir," she calmly said, "but I believe you should be aware of this report that has just come in."

She placed the A4 sheet of paper onto his desk and stood back.

"Summarise for me," he coldly instructed.

"As you are aware, I sent Bob Stevenson to Gartcosh with the victim's phone. He remained there and brought back this report. It's not officially typed up as yet in witness statement form, but it's a working copy that will permit us to proceed with a number of inquiries."

He couldn't fault her initiative and glancing at the report, saw a list of over a dozen phone number, most of which were ascribed to service providers.

Unwilling to admit his unfamiliarity with mobile phones, he stared curiously at her and asked, "What's your thought on these numbers?"

She remained pokerfaced, aware that the DI was uncertain how to proceed but reluctant to provoke another argument she bent towards the sheet of paper and using her pen as a pointer, replied, "These numbers here, sir, seem to be contract phones. We can contact the service providers and request they provide us with details of the account holders."

"Won't a warrant be required for such information?"

"Generally speaking, yes, but," she decided a little humility would go a long way, "but with your permission of course it's my intention to inform the companies that because this is a murder inquiry, time is critical in tracing these individuals."

"I see. Yes, I agree," he sighed then pointing to the sheet, asked, "These numbers that do not have a service provider listed alongside them. How do you propose to trace these account holders?"

"That's where we have a problem, sir. There are three numbers listed there that seem to be pay-as-you-go phones; what are colloquially called 'burn phones.' They are cheap and very basic and users can purchase them at most stores and do not require to provide personal details when doing so. They are topped up either by a credit card or by purchasing a credit voucher."

"Hmmm. That presents us with a problem, then."

"Yes, sir."

"Our technical people at Gartcosh; are they in any position to assist by identifying the users of these three phones?"

"Regretfully, no sir," Leitch replied, "however, what they did tell us is that the victims phone was last used on Friday evening to send a text message to this phone number," she pointed to one of the three pay-as-you-go phones.

Fitzpatrick stared curiously at her. "Do we have a copy of this text?"

Wordlessly she handed him a printout that read:

*dont forget to meet me. don't fuk me over. be nice and see wat you get and wat ill do for you like last time. Cxxx*

He was thoughtful as he read the text and about to comment on the victims spelling and grammar, but held his tongue for like Letch he did not wish another confrontation. Instead he said, "I assume there was no reply to this text message?"

"No reply, sir," she confirmed with a shake of her head.

He read the message again and softly smiled, telling her, "Well done, Detective Sergeant. It seems that we might just have made a little progress. All we have to do now is find the phone that received this message and we might have our killer."


Pulling into the drop-off bay at Glasgow Airport, Ellen Toner switched off the engine as Tom McEwan stretched across to retrieve his overnight bag from the rear seat and held it on his lap.

"I'm sorry we don't have more time together before you drop me off," he smiled at her.

"I'm only sorry that you hadn't time to eat anything," she shrugged. "Try and get something at the hotel."

"Wish you were coming too."

"So do I," she smiled and then on impulse, reached across to kiss him, placing her hand behind his head to draw him close.

He held her tightly and releasing her, reluctantly glanced at the dashboard clock. "I'd better watch my time. You know what the airlines are like for booking in early."

"You'll phone me and let me know you've arrived safely?"

The words were out before she realised what she had said, that she was worried about him; that she cared.

He smiled and releasing her, said, "Yes, of course I will," then eyes narrowing, took a deep breath as he blurted out, "Me and you, Ellen. This is going somewhere, right?"

She paused before answering, for she realised that to agree would commit her yet staring at Tom she knew that for now, she wanted him in her life.

"Yes, I hope so," she softly replied and gasped when Tom again reached over to hold her tightly before opening the car door.

He was out of the car, grinning happily as he turned to wave.

"I'll call you with any developments and…I'll see you tomorrow when I get back?"

"Yes, but after work; at my place," she added.

She watched him walk towards the main doors of the concourse, his bag slung across his shoulder. Taking a deep breath at the enormity of what she had just occurred, she switched on the engine and pulled out into the line of traffic.

It was some ten minutes of stop/start driving before Annemarie Turner found a parking bay near to the Royal Infirmary, for it seemed at that time of the evening everyone in Glasgow had a patient to visit.

Locking the BMW, she stood back to check there was no bumps or scrapes, but then frowned. Why did it matter if she scraped or bumped the car? She didn't know why she bothered worrying about it, for if Joyce's plan worked it was unlikely that Martin would drive the bloody thing again. She recalled how much time and money he spent on the car and with an almost triumphant smile, kicked at the tyre.

Embarrassed at her action she glanced about her, relieved that nobody had seen her little act of petulance and quickly made her way to the front door of the hospital.

Arriving at the Acute Receiving Ward, she saw that entry was by pressing the call-button and patiently waited till the door was opened by a young Irish staff nurse.

Explaining who she was and who she had come to visit, Annemarie was led to a single room where Martin lay unconscious, the oxygen mask still strapped to his face and an intravenous drip attached to his arm.

"Doctor asked that when you arrived, Missus Turner, that he be informed, so if you'd like to sit with your husband I'll just give him a call to get him here now," the nurse cheerily told her before closing the door and leaving Annemarie to stand nervously over the bed.

She stared down at her husband, but curiously felt no emotion; no pity, no hate. It seemed to her that in the last twenty-four hours Martin had become this gaunt stranger, no longer the abuser who she feared and loathed.

A tubular frame chair was in the corner. Laying her handbag on the floor, she carried the chair and placed it alongside the bed and sitting, continued to stare at Martin.

She glanced at the door to ensure it was closed before leaning forward to softly whisper, "I heard once that the last thing that goes is the hearing. If that is so, then listen to me, Martin." She licked at her lips, her heart beating like thunder in her chest. "It was me that did this to you. I gave you the pie that I poisoned. I wanted you dead; dead, Martin; dead. Can you hear me? Dead because of the horrible things you did to me and my daughters. The beatings, the abuse I suffered through the years because of you," she hissed, growing bolder as she leaned even closer. "I hate you, you *bastard*! I never had the courage to tell you this, but you are the worst excuse for a man, for a husband, for a human being that I can possibly imagine! You are a selfish, arrogant…"

The door behind her suddenly opened and in panic, she almost leapt from the chair.

"Oh, so I'm sorry," said the white coated man, "I didn't mean to startle you, Missus Turner. I'm Doctor Kane, the registrar that is attending to your husband," he introduced himself, but didn't offer to shake hands. His eyes narrowed. "Are you sure you are alright, Missus Turner? Can I get you a glass of water?"

"I'm fine," she gasped, her hand at her throat and tried to smile. The doctor stared at her, mistakenly believing that the shock of seeing her husband in such a poor state must be overwhelming the poor woman.

He remained standing while indicating Annemarie should again sit down and said, "We haven't previously spoken, Missus Turner, so if I might, I'd like to give you an update on your husband's condition." Not trusting herself to speak, Annemarie nodded.

Referring to Martin's chart, Doctor Kane described the treatment that was being provided and with honesty and compassion, told her the prognosis for Martin making any kind of recovery from the poison that he had ingested was slim to nil.

"To be perfectly frank, Missus Turner, it is very rare that anyone who has digested this particular mushroom survives the effect and if they should survive," he hesitated, "then the remainder of their life will probably be spent on dialysis and lifesaving medication." Horrified, her heart skipped a beat as the awfulness of Doctor Kane's statement struck her. Her eyes widening, she asked, "Then what you're telling me is that there is a chance he might...survive?"

"A very slim chance, Missus Turner and I assure you we are doing everything in our power to enhance his chances; however, our knowledge of this type of invasive damage to the liver and kidneys is extremely limited.

"How...how soon will you know? If he'll live, I mean," she said, her voice almost a whisper.

Doctor Kane felt awful, as though giving her false hope, but continued, for he quite naturally mistook her question as concern for her husband's life. Shrugging, he replied, "We just don't know, Missus Turner. As you can see, we have induced a coma to ease your husbands suffering..."

"What? You mean that he's probably in pain?" she interrupted.

"Oh, if he were awake, undoubtedly," he replied.

She rose and bending to lift her handbag from the floor, shook her head. "I'm sorry, I have to go; I have the children at home," she turned towards the door.

"Yes, of course," he stood to one side to permit her to pass.

Watching her hurry along the corridor towards the ward exit, he shook his head.

Poor woman, he thought, so very upset and yet he wondered at the fading bruise on her eye.

She didn't hear or see anyone or notice the curious stares as she stumbled through the hospital, the horrifying implication of the doctor's statement haunting her thoughts.

He might live!

Dear God, she unconsciously shook her head. If Martin pulled through, it will all have been for nothing! She could not face him returning home and even worse, if the doctor was correct and he survived the poison, he would be unable to work and would be housebound.

Her throat felt tight and her breathing became rapid and shallow.

She would be at his beck and call for every minute of every day for years to come!

Stepping through the sliding door of the main exit, the cold air hit her like an electric shock and she felt her legs shaking. Reaching out a hand towards the wall to steady herself, she thought she was about to pass out and her legs finally buckling beneath her, she stared blankly as she slid helplessly down the wall to sit on the ground.

"Here, hen, are you okay?" a passing ambulance man knelt beside her, his eyes expressing his concern.

She turned towards him, but was unable to speak and slowly closing her eyes against the enveloping darkness, she fainted.

DI Mickey Farrell decided there was little more he could accomplish on a Sunday night and with a sigh, reached for the mobile phone and dialled his girlfriend, Diana.

"Hi love, sorry I had to cancel today," he started, but was hushed when she replied, "Don't be silly. I know that you are on call and I expect it won't be the last time that our day gets interrupted by work."

He grinned and replied, "So you think you and I will have plenty of days together in the future, then?"

There was a definite pause before she replied, "I hope so. When do you finish work tonight?"

"I'm more or less done here. Why?"

"Well, I'm at home and haven't eaten yet, so why don't you bring something in?"

"See you in twenty minutes," he replied and had just ended the call when his door was knocked. He groaned when DC Kenny Ross stuck his head in.

"Sorry, boss, I know you're nearly knocked off."

"Yes, Kenny, what can I do for you," he asked.

"That was a call from DCI Massey to remind us she's the duty SIO for the city divisions this weekend and asking if you'd give her a phone. Says she's heard about the poison case and also said you'll have her phone number."

"Okay," he gruffly exhaled, wondering if the twenty minutes he promised Diana was a bit optimistic.

Lynn Massey answered on the second ring and from the background noise, Farrell realised she was in her car.

"What's the situation about the victim?" she asked.

"He remains critical, but other than that I've no further information, Ma'am."

"Right, well, I'm on my way to look in on the Kirkintilloch incident room for an update before I head home, Mickey. Anything else while I'm on the phone?"

"No, not really, but just to give you a heads up. I had a visit today from a young guy, a former cop called Tom McEwan. Says he works for your cousin, Martin McCormick whose firm represents Chrystons in Scotland."

"I haven't spoken with Martin for a while," she replied, "but I know Tom. He's a good lad. Was drummed out of the polis…"

"Yeah," interrupted Farrell. "We had a wee chat and he told me about that business with Poet Burns. Anyway, McEwan and some investigator he's working with from down south have a suspect, a female who *might* be Scottish. McEwan's convinced there's a Glasgow connection. He was quite forthcoming about what he's learned so far and gave me a copy of a CCTV photograph of the suspect, but he thinks the woman is wearing a disguise, so we're no further forward."

"What does he want in return for his information?" she asked for though she liked Tom McEwan she was mindful that he was he was no longer a police officer, but an employee of her cousin's firm whose agenda was completely separate to that of her officers.

"Nothing that he can't learn in the media, Ma'am," Farrell replied. "I gave him the name and address of the victim because he told me that he and your cousin who will represent Chrystons, intend visiting the victims next of kin some time tomorrow. The next of kin is the wife, by the way. According to McEwan their visit will be related to supporting or compensating the victim's family and won't interfere with my inquiry, so I don't see a conflict of interest there."

"Okay, thanks for that. I might just have a private word with Martin tomorrow morning and stress that he and McEwan stick to their own issues. Okay then, Mickey, should the status of your victim's condition change, you have my number."

"Right, Ma'am, I'll be in touch," he ended the call.

James Hardie rolled over on the bed and watched the naked Lesley Peters lift her underwear and dress from the floor of the hotel room before striding across the room to the en suite.

Turning onto his back, he sighed with pleasure. The woman was insatiable and for the past hour all his worries and concerns over this bloody poison business were forgotten at the thought of her writhing beneath him, satisfying him the way no other woman ever had.

He was still smiling when a few moments later she emerged dressed, then sitting on the edge of the bed, instructed him, "Be a darling, do my zip."

One hand tugged at the zip while the other slid round her slim body to caress her breast, but she clamped her own hand on top of his and half turning said, "James, we have to be careful. I'm not certain, but I think that Jackson suspects something."

He stopped and eyes narrowing, asked, "Why do you think that? Has he said anything?"

"No," she slowly shook her head, "but I just have this *feeling*; this sense there's something about his manner recently, the way he has become even more courteous."

Hardie smiled. Jackson Peters, for all his faults was perhaps the most courteous and polite man he had even met; sometimes *too* polite and in particular to the staff in the office, sometimes forgetting his status and theirs.

He replied, "He can't know or suspect anything, my dear, for if he did he would never permit you the freedom that you enjoy. He would certainly curtail your allowance and perhaps even question who you meet with and where you go. Has he done any of this, asked any questions of you?"

"No," she admitted and turned to face him, worry etched upon her beautiful face, "and I know it sounds silly, but in the past few months he hasn't even made any advances towards me. We haven't had sex…"

Hardie burst out laughing. "Have you considered his age, Lesley? My God, he's what…sixty something?"

"Sixty-two," she softly replied. "And let me assure you, James, Jackson is well into his prime. There has *never* been an issue in bed," she coyly smiled."

"Well then, there you have it. Maybe time has caught up with him and he's having a hard time getting it up, if you excuse the pun," he continued to smile.

"Yes, perhaps you're right," she nodded, but he saw he had not convinced her.

"Of course I'm right," he tried to sound cheery. "You've nothing to worry about."

He forced another cheery laugh and added, "And when this business about the threat to the company is over, when I assume the role of CEO and get rid of that shackle around my neck," he pulled her gently to him and kissed her forehead, "then there will be no more need to hide in hotels rooms. It will be you and me against the world."

Lesley smiled and again nodding, glanced at her watch. "I'd better go."

He watched her slip out of the door, blowing him a kiss as she left. Yes, he lay back down onto the bed. Lesley *was* quite a woman, but when he finally did achieve the top position and obtain a divorce, there would be many like her eager to share the bed as well as the income of the new CEO of Chrystons.

The plane landed ten minutes early and after disembarking, Tom McEwan was greeted at the domestic arrival gate by Gavin Blakestock.

"I know the Premier Inn has a restaurant, so I thought we could have a bite there and go over what we know so far," Blakestock suggested with a smile as they made their way to his car.

The Sunday night traffic was light and they made good time getting to the hotel and while Tom booked in at the reception, Blakestock secured a table in the near empty restaurant while Tom took his overnight bag up to the room.

"I'm driving, but I ordered you a beer," Blakestock smiled at the pint.

"Great, thanks. Now, you're up to date about all I know except my visit with the local CID in Glasgow," Tom began and related his discussion with DI Mickey Farrell.

"Do you know him from your time in the CID?"

"No, not personally," Tom replied. "Well, not that I recall meeting or working with him. I know *of* him. Coincidentally, the other investigator in the firm that I work with, John Logan; he's a good friend of Farrell and speaks highly of him. I know that Farrell was in the Drug Squad before I joined the surveillance unit and you know what it's like in a large Force, like Strathclyde Police was at that time. You get to know or cross paths with quite a number of detectives, but there's a lot you don't meet simply because of the size of the area that the Force covered. By all account and from what John has told me, Farrell is one of these…how can I describe him," he mused. "A sort of kick the door down to get the bad guy type of detective. Fearless and very competent."

"You think DI Farrell will keep you in the loop regarding any information he might acquire about our suspect?"

"Yes, I think so," Tom nodded. "It doesn't do any harm that his boss, DCI Massey, is a cousin of my boss."

"Right then," Blakestock smiled and reached for a menu. "My treat, young Tom. What you having?"

DS Anne Leitch was about to close the murder incident room for the night when to her surprise, DCI Lynn Massy pushed open the door and walked in.

Glancing about her, Massey saw that apart from Leitch, the room was empty and said, "Anne, sorry. Were you just about to leave?"

"No problem, Ma'am. What can I do for you?"

Massey dropped her handbag onto a desk and declining Leitch's offer of a seat, replied, "I'm just on my way home and thought I'd stop in to ask if there has been anything, any developments before I go home."

"Nothing," Leitch shook her head.

Massey sighed and with a grin, said, "Good, it's been a long day. I'll be pleased to get home to Greg for likely he'll have dinner waiting, but I'll wait and walk you out."

"I heard on the radio that you've got a poisoning case ongoing; something about a victim in the Royal Infirmary," remarked Leitch who walked round the HOLMES desks, switching off the terminals and desk lamps.

"Yes, apparently the man's condition is caused by a poisoned pie he ate and was sold by Chrystons; you know, the supermarket people and it follows a threat against the company."

"Any suspects yet, Ma'am," Leitch was having a final glance round the room before switching off the overhead lights.

"Not at the minute," Massey carefully replied and held open the door to permit her to pass through. "Mickey Farrell, the DI at Stewart Street has the inquiry and he's dealing with a former cop called Tom McEwan who is now working as a private investigator." She smiled and added, "Curiously enough, McEwan's working for my cousin's law firm."

In the corridor leading to the yard, Leitch stopped and stared at Massey. "If it's the same guy, I know Tom McEwan, Ma'am. He was a DC in my old division when I joined the police. A nice guy that didn't treat us uniform cops the way some of the CID did," she shook her head and her brow furrowed. "Didn't I hear he was dismissed from the police then reinstated or something?"

"Actually he resigned, though as I understand it there was some pressure for him to do so, then some years later he was exonerated. But no, he didn't rejoin the police."

"What's his interest in the poisoning case?"

"Well, it seems McEwan is acting on behalf of Chrystons doing some local inquiry in Glasgow. Mickey had a word with him and seems to trust him and I trust Mickey, so as long as he doesn't get in the way of the police inquiry, I've no objections."

Leitch held open the door that led to the yard where the cars were parked. "Well, Ma'am, if you do come across Tom, please give him my regards. He was a nice guy then and I can't think he'll have changed much."

"I'll be sure to do that, Anne," Massey brightly replied and bid Leitch goodnight.

## CHAPTER SEVENTEEN

The day dawned sunny and warm in Birmingham and in his bedroom, Jackson Peters dressed carefully. Today was to be an important day; perhaps even the day that his plan came to fruition. Selecting his favourite tie, he knotted it and slipping on his jacket, stood in front of the mirror and critically examined his appearance. Satisfied, he smiled and taking a deep breath, strode towards the bedroom door and pulled it open.

At the open door and before he stepped into the hallway, he stood and cocked his head to one side, hearing the maid in the hallway downstairs humming along to the radio that he could faintly hear was playing in the kitchen where the housekeeper was preparing breakfast.

Passing by his wife Lesley's adjoining bedroom door he stopped and listened, but heard nothing. He knew that her car was parked in the driveway and assumed she was home. Tempted though he was to knock upon her door and wish Lesley a good morning, he decided against it.

If it come to it, there would be time later to speak at length.

He couldn't explain his smile, but continuing down the wide stairs decided that a hearty breakfast was required for the long day that lay ahead.

DS Anne Leitch was again first into the office that Monday morning and gasping for a hot drink, she first headed for the kettle.

The murder inquiry wasn't foremost on her mind; she was more concerned that tonight she and her husband were due to attend the primary for their daughter's school report and she still had to make arrangements with her parents in Pollok about childminding her older girl. Though the police shifts had come on leaps and bounds in the last couple of decades when it came to accommodating their officers home lives, police work was still a twenty-four hour, seven-day job and major inquiries such as murder had no limitation on the hours the detectives and civilian staff often worked.

Her husband Alistair, bless him, did his best juggling his job and running the house as well as being there for the girls, taking and collecting them from their school, but even he needed a hand now and then.

Though her mind was occupied by that night's school visit, Leitch mechanically began her routine of switching on the computers then seated at her desk with a strong milky coffee, began to leaf through the returned Actions that sat in her in-tray.

She took a satisfying whiff of the coffee and read through the last of the Actions. There was nothing in any of the reports that required her immediate attention and placed the bundle into the tray marked for the analysts.

The door opened to admit two of the civilian analysts who chatting away together, stopped to wish Leitch good morning before making their way to the tea and coffee table.

Almost immediately in their footsteps and to Leitch's surprise, DI Murray Fitzpatrick opened the door and was making his way to his office when almost as an afterthought, he turned and nodded towards Leitch.

"Good morning, sir," she courteously acknowledged his nod, inwardly smiling that maybe DCI Massey's little chat with him had hit home after all.

She watched as Fitzpatrick closed the door behind him then turning, saw Bob Stevenson enter the incident room.

"Morning, Jumbo," she cheerfully called out.

"Sarge," he formally responded and headed for the kettle. Making himself a cup of tea, he joined Leitch at her desk and quietly asked, "How are things this morning, Anne? Anything new? Any developments?"

"Nothing," she shook her head and then asked him, "but I need a couple of detectives to call at the victim's school, this morning; interview staff and any pals that she had there. Do you want to be part of it?"

"Yeah, why not."

"Okay then. I'll work out who to send with you, so give me a couple of minutes and I'll ask the DI to brief you on any particular questions he wants asked."

"Oh, joy," was Stevenson's laconic response.

Leitch fought the grin that threatened to betray her agreement and rising from her chair, said, "Give me a minute and I'll ask him to speak to you."

The two wee girls were excited at getting a lift to school that morning. An emotional Joyce McKinnon watched her nieces as they entered the school gate, turning and shyly smiling and waving at her. She fought the tears that threatened to spill from her; they were such innocents and so pleased that their auntie Joyce promised that if they did well in class that day she would pick them up after school and "…just *might* have some sweeties for them."

Returning to her sisters house she made Annemarie some tea and toast that she carried upstairs on a tray to the main bedroom; the bedroom that had so recently been denied her by Martin.

Pushing open the door, Annemarie wearily sat up in bed, her eyes still showing the effect of the medication.

Joyce hurriedly laid the tray down onto the end of the bed and said, "Here, let me," as she propped the pillows behind her sisters back. "Now, doctor's orders, my lady. They told me you are badly in need of some rest so here's a nice cup of tea and some toast. Have that then get your head back down onto that pillow. I mean it, Annemarie," she sternly told her. "They wee girls need their mother and I need my sister and you will be no good to anybody if you don't look after yourself. Besides," she began to fold the quilt about her sister, "I'm here to take care of things."

She stepped across the room and drew a chair from under the window towards the bed and sat down, drawing the tray forward and handing the plate of toast to Annemarie.

"When I got the call last night from the hospital," she reached across and stroked at her sister's cheek, "I got such a fright. When they told me you had collapsed." She involuntarily shivered. "I just didn't know what to think. I just bundled the girls into my car and my God," she laughed softly. "It's a wonder the police didn't catch me, the speed I was doing to get to the hospital. So, tell me; what happened?"

Annemarie shrugged. "When the doctor told me that Martin might not die, that he might live, but be an invalid for the rest of his life, I sort of…" The tears threatened to overwhelm her. "I just felt that everything you had done, everything that you planned; what *I* did." She took a deep breath and shook her head. "That it had all been for nothing; a complete waste."

"Look, it's not over yet. The doctor was only offering an opinion, trying to keep your spirits up. I mean, for God's sake Annemarie, he's not going to say something like 'Sorry missus Turner, but your husbands on his way out' is he? It's his job to be upbeat, to try and be positive."

Annemarie stared at her, the toast in her hand forgotten. "Do you really believe that? That Martin might die?"

"I bloody hope so; that's what we planned, isn't it? To get you and girls free from him?"

Annemarie didn't immediately reply, but turned her head and staring blankly at the wall, softly replied, "I hope so Joyce or else I'll have him here in the house with me running after him for the rest of my life."

Ellen Toner arrived at work just as her secretary Wilma Clark was walking along Woodlands Road.

"Well, seems like the proverbial has hit the fan," Wilma shook her head.

"You've seen the news then?"

"Can't miss it," Wilma sniffed. "It's been the main item on the local radio and on the tele too. What have you heard?" she stared narrow-eyed at Ellen.

"Not much more than you, likely," Ellen fibbed with a straight face.

"What about that private detective, that Tom. Hasn't he been in touch?"

Ellen opened the office door and holding it open, turned to face the older woman who began to grin.

"Come on now, Ellen. He's sweet on you and you know it too," she continued to grin. "That doesn't mean to say he's going to share his information with me," she tried to play down her budding relationship with Tom McEwan, but Wilma, long in the tooth, would not be fobbed off. "You like him, don't you?" she teased Ellen whose blush answered Wilma's question.

They had been in the office less than five minutes when Wilma knocked on Ellen's door to tell her a general e-mail to all Chrystons stores had arrived from head office instructing that all food products were to be closely scrutinised for any indication of a black X or any signs of tampering to the wrappings.

"But we've not even opened yet and that will take hours," groaned Ellen.

Wilma glanced down at the e-mail printout in her hand and continued, "It also says that to facilitate this instruction, stores are to be closed for the duration of the search. Any items discovered that seem to be suspicious are to be carefully sealed and the head office notified immediately."

"Right," Ellen loudly puffed and shook her head, "lock the main doors and print out a sign to be displayed in the window informing customers that for the meantime, we're stocktaking. Don't mention anything about a search. Also, have the staff assembled in the rear loading bay for me to address them. After that…"

She was interrupted when her mobile phone activated and waving that Wilma carry on, saw on the screen the caller was Tom.

"Morning," she answered the call with a smile. "Where are you?"

"I've just arrived by taxi at the head office. Gavin Blakestock is meeting me in the foyer and we'll attend the meeting together," he replied.

She heard the sound of a diesel engine and Tom paying off the cabbie.

"How are things up there?" he asked.

Quickly she told him about the memo from head office instructing the immediate search of the food products and that having just arrived at the office, she had not yet checked the packaging code for the pie that was purchased in Glasgow.

"Don't worry too much about that now, but regarding checking the stock. That's useful to know," he said, then added, "I'll cut this short because I see Gavin inside the foyer. Listen, I'll be heading for the airport when the meetings concluded and when I arrive in Glasgow I'll likely be going with my boss to interview the victims next of kin. After that I'm not sure what I'll be doing, but somehow or other I'll try to get to visit you tonight."

"Okay," Ellen replied, "and if you haven't eaten, let me know," she said and ended the call.

She lingered in her office for a few moments, thinking about Tom. Like it or not Ellen Toner, she frowned, you're starting to fall for him.

Seated at the top of the table, both hands flat on the surface, Jackson Peterson called the meeting to order.

His fellow Directors were in a sombre mood as evidenced by the muted mutterings that preceded them into the boardroom.

To Peters right sat James Hardie wearing a dark blue three-piece suit, white shirt and with a vivid red coloured tie and matching handkerchief flowing from the top pocket of his jacket.

Courteous to a fault, Peters greeted each of the Directors by name and with a smile acknowledged the presence of the two investigators, Gavin Blakestock and Tom McEwan before thanking and politely dismissing the young woman who had served coffee. When the woman closed the door behind her, Peters began.

"Let us proceed, gentlemen," he started, but then paused and addressing the Director Frank Kennedy, smiled and asked, "For the purpose of the meeting, my dear chap. Would you be so kind as to take notes?"

Taken aback, Kennedy agreed then spent a minute fetching a pad from the cupboard at the end of the room and resuming his seat, took a pen from an inner pocket and nodded he was ready.

"Gentlemen," Peters said, "there is no need to revisit the unpleasant circumstances that necessitate this extraordinary Board meeting and of course you are all aware of the circumstances surrounding the poor man, the victim as it is, who it seems consumed a product purchased from our Argyle Street store in Glasgow that has led to his confinement in hospital. Mister McEwan," he stared down the table at Tom, "do you have an update regarding the victims current condition?"

"As of this morning, sir, according to the CID officer I spoke with, there is no change. By that I mean the victim, Mister Martin Turner, remains in an induced coma and there is still considerable concern that his condition will prove fatal." Tom glanced briefly at his notebook and continued. "Thanks to the Greater Manchester Police who conducted the initial examination of the chicken pie that was discovered in the Quay Street store and was confirmed by the toxicology department at Glasgow's Royal Infirmary, we now know that the poison added to both pies, that is those pies purchased in the Quay Street and Argyle Street stores, is a type of mushroom called Amanita Phalloides that is also known as Death Cap. Our research has indicated that ingestion of this mushroom is usually fatal."

He paused to allow this information to sink in and saw some of the Directors turn to stare curiously at each other for clearly, none of them had heard of the plant.

"I can also disclose that Mister Blakestock and I have managed to obtain a CCTV photograph," he lifted a number of copies from a brown envelope that he began to hand down the table to the Directors, "that seems to indicate a suspect who we also believe might be a Scottish female. Regretfully, we believe the woman is wearing a disguise. This photograph and a similar photograph that is not so clear, were obtained from the CCTV cameras located here in your 'Founding Store' and also at Glasgow's Woodlands Road store when the first threat was issued to your company; when the baby food jars were marked."

"Why do you believe the woman might be Scottish from a photograph, Mister McEwan?" asked a puzzled Director.

Tom smiled and explained, "Mister Blakestock traced an assistant at your 'Founding Store' who spoke with the suspect, sir. Moving on, the second threatening letter was handed into a newsagent in Oxford Street in Manchester. A local detective noted a statement from the shopkeeper who described the same woman, but regretfully there is no CCTV footage from that shop. I should also tell you that as we speak, the CCTV camera footage from the Quay Street store is being couriered down to Mister Blakestock who will view it to try and determine if the same described woman also visited that store. In our opinion, though, we believe it is the same woman who planted the poisoned pie in that store. The fact that in all instances it seems the same woman is involved in this threat causes us to assess that Penthesilea is in fact one individual and not as the threatening letters suggest, a group."

"That sound all very well and good, Mister McEwan, that you have what sounds like a female suspect," Hardie loudly demanded, "but how close are you to finding this woman?"

"Not close at all, sir," Tom replied and wearily shook his head, aware of the muttering that immediately commenced after his admittance. "However, now that the threat has become public knowledge Mister Blakestock and I are no longer restricted in our inquiries and we are both liaising with the local CID as well as keeping in touch with the Manchester police."

"If I may," Blakestock lightly touched Tom on the arm and slowly turning his head to stare at each Director in turn, he said, "You will recall gentlemen that as dictated by Mister Hardie, you blankly refused to permit my colleague and I to contact and utilise the services of the local constabularies. That said, admittedly we did speak to some trusted former colleagues in our efforts to trace this individual or group calling itself Penthesilea, but without success. Now," his voice grew firmer, "given that we have had what, three days to identify a suspect, this woman, I believe that we have done rather well and will continue to do well providing that we receive your full cooperation and support; such support permitting us to use and liaise with whatever agency will assist us in tracking down this individual and," his voice raised to a higher pitch, "I need not remind you that this Boards reluctance to inform the general public about the threat to *your* food products has resulted in a man…a man with a wife and two small children, I might add, being poisoned to the peril of his life!"

A tense silence fell upon the room, broken after a moment by Jackson Peters who calmly said, "You anger is well justified, Mister Blakestock. It is to our regret that we did not take cognisance of you and Mister McEwan's prior warning at the time."

It did not escape the notice of the Board that when making his statement, Peters gaze fell upon James Hardie who visibly paled and tight-lipped, seemed to shrink in his seat.

Taking a deep breath, Peters then asked, "Mister McEwan. I believe when you return to Glasgow it is your intention with…" he hesitated.

"Martin McCormick, the lawyer representing Chrystons in Scotland, sir."

"Indeed," he grimly smiled, "with Mister McCormick, to visit the victim's wife. I believe the term used is damage limitation."

"Yes, sir. Mister McCormick intends meeting with the victim's wife, Missus Turner, to offer her any financial support she might require for the time that her husband remains incapacitated."

"And what about after he's discharged from hospital? What then, if some ambulance chasing lawyer takes charge of the victim?" asked Kennedy. "What sort of court action are we looking at?"

"That might depend on whether or not the victim survives," mused another Director who slowly shook his head.

"In the meantime," Peters interrupted, "are you able to tell us what Mister McCormick's intentions are?"

"Well, by now I am certain the local media will have the victim's details, sir," Tom replied, "so I believe that Martin's keen to have Missus Turner sign a non-disclosure of information agreement, obviously subject to her husband surviving or not. As for costs, I'm sorry," he shook his head at Kennedy, "I have no idea what that will be."

"No, of course not," agreed Peters. "I believe, gentlemen that our main issue is damage limitation to our good name. As you will be aware, we have issued a memo instructing all stores to be searched for any other contaminated food products. There is nothing to suggest that this woman…this Penthesilea will not strike again and so," he turned towards Tom and Blakestock, "you gentlemen might wish to continue with your inquiries while we Board members discuss how to contain the damage." Smiling, he added, "And on behalf of the Board I wish to offer you both our sincere and grateful thanks for all your efforts to date and I look forward to your continuing reports."

While the two investigators left the room, some of the Directors arose to visit the adjoining toilet or to refill their coffee cups for they suspected a long morning lay ahead of them.

Detective Constable Bob 'Jumbo' Stevenson and his colleague, DC Gemma McNulty, arrived at the high school and after parking in the staff car park, made their way to the Head Teachers office. Identifying themselves, they were admitted to his inner office and broke the news to the shocked man of the murder of one of his pupils, Colleen Younger. He in turn summoned the Deputy Head Teacher who called for the dead girl's form teacher and Departmental Head, Charlie McFadyen, to attend the Head Teacher's office.

Crowded in with the four teaching staff, Stevenson repeated his news about the murder of Colleen Younger and requested that he and McNulty speak to any staff member or pupil who might have some knowledge of the victim's personal life.

His request was met with guarded suspicion and indecision by the Head Teacher who worried that permission should first be obtained from the councils Education Department, the teaching unions representing the large number of staff as well as the parents or guardians before any pupil could be interviewed on the school premises.

Bob Stevenson was a patient man and not given to telling lies, but was determined that he was not returning to the incident room to inform DI Fitzpatrick that he had been rebuffed from obtaining the statements by a bloody bureaucrat!

Adopting a pleasant if slightly indifferent manner, he shrugged and said, "Okay then, sir, if that's your decision. I'll just give my boss a wee phone call and let him know." He was reaching into his pocket and fetching out his mobile phone when almost jovially, he said, "This kind of reminds me of another murder I was investigating some years ago. That was a secondary school pupil too. You're in the teaching game so you'll likely recall what happened then, of course."

Needless to say the Head Teacher had no idea what Stevenson was talking about and stared curiously at him, slowly shaking his head. "Oh, you don't remember?" Stevenson stared innocently at the man and raised his eyebrows. "Well, it turned out that there were some pupils in the school who had information that identified the killer, but because the CID weren't permitted to interview them *at* the school, it wasted some precious time, hours really if I recall correctly, but enough time for the killer to strike again later that afternoon; murdered a wee lassie, as it happened. The Head Teacher, nice guy he was, but I can't seem to recall his name…" Stevenson sombrely shook his head. "Maybe you know of him, sir. The last I heard he's working in a pub; somewhere in Govan I think it was."

Behind Stevenson, Charlie McFadyen stifled a grin for he rightly guessed the big detective was lying and poker-faced, commented, "Oh aye, that was the school in Bearsden, wasn't it?"

Turning, Stevenson glanced at McFadyen and saw the subtle wink. "Aye, that's right. Bearsden," he nodded in agreement.

"Well," the Head Teacher hastily interrupted, "if your interview *is* time critical, DC Stevenson, I believe that *tempus fugit* so on this occasion, who exactly is it again that you wish to interview?"

Anne Leitch was pleased that the DI chose to remain for most of that morning in his room. Apart from the morning briefing when the morose Fitzpatrick had little to say other than instruct Leitch to keep him apprised of any developments, his absence permitted her to allocate the team with their Actions and update the running log.

Just before midday, the portly civilian station assistant entered the incident room to hand Leitch a dispatch that had arrived from the Forensics Department at Gartcosh.

The report the envelope contained confirmed that the minute sample obtained from under the victim's fingernail by Doctor Watson at the PM was indeed dried blood and not that of the victim. The report continued that the blood type and DNA extracted from the sample were now logged on the database at Gartcosh. Regretfully, the report concluded that the extracted DNA was not a match for any individuals' DNA that was currently on the database nor was the

DNA familial, which though did not absolve them, seemed to negate any immediate requirement to acquire DNA from the victim's siblings.

Rising from her seat, Leitch decided the report was significant enough to warrant the DI being told and first knocking upon his door, heard him call out and entered to find him poring over an Action report.

Laying the report upon his desk, she said, "With your permission, sir, I'd like to commence obtaining DNA samples for elimination purposes from any individuals the team interview who either had contact with or were known to the victim."

Sitting back in his chair, Fitzpatrick arched his fingers beneath his hawk like nose and replied, "Do you think at this stage, Sergeant, that procuring DNA samples from so many people is necessary?"

"Yes sir, I believe so."

"And if we were to obtain DNA from, let us say, every school pupil who knew or had contact with the victim, we could be literally talking about hundreds of young people without even adding any adults, yes?"

"Yes, sir," she replied and already could feel the chill of rejection running down her spine.

"And would you also agree the Forensic laboratory would quite likely be overwhelmed with all the DNA samples we submit?"

"Surely that shouldn't be a concern, sir? Not when…"

"Oh, but it *is* a concern, Sergeant," he coldly interrupted. "This murder inquiry like so many other police inquiries runs on a budget. I will not fritter away the teams' energy and the inquiry's financial resources on what is likely to be a waste of time. Bring me a suspect and yes, we will obtain DNA to compare to that DNA discovered under our victim's fingernails by Doctor Watson."

He paused and stared daringly at her, but she refused to be drawn into an argument.

"Now, is there anything else, Sergeant"

"No, sir, nothing else," she calmly replied and leaving, closed the door behind her.

Returning to her desk she could not decide whether the incompetent bastard just didn't realise that to ignore individuals interviewed by the team was a dreadful blunder or he was simply making a point to frustrate her.

## CHAPTER EIGHTEEN

Tom McEwan decided that there was no further need for him to hang about Chrystons head office and was grateful that Gavin Blakestock offered to run him to Birmingham Airport.

"You'll give me a call when you've spoken to the next of kin and update me regarding Mister Turners condition?" asked Blakestock as he fetched Tom's bag from the boot and then shook his hand.

"Absolutely," he nodded in reply and was turning away towards the main doors when Blakestock called out, "And don't forget to give Miss Toner a kiss from me!"

That caused Tom to stop and turning, waved with a grin before he went through the door.

There was an air of solemnity in the boardroom as the Directors resumed their sets. The fifteen-minute comfort break allowed them to gather their thoughts, speak with their Deputy Directors at their own Departments or call home.

As they once more settled themselves around the large table it did not escape Jackson Peters attention that James Hardie seemed to hold court with just two of his fellow Directors though curiously, Peters noticed, the other three of Hardie's previous supporters had drifted away from the group and were now in deep conversation with the Media and Public Relations Director, Frank Kennedy.

Peters wondered, was this James's supporters sensing the smell of defeat and were now drifting away.

Seated again at the top of the table, he called the meeting to order and glancing down at a report that lay before him, commenced with, "Gentleman, I have a number of issues that I must bring to the Boards attention." He slowly inhaled and continued, "Obviously in response to the media announcements, I am informed that the number of Chrystons customers complaining of nausea and other ailments has increased tenfold since our last meeting. Needless to say, it is assessed that a large number if not all of these complaints will likely prove to be unfounded and while some customers have alleged to attended at a doctor or hospital, none have been detained for any kind of treatment. On the plus side, this morning each of our stores completed a check of their food products and I am told by our own Mister Packer, who coordinated the search, that that no product was discovered that was marked with a tell-tale black X nor was any product discovered to have damaged wrapping. As a result of this information I have learned that all our stores are now re-opened for business."

He glanced up at the Directors and his brow furrowed before he continued. "I regret I am also informed that since the media announcements warning our customers and the public at large of the threat against us, the price of Chrystons shares has dramatically fallen and continue to fall as public confidence in our food products decline."

This comment provoked a mutter of dismay that stopped when Peters raised a hand and wryly smiled. "Let us not be surprised by this predictable fall in shares, gentlemen. We all expected this would occur. It would not surprise me if there were those among you who might consider that rather than selling, this could be the ideal opportunity to purchase more shares in our company."

Taken aback, the Directors turned to stare at each other, one shared thought in their minds; this disaster *might* just prove to be lucrative.

"Now, to other business," Peters glanced again down at the report, then sharply lifted his head to stare directly at James Hardie.

"Our private investigator was absolutely correct. We might not find ourselves in this situation, James, had you the foresight to notify the police both here in Birmingham and also in Glasgow."

His voice cut like a knife through melting butter as an icy chill fell upon the room. His fellow Directors waited expectantly, none daring to interrupt, defend or even look at the pale faced Hardie, who spluttered, "I beg to remind you Jackson, that you were not even in the country when this threat occurred! I made the decision..."

"And a bloody bad decision it was too!" interrupted Peters as he banged the table with a fist. "Don't you understand, James? My God," Peters rose slowly to his feet, his hands flat upon the tabletop and his eyes blazing as he stared at Hardie, "you are supposed to think these things through, not persuade this Board to collectively bury their heads in the sand and vainly hope that the threat would simply go away! How the *hell* did you expect just two men, competent though they might be, to solve this threat without the full force of the police to assist them?" He slowly sank back down into his seat, but continued to stare angrily at the red-faced Hardie. "Did you not realise that by immediately refusing to inform the general public and the police of the threat against the company, the damage that you have done? The damage that continues to be done? The possibility of law suits that might bring the company down?" He paused to let his words sink in as he slowly resumed his seat.

"James, James," he slowly shook his head, his voice now sad with disappointment, "I trusted and hoped that you would be a fitting successor to me when I retired, but now this."

"You agreed with me, that I had taken the correct course of action," Hardie had finally found his voice as he growled at Peters.

"No, James," he quietly replied, "let me remind you that what I did was confirm that in my absence, the Board accepted *your* decision, a decision that I questioned but did not overrule for my mistake was in trusting your judgement. I also recall your vehement response when our investigator Mister Blakestock informed you that he had disclosed the threat to some former, but trusted police colleagues. You were almost apoplectic with anger."

"I still maintain I made the correct decision!" snarled Hardie.

"Though on hindsight, perhaps not," Peters coolly replied, then before Hardie could continue, quickly added, "I also recall how opposed you were to paying the demanded money to the women's charities."

"That would have been surrendering to terrorism!" Hardie barked, unaware that Peters had deftly changed the subject and turning, sought to seek support from his fellow Directors, but they all turned away for they now realised to a man where the wind was blowing.

"Perhaps," Peters pursed his lip and shrugged as he replied. "But had you considered that the payment demanded by this Penthesilea offset against the financial loss we will endure, would have been minimum. However, consider this," his gaze swept slowly across the Board members. "Had we made that payment, we could have involved the police who would undoubtedly pursued the individual or individuals threatening the company and even if the one million pounds was never recovered, supporting these women's charities would have resulted in a massive PR coup for Chrystons. Now, our profit loss will run to at least untold millions, but worst of all our credibility as a food product company might possibly take several years to recover."

He paused again to permit the Directors to consider his speech.

Staring at Jackson Peters, James Hardie realised that he had been completely outmanoeuvred, that the blame for this disaster was being placed firmly at his feet. No matter how he tried to defend himself, he had lost the support of his fellow Directors. The possibility of attaining the position he craved, that of CEO was now gone and with a shock he realised that even his position as the Director of Operations was untenable.

If he wished to save face, he now had no choice but to resign. Slowly and a little unsteadily, he rose to his feet as watched by the Board members, he buttoned his suit jacket and taking a deep breath, walked wordlessly slowly from the room.

A moment passed before Peters said, "A little dramatic, but I take it that James is now gone from the Board. Now gentlemen, let us discuss how we might recover from this disaster that threatens to overwhelm us."

The Head Teacher suggested that for their interviews, the two detectives use a classroom that was currently being used to store school furniture.

DC Bob Stevenson agreed with his neighbour, DC Gemma McNulty that it would be time consuming interviewing the all victim's classmates and decided instead to interview the members of staff who had taught Colleen Younger.

In the interest of expediency, they also agreed to conduct the interviews independently of each other and would therefore be able to confer with two teachers at a time.

With so much furniture available, the detectives were able to set up two interview areas at each end of the room and with the cooperation of the Deputy Head Teacher, arranged a rota whereby the staff attended the room two at a time.

"Just like the Ark," grinned McNulty.

Stevenson nodded and regretted that neither he nor DS Leitch had the foresight to send more detectives for he realised that it would take several days to conduct in depth interviews. Instead, he and McNulty were obliged to simply note personal details and ask the most basic of questions.

It was Stevenson's good fortune that his first interview was with the Head of the Mathematics Department, Charlie McFadyen.

Greeting the heavy-set McFadyen and indicating he sit down and after noting his personal details, Stevenson said, "Thanks for your support back there, with the Head I mean."

"No problem," McFadyen smiled. "He's not a bad guy, but a little afraid of making mistakes. Worries too much about his pension. Other than that though, he more or less leaves us alone to get on with our job." His face turned cloudy as shaking his head, he added, "Bad business this."

"Aye, murder is a bad business, but even more so when it's a child," Stevenson agreed.

It didn't escape his notice that McFadyen raised his eyebrows and so he asked, "What?"

McFadyen took a deep breath and said, "Colleen Younger. She was sixteen, as I recall. Sixteen going on thirty."

"She was obviously known to you, then."

"Aye, well known since the day she arrived from primary school. I knew her brothers too. They were also pupils here. Not a popular family with the teaching staff." He paused and continued, "Colleen herself is…sorry, I should say was…" he stopped again and rubbed wearily at his brow, "was not what you might call an out and out troublemaker, but a girl who hated school and had little ambition other than to leave. There are some kids who simply refuse to be taught; they know better than their teachers and to them school is a stopgap that is to be suffered, between birth and going out into the wide world."

"If she was sixteen, couldn't she just leave?"

"She decided to finish the term. You must understand that I'm speculating, but even though she hated being here, I think it was preferable to the home life she had. Have you met the family, her brothers and her mother?"

Stevenson nodded with a sigh, recalling with clarity the Younger house and understood McFadyen's opinion.

"Well, being at school got her out of the house and besides, her friends are in the school during the day anyway."

"Her pals," he slowly nodded. "That will likely include boys too, I suppose?"

McFadyen stared at him and hesitated. In the twenty minutes since the detectives had arrived at the school, his mind had raced and was still in turmoil. All weekend he had given much thought to the allegation that a pupil was in a romantic liaison with a member of the teaching staff…and now this.

The news that Colleen Younger had been murdered shocked him to the core.

Even if the story overheard by the Prefect and told to her form teacher Julia Carson, were true, he had no way of knowing who the pupil or teacher in the alleged relationship was. And besides, he told himself again, it might not be related to the murder of Colleen.

But should he tell the detective of the allegation; was he permitted to make that decision? Naturally, he had informed the Deputy Head of what had supposedly been overheard, but as he correctly predicted, the useless woman had dismissed the allegation almost out of hand as some sort of teenage fantasy.

He worried that if he were to inform the detective of the allegation it could perceivably mislead the CID, perhaps even throw the murder inquiry off on a tangent pursuing the allegation about teacher who might have nothing whatsoever to do with Coleen's murder.

But that was not his decision.

He felt that to inform the detective would relieve him of the burden of knowing and inwardly realised that it should be the CID to decide if his information was of any use.

Taking a deep breath, he slowly exhaled and leaning forward, he glanced nervously to the other end of the room where a colleague was being interviewed by McNulty. Staring Bob Stevenson in the eye, his voice low, he said, "It might be a waste of your time and it could be nothing, but I have something to tell you."

She had just quietly looked in on the sleeping Annemarie and was coming down the stairs when Joyce McKinnon's mobile phone activated and pulling it from her jeans pocket, recognised the caller's number. She couldn't help but smile and answered, "Good Morning, Sandy. How are you?"

"More to the point, how are you?" he replied. "I hear from your secretary that you're taking some time off. I haven't scared you away from work, have I?" he joked, but she thought there was a little unease in his voice.

"No," she unconsciously shook her head and slowly sat down onto the second step, resting her elbow on her knee and her chin in her hand. "I'm staying with my sister for a few days. In Glasgow," she added, but didn't think it wise to provide the address. "She's been a little under the weather and her husbands in hospital, so I thought I'd move in and take care of her daughters. Give her a wee break."

"Oh, right. Anything I can do?" he asked.

"No," she was a little taken aback at his offer, "not really."

There was an uncomfortable silence that lasted more than a few seconds before he said, "Well, I just thought I'd give you a call. See how you were doing. That you were okay."

A little more hurriedly than she intended, she said, "I enjoyed our night," then unaccountable blushing, added, "Well, I mean I know that I wasn't the best of company…"

"I enjoyed it too," he interrupted her. "being with you, I mean. I'd like to do it again. Going out, I mean. For dinner. If you would like to."

God, she thought, why is this so difficult, then inhaling, said, "Sandy. I've been a little distracted recently. Things I've had to do; for my sister, I mean. When I'm done here and back at work, perhaps we could…I don't know. Maybe see each other a little more. Outside work, that is. If you want to."

"Yes, Joyce, I'd like that. To see more of you. Outside work," she could almost hear the pleasure in his voice.

"Look, why don't I give you a call when I'm moving back home, back to my flat. If you like, you could maybe pop up one night. For a drink. Or something to eat, if you like?"

"Yes, that sounds like a plan. Right, I'll let you get on," he said, and ended with, "Stay in touch, Joyce. Please. Oh, and I hope your sister feels better. And of course," he added almost as an afterthought, "her husband, too."

She sat for a moment staring at the blank screen and for the first time in weeks, smiled with real pleasure, buoyed by the realisation that Sandy Munro apparently had a real interest in her; for that brief moment Annemarie and her predicament forgotten.

The consultant leaned over Martin Turner and prised open his eyelid. With a pencil torch he examined the eye and repeated the exercise with the other eye.

"Hmmm," he said as he stood upright.

The young registrar stared expectantly at the consultant who turned and said, "Well, he's still alive then."

Beside the registrar, the staff nurse inhaled and angrily thought, the salary that sod gets and all he can tell us is that the patient is alive. I'm bloody underpaid, I am.

"But no change," the registrar ventured.

"Apparently not," the consultant shrugged and shook his head and added, "but perhaps that's a good thing. His condition doesn't seem to have deteriorated and while of course he remains unconscious, there is only so many tests we can perform. Let's continue with the Silibinin meantime and I'll review him again before I leave today. Staff," he turned to the young woman, "Mister Turner's wife. Has she visited recently? I would like a word with her."

"The ward Sister received a phone call this morning from a relative. Missus Turners sister I think it was, sir. She informed Sister that after her last visit, Missus Turner collapsed outside the casualty ward. As far as I am aware, she was treated for shock and told to get bed rest. I believe the caller said there will be a visitor some time this afternoon, but nobody has yet arrived."

"Right, I see," he stroked his chin. "What about reporters. Have they caused any further trouble trying to get into the ward?"

"No, sir," the nurse replied with a smile. "Not after Sister had a word with them about calling the police."

"Good, good," he nodded, but startled when the patient uttered a loud and sharp scream and began to violently shake on the bed. The registrar quickly moved towards Martin and called out to the nurse, "He's fitting." Grabbing at Martin, he struggled with the nurse to turn him onto his side while the consultant reached out in an attempt to hold the convulsing mans legs that were thrashing about on the bed.

"It seems to be some kind of grand mal seizure," grunted the consultant as with some effort, he managed to restrain Martin's legs then just as quickly as the fit begun, Martin wheezed and with a groan, his body relaxed.

The consultant stared at the registrar and with a relieved sigh, hesitantly withdrew his hold upon Martin. Shaking his head, he said, "I want this man to have an MRI. Set it up and have the results forwarded to me *post haste*, if you please."

When he landed at Glasgow Airport, Tom McEwan was a little surprised to find Martin McConnell waiting for him at the domestic arrivals gate.

"I thought rather than you having to get a taxi to the office and incur Martha's rage with your expense sheet, I would pick you up and we could head straight for the interview with the victim's wife, Missus Turner," McCormick grinned at him. "Now, what's the latest from your meeting at Chrystons?"

Walking to the car park opposite the Terminal building, Tom provided McCormick with an overview of the Board meeting.

"I had a look on the Internet before I left the office," McCormick said. "Chrystons shares in the market have dipped to their lowest ever. Some of the pundits on this mornings news programmes are predicting they might not survive the drop and the word is that their competitors are lining up for a takeover bid," he added.

"Is the warning about the poisoned food products still running in the media?" Tom asked.

Opening the driver door of his car, McCormick nodded and replied, "Every hour in the radio news bulletins and it's hit the newspapers too, of course. I spoke earlier this morning with your friend, Miss Toner at the Woodlands Road store. She told me that so far this morning she's had two customers in complaining that either them or family members felt unwell after eating food bought from her store."

"How did she handle that?"

"Took their details," he started the engine, "though only one of the customers brought back the remains of the food and the packaging. Miss Toner has instructions from her head office to forward every complaint to her head office and that includes the food and packaging. She believes that once the complaints are assessed, it's likely that we as the Scottish legal representatives for Chrystons will be contacted by the head office and asked to make inquiry into the complaints. If nothing else, it's more work for us," he grinned as they passed through the security barrier.

"Did she make any comment about the customers or their complaints?"

McCormick gave him a wry smile and replied, "She's of the opinion that they're both at it. Said one of the customers is known to her staff and lives locally; described her as heavy bevy woman that's frequently in hovering about the drinks aisle. Nevertheless, she is instructed by her head office to simply note the details of the complaints and pass them on and not to challenge the customers about the complaints."

Tom was tempted to ask if Ellen had mentioned him, but decided that this wasn't the time to disclose his interest in her to Martin. "What about the victim, Martin Turner. Any further news on him?"

"I phoned the Royal this morning, but when I was put through to the ward, the nurse I spoke with told me she can't give out any information unless it is to a family member," he sighed. "I'm guessing, but I think the hospital has probably been inundated with calls from the media about Turners condition, so quite rightly the hospital isn't giving out any information."

He turned onto the east bound lane of the M8 and continued. "I also had an interesting phone call this morning from my cousin Lynn Massey. She's heard from one of her DI's at Stewart Street…"

"That will be Mickey Farrell. I met with him before I flew south," Tom intimated.

"Yes, well, Lynn learned of your interest in the case from this guy Farrell and wanted to assure me that she would not interfere in your inquiry provided," he paused and turned briefly towards Tom to stress again, "*provided* we keep Farrell updated with anything we learn that might identify the culprit who is responsible for poisoning Martin Turner. Needless to say I agreed and Lynn has in turn agreed that anything the police discover that might assist us, she has no problem with us being kept in the police investigation loop."

McCormick continued, "I called Missus Turner this morning to set a time for our interview. It wasn't her, but her sister that I spoke with, a Miss McKinnon. She's agreed that we can call at the house, but she isn't certain if her sister will be up for an interview. Apparently Missus Turner collapsed yesterday when she visited her husband in hospital and the doctor recommended she take some time in bed."

"Do you think it's a ploy?" Tom asked. "I mean, pretending to be ill on the back of her husband consuming the poison; setting herself up for a claim against Chrystons for what, emotional distress or something like that?"

"Could be," McCormick mused, "but lets not make any hasty decisions until we have spoken with her."

"How do you propose to deal with her today?"

"Well, while you were in midflight, I spoke with Gregory Packer, the guy who first contacted me…"

"Yeah," Tom interrupted as he turned towards him, "I know who he is. He's the Deputy Operations man. He met with me when I first travelled down to Birmingham. Nice enough fellow I thought, but a little lacking in confidence considering his position in the company." McCormick nodded and then said, "What you might *not* know is that since this morning, he's no longer the Deputy Operations man. It seems his boss Mister Hardie has resigned," and before Tom could ask, added, "I don't know any details, but suffice to say that Packer is now the acting Director of Operations and as such is our contact regarding any further issues we deal with on behalf of Chrystons, here in Scotland."

"Wow, so Hardie's gone," Tom slowly replied, his curiosity eating at him. "He was at the Board meeting this morning. I wonder what happened there?"

"What about the threat from this Penthesilea," McCormick interrupted his thoughts. "What do you think will be the next demand?"

"Hard to say, but with the publicity surrounding the poisoning of Martin Turner it's likely that whoever is behind the threat must realise they have lost any suggestion of public sympathy. That and though we can't for the minute prove it, Gavin Blakestock and me are both of the opinion that our female suspect *is* Penthesilea; that it's one individual and not a group."

"Oh, well that's a step forward at least, but what do you mean by losing public sympathy?"

"Well, think about it. If the threat is *really* designed to help the women who have supposedly been exploited by Chrystons and that threat became public knowledge, Chrystons as a company would be reviled for their sexism, both socially and by its customers. However, Penthesilea would be hailed as the individual or group who had exposed Chrystons; perhaps even extolled as the individual or group who were fighting for women's rights."

"But now that they carried out their threat…"

"The media will lambast them or her, I should say, for the criminal she is," Tom nodded.

"You still believe in your theory that there is another agenda, this second agenda you told me about?"

"I can't explain it, Martin," he slowly shook his head, "but I have this gut feeling that there's more to the threat against Chrystons than what we already know."

"Back to Missus Turner," McCormick slowly said. "Gregory Packer has related an instruction from the CEO, Mister Peters, that we are to be totally upfront and honest with Missus Turner and if her husband dies as the doctors expect he will, Peters wants us to assist Missus Turner with any legal or other expenses in the interim. According to Packer, Peters does not wish the already negative media campaign to worsen and expressly directed that our dealings with Missus Turner be as positive and transparent as possible." He turned briefly to smile at Tom and added, "We must be seen to be the good guys, particularly if she has been in touch with the media, so no badgering the woman."

"Even if we suspect that she might be a money grabbing lady who is out to screw Chrystons for millions?"

"Even that," McCormick sighed.

"Hmmm, then this visit might be interesting," Tom shrugged.


Driving from the private car park that served the senior management of Chrystons, James Hardie's shock at his unwarranted treatment by Jackson Peters turned from surprise through to anger and finally settled on outright hatred for the man.

That he, the only hope the fucking company has of coming out of this debacle, should be treated like some sort of...of...manager!

He was a Director, for Christ sake! How *dare* Peters treat him like that; ridiculed and humiliated in front of that sycophantic bunch of shits!

He banged a fist off the steering wheel and oblivious to the other road users, raced towards his home in the fashionable Westfield Road area of Birmingham.

Turning into the drive, his anger had not abated and a dozen ideas of how to get even with Peters were already racing through his head.

He would destroy the bastard, of that he was certain!

He slowed up as he approached the front entrance to the large house, surprised to see two men, one white and the other a black man, both wearing dark suits, white shirts and dark ties and curiously, black framed sunglasses, stood in the portico on either side of the door.

He stopped the car and getting out, warily approached them.

"Can I help you?" he asked, adopting a firm voice.

"Mister 'Ardie," asked the tall and heavily built black man, a Londoner he guessed from the way he dropped the H in Hardie.

"Yes, that's me; who the devil are you and why are you stood here at my house?"

The black man turned and smiled at his companion who was equally as tall and large.

"My associate and I are representatives of the law firm engaged by your wife, Missus 'Ardie," the man replied, "here to ensure that you comply with this."

He reached into his inner suit pocket and handed Hardie a folded document.

Puzzled, Hardie took the document from his hand and opening it, saw it to be three A4 sheets of papers stapled at the top left hand corner, but it was the bold upper case typed heading that attracted his attention. His eyes opened wide and his head shot up as startled, he gasped, "But this is an injunction and it…it bans me from my own home!"

"Yes, sir," smiled the black man. "Granted this morning on behalf of your good lady against you by the Crown Court in Birmingham, because Missus 'Ardie fears for her safety…from you," he added with a tight smile.

"But…but…I don't understand!"

"I fink if you read it through, Mister 'Ardie, it will all become clear," the man smiled again and turned to theatrically wink at his companion who stood with his hands clasped in front of him, stared menacingly at the confused Hardie.

"I'll bloody sort this out," he made to step towards the door, but both men closed together shoulder to shoulder in front of the door to block him and timidly, he quickly stepped back.

"I fink Mister 'Ardie you should leave, sir. Just in case you come to some 'arm, if you know what I mean, sir."

"Are you threatening me?"

"Oh no, Mister 'Ardie, but let's put it this way. Your good lady has changed the door locks and that there," he pointed to the document in Hardie's hand, "forbids you from contacting Missus 'Ardie other than through her solicitor, whose name is on the injunction. Oh, and by the way," Hardie could see that both men were now struggling to keep from laughing as the black man went into his jacket pocket, "your wife gave me these for you to peruse, Mister 'Ardie," and handed him a bulky cardboard envelope. "I should add I'm to tell you that those are copies, Mister 'Ardie. I understand your good lady and her solicitor have their own copies if you need any more," he smirked.

"By the way, sir," the man pointed towards the entrance gates at the bottom of the driveway, "At the request of your good lady, me mate and me took the liberty of dropping your suitcases down there for you. No need to thank us," he raised a hand. "You can pick them up on your way off the premises…sir."

His hands shaking, he turned and saw three suitcases sitting forlornly where the man pointed and then head bent, slowly opened the cardboard envelope.

He almost fainted with shock.

Watched by the grinning men, he saw with horror the envelope contained a number of coloured photographs that clearly showed him and Lesley Peters naked and in sexually compromising positions.

Stunned, the photographs fell from his hands and turning, he almost fell into the driving seat of the car.

Turning out of the ornate gateway into the quiet suburban road, the suitcases ignored, James Hardie was slowing coming to realise that not only was he resigned from his Directorship at Chrystons Supermarkets (PLC), but that he was now homeless and though he was not yet aware, soon to learn that his private and what he believed to be his secret and private bank accounts, had been frozen by the same Court that issued his wife Margo with her injunction.

Joyce McKinnon had decided to tidy the front room, but entering the room glanced around her and sadly shook her head. The room needed no tidying for her sister Annemarie had been so cowed by her husband Martin, so frightened of his pernickety ways there was not the slightest, minute dust to be found and the room was spick and span. Sighing, she lifted the couch cushions and plumped them up. She heard the creak of floorboards and movement from upstairs and making her way into the hallway saw Annemarie, wearing an old and worn terry bathrobe, slowly coming downstairs.

"You look terrible. You should be lying down, taking it easy," she rebuked her sister.

Annemarie stopped midway and pushing her hair back from her face, yawned and smiled. "I've had more than enough rest for today. In fact, that is the longest I've stayed in bed since…God, I can't remember when."

Her face grew serious as she asked, "Has there been any word?"

"No," Joyce sighed. "I phoned the ward earlier this morning and explained that you are unwell and told the nurse I spoke with that I'll visit him tonight."

"Do you really need to?"

Joyce, her chin resting on her arms as she leaned on the lower banister, stared up at her and replied, "We have to keep the illusion going that we are a concerned family. It would look suspicious if we didn't visit him. Besides, we need to know what's going on, whether he's going to…"

"To die," Annemarie finished for her.

"Yes, Annemarie, to die."

They didn't speak for a few seconds then Joyce brightly said, "Well, as long as you're up, do you think you might manage some lunch?"

"I can try," Annemarie forced a smile and continued to come down the stairs, but then Joyce turned and said, "I forgot to mention. You had a phone call from a solicitor, some guy called McCormick that's acting on behalf of the store, Chrystons, where you bought the pie. He asked to speak with you; says the company would like some more details about the purchase and to find out if you need any help at the minute."

Annemarie frowned. "You don't think that they might suspect something, that they…"

"No, absolutely not," Joyce confidently shook her head. "We discussed this, remember? It's probably likely that Chrystons are covering their back. They sold…" she stopped and sadly smiled, "or think they sold a poisoned pie. They are taking a bit of a beating in the news because of it and I'm guessing that this lawyer, McCormick has been told to do some damage limitation. All you have to do is remember the story we agreed; that you were with the children in the city, you visited the Argyle Street store and bought your husbands favourite chicken pie that you later cooked that night for his dinner. If they ask for details, you remember dropping your handbag at the front door. Don't elaborate, just keep to the details we spoke about, okay?"

Her eyes narrowed. "That reminds me. Did you keep the till receipt?"

"Yes, it's in my purse."

"Good," Joyce smiled. "The receipt will have the time and date on it and the lawyer can verify your presence in the store by matching the receipt to the CCTV cameras."

She moved towards Annemarie and hugged her. "Don't worry, sis. It will all turn out fine."

"Yes," she quietly replied, "just as long as he never comes home, you mean."

While James Hardie was panicking about his future, his nemesis Jackson Peters had just returned home from the Board meeting and learned from the housekeeper that Missus Peters was at the gym. From previous habit Peters guessed it would be a full hour or more before she returned and instructed the housekeeper to pack his wife's clothing and jewellery into her suitcases and to leave them outside the front door.

Suspecting there was something afoot, the housekeeper wisely made no comment and did as she was told while the recently arrived locksmith worked quickly at changing the locks on the doors.

It was about twenty minutes after he returned home that Peters solicitor arrived and confirmed at the Court that morning the divorce paperwork was lodged and the injunction granted pending the divorce action against Lesley Peters.

With his client's permission, the solicitor suggested he remain in the house to personally serve the papers upon the adulterous Missus Peters when she arrived home. The solicitor also confirmed that instructed by his client, Lesley's personal bank account was cancelled and all funds transferred to Jackson Peters own account, thereby leaving his soon to be former wife with no immediate income.

"Perhaps you might consider some small gratuity, just as a goodwill gesture," suggested the solicitor.

"She can sell the car, her designer clothing or her jewellery," was Peters only response to this request for after all, he was not so heartless he would leave her completely bereft of some form of revenue.

"Jackson, do you wish to see Lesley when she arrives?" his old friend asked.

"No, she is no longer welcome and not to enter the house," he firmly instructed and handing the solicitor a cardboard wallet of photographs, added, "However, perhaps you might be good enough to provide her with her own copies. She may wish to refer them to her solicitor should she foolishly choose to defend the action."

The arrangements made, he permitted himself a large cognac and settled into his comfortable chair in his study to patiently await the fracas that was soon to arrive at his front door.

Detective Constable's Bob Stevenson and Gemma McNally arrived back at Kirkintilloch office and while McNulty headed to the Ladies, Stevenson made his way to the incident room to return their completed Actions.

"Anything of interest," Anne Leitch stared up at him.

"To be honest, Anne, we really need a team at the school if we're going to conduct in-depth interviews with both the staff and any pupils that knew our victim. Gemma and I managed a few staff interviews, but we only scratched the surface."

"Okay, point taken, but did you learn anything of use?"

"No, not really," Stevenson shook his head, "though I did have an interesting discussion with one of the departmental heads, a Mister McFadyen. Seems that one of the school Prefects was in the girls' toilets and overheard some pupils giggling about one of them shagging a teacher. No names or descriptions of the teacher or the pupil allegedly involved..."

"A male teacher?"

"You know," Stevenson looked thoughtful as he shook his head, "I presumed it was a male, but on hindsight I think I'll give McFadyen a phone just to confirm that."

As it didn't seem to be directly connected with the murder, Leitch was losing interest in the supposed shenanigans at the school, but asked, "What are the school doing about it?"

"According to McFadyen, nothing. He seems to be a decent guy and he's a bit peeved that after bringing it to the attention of the Deputy Head, she is content to simply treat it as a schoolgirls fantasy."

"So, really nothing for us to investigate?"

"No, I suppose not," Stevenson replied and placing the Actions down in front of Leitch, he added, "Apart from that little juicy bit of gossip, like I said we need more bodies down there to conduct better more interviews."

"Right, leave it with me and I'll put it to the DI."

"Anything else happening?"

"No, stalemate so far, but the substance discovered under the victim's fingernails is in fact blood and the Lab have obtained DNA from it. I asked the DI if we could begin conducting elimination DNA samples, but he flatly refused."

She saw Stevenson was grinning at her.

"Do I sound annoyed," she asked him.

"Just a wee bit," he confirmed.


Charlie McFadyen felt guilty about relating the allegation to the detective about the pupil and the teacher; a little like he was adding two and two together and coming up with five. However, telling the big detective brought back his indignation that if the allegation were true, no bugger was doing anything about it.

The more he thought about it, the angrier he got and so made the decision that without informing the Deputy Head, he would himself interview the Prefect, but to negate any allegation that might arise from the interview thought it would be prudent to have the form teacher, Julia Carson, sitting in his room when he spoke to the lassie. Now seated at his desk, he stared at the nervous teenager.

"Am I in trouble, sir?" the young girl asked, the wariness obvious in her eyes.

"No, not at all," he waved his hand in front of her and smiled. "In fact, I'd like to commend you for bringing this information to Miss Carson here," he nodded to the teacher. "The reason I'm speaking with you is to clarify what you think you heard?"

"I didn't *think* I heard it, sir," the Prefect replied, a little annoyed at the inference she might be fibbing. "I *did* hear it."

"Well, can you tell me again what you heard?"

The girl turned to glance at Carson before replying, "Well, like I said before to Miss Carson, I was in the girls' toilet on the first landing; in a cubicle, you know…" she blushed, unaware that McFadyen already knew of her smoking.

"I have two daughters slightly older than you," he refrained from smiling. "There's no need to explain why a young lady visits the toilets."

"Yes, sir," she nodded.

"Now, tell me exactly what you heard?"

The girl took a deep breath and said, "Well, I was just about to leave the cubicle when I heard what sounded like three girls talking. I knew that they weren't sixth year, I think they sounded more like third or fourth year; you know, not that mature? Their...their language was, well, you know..." she shrugged.

"Juvenile?"

Quite unabashed she replied, "Yes, sir, council girls, I'd say. Plenty of fucks and bastards and words that *I* wouldn't normally use."

"Ah, yes, I *think* I understand," he replied, forcing himself to remain pokerfaced while conscious that in the corner, Julia Carson's face turned red at the Prefect's fruitful language.

"Anyway," the girl sat forward, now eager to relate her story, "I heard one girl say that she was shagging a teacher. The other girls tried to persuade her to say who the teacher was, but all she would tell them was that she screwed the teacher in the back of his fancy beamer."

McFadyen's eyes narrowed. "His beamer? You're quite certain that's what was said? The word beamer was used?"

"Oh, yes sir," the girl enthusiastically nodded her head, then slowly turned towards Carson. "I did say beamer, Miss. Don't you remember?"

He glanced sharply towards Carson and said, "You never mentioned a beamer, Miss Carson."

"I'm sorry, Mister McFadyen," she stuttered, clearly embarrassed. "I don't drive...well, actually I'm taking lessons," she gushed then seeing McFadyen's irate face, mumbled, "I thought that the word beamer simply meant a car. I didn't know...didn't think..." she lamely finished.

A beamer, he slowly shook his head; a BMW.

From memory, there were a number of such vehicles parked in the staff car park. It wouldn't be too difficult to identify those male teachers who drove such vehicles, he thought. He turned again to the Prefect and asked, "The girl who was supposed to be having this…this relationship with a teacher. Did you know her voice or would you recognise her voice again?"

"No, sir, I don't think so," the girl slowly replied, "but she did say that she was meeting him again, the teacher I mean."

"Did you happen to hear when or where?"

"No, sir," the girl shook her head.

Staring anxiously at McFadyen, Carson shook her head as though this latest titbit was news to her.

Privately, McFadyen thought that Carson had just been too eager to pass the information along and hadn't taken the time to properly listen to what the Prefect told her.

"Well, thank you. That has been most helpful," he nodded to dismiss the smiling girl while Carson stood hesitantly, unsure if she should remain or go. "Thank you, Miss Carson," he forced a smile to dismiss her too, but really wanted to kick her stupid backside.

After both the young women had left his room, he considered what he should do with this new found information, but whatever he decided, he realised he would be better keeping the Deputy Head out of the loop.

## CHAPTER NINETEEN

In his first floor, two-room office in the Sparkbrook area of Birmingham, Gavin Blakestock sipped at a mug of strong, black tea while he brooded over the synopsis of information that both he and Tom McEwan had so far acquired.

The owner and sole Director of Blakestock Inquiry Agency, he was also the principal and only investigator and lone intelligence analyst and lorded it over his one member of staff; his wife Celia who acted as his receptionist, telephonist, office cleaner, accountant, typist, and chief bottle washer, though not necessarily in that order.

Following his retirement from the West Midlands Police with the rank of Detective Superintendent, the restless Blakestock first turned his hand to doing nothing; a job that lasted all of one week before his frustrated wife convinced him that as twenty-five of his thirty years' service was spent in CID units, he should put that experience to better use and suggested he set himself up as a private investigator. In the seven years since they had jointly made that decision, he had never been happier; even more so when his still very attractive wife of thirty-eight years agreed to work with him, telling him, "I've endured those years of you working all sorts of hours, Gavin Blakestock and I hardly ever saw you for weeks on end. At least now we can finally spend our time be together and I can also keep my eye on you!"

"Penny for them," she said from the door of his office, then leaning heavily on her cane, shuffled through to painfully slump down onto the chair opposite his desk.

He glanced at her, at the weariness that lined her face. He hated seeing her like this and again felt helpless that there was so little he could do to ease her ache.

"That hip bothering you again, love?"

"It's the weather," she sighed glancing through the window at the falling rain. "It always comes on worse during the wet weather."

"Perhaps we should seriously consider having that operation," he quietly suggested.

"We? There's no *we* about it, Gavin Blakestock. It's me that would go under the knife. No, time enough in the new year."

"You said that last year," he huffily reminded her, but his comment only provoked a grin.

"That the Chrystons report?"

"Yes," he nodded and laid the paperwork flat onto his desk. "That young Scots lad, Tom. He's certainly very bright and astute. I like him. I could have used a couple more like him when I was serving with the CID," he mused.

"Do you think he is on to something? What you told me, about the threat being more than just the demand for compensation for the women employees?"

"I do, love. I have to admit though," he wheezed, "it was Tom who got us thinking that way. Smart of him it was too."

Celia shook her head and said, "That poor man who was poisoned. Is there any word on his condition?"

"Still alive as far as I'm aware, though from what Tom was telling me his prognosis isn't great. If he *should* survive the poisoning, he's likely to be left with serious internal problems that today's medicine won't cure."

"And he's married, you said?"

"Yes. A wife and two small girls. Tom McEwan and his boss should be on their way there now to meet with the wife; try and determine what help they can provide during this…"

His eyes narrowed and he peered down at the report, then lifted it from the desk. "I wonder…" he muttered.

"You've got that look in your eyes, Gavin Blakestock," she teased. "What are you thinking?"

He was reaching for his mobile phone and punching in the number before he replied, "A thought has just occurred to me. I hope I can catch young Tom before he goes to the victim's home to speak with the wife." His eyes widened and he said, "Tom? It's Gavin. Can you speak?"

"Hello, Gavin. Yes, Martin and I are just pulling up outside Missus Turner's house. What's up?"

"This idea you have, that there's more to the threat than just the female employees being compensated."

"Yes," McEwan slowly drawled, "go on and Gavin, I've put you on speaker to allow Martin to listen in."

"Okay; hello Martin," Blakestock formally greeted McCormick, then continued. "I might be coming at this from the wrong angle, thinking outside the box as it were, but continuing your thought and your comment about a second agenda; what if the threat against Chrystons isn't the primary threat, that the company is not the principal target? What if your second agenda is our victim and *he* is in fact the primary target for the poisoning? Based on that supposition, if the victim is the target for the poisoning, it could be that the Scottish woman we're looking for is the victim's wife."

There was a stunned silence and then Tom replied, "You're thinking that it might be a scam by the wife to extort money from Chrystons and do away with her husband too?"

"Be honest with me, Tom; does it sound too far fetched?"

"No, not at all," he could almost hear the tension in Tom's voice. "It's obviously something that we must consider. Look, Gavin, I can see someone looking out of the window at us, so I'll cut this short, but as soon as I'm out of the house I'll call you with a description of Missus Turner and bring you up to date with how we get on."

Blakestock ended the call and paused before he quietly said to his wife, "That's the worst part of this job; the waiting."

Detective Inspector Murray Fitzpatrick sat brooding morosely in his office, wondering if he had been too quick to dismiss DS Leitch's suggestion that the inquiry team begin to acquire DNA samples from witnesses for elimination purposes.

It had always been a source of pride that he kept his inquiry budget to a minimum and it irked him when he had either to request further detective resources or ask that…that woman Massey for Forensic or logistic support.

Try as he might, he was unable to hide his dislike for Lynn Massey and was acutely aware of her feelings abut him. His anger brought on the ache in his chest and he reached into the drawer to fetch the small plastic bottle. Tipping out two of the red coloured pills, he swallowed and washed them down with a little water from the bottle he kept in the drawer.

Within a few minutes, he felt better and reaching for the phone, dialled the internal number for DS Leitch.

His office door knocked then Anne Leitch popped her head through and said, "You wanted me, sir?"

He held up a report and said, "This Action that was submitted by DC Stevenson. He spoke with a teacher at the victim's school who confided that there was some sort of inappropriate relationship taking place between a teacher and a pupil. Just how much do we know about that?"

Leitch pursed her lips and shaking head head, replied, "It was an allegation, sir. Nothing to suggest it might have been the victim. Do you want some further inquiry made?"

Fitzpatrick sighed and said, "So far, Sergeant, we have very little to go on. It might do no harm to have DC Stevenson contact the teacher again and elicit what detail he can if nothing more than eliminating the possibility it might have been the victim."

Leitch nodded and inwardly thought, good idea, but annoyed that she hadn't taken as much notice of Jumbo's report than had the DI.

"I'll get Jumbo…I mean, DC Stevenson on to it right away, sir."

Returning to her desk, she reached for the phone to call Stevenson, but stopped when she saw him and his neighbour, Gemma McNulty push open the door and enter the incident room. "Jumbo," she called out and beckoned him over to her. "That teacher you spoke with at the school who made the allegation about the teacher and..."

"Mister McFadyen," he interrupted her. "Funny you should mention him, Anne. He's just sent me a text message asking if I'd call back at the school. Seems he's got some further information for me."

"Right then, I'll have an Action created for you to follow up speaking with him. Let me know pronto what you learn," she lowered her voice. "The DI has an interest in it."

"On it," he smiled and calling out to McNulty, left the incident room.

Across the city, DI Mickey Farrell's inquiry was currently at a dead end. Other than having a man lying seriously ill in the Royal Infirmary and being aware that Martin Turner was the victim of a threat against Chrystons, Farrell was no further forward to finding the culprit or culprits who had committed the crime. Sat with his feet up on top of his desk, his tie undone, the remains of a pie and chips wrapped in its polystyrene container stuffed in the bin beside him and a large mug of coffee at his elbow, he was thoroughly pissed off. The interview with the victim's wife, Annemarie Turner had proved fruitless; unable to tell him anything other than last Saturday she had bought the poisoned pie in the Argyle Street store and served her husband with the pie that night. That and the Forensic examination of the wrapper had proved useless.

Her sore eye bothered him, though. It was quite evident that somebody, her man if she was to be believed, had given her a dull one. The eye was turning rainbow coloured, suggesting it had occurred a few days earlier; certainly less than a week anyway.

He hadn't pursued the reason for her husband punching her to the face simply because Farrell was a man and in his book men didn't hit women, so there was *no* reason to lift a hand to hurt a woman. And that, according to the rules Mickey Farrell lived by, was that. He shook his head as though to clear it of his thoughts for even thinking about the woman's sore face had made him unaccountably angry.

It had occurred to him that perhaps Missus Turner had deliberately and knowingly poisoned her husband, but there were several reasons that refuted that idea.

She had purchased the pie on the Saturday, evident from the time and date on the till receipt and the CCTV recording that confirmed her and the wee girls' presence in the store and that was prior to the public alert by Chrystons about the threat of the contaminated food. Besides, the packaging she had retrieved from her recycle bin and handed to him and Willie McGuigan was clearly marked with an X; again this information was prior to it being broadcast.

No, he slowly shook his head, Missus Turner could not have been privy to any prior information about the poisoned chicken pie that she served her husband.

However, if like she said it was her husband that battered her, he suppressed a grin, then serving the bastard with poisoned pie couldn't have happened to a better man.

Martin McCormick had pulled up behind the Ford Fiesta that was parked across the driveway and walking up the path to the front door, both men could not but admire the highly polished BMW car that sat behind the rusting Ford Escort.

It was Joyce McKinnon who opened the door to admit them, explaining that her sister Missus Turner was in the front room.

"My nieces are at school and I'll be leaving shortly to uplift them, but I'll get you a coffee or tea the before I go," she courteously offered as she led them into the room, but both men declined. She did not follow them into the room, but closed the door behind them.

Annemarie, now dressed in a plain white blouse and black, knee length skirt, her shoulder length auburn hair neatly brushed and tied back with a white ribbon, stood up from the armchair as both men entered.

Tom immediately saw how attractive Annemarie Turner was and though she looked pale and drawn, he was certain that despite the fact she had skilfully applied makeup, there appeared to be some bruising to her left eye.

"Please sit down," she smiled nervously at them and smoothing down her skirt, sat down on the edge of the armchair, her knees primly together and her hands clasped upon her lap.

The two men sat side by side on the couch and once seated, McCormick placed his briefcase upon his knees and withdrawing a legal pad and a pen, rested the pad on top of the briefcase.

In the car, they had agreed that McCormick would conduct the interview with Missus Turner and it was he who introduced them both, describing Tom as his firms' investigator.

"Tom is currently liaising with Police Scotland, Missus Turner, to try and identify who is responsible for what happened to your husband," McCormick explained and then asked how Martin was. "There has been no change since my sister Joyce phoned a few hours ago. I took unwell yesterday when I visited him," she quietly replied, "and I was briefly admitted to the casualty when I fainted at the entrance. I feel a little foolish about it all," she blushed. "My sister came to the hospital with my daughters and brought me home. She's been running about after me," she smiled with a sigh. "After she walked the girls to school this morning she went and fetched Martin's...the car from where I'd parked it at the hospital. The doctor at the casualty department said I wasn't to drive, that I was suffering from delayed shock and instructed that I am to rest. Joyce will go and visit Martin tonight and we'll get an update from the doctor then."

"I understand your husband is a teacher?"

"Yes, he teaches maths at the secondary school in Ryehill Road in Barmulloch."

"I presume the school is aware that he is currently confined in hospital?"

She softly smiled and replied, "Joyce spoke this afternoon with the Deputy Head so yes, the school is aware."

They heard the sound of the front door closing and assumed that the sister was off to collect the children from their school.

"Okay," he smiled, "let me explain the purpose of our visit today. Quite simply Mister McEwan and I act in Scotland on behalf of Chrystons Supermarkets (PLC)."

He didn't get any further for Tom McEwan butted in and said, "Missus Turner, your sister told us that she's away to collect your daughters from their school. You've said that you had a bit of a fainting fit yesterday at the hospital. In the interest of fairness to you, perhaps we should wait until your sister returns then she can sit with you while Mister McCormick explains any further." He smiled and added, "It wouldn't be proper if you've been unwell; we wouldn't like anyone to think that we were taking advantage of your situation."

"Yes, of course, you're right," she smiled and then a little hesitatingly, asked, "While we're waiting, would you like tea or perhaps coffee?"

Both men agreed this time and asked for coffee and when Annemarie had left the room, a puzzled McCormick quietly asked, "I suppose you have a good reason for waiting?"

"I'd like to get a proper sit-down with the sister. It will be handy if we could speak to them both and try to assess if Gavin Blakestock might be on to something."

"Okay," McCormick slowly agreed, but warned Tom, "Just don't get them riled up. I don't want us getting tossed out on ear because we've upset them by suggesting they might be implicated or something," he hissed.

"Okay, boss," Tom agreed.

A few minutes later the door opened and Annemarie, carefully carrying a tray, set it down onto a small side table before handing them a coffee.

They chatted informally for almost fifteen minutes, mainly about bringing up children before they heard the sound of the door opening and listened to the noise of two, squealing girls in the hallway.

The door opened and the two girls, shepherded by their aunt, shyly entered to stand by their mother who wrapped an arm about their waists.

"My angels," she proudly called them, then Joyce said, "Right you two. Just like we agreed. Upstairs to do your homework and if there is no noise, there will be a chocolate treat."

When the girls run from the room, Annemarie called to her sister, "Mister McCormick's colleague suggested that we wait till you returned, Joyce, so that you could sit with me."

"We thought that would be advisable," McCormick confirmed.

"Give me a minute till I sort the girls out and I'll be right back," Joyce replied and

a couple of minutes later, returned from upstairs and settled herself in the second armchair.

Glancing at her, Tom McEwan decided that like her older sister, Joyce McKinnon was a fine looking woman, but wondered at the absence of any rings on her left hand.

"I understand, Missus Turner, that you have been interviewed by the CID?" McCormick asked.

"Yes, by a Mister Farrell and another detective. They came to the house and took away the wrapper that was on the pie. Oh, and my till receipt. From Chrystons, in Argyle Street. Where I bought the pie."

"I see," he made a notation on his pad, then said, "My purpose in being here is as I said earlier, to represent the interest of Chrystons. Now, you must be aware of the media interest in your husbands unfortunate…illness as a result of consuming the pie purchased in Chrystons. Needless to say, Chrystons feel awful that this has occurred, but of course they do not sell poisoned pies; the pie was unlawfully tampered with and the poison added to the product, then the pie was replaced for sale to be purchased by an unsuspecting customer; in this case, by you."

He paused and then carefully told them, "Now, while the investigation proceeds to identify and arrest whoever did this, Chrystons are not in a position to make any settlement with you until this issue is resolved."

Tom glanced at both Annemarie Turner and her sister and formed the opinion that while neither had so far asked any question, both were listening intently and he assumed saving their questions till McCormick had completed his address.

"However," McCormick continued, "I am instructed by the Chief Executive Officer for Chrystons, Mister Peters, that while the company do not at this time accept any liability or responsibility for your husband's condition, the company are willing to forward to you a remuneration to assist you with any fees that you incur as a result of your husband's incapacity at this time. In short, Missus Turner, as a gesture of good faith the company will assist with any bills, whether they be medical, transport or anything that is incurred until your husband returns to work."

"What about funeral bills!" Joyce McKinnon unexpectedly snapped at him.

An awkward silence fell upon the room, broken when McCormick nodded and replied, "Yes, Miss McKinnon. If the very worst occurs; funeral expenses too."

"And are you here to ensure that my sister doesn't upset your apple cart? That she doesn't make a fuss? That she doesn't get herself a lawyer and sue the arse off your company?"

"Joyce, please," Annemarie nervously extended a hand to calm her sister, but Joyce was on a roll and nostrils flaring, stared aggressively at McCormick.

"Your company…"

"Chrystons," he quickly corrected her.

"Whatever! Chrystons sold my sister a poisoned pie that she unwittingly served to her husband. Let me ask you this, Mister McCormick," she was now on the edge of her seat, "if you were a lawyer representing my sister, what would *you* suggest she do?"

"But I'm *not* representing your sister, Miss McKinnon, so it's a moot point," he replied. But Martin McCormick was no fool and returning her stare, he calmly continued, "What I *am* trying to convey to Missus Turner is that on the instruction of Mister Peters…"

"Yes, the CEO. I know about him," she interrupted and nodded.

"Mister Peters wishes that all assistance be provided to your sister and when the matter of the poisoned food products is resolved, I am instructed to discuss with Missus McKinnon some form of compensation."

He could see that Joyce was again about to speak, but holding up his hand, firmly added, "I agree. Missus Turner is quite at liberty to engage legal representation, however, I wish to remind you that while Chrystons has accepted liability for selling the product, it was *not* Chrystons who poisoned the pie, Miss McKinnon. That was an act of criminality by a third person or persons who are now actively being sought by the police as well as private investigators, appointed by Chrystons. Now, in my experience if you advise your sister to pursue a lawsuit against Chrystons, there is more than a strong possibility that a court will find in favour of Chrystons and I use a metaphor merely as an example; if the driver of a stolen car runs down an old woman on a pedestrian crossing, does the court convict the driver or the owner whose car was stolen?"

Tom McEwan stared from McCormick to Joyce, wondering where the hell *that* had come from, but seeing the expression on her face realised McCormick's example had effectively hit home.

"So, Mister McCormick," Annemarie quietly addressed him, "am I to understand that while Martin remains in hospital, any bills that result from his confinement, loss of salary if the period exceeds three months, that sort of thing, will be covered by Chrystons?"

"As a gesture of goodwill by Chrystons, most assuredly, Missus Turner. I will be your point of contact for any news regarding your husband or any hardship that you and your children suffer as a result of his illness."

"Well then, one final query, Mister McCormick," she peered questioningly at him. "Can I trust you?"

He softly smiled and holding up his legal pad, replied, "As likely you saw, I made some notes. Upon my return to the office, Missus Turner, I intend dictating a letter that will contain all I have said and written; a letter that I will sign and have returned to you by first class post. I am trusted by Chrystons to represent them and if Chrystons do not hold up to the agreement that have asked me to propose to you, then you have my word…and that will also be included in the letter…my word that I will represent you in any action you decide to take against Chrystons."

"Isn't that some sort of conflict of interest," Joyce asked, her expression indicating her puzzlement.

"If Chrystons withdraw or fail to honour their promise to your sister, Miss McKinnon, I will no longer represent them; so no, there will be no conflict of interest for they will also be failing me," he replied.

Joyce continued to stare at him, then lowering her head, slowly shook it before commenting, "Well, if you *are* to be believed, I don't suppose there is anything else to say, is there?"

He turned towards Annemarie and asked, "Any further questions, Missus Turner?"

"No," she shook her head.

"Perhaps I might ask you a question, Missus Turner," Tom said. "Have you ever been employed by Chrystons?"

Joyce rose quickly to her feet, her fists clenched and tensely replied, "Are you tying to accuse my sister of something?"

"No," he shook his head, "but it's my job to ask the hard questions, Miss McKinnon. I've a job to do and that includes eliminating all persons who are directly or indirectly involved in this crime as suspects. It's a simple enough question."

"No, Mister McEwan," Annemarie interrupted, her hands raised towards Joyce to calm her and shook her head. "Before I married I was employed as a perfume and cosmetics sales assistant in Buchanan Street. I have never worked for Chrystons."

That explains the cover up for that bruising, he mused, then turned towards Joyce who remained standing with her arms folded, but before he could ask, she sharply said, "I'm a senior lecturer at the City College in Food Sciences and no, I have never been employed by Chrystons either!"

"Thank you, ladies," he smiled and turned to McCormick who eyebrows raised at Tom, returned the legal pad to his briefcase and rising to his feet, said, "Well, Missus Turner, Miss McKinnon, I hope our visit has not been too awkward for you and I wish to reiterate to you, Missus Turner," he handed her a business card, "that if there is anything that Chrystons can do for you, please call my office and ask for me personally."

It was Joyce who wordlessly showed them to the front door, closing it a little too loudly as they left the house.

"Well," McCormick grimaced as they made their way down the garden path, "under the circumstances that didn't go too badly, I suppose."

Tom saw that the Fiesta across the driveway was now facing the opposite direction and guessed it was Joyce McKinnon's car. That's when he had an idea.

"When we get into your car, Martin, give me a minute before you drive off," he said.

"Why?"

"I want to take a note of the registration numbers of the beamer, the Escort and this Fiesta," he replied as he rounded the Fiesta towards Martin's car and opened the passenger door.

"What for?"

Now seated in Martins car, Tom withdrew a notebook from an inner jacket pocket and scribbling on it, explained, "I'm thinking that a wee check registration with my mate Danny McBride might be useful."

"To check if the cars are owned by the family? I don't see that…"

"No, not owned by them. I was thinking more ANPR."

"Isn't that the…"

"Automatic Number Plate Recognition, yes. It's occurred to me that at the outset of this business whoever delivered the message and the marked pie to the Birmingham store might have driven down there and also driven to Manchester to place the pie in the store there too. I can't say for certain where the ANPR cameras are located in Scotland, but I do know that there are several thousands of cameras throughout the UK. I am also aware from my days in surveillance that some are located on the M74 at the border to monitor the registration numbers of vehicles known to be used by travelling criminals, predominantly drug couriers. I'm not an expert on the system, but I do believe that the number plates that are captured by the cameras are recorded onto an ANPR database and if they are not used for intelligence of as evidence, retained for a length of time before being discarded. What I *don't* know is how quickly Danny can have these registration numbers searched on the ANPR database for a result."

"But you think that there is a likelihood if your mate Gavin Blakestock is correct and that if the wife is involved, she might have used one of those vehicles to travel south?"

"Won't do any harm to check," Tom's eyes narrowed as he pondered something else that had struck him.

"Well," McCormick grinned, "if Missus Turner travelled down in that old Escort, I'd guess she was taking her life in her hands."

Tom didn't immediately reply and pulling away from the house, McCormick risked a quick glance and said, "What?"

"The sister, Joyce McKinnon," Tom slowly said. "She told us she knows who Jackson Peters is and also that she's a lecturer in Food Science. Remember, both letters were addressed to Peters and that sets me to wonder; why would she know who Peters is and who would be ideally placed to provide information about a food colouring called Lutein that was used in the first threat or even have knowledge of a mushroom that we now know as Death Cap?"

## CHAPTER TWENTY

She glanced up from her desk when the door opened and watched as Bob Stevenson and Gemma McNulty strode quickly over to her and her senses picked up on their excitement.

"Might have something, Anne," Stevenson said, his eyes bright as he added, "Can we tell you and Fitzpatrick together?"

"Okay," Leitch agreed and arising from the desk, led them to the DI's door.

"Come in," Fitzpatrick called out, his eyes betraying his curiosity when the three detectives entered the room together.

"Sir, it's about that action you had us raise," Stevenson began and then, his face the picture of innocence, said, "do you mind if we bring some chairs in?"

Before Fitzpatrick could respond, the large man had turned and was back out of the door, returning a couple of minutes later carrying a chair for him and McNulty while the sober faced Leitch took the hint and settled herself in the chair opposite the DI's desk.

"We returned to the school to re-interview Mister McFadyen, the Departmental Head for maths," began Stevenson. "He was quite frank when he told us his boss was unwilling to make further inquiry about the allegation of the relationship between a pupil and a teacher, presuming that was because of the interest it might attract from the councils Education Department. However, McFadyen is outraged that nothing is being done and took it upon himself to re-interview the young girl who had overheard the allegation. It seems he was correct to do so for he learned that the 'fancy car' mentioned when the girl told her form teacher is a beamer, a BMW."

"And that tells us what?" Fitzpatrick asked, his eyes shining brightly in anticipation that this information was leading somewhere.

"McFadyen checked the schools staff personnel records for it seems that the staff have to register their vehicles for parking purposes within the school. Something to do with the councils' insurance. Anyway, there are three BMW's registered to park in the school staff car park; one registered to a female teacher and the other two BMW's to male teachers."

"Go on," Fitzpatrick nodded.

"One teacher drives an old four door M3 with leather sports seats that McFadyen describes as a lovely, well maintained vehicle the other teacher rides a BMW motorcycle."

"The M3 vehicle. Who is the current keeper?"

Both Fitzpatrick and Leitch watched as Stevenson took a deep breath and glanced briefly at McNulty before shaking his head and replying, "Therein lies the problem, sir. The registered keeper of the M3, the teacher; it's a Martin Turner and according to McFadyen, Turner is currently detained within the Royal Infirmary. He's the man that is in the news; the man who was poisoned by the chicken pie bought in Chrystons."

Fitzpatrick stared in silence at Stevenson, who long in the tooth refused to be intimidated by the DI and stared back.

"In what way do you believe this relates to our murder inquiry, DC Stevenson?"

"I believe that if a teacher is having an inappropriate relationship with a pupil and fears that relationship might be disclosed, there is a likelihood that teacher could resort to violence to keep the relationship secret. We have Turner's address where he lives with his wife and children, sir. I can't think of any reason why we don't make some discreet inquiry with Turner's wife regarding her husband and even perhaps obtain her permission to have a look at his car."

Fitzpatrick slowly turned towards Leitch and to her surprise, asked, "Do you agree Sergeant Leitch?"

She stared back at him and nodded. "Yes sir, in light of the fact we have very little other evidence to the contrary and no other definite line of inquiry, I believe that for the time being we pursue this as a line of inquiry. If it should turn out that there is no connection to the murder, then nothing is lost."

The DI continued to stare at her for a few seconds after she had finished speaking, then gave her an almost imperceptible nod.

"I agree," he said at last then added, "As it is unlikely we will be able to interview this man Turner, we will instead interview his wife and request we search and test his car for any trace of contamination by our victim. I must stress that as Turner has attracted a lot of media attention and is the victim of the poisoning, we should handle this issue with the maximum sensitivity and sympathy for the mans wife and children. I do not want an irate media descending upon this office accusing us of bullyboy tactics while the woman's husband lies seriously ill in hospital, is that absolutely clear, Sergeant?"

"Of course, sir," she replied. "With your permission, I'll attend to the matter personally."

"Good. Now, regarding the cross over with the poisoning inquiry, I will contact Stewart Street and speak with…"

"I understand it's DI Mickey Farrell who has the poisoning inquiry, sir," Leitch interrupted.

"DI Farrell," acknowledged Fitzpatrick, his eyes narrowing and almost spitting the name out, leaving those present in no doubt of his opinion of Farrell. "In that case I will contact the Detective Inspector and inform him of our interest in his victim. In the meantime, also raise an Action to interview Turner's next of kin who presumably is his wife and should you believe that Turner indeed is a suspect for our murder, prepare a Sheriff's warrant to be signed in the event we need to seize the BMW vehicle for a Forensic search."

"Sir," Leitch and was about to rise from her seat when the door opened to admit a nervous looking civilian station assistant.

"Sorry, sir," he addressed Fitzpatrick, blushing with embarrassment.

"Yes?"

"It's about the murder, sir. There's two lassies, eh, I mean, two schoolgirls in at the bar. They're asking to speak with someone about the murder. Say they were pals…I mean, friendly with the victim and have some information."

Fitzpatrick, his voice deliberately monotone, turned towards Leitch and said, "Deal with this, Sergeant, and let me know what information these two schoolgirls purportedly have."

Ellen Toner's day had been more stressful than she anticipated when she walked through the stores staff door that morning.

She had spent most of the day fobbing off inquiries from the very few curious customers who visited the store, wondering what foods were safe as well as assuring anxious staff members that no, Chrystons were not about to fold overnight leaving them jobless.

The problem was that while she was confident in telling the customers the food was safe, she was not so assured telling her staff they would continue to be employed.

Now in her office sharing a coffee with Wilma Clark, she longed for the end of the day when she could close the doors and head home for a nice, warm and relaxing bath. Her mobile phone chirruped and she was about to groan, but heaved a sigh of relief when she saw the caller to be Tom.

As if on cue, Wilma winked and decided that some paperwork in the outer office required her attention, closing the door behind her.

"Hi there, how has your day been?" she asked him and guessed he was in a moving car.

"Probably better than yours," he replied before adding, "you sound tired."

"More than I care to admit," she stifled a yawn. "Any news?"

"Possibly. I'm with my boss, Martin," he said, the warning clear.

"Okay," she slowly drawled. "Will I see you later?"

"That's why I'm calling. I was considering picking up a takeaway and calling into yours. When will you be home?"

She glanced at her wristwatch. "I'm locking up in half an hour, then home for a bath and…" she smiled. To much information there, my girl she told herself. "Say, home in about one hour at the earliest; an hour and a half at the latest."

"Right then, see you in an hour and a half. Chinese?"

"That'll do for me," she agreed and ended the call.

Sipping at the remains of her coffee, she thought about Tom and wondered that in such a short time, she had come to like him so much.

No, *like* isn't the word for it, she self-consciously admitted; Tom McEwan was someone that she wanted to see more of and to be with and fervently hoped he felt the same way about her.

The staff nurse checked the intravenous drip attached to Martin Turner's left arm and replaced the bag then marked the change on his chart.

Muttering incoherently in his sleep, he continued to agitatedly twist and turn as though fighting an inner demon.

"Poor man," mumbled the nurse and then as she bent over to straighten the sheet under his chin, quite clearly heard him softly whisper, "Please, no Colleen."

Together with Frank Kennedy, the Media and Public Relations Director and the newly appointed Director of Operations, Gregory Packer, Jackson Peters prepared to meet the media representatives in the company boardroom.

With his prepared statement in his hand, Peters sat down at the top of the long table with Kennedy seated to his right and Packer seated to his left.

"Ladies and gentlemen," he began to a hushed and packed room, "first, thank you for attending this meeting. I will now read my prepared statement and my fellow Directors and I will thereafter respond to your questions." He forced a smile and without referring to the paper in his hand, began. "As you are already aware, Chrystons Supermarkets (PLC) were the target of a criminal attempt by an individual or group calling themselves Penthesilea to extort one million pounds from the company; such monies to be divided among twenty charities that were named by the extortionist or extortionists. Make no mistake, ladies and gentlemen, this was *not* a Robin Hood scheme, but a cold and calculating plot that threatened the safety of our customers and the livelihood of our many thousands of staff and has to date resulted in the attempted murder of an ordinary and entirely innocent member of the public."

Glancing at the reporters, he could see that already they were struggling against restraint and desperate to quiz him.

"The correct decision was made by the Board of Chrystons not to acquiesce to the threat, however, a bad decision was also made at that time *not* to inform the police. I can inform you that with my unfortunate absence at the time the threat was first received, the Director who was behind the decision not to inform the police has since resigned." He took a deep breath and continued. "It is to our shame and deep regret as a company that we delayed in seeking the professional assistance and advice of the police, but I assure you that upon my return from abroad and becoming aware of the circumstances, I as CEO immediately instructed that we fully cooperate with both the West Midlands Police, the Greater Manchester force and their northern colleagues, Police Scotland."

To his right, Kennedy slightly bowed his head, aware that Peters was perhaps gilding the lily to enhance his part in the issue, but thought it prudent to keep that information to himself.

A couple of hands were raised, but Peters raised his own hand to quell their questions and continued, "As a result of this poor decision by the former Director, the public were not immediately informed of the threat and I also regret that a customer in Glasgow, a Mister Martin Turner, was the victim of a poisoned food product sold by Chrystons. Our Scottish legal representatives have since contacted Mister Turners family and will remain in contact with them to offer every assistance at this distressing time." He paused to permit the reporters to take notes and then again continued. "Since Mister Turners admission to hospital where he remains in a critical condition, Chrystons has not received any further threat from the individual or group called Penthesilea. It might be that the threat will continue," his voice became steely and laying the prepared speech down onto the table, gazed narrowed eyed about the room and slightly raised his voice. "But let me categorically assure our customers and the public at large that Chrystons Supermarkets (PLC) will *never* yield to any form of terrorism and we will continue to cooperate and support our police services. I must also assure our customers and the public that we will take every opportunity to pursue by any legal means necessary any individual or group who believe that they can threaten this esteemed company, our dedicated staff and our loyal customers."

A silence fell across the room for a few seconds before the reporters beginning to clamour for his attention, started to shout questions at him.

Jumping to his feet, Gregory Packer raised both hands and calling for silence, pointed to the senior crime reporter for the most prominent Birmingham evening newspaper.

"Mister Peters" the balding reporter got to his feet, "you referred to a Director who has since resigned. Rumour has it that the Director is James Hardie who rumour also has it was implicated in an affair with your wife. Can you comment on that, sir?"

He had expected that this question would be asked and just prior to the news conference spent a full five minutes in the privacy of his private bathroom in front on the mirror, practising his reaction and the expression he would adopt.

Gritting his teeth tightly, he forced himself to seem shamefaced and slowly nodding, replied as though the admission was causing him anguish, "Sadly, I can confirm that I recently learned Mister Hardie and my wife were engaged in a long term extramarital affair. However, while Mister Hardie is now no longer associated with this company, I can assure you that his liaison with my wife had nothing to do with his resignation, that the two issues are completely unrelated. However, as a result of the poor decision he made in this issue of the threat, it is my duty and that of my fellow Directors to repair the damage he did to this company prior to his resignation. As for my wife, I can confirm that after becoming aware of her adulterous behaviour with Mister Hardie, we have mutually agreed to separate and are no longer living together."

And that announcement, he inwardly thought, should put paid to both those devious bastards!

DC Gemma McNulty had taken the girls details and now sat opposite the teenager while her colleague interviewed the other pupil in an adjoining room.

"So you and Colleen Younger were in the same year, the same classes?"

"Yeah," the girl replied, clearly edgy and chewing at her bitten fingernails, "me, Coleen and Shiv…I mean, Siobhan."

"So, Pauline, what is it that you want to tell us? You apparently told the bar officer you had some important information?"

"Where's Siobhan," she nervously asked.

"She's being spoken to by my colleague. We don't interview potential witnesses together," McNulty smiled.

She watched as Pauline twisted her hands together and heard the rhythmic tapping of the girl's foot under the table.

"Will I need to go to court? I mean, will I get my name and my picture in the papers and be on the tele?"

"If what you tell me is of use, the Procurator Fiscal might use you as a witness, Pauline, but first you need to tell me what you know, okay?"

She watched impatiently as the girl bit at her already chewed fingers.

"Look, hen, if what you know is important it might help us catch who murdered your pal. You were pals with Colleen, weren't you? I mean, you want to catch who killed her, don't you?" encouraged McNulty.

She watched as Pauline's throat tightened.

"Will I get into trouble because of what Colleen told me…us, I mean?"

"Why would you be in trouble because of what Colleen told you?"

"I don't know," the girl shrugged. "Maybe because we should have come forward earlier."

"But you're here now, Pauline. So, what is it that you want to tell me," McNulty forced a smile for she was becoming a little irritated with the girl.

Pauline bit at her lower lip then leaning forward, as though confiding something terrible, replied, "Colleen boasted to me and Shiv that she was shagging a teacher."

McNulty fought the excitement of what she was hearing and in a calm voice, asked, "Did Colleen say who she was shagging? The teacher's name or anything about him?"

"No, nothing like that."

"Did she say what school he taught in?"

"No," her brow furrowed, "I just took it that he was teaching in our school. That's why Colleen was so excited."

"Did Colleen describe him, tell you *anything* about him? Anything at all?"

Pauline vigorously shook her head. "All she would tell us, me and Shiv, was that he had a fancy car. That she did it in the back of the car with him."

"What kind of car?"

"I dunno; I don't think she said," Pauline's eyes narrowed as she tried to remember, "but I do remember her saying she was meeting him again that night."

"What night, can you remember?"

"I'm not sure, but I think it was a Thursday or maybe Friday."

"Where did she tell you this? You and Siobhan?"

"In the loo; the girls' toilets. Told us she'd rip us if we told anybody else."

"Rip you?"

"Aye, you know. Batter us."

"Were you frightened of Colleen?"

"Are you for real, miss? She was a fucking madwoman! Came from a nut job family, she did. Do you not know about the Younger's? They're the talk of the scheme, particularly that psycho brother of hers, Sean. He's a real headcase."

McNulty was taking notes when Pauline volunteered, "He wasn't her first, you know."

A cold chill gripped her heart for McNulty immediately suspected there might be other teachers involved and staring curiously at the young girl carefully replied, "What do you mean, not her first?"

"Well," Pauline was now right into the swing of her tale and leaning forward, her elbows on the table, continued, "If she was telling the truth, Colleen had shagged a couple of guys before. Not that she would tell us who they were, but she was always boasting that she could go into the town at night and get into the pubs no bother and guys would buy her drinks. And if she liked them, the guys I mean…" Pauline smirked, "well, you know."

McNulty didn't know, but could guess what Coleen Younger had got up to in the city's pubs. Curiously, an odd sense of relief flooded her that Colleen Younger's previous paramours apparently were not from the schools teaching staff, yet she felt so very sad that the young girl had apparently trawled the pubs seeking the affection she should have received at home. With a sigh she concluded the interview and leaving Pauline in the room, went searching for Anne Leitch.

He was sitting with Martin McCormick and just finishing a coffee when his mobile phone rung.

"Danny," he greeted his old friend. "Have you any news for me?"

"You owe me big time, McEwan," McBride snorted. "Have you *any* idea how many favours I had to pull in to get this information?"

"Oh, I take it that you can't just tap the information into a keyboard and up it comes, then?" Tom innocently replied.

"If only it were that simple," McBride sighed, then continued. "Right, got a paper and pencil handy?"

"Okay, shoot," Tom replied, dragging McCormick's legal pad across the desk.

"The Ford Escort and the BMW are both registered to Martin Turner at your victim's address. The Ford Fiesta is registered to Joyce McKinnon at a flat in Peel Street in the west end of the city. Now, starting with the Escort. It hasn't been road taxed or MoT'd for well over a year and there's nothing on the ANPR database for it. The BMW is currently road taxed and MoT'd," then he paused.

"And?" Tom asked. He could almost hear the grin on McBride's face when the DI slowly replied, "The dates you have given me for when you believe the threats were posted at Birmingham and Manchester…"

Again McBride paused, savouring the moment.

"Come on, stop teasing me," Tom excitedly said.

"So, tell me about this bird that you're seeing?"

"What?"

"McEwan, you dullard, have you any idea what kind of interrogation I endured from Brenda with that parting comment when you mentioned going out on a foursome?"

"What?"

"Just tell me her name and where you met her, McEwan, before I tell you anything else," demanded McBride.

Tom glanced quickly at McCormick and unaccountably blushed.

"Ellen Toner. She's the manager of Chrystons on Woodlands Road. Now for heavens sake, Danny, what else do you have?"

Laughing, McBride replied, "So it *is* the store manager after all, eh? I'm firing you right into Brenda and boy, will she set about you when she sees you next. Right, your checks. Ready?"

"Shoot."

"On the first date you gave me, the Fiesta was recorded crossing the border into England at seven-seventeen that morning. Later that morning the same car was registered travelling between a set of average speed cameras that were set up at a road works two miles outside Birmingham, near to Spaghetti Junction. You *do* know where that is?"

"Of course I do," Tom impatiently replied.

"The car tripped a second set of average speed cameras just over two hours later, but this time it was northbound and the last recording on that date is when it triggered the ANPR cameras at the border, again northbound. When it passed through the average speed cameras, the car was travelling within the speed limit of the cameras and was not in excess of the limit, so no penalty was incurred."

"The registration number. No chance it could be a mistake," Tom excitedly asked.

"No chance, Tom. Remember, the evidence of these cameras is used in court, though mainly for speeding violations. Now, are you ready for the rest of the good news?"

"Go ahead," Tom replied, pen at the ready.

"The following Saturday, the second date you gave me the Fiesta tripped the ANPR cameras, again at the border heading south," and related the time. "An hour later the car was recorded travelling through road works, once more by average speed cameras, on the M62 towards Manchester. It tripped a second set of average speed cameras travelling south on Bury New Road and what I'm told by these buggers here," his voice faded slightly as he turned his head away from the phone towards his staff, "is that Bury New Road leads into the heart of Manchester city centre. I've a third recording of the car travelling north across the border just over two hours later. Just as before though, no penalties incurred because the car maintained the speed limit between the cameras."

Tom wheezed, stunned at the information that McBride had provided.

"Don't suppose your fancy cameras can tell me who the driver was or possibly even caught a photograph of the driver?"

"We're good, McEwan, but not good," McBride laughed and added, "Now, is that of any use to you."

"Better than I hoped, Danny, and well worth a night out with Ellen and I when you and Brenda arrange for a babysitter."

"I'll hold you to that, buddy and for the favours I called in, you're paying," McBride laughed and ended the call.

He pushed the legal pad across the desk towards McCormick and said, "Danny McBride came through. Those are the times that the ANPR and average speed cameras on the motorways and roadwork's recorded Joyce McKinnon's Ford Fiesta travelling down to both Birmingham and Manchester and travelling back."

McCormick slowly nodded and then staring at Tom, asked, "Nothing to indicate who the driver was? Missus Turner or her sister?"

"No," Tom shook his head and stabbed a finger at the first date he had written. "I could check if McKinnon was at the college on that day, but even if she was off work, it doesn't prove she was driving the car. She could just as easily have been watching her nieces while Missus Turner drove south."

"In short though, there's a strong possibility that one of them is responsible for travelling to Birmingham on that date…"

"And I think it was McKinnon," Tom interrupted.

"Why do you think that?"

"If my suspicions are correct, I don't think that Missus Turner's husband would permit his wife to be away for most of the day. Even if he was teaching at the school who's to say he wouldn't phone home or even travel home early looking for her. No, I suspect it was McKinnon who drove south and delivered that letter and placed the marked jar with the Lutein in the 'Founding Store' opposite the company's head office."

"And the marked jar in the Woodlands Road store?"

"Could have been any one of the two of them at any time on that day," Tom pursed his lips, "but again I think it was the sister because I don't see the two of them having the same disguise. According to the CCTV photos we have, the disguise looks to the same that was used in both the Glasgow and Birmingham stores."

"They might have shared the disguise, "McCormick mused, then added, "But you are convinced they are acting together?"

"Yes, I think one or both drummed up this scheme to knock off the husband and screw Chrystons for a fortune. Unfortunately for them, with your statement that no court would award them the kind of money they probably thought they would get you kind of put paid to their dream of a large payout."

"How do you want to handle this?"

Tom sighed and replied, "Before I make any kind of decision, I had better contact Gavin Blakestock and update him." He smiled. "He'll be pleased to know that his hunch paid off."

"Well, you're the investigator, Tom. Just keep me apprised of what you decide and as far as representing Chrystons goes, as long as your decision does not affect the company or our firm here, I'll stand by it."

DI Mickey Farrell almost threw the phone down in disgust. Shaking his head, he quietly seethed at the arrogance of Murray Fitzpatrick. The nerve of the skinny wee bastard, calling him up and telling him what *he* wanted Farrell to do.

Still, he calmed slightly, if Fitzpatrick was correct and Martin Turner *is* a murder suspect, it would do no harm to visit the wife again and maybe conduct a more in depth interview about her husband; probe their relationship a little deeper, he thought, recalling the woman's sore eye.

The door knocked and opened to admit Lynn Massey and as always, the DCI looked like she had just stepped off a Vogue fashion shoot. Pulling out the chair from opposite Farrell, she sat down and almost with a twinkle in her eye, said, "I hear Murray Fitzpatrick has a suspect for his murder."

"Okay, very funny," Farrell shook his head. "So, where does that leave me? Do I continue with the poison inquiry or do you want me to hand it over to that wee…DI Fitzpatrick," he almost groaned as he corrected himself.

Suppressing a grin, Massey replied, "No, you stick with the poison inquiry, Mickey. If DI Fitzpatrick's suspect turns out to be dud information, you continue what you're doing. If on the other hand this man Turner proves to be a strong suspect, well, we'll review that at the time. Anyway while I'm here, is there an update re the poisoning inquiry?"

"Nothing, Ma'am," he shook his head. "Turner's condition continues to slightly deteriorate, but the last I spoke with the consultant and that was about," he glanced at his wristwatch, "two hours ago, he tells me that he's a little surprised Turner hasn't turned his toes up yet. Even suggested if he makes it through the week there is a slim possibility he might survive, but with untreatable organ damage and even a further possibility of brain damage. Either way, he won't be playing five a sides again anytime soon," he snorted.

Charlie McFadyen sat troubled in his office, the last of the pupils and most of the staff now gone home. Outside his door, he could hear the cleaners working their polishing machines along the vinyl floor of the lengthy corridor.

Again he worried if he did the right thing and wearily rubbed at his forehead. If the Deputy or worse, the Head Teacher discovered he had gone against their instruction and spoken with the CID; well, it had been a long time since he had heard of a teacher being sacked for that sort of thing, disciplinary behaviour they called it, but it wasn't unknown. He shook his head, wondering what the devil possessed him to take such a risk; a risk with his long and so far exemplary career.

But he knew why he did it for no matter what direction or instruction he received from his management, he could not go against his own conscience.

No, he could never let a bloody thing like that go.

To often he had seen examples of his profession being eroded because senior management decided to turn a blind eye, frightened to make waves, worried about their jobs and their pensions; bloody political correctness, he silently fumed. Well, if what he did was disclosed then hell mend them, he angrily thought…then startled when his mobile phone rung.

"Mister McFadyen, DC Bob Stevenson. Thought I'd give you a wee call, sir."

"Yes, Mister Stevenson," his heart sank as he rubbed at the dull ache in his forehead. "What can I do for you?"

"Well, actually I'm calling without official permission as it were, Mister McFadyen, so I'll be grateful if you treat this call as completely confidential."

"Confidential? Yes, of course. May I ask why?"

"Mister McFadyen, I'm not unaware that you took a bit of a chance informing me about the allegation of the relationship between a teacher and a pupil and I'm guessing what you told me could get you into a wee bit of bother if your boss was to find out. Well, sir, I'm phoning to let you know that because of what you told me and certain other information that has arisen, you have progressed the murder inquiry to a new level, Mister McFadyen. Without your information we might still be blundering about. I know that you won't want it disclosed and that you won't want any credit, so I'm phoning to personally thank you on behalf of the inquiry for what you did. Thank you. We're very grateful, sir."

Stunned, McFadyen could only bluster, "Yes, well, thanks for letting me know, Mister Stevenson."

When the call ended, he slipped his jacket on and grabbing his briefcase, headed out of the door, his step a little lighter and his morale much improved.

Regardless of their aunt's stern warning, the girls were happily running wild throughout the house.

"Let them be," smiled their mother, just so pleased to see her daughters in high spirits and waving as Joyce drove off to the hospital for the early evening visit with Martin.

Her sister had been gone just five minutes when DS Anne Leitch and DC Gemma McNulty called at Annemarie Turners door.

She wasn't unduly worried and half expected the CID to arrive again anyway and invited the two officers into the lounge, urging her curious daughters to go and play upstairs.

"Missus Turner, I regret visiting you at this time when I understand your husband is currently incapacitated and detained in hospital. That's correct, yes?"

"Yes, but you know that," Annemarie frowned, a little puzzled by the comment. "Mister Farrell was here on Sunday evening with one of your colleagues and…" she stared apprehensively at Leitch. "You're not with Mister Farrell, you're here about something else, aren't you?"

Leitch nodded and replied, "Perhaps you might wish to sit down, Missus Turner."

Annemarie's stomach was in knots and her mind raced.

They know, she thought! They've found us out!

Her face paled and panicking, thought she was about to faint.

Leitch and McNulty together reached for her and each holding an arm, helped her sit on the couch.

"I'll get some water," McNulty said and left the room.

Annemarie started shaking and tightly gripped her hands together as McNulty returned with a mug from the draining board filled with cold water that she handed to her.

She held the mug in both hands and slurped at the icy cold water, spilling some down the front of her blouse. Tears stung at her, her first thought being what was to become of her daughters when she went to prison.

As if from a distance, she heard Leitch say, "Missus Turner, are you okay? Do you want a doctor?"

"No," she gasped, "I'm fine. Really. I'm fine," she repeated, then began to softly weep, her shoulders shaking as she drew her legs up and leaned forward to hide her face in her hands.

Leitch and McNulty stared at each other then as if by mutual agreement, both sat in the armchairs to await the distraught woman composing herself.

Breathing deeply, Annemarie sniffed and accepted a paper handkerchief that McNulty handed her from her handbag.

"Thank you," she sobbed and taking a further deep breath, despairingly asked, "What is it that you want to know."

With a further glance at McNulty, Leitch said, "Missus Turner, It's about your husband, Martin. On top of what you are going through, I have to inform you that my colleague and I are from Kirkintilloch CID and investigating the murder of a sixteen-year-old schoolgirl, Colleen Younger. Does that name mean anything to you?"

She stared in confusion. Murder? A schoolgirl? What the…

Like a thunderbolt, it struck her and she sat upright. This wasn't about the poisoning of Martin. This was about something else; a murder.

"No," she stammered, "I don't know anyone by that name."

"Your husband never mentioned a pupil by that name?"

"No, not to my knowledge. No, never," she almost whispered then added, "Martin never discussed his work."

"The BMW car that is in your driveway, Missus Turner. Who uses that car?"

"It's Martin's car. The car he drives. I'm not allowed to…," she shrugged, then continued, "No, I did drive it. Once. When I visited Martin yesterday. God, I don't even know if I'm insured to drive it," she mumbled, fearfully staring at Leitch. "Then I..." she took a deep breath. "I fainted at the hospital. Shock, the doctor said, and I was brought home by my sister, Joyce in her car. Then later, Joyce got a taxi to the hospital to fetch it; she drove it just the once, when she collected it from the car park near to the hospital and brought it home here. I've been told to rest at home and that's why Joyce is away to visit Martin instead of me," she said, unable to stop herself from rambling.

"So, the car, the BMW outside in the driveway. You're saying that the only person who drives the car regularly is your husband. Is that correct?"

"Yes. Why?"

"Missus Turner. Would you have any objection to my colleague and I having a quick look at the car? At the inside?"

"No, I don't think so," she shook her head, then her curiosity got the better of her and she asked, "Why do you want to see the inside of the car?"

Leitch took a few seconds before answering and replied, "Missus Turner, I don't wish to alarm you or distress you any further, but there has been an allegation about a male member of your husband's school who drives a BMW. We the police are simply carrying out checks on all teachers who own BMW cars. There's nothing to imply that your husband is a suspect," she forced a smile to maintain the lie.

Annemarie didn't immediately respond, but her thoughts turned back to Martin's curious behaviour that day; that Friday evening…the day before she poisoned him.

"And this inspection of Martin's car is to do with a murder. Of a schoolgirl. That's what you said."

"Yes, I'm afraid it is."

Her eyes narrowed as it came to her then. The smell of cheap perfume from him, the frantic cleaning of the car interior with her bleach, the spots of blood on his fawn coloured jacket and his chinos.

Idly she stroked at her bruised eye, her face turning grey as she stared at Leitch.

"I'll get you the car keys, but first I have something that I should show you," she began to rise from the couch, aware that her legs were shaking.

"Something in my wash basket."

Tom McEwan was like a toddler on sugary sweets when he spoke with Gavin Blakestock, telling the older man of his call from Danny McBride and congratulating him on his hunch that seemed to prove that one or both of the two women were probably responsible for the threat against Chrystons.

"But you're not certain which woman, Tom, though you are of the opinion that it's probably the sister, this Joyce McKinnon?"

"She sounds to have had the best opportunity, Gavin. I'm guessing if Missus Turner's eye is anything to go by that her husband is an abuser and likely keeps a tight rein on her. I don't see him permitting her to gallop off to England alone. No, I think it's the sister, but probably they are colluding."

He recounted Martin McCormick's warning to the women that it was unlikely they would financially benefit from the scheme and that drew a chuckle from Blakestock.

"So, what do you think, Gavin; should we challenge the women ourselves or turn them over to the local cops here?"

"Let's think about it, chum" he heard Blakestock quietly respond and imagined the older man was weighing up the advantage of confronting the women against simply turning them over to the police. "What evidence do we have other than your man McBride's ANPR recordings and even that was obtained on the old pals' network, not officially. Besides, we have no other evidence other than a couple of suspect CCTV photos that show a grey haired woman wearing a dowdy coat and the suspicion of a Scottish accent. From what we both agreed if it *was* Joyce McKinnon in disguise, she sounds an attractive woman from your description and without the disguise is unlikely to be identified by the young shop assistant at the 'Founding Store'. No, what we know and what we can prove are two completely different issues, young Tom."

Blakestock paused and asking him to wait a minute, could be heard conversing with a woman. Returning to the phone, he said, "Tom, I've just had a word with my better half Celia and she's now booking me an early morning flight to Glasgow. If you agree I think that both of us should challenge the women together, see what we can turn up. If they deny they are Penthesilea, nothing lost but they will know *we* know about their plan and hopefully it will put an end to this business. Remember, though I'm conscious we're both former coppers, Tom, our allegiance is now with our client. We work for

Chrystons who have engaged us to identify the culprits threatening their business, to identify whoever Penthesilea is. Once that is done and with the consent of the client, then we can turn over what we know to Police Scotland and let them deal with the criminality; they can take it from there regarding the poisoning of the husband. How does that sound to you?"

Tom unconsciously nodded as he smiled and replied, "Sounds like a plan, Gavin. Text me your arrival time and I'll pick you up from the airport."

## CHAPTER TWENTY-ONE

She didn't understand why her heart skipped a beat when she opened the door to Tom McEwan, but with a smile invited him through to the lounge where she had set the table for dinner, aware that she was gibbering like a budgie about nothing in particular.

Taking the paper carrier bag containing their meal from him, she placed it onto the table then was surprised when Tom gently took her by the hand to draw her to him and holding her close, run his fingers lightly down her cheek.

"Look, Ellen," he stared at her, their faces just inches apart, conscious of the subtle scent of her perfume, "I realise that we've only known each other for such a short time, but I was wondering…" he hesitated and she watched him biting at his lower lip.

"Yes?" she prompted with an expectant smile.

He cleared his throat and continued, "I like you, Ellen, more than I realised at first. Really like you. So, I was wondering…" but again he stopped short.

She shrugged as though unaware of what he was trying to tell her and though her heart was racing, said, "Tom, what is it that you asking me?"

He took a deep breath and exhaling, replied, "I want to see more of you, be with you. I want us to be together. In a relationship."

"But aren't we already seeing each other?" she teased him.

"Yes, but what I mean is…"

She raised a forefinger to his lips stop him, then placing her hand behind his head drew her to him to kiss him.

"Yes, I'd like us to be together too," she softly replied before reaching for his hand and the meal for the moment forgotten, led him through the door towards her bedroom.

Waiting to be admitted, Joyce McKinnon was nervous while she stood in the corridor outside the Acute Receiving Ward. The buzzer unlocking the door startled her and pushing her way through, she was greeted by a smiling nurse who first satisfying herself that Joyce was not a reporter, informed her that Mister Turner was in room seven and pointed to the end of the corridor where Joyce would find Martins room on the right.

Before she entered, she stood watching the unconscious Martin through the door window, seeing him writhing in the bed that had low cot rails to prevent him falling out.

She felt no sympathy for him and bracing herself, pushed open the door.

The perfunctory visit, she had agreed with Annemarie, was twofold; it would seem odd if he did not receive a visit and it was also necessary to avoid any suspicion by the medical staff or police if his wife displayed no interest in his condition. As Annemarie was under doctors' orders to rest, it therefore fell upon Joyce to conduct the visit, a task that quite simply disgusted her.

Standing over the bed she stared down at the comatose man, hearing him softly moan and mumbling in his troubled sleep and watching as his face contorted in pain.

She turned to ensure the door was closed and bending over him, whispered, "I hope you are in real agony, you selfish bastard! I hope that each time you hurt my sister and my nieces is coming back to you tenfold and I want you to know that it was Annemarie and me that did this to you! I want you…"

His bloodshot eyes suddenly opened and he stared up at her.

Startled, she almost jumped back with shock as Martin, his teeth gritted in pain, saliva dribbling from the side of his mouth, tried to speak.

She slowly exhaled, calm now and again leaned towards him and forcing a smile, said, "Hurts, does it? Good. Why don't you just die, you *bastard*!"

The door opened behind her and a young and slightly dishevelled man with unruly dark hair wearing a light coloured turtle neck sweater and scruffy corduroy trousers, a doctor she presumed if the stethoscope round his neck was any indication, entered and with one hand on the door handle, asked, "Missus Turner?"

"No, I'm her sister, Miss McKinnon. My sister isn't well. That's why I'm here," she lamely finished, casting a nervous glance down at Martin whose eyes were still opened and whose teeth were tightly gritted as he continued to stare menacingly at her.

"Ah, I see. But you *are* family so perhaps I might have a quiet word?" he stood to one side to permit her to pass.

With a backward glance at the now semiconscious Martin, Joyce followed the doctor a short distance along the corridor to a small almost claustrophobic room with medical leaflets pinned to a notice board on one wall; a doctors' room she thought it was, where he invited her to sit on the plastic backed tubular framed chair and then squeezed himself to sit behind the small table that littered with a half dozen used plastic coffee cups and biscuit wrappers served as a desk.

"I trust that Missus Turner isn't too unwell?"

"No, it's the strain of the last few days," Joyce replied, inwardly thinking not the last few days, but the last eleven years.

"Good," he replied then added, "My name is Doctor Kane. I'm the registrar and currently dealing with Mister Turner. Now," he shuffled some paperwork on the table before continuing, "I have to inform you, Miss McKinnon that your brother-in-laws condition continues to give cause for concern and while he seems to be stabilised for the minute, we are uncertain if indeed he will survive the deterioration that the poison has inflicted upon his internal organs. Those organs I speak of, unless you are already aware…?"

"No," she shook her head, deciding it would be prudent to deny any knowledge of what effect the poison has on the body.

"Well, our MRI scan has detected severe damage to both his liver and kidneys as well as the strain his condition has placed upon his heart. I regret he has already suffered a number of seizures brought on by dehydration and as you probably noticed when you were within his room we are now constantly hydrating Mister Turner. Shortly after admission he was fitting very badly and was placed in an induced coma, however, we have brought him out of the coma and," he smiled softly, "you were fortunate to see him awake for your visit, though of course he isn't able to communicate at any level at this time." His face became grim as he added, "That all said though, I cannot in good faith offer you any hope for his continuing survival."

"So, he might after all…die?"

"Ah, yes, that *is* the prognosis, but there is some light," he smiled and slowly nodded as though to reassure and comfort her. "The nature of the condition is not unknown to medical science and to be perfectly frank, previous recorded treatment is not generally effective in preventing death. However, forgive me if I describe this in layman terms…"

Joyce forced a smile and replied, "I would much prefer it if you did explain in simple English, Doctor Kane."

"Yes, well, as you might already be aware the condition is gastrointestinal. The consultant and I agree that the consumption of alcohol Mister Turner apparently consumed shortly after his intake of the poison seems to have set off a gastric reaction whereby he quite literally vomited much of the poison and combined with the subsequent bout of diarrhoea, more or less flushed most of the poison from his system."

He saw her face pale and assuming his explanation was too graphic, apologised for upsetting her.

What he could not know was that Joyce and Annemarie's worst fears were being realised; that after all their planning, all their efforts, Martin might just live.

"If he were to survive, Doctor Kane, what would be his quality of life?"

"Hard to say, Miss McKinnon. I suspect that if Mister Turner is stabilised there is every likelihood that he will require constant nursing attention." He leaned forward, steepling his fingers under his chin and continued, "I fear he will never work again. His quality of life will be harshly impaired and there is more than a strong possibility he will be unable to work or perform any of the motor functions that he previously enjoyed."

"You're suggesting he might be disabled, a permanent invalid? A paraplegic, even?"

"Yes," he nodded, "I'm afraid so and that is *if* he survives."

Dumbstruck, she sat motionless staring sightlessly at the wall.

"Miss McKinnon? Wait here," he said and left the room, returning a moment later with a small plastic beaker of water and said, "Here, drink this."

Shaking, she held the cup on both hands yet still managed to spill some of the water onto the front of her blouse.

Doctor Kane wordlessly handed her a paper towel and then said, "I'll leave you for a moment to compose yourself. I'll be right outside should you need me," and again left the room.

He could not know that in that instant, she made her decision.

She fought the tears and braced herself for her mind was made up.

Annemarie and her nieces would never have to endure Martin returning home.

Her sister would not again be the skivvy that he had bullied and demanded of her for the last eleven years.

No matter what happened to her, no matter what she would be forced to endure, she would not permit him to further ruin Annemarie's life. She would confess to everything, persuade the police it had nothing to do with Annemarie, convince them it was all her idea.

She took a deep breath, somehow relieved that the decision had been made. All she had left to do now was if the opportunity presented itself before she left the ward, she would return to visit Martin and in the quiet of his room, use his pillow to smother him.


In the driveway outside the house DS Anne Leitch used her mobile phone to call DI Fitzpatrick, conscious of her excitement yet forcing herself to be calm.

When he answered, she said, "Sir, it's me. I'm outside the house at the minute. DC McNulty is sitting with the wife and I've good news."

"And that news is?" was the monotone response.

"Missus Turner has handed us a pair of trousers and a jacket that she said her husband wore the night that our victim was murdered. There seems to be some spots of blood staining on both items of clothing."

Seated at his desk, Fitzpatrick's eyes narrowed at the news. "What is the wife saying to it, Sergeant?"

"The wife has been very cooperative, sir. Unusually so, I'd say. It seems her husband is an abusive man. She claims her husband has previously and regularly assaulted her and if she's to be believed she's sporting a black eye where she alleges he punched her to the face."

"And the car, the BMW?"

"I'm standing here staring at it, sir. Missus Turner says that last Friday night after he returned home in the BMW her husband caught her in the car switching off the interior light. She told me she thought the car smelled of urine. When she went back indoors that's when her husband punched her because she had been in the car. She says he's paranoid about the car and doesn't let her or their children into the car at any time. The next morning, last Saturday morning, she saw him washing out the rear interior of the car with a basin of soapy water. Missus Turner gave permission for me to inspect it and when I opened the door it seems obvious to me that it has been thoroughly cleaned by bleach, if the smell is anything to go by. In the meantime, I've closed the door and would suggest we have a Traffic Department low loader bring the vehicle to their garage and have it Forensically examined there. The only downside is that since last Friday Missus Turner drove the car to the Royal Infirmary and her sister collected it from there, but other than that no one else has been in the car."

There was a pause before Fitzpatrick replied, "Seize the car and I agree about the low loader. Leave me to arrange that. Anything else?"

"Just a little thing, might be nothing. She's suspected for some time that her husband has been going out and seeing other women. She says on the Friday night when he came home he was smelling of a cheap scent, not one she recognised and he had a fresh cut on his cheek."

"Are you telling me this woman is some kind of expert on perfume," Leitch could almost hear the derision in his voice.

Smirking, she replied, "Well, sir, as a matter of fact she is or rather, she was. Prior to her marriage, Missus Turner told me she was employed on the perfume counter of a prestigious Glasgow store and though she admits she is a little out of touch with the current market, she's confident she can recognise a cheap scent from an expensive perfume." There followed a slight pause and before Fitzpatrick could respond, Leitch added, "In fact, sir, Missus Turner has suggested if we can provide her with a sample of the scent used by our victim, she should be able to recognise it."

"What," he exclaimed, the doubt in his voice obvious, "you mean if we provided her with several samples of women's perfumes she could pick out the scent she smelled on her husband?"

"Yes, sir, she's confident she can."

"Hmm, well, I don't suppose it would do any harm to send an officer to collect the victim's perfumes from her home," he sighed. "You can arrange that, can't you Sergeant?"

"Yes, sir, of course and don't forget too there's the cut on her husband's cheek. We have the small sample of blood that was obtained by Doctor Watson at the PM from under the victim's fingernail. If we were to match the sample with Turner's DNA it might prove pretty conclusive."

"Indeed," he replied and Leitch irately thought the stupid bugger had not been listening, that he hadn't even given the fresh cut on Martin Toner's cheek a consideration. Bloody hell, she angrily thought; hasn't he any idea how important that is?

"This woman seems particularly keen to assist us, Sergeant," he broke into her thoughts. "Why is that?"

Leitch turned towards the house and thoughtfully replied, "I think that Missus Turner has had a bad life with her husband, sir. It seems to me that…"

The door opened and McNulty stepped out holding a briefcase.

"Can you hold on, sir. DC McNulty wants a word."

Indicating that McNulty be careful what she said, that Fitzpatrick was on the phone, Leitch questioningly raised her eyebrows.

McNulty, wearing blue coloured Forensic gloves, held up the old, brown leather briefcase and said, "Missus Turner informed me that her husband keeps his mobile phone in here, but there's no trace of it. She's had a quick look in his room but can't find it there either and suggested we might want to look in the car."

"No," Leitch shook her head, "I don't want to open the car again in case we contaminate it any further before the Forensics go over it. I'd rather leave the search to the Forensic team." Her brow furrowed. "Wait a minute, I've got an idea. Get your mobile phone ready," she instructed McNulty and returning her own mobile to her ear, said, "Sir, that list of phone numbers. Can you read out the phone number that our victim sent the text message to. The text she sent on the night she was murdered."

"Yes. Wait a minute," was the impatient reply.

She heard him shuffling papers.

"Right, here it is," said Fitzpatrick and slowly read out the digits that Leitch repeated to McNulty who punched the numbers into her keyboard and then pressed the green send button.

They stood perfectly still, ignoring the noise of the street.

Fifteen tense seconds passed then Leitch and McNulty grinned together when they heard the muted sound of a phone chirruping from inside the BMW.

In bed together, Tom McEwan and Ellen Toner lay facing each other, their fingers entwined.

He smiled and said, "What say I get up and bring you a cup of tea or coffee."

"What say I refuse because I've got something else in mind," and grinning, pushed up from the bed and eased herself across to straddle naked on top of his chest, her hands pinning his shoulders to the bed, her hair falling about her face.

His brow furrowed and adopting a frown, replied, "Yes, you're right. Something's just come up."

She playfully slapped at his head and was leaning over to kiss him when they heard the sound of his mobile phone ringing from his discarded clothes.

He stared at her and was about to tell her to ignore it when she leapt from the bed and began to rummage through his clothes, finding his phone in his trouser pocket.

Leaning on one elbow, his head cradled in his hand, Tom watched her with a smile before saying, "Unless it's an emergency, throw the phone into the toilet," he joked, but his brow furrowed when Ellen replied, "The screen says you missed a call from a Mickey Farrell. Didn't you say he's…"

"Yeah, he's the DI at Stewart Street. I'd better take the call," he sighed and then standing upright from the bed, wrapped the quilt cover about the naked Ellen before taking the phone from her.

"I'll quickly shower then get that dinner heated and organised," she smiled at him before heading to the small en suite.

Less than five minutes later, wrapped in a bathrobe, she opened the en suite door to find Tom still sat on the edge of the bed, but now wearing a bath towel wrapped about his waist.

He stared curiously at her and shook his head.

"I spoke with DI Farrell. Big, *big* development," he said. "You're not going to believe this, Ellen, but it seems that Farrell was contacted by a DI who is running a murder inquiry. A schoolgirl discovered on Saturday morning in woods, somewhere in the north of Glasgow."

"Yes, I heard about it on the radio. Why? How is that related to your inquiry?"

He stared at her, still confused at what Mickey Farrell had told him before replying, "According to Farrell, the SIO…"

Her eyes narrowed and he smiled. "The Senior Investigating Officer for the murder," he explained.

"Oh," she simply replied.

"Anyway, the SIO informed Farrell that Martin Turner is the primary suspect for the schoolgirls murder. Farrell will remain as the SIO for the Scottish side of the threat against Chrystons and the poisoning inquiry, but any further inquiry that involves Martin Turner will need to be through the murder inquiry team."

"Does that cause a problem?"

"Well," he nodded, "it just might if Gavin and I intend interviewing the wife and her sister. Farrell said the SIO for the murder inquiry…" he smiled again. "Well, lets just say his language betrayed his dislike for the man and inferred the SIO isn't easy to get along with. It might mean me making a call to my boss, Martin McCormick and seeking his assistance."

She moved towards him and cradled his head against her bosom, stroking at his hair.

"Well, make your call and remember, if anyone can persuade this SIO person to assist you and Gavin, I'm sure you can," she murmured.

He drew a deep breath, smelling the freshness of her skin and the scent of her soap and becoming aroused tried to wrap his arms about her waist. Laughing, she pulled away from him and coyly said, "Shower first, make your call, then dinner. After we've eaten we can talk about what to do for the rest of the evening."

Following DS Anne Leitch's phone call to DI Fitzpatrick, the incident room within Kirkintilloch police office became a hive of activity. For too many days the detectives and civilian staff had toiled at dead ends. Dozens of Actions were investigated and concluded and resulted in nothing of evidential value to indicate who murdered sixteen-year-old Colleen Younger.

Now morale was high and the end, the team believed, was at last in sight.

The team had a suspect, but more importantly, they had circumstantial evidence that if proved positive by the Forensic laboratory at the Gartcosh Crime Campus would evidentially implicate that suspect in the murder. That and the statements from the victim's friends confirming the victim's statement she was having a sexual affair with a schoolteacher.

Reacting to an earlier phone call from Mickey Farrell, DCI Lynn Massey arrived and immediately sensed the buzz in the room. Nodding and smiling at the staff as they busied themselves, she strode to DI Fitzpatrick's office and knocking, opened the door. Deferring to her rank, Fitzpatrick stood and nodded a greeting.

"I hear we have a result, Mister Fitzpatrick," she smiled at him as she sat in the chair opposite him.

"While I am of course not one to usually base my conclusions on that of an overexcited Detective Sergeant," he dryly said, "it would seem so, Ma'am. Reluctant as I am to formally declare a suspect until such times I have the paperwork confirming it, Martin Turner, a forty-year-old teacher who is on the staff at the victim's school is in the frame, as it were."

Massey stared at him, resisting the urge to respond to his derisory comment about Anne Leitch and instead said, "So we are talking about the victim for the poisoning case, the man…"

"Indeed it is, Ma'am," Fitzpatrick nodded as he interrupted. "I instructed my officers to make inquiry at the victim's school and in particular, to seek out any suggestion of any association with any men employed at the school. It seems my instinct was correct. Martin Turner taught the victim mathematics.

Massey suspected that Fitzpatrick was embellishing the truth for she did not believe him to be so intuitive. No, there was more to his story than he was telling; of that she was certain.

"Now that I have identified Turner," he continued, "I called Detective Inspector Farrell at Stewart Street and apprised him of my findings and requested of him that he stand down regarding Turner as his victim. I will of course now pursue Turner as the primary suspect in my murder inquiry."

"Is the evidence that you have so far attained eyewitness or circumstantial?"

"At this time, purely circumstantial," he waved his hands, "however, I am confident that the results of DNA testing upon the bloodstained clothing that I instructed my officers to seize from the suspects home will confirm my suspicion that he is indeed the killer. There is also the matter of a text message sent by the victim on the evening of her murder to a mobile phone; a phone that I ordered DS Leitch to search for. The phone is apparently within the suspects BMW vehicle. Along with the bloodstained clothing seized from the house I have arranged for the vehicle to be taken for Forensic examination." He glanced down at a page of notes he had made and continued. "There is also a suggestion by his wife that on the night he returned home, the night our victim was murdered, the suspect bore a fresh cut to his cheek. As you are likely aware, Doctor Watson recovered a minute sample of blood from underneath our victim's fingernail that I will arrange to have compared with the suspects DNA. Of course, once the Forensic results are returned to me I will make plans to have Turner formally arrested, though of course it will likely mean a police presence by his bed until such times he can be removed to a prison hospital facility."

Aye and it's all me, me, me, thought Massey, but who retained her composure and said, "It seems that you and your team are to be congratulated, Mister Fitzpatrick. When will you be ready to release details of your arrest to the media?"

"As I say, Ma'am, I expect the DNA results within the next two hours. With your permission I will call a briefing here at Kirkintilloch office and break the news to the media. Will you attend?"

"Yes, I'd be pleased to support you, Mister Fitzpatrick," she calmly replied and smiled, but thought you're fucking right I'll attend, for no way was she letting this buffoon claim credit for his teams' hard work. She knew Fitzpatrick of old and the man wasn't averse to self publicising.

Her mobile phone rang and politely excusing herself, returned to the incident room to take the call.

With a smile, she greeted the caller with, "Hello Mister McCormick. What can the police do today for my wee cousin?"

"Actually, what *you* can do is give my investigator a helping hand, Lynn, if it doesn't interfere with your murder inquiry."

"Are you calling in a favour?" she teased him.

"No, not a favour, you know I wouldn't do that…"

"I'm kidding, wee cuzz. So, what is it that I can help you with?"

"Well, as you are aware, my guy Tom McEwan is currently acting for Chrystons in the poisoning inquiry, but he's spoken with your DI Farrell who suggested that there might not be the same cooperation with the SIO of the murder inquiry team; that he will no longer have access to the family of the poison victim."

"He's not far wrong," she sighed and with a quick glance to ensure she was not being overheard, added, "regarding the SIO I mean. Leave it with me, cuzz. I'll inform DI Fitzpatrick that McEwan is vetted by me and provided he does not seek information about the murder of Colleen Younger, he can continue to interview the family about the poisoning." Her eyes narrowed and she added, "Tell McEwan if he calls into the murder incident room he is to speak with DS Anne Leitch. As I recall, Anne knows McEwan, so she can be his point of contact for interviewing the family."

"Great, cuzz. I'll pass the news along and thanks."

"You're more than welcome," she smiled as she ended the call then turning towards the DI's room, sighed in anticipation of the scowl when she gave Fitzpatrick the news.

Doctor Kane, believing that Miss McKinnon needed some time to take in the devastating news about her brother, arranged for a nurse to bring a cup of tea to the small cramped room while he scurried off to attend to a crisis in an adjoining ward. Now the tea lay cold and untouched as she steeled herself to murder her brother-in-law, Martin.

Her throat was dry, her hands trembled and her knees shook beneath the table.

She forced herself to rise from the chair and almost stumbling in the small room, opened the door to the corridor outside. Two nurses, each carrying small cardboard boxes and speaking quietly passed her by without a glance as they made their way towards Martins room door, but to Joyce's relief they passed by without entering and turned a corner out of sight.

She took a deep breath and ensuring the corridor was now empty of nursing staff, walked purposefully towards his room.

Annemarie, standing with her arms folded, watched from the front room window as the two officers who had arrived on the low-loader that now carried the BMW on it's trailer, covered Martin's car with a large grey coloured tarpaulin and tied it down. Upstairs, she could hear her daughters running back and forth and laughing loudly as they chased each other across the room. Without turning, she asked Leitch, "Where are they taking it?"

"It will be taken to a covered garage, presumably at the Crime Campus out in Gartcosh where the Forensic people are based and where the car will be subjected to a Forensic examination, Missus Turner. My colleague DC McNulty will go with the guys in their truck to record any items the Forensic people find in the car; any evidence I mean. We call it continuity of evidence."

"Evidence like his phone?"

"Yes, like his phone."

Annemarie sighed heavily, continuing to watch as grinning broadly, one of the officers helped the young woman detective climb into the high cabin of the truck, hitching her skirt above her knees to mount the high step. The officer then handed the detective two large paper bags that she knew contained Martin's trousers and jacket; the trousers and jacket that were bloodstained.

"Do you think he did it? Killed that girl, I mean?"

Sat on the couch, Anne Leitch shook her head and replied, "I can't say, Missus Turner, that's for a jury to decide. All I can tell you is that from what you told us and with the blood staining on his clothes and the likelihood that his mobile phone was in contact with…with the deceased, it seems increasingly likely your husband, if not the killer, has some knowledge of the murder." Her brow creased and she asked, "What do you think, Missus Turner? Is your husband capable of murdering someone?"

The truck pulled away with a roar, but she continued to blankly stare through the window. They need another wash, she rubbed vigorously with a finger at a smudge in the corner of the glass. He would go mental if he saw that, she thought.

"Murder someone?" she repeated Leitch's question.

She paused, then nodding, replied, "Oh yes. Martin is perfectly capable of killing someone. But it would need to be someone who couldn't or wouldn't fight back; someone like me," her shoulders heaved as the tears began to freely fall from her and rolled down her cheeks.

Leitch rose to her feet and slung her handbag across her shoulder. "Missus Turner, you must realise that you have been very helpful. However, there will be a time when you will require to be formally interviewed, but I don't think that this is the time or the place." Her head turned towards the ceiling and her eyes softened as she listened to the girls laughing while they played upstairs. "What I'll do is arrange to have you brought to the office some time tomorrow at a time that is convenient for you. Perhaps when the girls are at school. I'll personally call you later today to arrange a time and get you picked up from the house here. Is that okay with you? Missus Turner?"

She turned, sniffing as she used her sleeve to wipe at her wet cheeks. "What? Yes. Of course. Tomorrow."

"Right then, I'll be off," but she hesitated, one hand on the door handle and said, "Missus Turner? Will you be okay? Do you want me to wait here till your sister returns? It won't be any bother, I assure you."

"No," Annemarie shook her head, "I'll be fine, honestly," she forced a smile.

"Okay, Like I said I'll phone some time later this evening with a time to have you picked up tomorrow."


Her hands trembled as she pushed open Martin's room door.
She saw that once more he had lapsed into unconsciousness.
Warily, she stepped into the room, her eyes upon him and quietly closed the door behind her.
She stood watching him breathing as some dream haunted him for he shuddered and occasionally writhed on the bed, muttering incoherently in his sleep.
She thought he whispered something, for it sounded like a mans name. Colin or some name like that.
She closed her eyes, gripping her hands tightly to stop them from shaking, willing herself to do what she intended, yet fearful that her nerve would break and she would run from the room.

She took a deep breath and almost as though it had a will of its own, her hand dropped her bag onto the floor and her legs propelled her towards the bed where her shaking hands slid the pillow from under Martin's head.

Now grasped tightly in both hands, her knuckles white and her fingers tense, she hovered over his sleeping form and with the pillow held over his face prepared herself to push down hard.

The phone clamped to her ear, Annemarie called again to the girls to be quiet, that she was trying to make a call and unconsciously muttered, "Come on, Joyce, pick up."

With sudden determination, she pushed the tightly gripped pillow onto his face and gritted her teeth. Almost immediately, he began to writhe and squirm, but she held the pillow firmly on his face, the tears welling at the enormity of what she was doing.

She almost fainted and inhaled in shock when her mobile phone rang in her handbag.

Startled, still grasping the pillow, she stepped back just as the door opened and a young nurse entered, a hesitant smile on her face.

"I'm sorry, I didn't know Martin had a visitor," she began, staring inquiringly at Joyce who almost guiltily still held the pillow in both hands.

"He...he...he seemed uncomfortable," she gasped. "I thought if I..."

"Here, let me," the nurse smiled sympathetically and took the pillow from her hands. "That's why the pay me the big bucks," she grinned and sarcastically added, "...as if."

Her hands under his neck, the nurse slid the pillow beneath Martin's head and gently pecking his cheek between her forefinger and thumb, said, "There you are, sweetheart. That's better now, isn't it?"

Joyce, her mouth open and face pale, stepped further back against the wall and lifting her handbag from the floor, anxiously fetched out her mobile phone. Stepping through the door into the corridor, she slumped against the wall; her legs shaking while her heart raced and close to tears, she bit at her lip.

She had failed.

The bastard was going to live after all.

Glancing down at the screen she saw the missed call number was from Annemarie's house and slowly letting out a breath, pressed the green button.

Her sister answered almost immediately.

"Joyce, you have to come home," she whispered, "I've had the CID here again. Oh, my God, Joyce. You need to come back here right away."

"What...Annemarie, slow down. Was it about Martin again? The poisoning? Do they..."

"Joyce, it isn't about that, you know...that thing. No, it was about Martin this time. They think he killed someone. A girl from his school. Joyce, they think he's a murderer!"

## CHAPTER TWENTY-TWO

Stood in the waiting area outside the domestic arrivals doors, Tom McEwan scanned the redeye crowd of passengers and waved a greeting at Gavin Blakestock.

The grey-haired man, suavely dressed in a tailored suit and carrying a briefcase, looked every inch the successful businessman as he returned Tom's wave and greeted him with a handshake.

"Have you had breakfast, yet?"

"Just a coffee on the flight," Blakestock replied, "and between you and me, young Tom, the bloody cabin crew should have been wearing masks, the price they charged," he scowled.

"Right then," Tom grinned, "we'll head into the city and I'll treat you to a Wetherspoons Scottish fry-up first and bring you up to speed on what I've learned to date." Leading him to his car in the car park opposite the terminal entrance, Gavin scowled and casting an eye at the low cloud cover, remarked, "The weather forecast for Glasgow was sun, but I expect we're in for a shower."

"That's the thing about living up here," Tom grinned. "The predictable thing about Scottish weather is it's unpredictable and the best weather forecast is sticking your head out the window and having a wee look."

Twenty-five minutes later and seated in the large Wetherspoons in Bothwell Street, they thanked the young waitress who delivered their breakfast with a smile.

"Well," Tom began, "as you know from our telephone conversation late last night, our poison victim Martin Turner is now the primary suspect for the murder of a schoolgirl here in Glasgow."

"This is too much of a coincidence, Tom. Our victim is a murder suspect? And you still believe that his wife and sister-in-law, either one or both colluding together, is responsible for poisoning him?"

"I do, Gavin, yes," Tom confirmed with a nod. "What I *don't* believe is that poisoning Turner has anything to do with his being suspected of the murder. Too much a coincidence or not, I'm of the opinion that the two incidents are completely unrelated."

"Well, the interview should prove interesting," he shook his head, then turned towards his plate. "This breakfast is just the job," Blakestock sliced into his black pudding, "and bugger the arteries. I'm really enjoying this," he added with a grin.

"Yes, well," Tom smiled, "moving on. My boss pulled in a favour with his cousin who is the DCI in overall charge of both the murder and the poison inquiries. She's agreed that with the permission of the murder SIO, we can still interview Missus Turner and her sister, Miss McKinnon."

"Without the presence of the police in the room?"

"Ah, there's the hiccup. A police office *is* to be present," Tom replied. "However, my point of contact will be a former colleague, Anne Leitch, who is a DS working on the murder. I phoned her and Anne's agreed to meet us at Missus Turner's home and I've requested that Missus Turner's sister also be present when we conduct our interview. Apparently Joyce McKinnon is living there for the time being, to help out while the husband is in hospital."

"And Missus Turner and her sister have agreed to be interviewed by us?"

"Well, now," Tom grimaced, "Anne informed both women that we will be present, but *not* why we wish to speak with them."

"Does your friend know of our suspicions that both these women are possibly responsible for the husbands poisoning?"

"I kind of neglected to mention that," Tom drew a deep breath. "What I'm hoping is that we might persuade Anne to give us five minutes alone with the women to put our suspicions to them."

"I see," Blakestock slowly replied, his eyes narrowing. "What will be the reaction from your friend if she finds out that you have deceived her?"

"I don't think she'll be pleased, but I'm conscious of what you reminded me, Gavin. We work for Chrystons in this issue. If the CEO, Mister Peters, decides to inform the police of what we have learned then Anne Leitch will be the first officer I inform."

"And the time of this meeting?"

Tom glanced at his wristwatch and replied, "One hour from now. Time enough for another mug of coffee."

Sat at his desk in the head office in Birmingham, Jackson Peters scanned the report in front of him.

The outlook over the next year was bleak with projected profits for the company at best breaking even; at worst…he shook his head at the thought.

Yes, he silently nodded, it was to be a hard time ahead and not least for the eleven thousand or so staff employed by the company.

Once more he read the report from the Director tasked with the responsibility of managing the huge personnel department; the moneysaving report that advocated downsizing the staff and the dismissal of what the Director termed as the more menial employees who worked in the storerooms and included the discharge of the student and housewife part-timers and ending the management graduate programme for which Peters had been so proud to inaugurate some years previously.

He slowly laid the report down onto his desk and considered it.

Of course, it made sense for if the company were to survive it would need to cut back on its massive staff expenditure.

And yes, if he agreed with the report then no doubt the unions would protest, but that was an issue he could deal with for he believed he had a good rapport with the unions and besides; the union could not dismiss the plan if it saved most of the jobs rather than all the employees lose their employment.

What he could not deal with was his conscience.

So many people relied upon both his and the Boards decisions, so many families relied upon the salaries the company delivered, so many students relied upon the income that guaranteed their domestic survival throughout their college and university years.

He shook his head wearily at the huge responsibility upon his shoulders and lifted the single page that he had printed late last evening from his computer.

And now this.

His investigator Gavin Blakestock had e-mailed him to inform him of Blakestock and the young Scotsman's belief that they had identified Penthesilea; a woman living in Glasgow who was either individually, but likely jointly responsible with her sister for causing all this chaos.

According to Blakestock, the women's motive was for the moment unclear, but it was his intention to travel to Glasgow and with his colleague, meet with and confront the women together.

The e-mail concluded that Blakestock would contact Peters when the meeting was over.

The page slipped from his fingers onto the desk and he smiled.

The media, initially outraged at the threat from Penthesilea, had latterly been kind to him and to Margo Hardie.

No, he thought, not kind, more sympathetic, accusing both her husband James and Lesley Peters of being philanderers and James in particular for the problems that now beset the company.

The photographs his lawyer had with Peters permission indiscreetly disclosed to a local reporter merely encouraged the public anger that settled upon James's shoulders after failing to divulge the poison threat to the general public.

Ironically, the woman or women responsible for the issue, this Penthesilea, had served a purpose of which she or they knew nothing of.

Their threat to Chrystons had permitted him to not only get rid of an internal threat from James Hardie, but also relieve himself of a woman who attractive and desirable though Lesley undoubtedly is, would sooner or later have left him and taken much of his fortune with her.

Curious that things should turn out this way, he sighed and again lifted the report from the Director of Personnel.

He reached for his gold plated pen and with bold strokes, penned and signed an addendum that quite categorically instructed there would be no lay off of staff, that regardless of whatever might come and even if from Director down there was to be wage reductions, no one would be dismissed from Chrystons.

That done, he rubbed at his forehead and with a sigh, drew a sheet of paper to him and commenced an internal letter to all the staff informing them that though hard times lay ahead, Chrystons as a company and the loyal staff who had worked so hard and so diligently to make it the high street store beloved by so many millions of customers, would remain together, that they would survive this issue.

Ten minutes later he re-read the letter and with a satisfied smile added am instruction to the Director that the internal letter also be discreetly released to the press.


DS Anne Leitch pushed open the rear door to the car park and was walking to a CID vehicle when she heard her name called.

She turned and hand raised to shade her eyes as she squinted in the sudden burst of sunshine, greeted Lynn Massey.

"Good morning, Ma'am. I'm just off to meet with Tom McEwan and some English guy, but DI Fitzpatrick's at his desk."

"No problem, Anne. I thought I'd call by and get an update. I understand that the DNA results have come back regarding your victim being in the suspects car."

"Yes, Ma'am. Turner cleaned the inside of the vehicle and apparently did a good job, but not good enough," she smiled. "Forensics found skin cells and some strands of blonde hair that matches our victim's DNA. There was also a very slight trace of the victim's blood on the plastic in the car at the rear door; presumably from the head wound she suffered. It all proves she was in the car, but not murder, however, DI Fitzpatrick is applying for a warrant to obtain Turner's DNA and we're confident we'll get a match for both the blood under our victim's fingernail and the skin cells removed from her neck. That and the Forensics found the mobile phone the victim had used to communicate with the suspect."

"And this was all DI Fitzpatrick's discovery," mused Massey, keenly watching for a reaction from Leitch, who stared curiously at her and replied, "Ma'am?"

"Well, I'm led to understand that it was the DI's idea to trawl the school staff looking for an association between an adult male and the victim…or isn't that correct, Anne?"

Leitch flushed and her nostrils flaring, angrily said, "Ma'am, that was a good piece of detective work by Bob Stevenson. He's the guy who persuaded one of the teachers there to speak out and trusting Bob, the teacher risked his career by going against his managements instruction and provided us with information about Turner and his BMW."

"And the business with the mobile phone. Wasn't that the DI's idea too?"

Leitch paused, now aware she was being grilled, softly replied, "My idea, Ma'am. But then again, I'm a team player so it's not in my nature to take credit or look for individual praise."

Massey nodded, aware that the younger woman was now tensely wound up and regretting her bull nosed attempt at finding out the truth. What she had learned from Leitch's angry responses was Fitzpatrick was full of shit and inwardly promised herself that she would deal with the deceitful bastard.

"Needless to say, we did *not* have this conversation, Detective Sergeant Leitch. Is that clearly understood?"

"No idea what you're talking about, Ma'am," Leitch shook her head.

"Tom McEwan," she smiled, assured now of Leitch's discretion. "I'm assured that he's a good man, so I'll be grateful if you do what you can to assist him."

She watched as Leitch turned away to walk to her vehicle and thought she had better watch what she said to Fitzpatrick for no matter that she believed Leitch, any hint that she had questioned the DS would likely spell trouble for the younger woman.

Pushing her way through the door and into the corridor that led towards the incident room, Massey went over in her head how she would raise the lies that Fitzpatrick had told. No, not lies *per se*, she corrected herself, simply a departure from the truth.

Nodding at the greetings that were directed at her, she prepared herself for confrontation and knocking on Fitzpatrick's door, entered the room.


They had sat all night discussing why the police and the man called McEwan, who worked for the lawyer representing Chrystons, wished to meet with them both.

Now, the girls driven to school by Joyce, they sat facing each other in the kitchen, nursing a mug of tea and wondered yet again.

"Do you think they know?" Annemarie asked again.

Joyce shrugged and shook her head. "Look, all we have to do is deny everything. Martin being suspected for murder, that changes things, Annemarie. God, when I think of how close I came to smothering him…" she shook her head again. "It would all have been for nothing. No matters what happens now," she reached across and tightly gripped her sisters hand, "you and the girls are free of him. The police won't let him come home now. Not if he's murdered a young girl. Don't you see? Everything we did, everything we planned," she softly laughed, "it was all for nothing. If we had known he was going to kill that girl…"

"But Joyce, we *didn't* know," she bitterly replied, "how could we? And now we still have it hanging over us. Threatening that company, poisoning him. We could still go to prison!"

"I won't let that happen, I promise you."

"Promise me? How can you promise me, Joyce?" she was becoming distraught, but could not help herself and her body began to shake.

"Annemarie, pull yourself together!"

"I could lose my daughters! I could…"

"Annemarie!"

She stared at Joyce, eyes narrowing with a sudden realisation. "You can't! We did this together! It was me that served him the pie!"

"It was my idea, my plan," her sister wearily replied. "All they need to know is that I'm responsible. You'll tell them that I bought the pie for you as a gift for Martin. You'll tell them…"

"I won't! You're not going to prison alone! I…I…I won't let you!" she rapidly shook her head.

"And what about Paula and Carol? We have no one to care for them, no other family, Annemarie," Joyce tightened her grip on her hand.

"I don't need you to martyr yourself for me. Think about what would happen to them if we both were sent to prison. They would be taken into care. Fostered if they were lucky, but likely separated. Is that worth being a martyr?"

"It's not right. You did all this for me, for us."

"Yes and I'd gladly do it again, sis," she smiled, aware that both were now crying.

She took a deep breath and releasing Annemarie's hand, smiled through her tears and said, "I think we should wash our faces before they arrive; make ourselves presentable, eh?"

Tom McEwan was driving through the city towards Glenhead Street when Gavin Blakestock's mobile phone activated.

He stared curiously at the screen then answered the call with, "Mister Peters, good morning sir. I didn't expect to be speaking with you until after Tom McEwan and I interviewed the women."

"I assume you are currently travelling in a vehicle with Mister McEwan. If no one else is present, can you put me on speaker please."

"Yes, sir, of course," he shrugged at the puzzled Tom and pressing a button on the keypad, said, "That's you on speaker, Mister Peters. Go ahead."

The next few minutes of the journey was spent listening to Peters instructions regarding the interview they were to conduct with the two women.

Surprised and a little disconcerted, Blakestock said, "I'm sorry, Mister Peters, but I'm confused by those instructions and I'm certain that Tom is too."

Similarly confused, Tom nodded in agreement.

"I understand what you are telling us, but I don't understand why you are telling us this. Is that *exactly* how you wish us to handle this, sir?"

"Yes, Mister Blakestock. Exactly as I have described. Once you have conducted your interview, I suggest that you and Mister McEwan join me in a telephone conference and I will explain my reasoning for those instructions"

Blakestock took a breath and replied, "Well, sir, you're the boss. As agreed, I'll call you when the interview is completed and let you know what occurred."

"Thank you Mister Blakestock and of course, you too, Mister McEwan."


DS Anne Leitch was still fuming when she pulled up outside the Turners house in Glenhead Street. If the neighbours were curious about the comings and goings of the CID and wondering about Martin Turner's car being taken away, they certainly didn't show it, she thought and glanced again at the house windows that overlooked the street.

She remained seated in the car, having decided to call at the house when Tom McEwan and his associate arrived.

To pass the ten minutes that remained before the agreed time Tom would arrive, she called the incident room and learned that the warrant to obtain Martin Turner's DNA had been approved and that Bob Stevenson and Gemma McNulty were now en route to the Royal Infirmary to collect the specimen from Turner. Once that was done, the detectives would speedily travel to Gartcosh and hand the DNA specimen to the Forensic laboratory for comparison with the DNA seized from Colleen Younger's body.

"It shouldn't take long for the comparison after that, should it?" asked the civilian analyst on the line.

"Hopefully not," Leitch replied, "and certainly not if they only have the one DNA sample to test. Oh, oh, here's my meet," she said and watched as Tom McEwan smoothly brought his blue coloured Toyota Yaris to a halt in front of her CID car.

Getting out of the car she greeted Tom with a handshake and a grin and was introduced to Gavin Blakestock, who immediately charmed her with a huge smile and said, "Had I known all Scottish detectives were so lovely, I'd have transferred up here when I was a much younger man."

They stood for a few moments in the street, conscious that the curtains in the Turners front room twitched and deciding who would take charge when they were in the house.

"So, it's true about Turner murdering the schoolgirl?" Tom asked.

"Oh, yeah, it's true," Leitch nodded. "By all accounts from what we've learned, he is a right mean bastard too. The life he gave his wife and those wee girls," she shook her head. "Apparently he treated them very badly. I've seen women who have lived with abuse and been traumatised and in my opinion, Missus Turner is probably the most abused victim I've ever come across," she added with some feeling. "Why she never left him, God knows, but sometimes it's easier said than is actually possible."

Her remark caused Tom to quickly glance towards Blakestock.

They stood for a few seconds, allowing Leitch's information to sink in then all agreed that as the serving officer, Leitch would begin by introducing Tom and Blakestock and also use the visit to update Missus Turner with any questions that she might have; but only questions that would not impede with the murder inquiry.

Tom then asked, "Anne, I know that your DI said you are supposed to be present when we speak with Missus Turner, but could you possibly consider giving Gavin and I five minutes alone with her and her sister?"

"What are you not telling me?" she countered, her eyebrows narrowing with suspicion.

Tom hesitated. To disclose their suspicions to the detective would oblige her to report the information to her boss, but he did wish to compromise her by asking her to remain silent on the matter nor did he wish to take advantage of their friendship by asking that of her. Instead he carefully replied, "There are certain facts regarding the threat to Chrystons that are available to Gavin and I that I assure you, Anne," he shook his head, "do not in any way hinder your inquiry. Nevertheless, if I were to disclose these facts in front of you it would oblige you to act upon what you hear."

She stared at him, trying to assess if he was telling the truth then remembered that this was Tom McEwan; a man she liked and had admired when he served as a police detective. Besides, while Fitzpatrick had categorically instructed she was to remain in attendance when the two civilian investigators questioned both Missus Turner and her sister, her earlier conversation with DCI Massey had infuriated Leitch so much that she decided, fuck Fitzpatrick.

"If I have your word, Tom," she slowly nodded, "then I'm certain that after we meet with Missus Turner and I speak with her, I might have to leave you to make a five-minute phone call."

"You have my word," he smiled in gratitude.


"They're just standing talking in the street," Annemarie whispered as furtively, she hid behind the front room curtain.

"What the hell are they waiting for," hissed Joyce, sat nervously on the couch, twisting a handkerchief in her hands, "and who's the older guy?"

"I don't know," Annemarie shook her head. "He wasn't here the last time, when the lawyer came, but I recognise the guy with the woman detective. He's the one called McEwan. He's definitely the man who visited with the lawyer…wait. They're coming up the pathway," she stumbled back from the window, smoothing down her skirt and clearly as nervous as her sister.

"Wait till they knock on the door," Joyce licked at her lips, her mouth unaccountably dry.

Even though they expected it, the loud knock startled them both and taking a deep breath in an effort to compose herself, Annemarie left the room to admit them.

Joyce stood expectantly, her hands clasped in front of her.

Annemarie returned to the front room, followed by Leitch and the two men.

"Missus Turner, I believe you already met Mister McEwan. This is his colleague, Mister Blakestock."

"How do you do, ladies," Blakestock smiled at the women in turn and transferring his briefcase to his left hand, extended his right hand as he added, "I'm so grateful that you permitted Mister McEwan and I to visit you both."

"Please," Annemarie feigned a smile and indicated they sit.

"I'll fetch another chair from the kitchen," Joyce said and hurried from the room.

Leitch and Annemarie sat on the armchairs while the two men shared the couch, but no one spoke till Joyce returned with the kitchen chair and was seated.

"Missus Turner," Leitch began, "I have some further information that I have been instructed to disclose concerning your husband. If you wish we can step into another room."

"No," Annemarie shook her head and turned to glance at Joyce. "There's nothing that you have to say that I won't share with my sister."

"And what about these gentlemen?" Leitch nodded towards the two men.

"Frankly, I'm beyond caring what people hear about Martin," she swallowed with difficulty. "Please, tell me what you have to say."

Leitch slowly nodded and replied, "As we speak, Missus Turner, two of my colleagues are attending at the hospital where they will present a warrant to staff and obtain a DNA sample from your husband. This sample will be compared to evidence that the police already have and I am confident that once the comparison is made it will confirm your husband is the primary suspect for the murder of Colleen Younger. In that event your husband will be formally arrested and while he continues to be detained in hospital, a police presence will be in place. Unfortunately, any visits you should make thereafter to your husband will be in the presence of an officer. However, once he is declared by the physicians to be fit to be moved he will be transferred to a prison hospital facility. During that period a report will be submitted to the Procurator Fiscal who will arrange with Crown Office for a court date to be arranged. I would suggest that in the interim period, you make arrangements for your husband to be legally represented. I'm sorry to break this news, Missus Turner…" she glanced at Joyce and continued, "I know that your sister is here to support you, but please be assured if there is anything that I can do to help, I'll leave you my card and I urge you to contact me. Also, because of the visit today, I'm deferring obtaining a formal statement from you meantime and suggest I contact you later this afternoon to rearrange a time. Is that okay with you?"

"Yes," Annemarie quietly replied.

"Miss McKinnon," she turned towards Joyce.

"Yes, of course," she nodded and stiffly added, "Thank you and I'll see that Annemarie gets in touch with a lawyer."

"Right then," Leitch stared meaningfully at Tom and then glanced at her wristwatch. "I'll need to check in with my office, so if you ladies will excuse me, I'll just make a phone call."

Rising, she left the room.

It was Joyce who opened the conversation, moving from the kitchen chair to sit demurely in the armchair facing the men. Her initial nervousness now past, she stared from one man to the other then said, "You're not here because of Martin, are you? So, what exactly do you want from my sister?"

They had earlier decided that Gavin would speak for them both and Tom would interject with any comment he believed relevant.

"No, you are correct, Miss McKinnon," Blakestock softly replied with a slow shake of his head as he stared at her. "We're not here about Mister Turner. We're here about Penthesilea."

Had he suddenly rose from his seat and screamed at them, he could not have shocked them more.

Annemarie's head whipped round to stare at Joyce, who visibly paled and said, "I…I don't know what you mean," she stuttered, her knuckles white as her fists clenched in her lap.

"Joyce!" Annemarie cried out, her composure shattered by that one word.

"We have evidence, Miss McKinnon, that indicates your vehicle was used to convey either you, your sister Missus Turner or both of you to Birmingham and Manchester. Our question is, are you both involved or is it your sister who is responsible for poisoning her husband?"

During breakfast at Wetherspoons, both he and Tom had discussed Blakestock's opening statement at length and knew they were gambling, but decided that the accusation would at worst provoke a denial, a defensive comment.

A subdued few seconds passed before a startled Joyce replied, "What evidence? I don't know what you mean?"

Blakestock didn't immediately respond, but theatrically shook his head and lifting his briefcase from the floor beside him, reached in and withdrew a single A4 sheet of paper; a sheet of paper upon which Tom had typed then printed from Ellen Toner's computer the previous evening.

Handing the sheet to Joyce, he said, "Miss McKinnon, on this paper you will find times, dates and locations when your vehicle was monitored travelling first to Birmingham and some days later, to Manchester. This information was provided to us by the computer database connected to the Automatic Number Plate Recognition that records the movement of all traffic in the United Kingdom. As you can read at the top of the sheet, your registration number is clearly outlined. I must also inform you that we have witnesses from both locations who spoke with you when you wore your disguise, in Birmingham a young shop assistant and in Manchester, an elderly shopkeeper who…"

"Enough!" she snapped, slowly exhaling, the defeat clearly etched upon her face. Tense seconds passed before she slowly asked, "Am I under arrest?"

Once more, Blakestock didn't immediately respond, but turned to Tom, his eyebrows raised. Tom took his cue and said, "We're not the police, Miss McKinnon. However, our remit is to hand all this evidence to Police Scotland and it will be their decision whether or not to proceed and charge you with attempted extortion as well as the attempted murder of Martin Turner and…"

"It wasn't just Joyce…"

"Annemarie!" her sister snapped at her and rose to her feet, her hands raised to prevent Annemarie saying more. "Don't say another word!" Turning to the two men, she continued. "It was all my idea.

My sister knew nothing of this. I planned it all, everything. I can give you details."

"And you hoped to achieve what, exactly?" asked Blakestock. Miserably she slumped down into her chair, the tears burning at her eyes. "I wanted him gone, dead; out of Annemarie and my nieces lives." She choked back a sob and shook her head. "You can't imagine the life that he gave her. A decade or more of abuse, physical and verbal. Treated her like a fucking slave. Threatened that he would take the girls if she tried to leave him. He is the nastiest, meanest, most brutal man I have ever known."

"Why Chrystons?" Tom asked.

She looked at him as though puzzled and then shrugged. "No particular reason. I thought if I chose a large chain like Chrystons with their outlets all over the UK then it would make it harder for the police to track us…" she took a sharp intake of breath and added, "I mean me, to track *me* down."

"I believe you have a background in food technology, Miss McKinnon, so I suppose you obtained the Death Cap from your college store?"

She saw no point in holding back and replied, "Yes. The college keeps all sort of prohibited food stock for research purpose. It was relatively easy to procure some Amanita Phalloides from the store." She glanced sharply at both men and quickly added, "I never meant for anyone else to be poisoned. It was my plan for Martin alone to eat the pie. I swear. I could never live with myself if anyone else was…was, you know…"

"Poisoned?" Tom prompted her, then asked, "When you were in Manchester, you handed the second letter to a shopkeeper. Why was that?"

She gave him a half smile and again shrugging, replied, "I panicked. That's all there was to it. I had planned to deliver the letter to…"

"The BBC Radio building?"

"Yes," she stared at him, surprised. "How did you know?"

"We worked it out," he said with a soft smile, pleased that his intuition had been correct.

"Anyway, the building was gone and I'd already planted the poisoned pie in the Quay Street store…"

"Where the cashier challenged you about your Scottish fiver," interrupted Blakestock.

"Yes," she softly smiled and shook her head at the memory of her alarm "Anyway, I was panicking in case someone bought the pie before I could warn the police so I just wrote that the envelope was to be delivered immediately to the police…" she stared at them in turn, her face registering her shock. "Oh my God! Oh, please! Don't tell me someone bought that pie!"

Blakestock quickly raised his hand to assure her, "No, Miss McKinnon, the pie was discovered before it was purchased. However," his face darkened, "it was by the grace of the good Lord that no one *did* buy that pie or you could be facing a murder charge in England, young lady!"

Tom turned towards Annemarie and addressing her, said, "You were complicit…" he paused, "You were involved too, weren't you?" Before her sister could intervene, she nodded. "It's like Joyce told you. I was at my wits end. It wasn't just me that was suffering, but my girls too. You can't believe the life they had living with him in this house. When they were not at school, they were virtually prisoners, confined to playing in their room where he wouldn't have to listen to or see them." She paused to regain her composure.

"When he was…hitting me, they would hear him. The things he did to me, the names he called me," she shuddered at the memory. "Nothing would please him. When he arrived home I was…" she stopped, her throat tightening, trying for the word, then said, "*required* to meekly stand by the door while he inspected the house; running his fingers up and down skirting boards searching for dust. If he found something that displeased him…" she slowly pointed to the fading bruise at her eye, "this was just a token to what he was capable of. I had no friends, no one to turn to; he even banned Joyce from the house and me from contacting her."

"Could you not just leave him?" Tom asked.

"Haven't you been listening?" she snapped back. "He controlled my very life! He used my children as leverage against me!" Teeth gritted and fists clenched, she continued, "No matter what I had to endure I would never…*never* leave my children with Martin!"

A palpable silence fell in the room, broken when Joyce stood and said, "I'm willing to go with you to the police, but my sister isn't implicated in this. I will admit anything you want, sign anything that has to be signed, but you cannot involve Annemarie. Christ, hasn't she been through enough?"

"Joyce…"

"No, Annemarie. I gave you the pie to serve to Martin. You had nothing to do with it."

"You are aware we have your sister on CCTV purchasing the pie in the Argyle Street store," Tom calmly reminded her.

That startled her and eyes widening, her lips began to tremble as she stared in shock at Annemarie, but then her eyes narrowed and she retorted, "That was a different pie! You can't prove it was the same pie Martin ate."

"I also understand Missus Turner admitted to the detectives who she spoke with here in her home that the pie she served was the one she purchased. How do you explain that, Miss McKinnon?" he challenged her.

She sat back down, totally defeated her elbows on her knees and her head in her hands. Annemarie left her chair and kneeling beside her sister, began to softly stroke at her hair. Turning to the two men, she asked, "What will happen to us?"

Blakestock glanced at Tom before answering. "Let's suppose you got away with poisoning your husband, Missus Turner. What money did you think you would collect from Chrystons?"

"Money?" she almost spat out. "This wasn't about money! I don't care about money! All I wanted was a life for me and my girls. I've lived for what seems like forever on the breadline; on what money Martin decided I needed to buy his food, to clean and heat his house. The girls and me, we had the cheaper foods, the charity shops clothes while he spent his salary on himself, his fancy car, his nights out chasing his women. Money? I never wanted Chrystons money, Mister Blakestock. I just wanted a life for me and my girls. Is that too much to ask?"

Joyce McKinnon had now completely broken down and hugging her sister, was sobbing.

"So," Annemarie asked again, "what happens now?"

Blakestock shook his head, surprised that he found himself acutely embarrassed.

Scratching at a sudden itch at the back of his neck, he replied, "We will report what we have discovered to our boss, Jackson Peters who as you already know is the CEO of Chrystons. It will be his decision whether or not to inform the various police forces where you have committed crimes, Missus Turner and," he raised a hand to forestall

Joyce McKinnon's protest, "we will also report to Mister Peters that you Miss McKinnon are accepting full liability for the threat against his company."

"Can we expect the police to be calling today?" Annemarie asked, her voice breaking. "I only ask because, well, I would like some time to…I don't know; some time to spend with my girls, make some arrangements for them."

"Give me a couple of hours," he replied, "and I'll phone you here at the house. In the meantime, I want both your word that you will *both* remain here in the house. Do I have it?"

She nodded in agreement for her and Joyce.


When they were seated in the car outside, Tom saw that Anne Leitch had apparently not waited for them, but driven off. Turning to Blakestock, he asked, "Why didn't you tell them when we were in there?"

Blakestock took a deep breath and slowly shook his head. "Like it or not, young Tom, and regardless of why they did it they tried to murder a man and almost caused the downfall of a large company. They're in pain at the minute and hell mend them, so they should be," he remarked, his voice angrier than Tom had previously heard. "Still," Blakestock continued, his voice a little softer now, "I do understand why they did what they did. My God, if it was me, I would have poisoned that bastard myself," he said with some feeling.

Tom grinned and said, "Right, while we're sitting here, why don't we call Jackson Peters and hear what he has to say?"

Blakestock nodded and dialling Peters number, pressed the speaker button and said, "We've conducted the interview, Mister Peters, and left the house, In fact, we're in the car outside. I am pleased to inform you that both women have admitted their complicity in the threat to Chrystons. However, from what they've said and what we know, it seems there is no family to care for Missus Turners two children so it's the sister, Joyce McKinnon who wishes to accept full responsibility and thereby save the children's mother from going to prison. What I should add is that both Tom and I are satisfied or as satisfied as we can be that this was never about Chrystons or the money. You recall Tom and I spoke of a second agenda?"

"Yes, Mister Blakestock, I do recall."

"Well, in short, the man who was poisoned, Martin Turner, apparently is a domestic abuser who treated his wife and two daughters very badly and has done for ten or eleven years or thereabouts. In despair, the wife and her sister colluded to do away with Turner, though as you know he survived their attempt, but remains seriously ill in hospital and might indeed continue to survive."

"That I believe is the current prognosis," Peters replied.

"We've also spoken with a detective officer who assures us that Turner, who she describes quite frankly as a bad bastard, is most assuredly responsible for the local murder of a schoolgirl with whom he had been having an illicit affair."

"And do you both believe that the sister, this woman McKinnon, is willing to sacrifice herself, to openly admit her guilt and face the consequences, for her sister?"

"Yes, well, we're convinced that neither Missus Turner nor her sister fear for what happens to themselves, but are sick with worry about what will become of Missus Turner's two daughters. The girls are young, ten and eight years respectively and if *both* women are imprisoned, the girls are likely to be made wards of the local social services."

There was a lengthy silence, causing Blakestock to check that the line was still connected before Peters responded with, "Your report presents me with quite a dilemma, Mister Blakestock."

"And why is that, sir?" Blakestock turned to stare in puzzlement at Tom.

"As you are aware, the company has taken quite a beating over this affair. However, I am confident that within a year, two at the most, we will resume our rightful standing as one of the premier companies within the UK. Now, I have given this issue much thought and I am advised my fellow Director Mister Kennedy, who is responsible for the Media and Public Relations, that interest in the threat against Chrystons is receding. That, gentlemen, is a good thing for the company, I assure you. However, if one or both these women are brought before a court there is little doubt that there will be a tremendous resumption of media interest in Chrystons and much unwarranted publicity that will remind a sceptic public of the threat against our food products; a reminder that the company can best do without."

"Mister Peters," Tom butted in, "unless I'm mistaken, are you suggesting that we simply ignore what these women did; ignore the fact that they attempted to murder a man?"

"What I'm *suggesting*, gentlemen, is that we act according to our conscience. My understanding is that having identified these two women they will never again threaten Chrystons. Am I correct in that assumption?"

"Yes, sir, we believe that to be correct," Tom turned to Blakestock as he confirmed for them both.

"So, you gentlemen have completed your main task on behalf of the company by identifying and neutralising Penthesilea. Agreed?"

"Yes, sir, agreed," this time Blakestock spoke for them both.

"And this man Martin Turner. By your own description he seems to be a veritable rogue and despicable sounding fellow. Agreed?"

"Yes, sir," Blakestock slowly replied.

"Well then gentlemen, as the attempt on his life has apparently failed and as your employer, I see no reason to involve the police in what sounds to me to simply be a domestic matter where a wife who, according to you Mister Blakestock, has endured eleven years or so of suffering and at last fought back. Sounds to me that this chap Turner deserved exactly what happened to him. Would you agree?"

Blakestock suddenly grinned and turning towards Tom, saw that he too was shaking his head and smiling.

Almost in unison, they both said, "Agreed."

"Then, gentlemen, we are unanimous, so a task concluded with a positive result and well done to you both. I will assume that this agreement will be maintained by us three alone. I thank you again and will of course be in touch," said Peters and ended the call.

"Well, young Tom," Blakestock continued to grin, "I suppose we had better return to Missus Turner and warn her and her sister that in future, they had better behave themselves...or else."

## PROLOGUE

The funeral service for the murdered schoolgirl Colleen Younger attracted several hundred mourners, the vast majority of whom were pupils from the dead girl's school. A hysteria of tears overtook many of the teenage girls that seemed to intensify just as they passed the television crews who were in attendance filming the cortege as it wound its way to Sighthill Cemetery.

As custom dictated, a small purvey was held in a local hostelry of ill-repute where after a few hours, the police and several ambulances were called to a violent disturbance. As well as several casualties who suffered wounds ranging from broken noses to multiple stabbing, a number of individuals were arrested for charges that included serious assault, offensive weapons and breach of the peace and included the brothers of the deceased, Sean and William Younger.

In the fullness of time, the Crown Office in Edinburgh fixed the date whereby the accused Martin Turner faced trial at the High Court in Glasgow for the murder of sixteen-year-old Colleen Younger, a pupil at the school where Turner taught and with whom it was alleged Turner was having a sexual relationship.

Unable to physically attend the court, His Lordship presiding instructed that doctors and psychiatrists acting for both the Crown and Turner's defence counsel ensure the accused was competent and mentally fit to participate in the trial from his prison hospital bed via a live television link.

The trial attracted widespread media interest, not least because Turner himself had been the victim of a failed murder attempt by a mysterious group calling itself Penthesilea who had since their failed extortion attempt and poisoning of the pie that so incapacitated Turner, disappeared from all but police criminal files.

The trial was set by the Crown Office to be completed in two weeks. However, almost from the outset Turner's defence team realised the overwhelming circumstantial DNA evidence and in particular, that of the miniscule blood sample discovered beneath the victim's fingernails that proved to be Turner's, could not be successfully contested and thus admitting his client's guilt, his counsel made much of Turner's incapacity and begged the mercy of the court.

His Lordship, acutely conscious of the extreme public outrage at the crime and in particular, Turner's betrayal of trust in seducing his teenage pupil, took no cognisance of the accused's profound disability and sentenced him to a minimum of twenty-two years, remarking in his summing-up that if the physicians were to be believed it was unlikely that Turner would survive for half of that time.

Detective Inspector Murray Fitzpatrick, the SIO who conducted the successful murder inquiry that led to the arrest of Martin Turner, suddenly and inexplicably retired from the police. It was wryly rumoured that his decision was made immediately following a lengthy and noisy argumentative disagreement with his senior officer, Detective Chief Inspector Lynn Massey.
In any event no farewell reception was held for the unpopular Fitzpatrick because, it was jokingly said, no telephone kiosks were available as the venue.

Annemarie Turner never again visited nor contacted Martin during his pending trial nor after his conviction and her divorce was not contested.
Shortly after her husband's conviction she reverted to her maiden name McKinnon, sold the story of her eleven years of marital hell to a popular women's magazine for an undisclosed sum and for a very brief period appeared on a number of daytime television programmes where she openly discussed her abusive relationship.
Several months after the trial concluded, Paula and her sister Carol were flower girls at their auntie Joyce's small, but intimate civil ceremony when she married her fellow lecturer, Sandy Munro.
At Joyce's insistence, Annemarie walked the bride down the aisle.

Gavin Blakestock was surprised but delighted to learn that the fee for his successful investigation on behalf of Chryston Supermarkets (PLC) greatly exceeded the invoice he submitted to the company.
His wife Celia, in her role as his company accountant, thought it odd that it was Mister Peters the CEO himself who had personally signed the cheque.

Martin McCormick was equally surprised when the cheque arrived at his office in payment for his firms' investigation carried out by Tom McEwan.
The hand written note from Mister Peters addressed to McCormick that accompanied the cheque requested that a substantial part of the

fee be delivered to Mister McEwan for what Peters described as 'personal services.'

McCormick was wise enough to realise that whatever business Tom carried out with Gavin Blakestock, if that business satisfied Jackson Peters and did not in any way compromise McCormick's firm, then what he didn't know couldn't hurt him and duly credited Tom's account with the sizeable sum.

Detective Inspector Mickey Farrell was left with an open and unsolved inquiry regarding the poisoning of Martin Turner. Who Penthesilea were and why they had suddenly ceased their activities worried him; but not for too long. The crime in Glasgow city centre was enough for him to deal with and Farrell had little time to spend worrying about an issue over which he had no control. The paperwork was logged and filed and with the victim himself serving a life sentence, all but forgotten.

Jackson Peters remained a further ten months as CEO of Chrystons, during which time he saw the company slowly recover from the menace of the extortion that had threatened to destroy it. Satisfied that profits were on the rise, albeit slowly and immensely proud that he had staved off any staff dismissals, Peters finally stepped down from the Board and was succeeded by the Director who was his friend and main supporter, Frank Kennedy. The accolades he received from his fellow Directors as well as the rank and file staff of Chrystons both surprised and delighted him. Now happily divorced from Lesley, he retired to a villa in the South of France where rumour had it that a regular visitor was the glamourous Margo, the ex-wife of his former Director of Operations, who according to a fashionable magazine was often seen at functions on the arm of Jackson Peters.

To cement the relationship that now existed between them, Tom McEwan introduced Ellen Toner to his daughters and was pleased that his daughters readily accepted Ellen as their father's new partner.

Patsy Younger, the drug and alcohol addicted mother of the murdered schoolgirl Colleen Younger, was dismayed that her application for Criminal Compensation for her daughter's death was summarily denied.

*********

Needless to say, this story is a work of fiction. As readers of my previous books may already know, I am an amateur writer and therefore accept that all grammar and punctuation errors are mine alone. I hope that any such errors do not detract from the story.
If you have enjoyed the story, you may wish to visit my website at:
www.glasgowcrimefiction.co.uk

The author also welcomes feedback and can be contacted at:
george.donald.books@hotmail.co.uk

Printed in Great Britain
by Amazon